HIGHLAND KISS

"What is this?" he asked, plucking at the laces on her shift until they started to come undone.

" 'Tis what a genteel wife would wear to bed," Gillyanne replied.

"Aye? I am to just fumble my way around it, am I?"

She gasped when he suddenly grabbed the shoulders of the shift and yanked them down until her arms were pinned to her side; not painfully so, but it would take a lot of wriggling to get them free. Gillyanne felt no fear, knew deep in her heart that Connor would never hurt her. What she did feel was intrigued and just a little aroused. She had turned into quite a wanton, she thought with an inner, slightly rueful smile.

He kissed her and Gillyanne let the sensual magic of that kiss flow through her. The feel of his broad chest pressed against her was enough to make her ache. Gillyanne tried to move her arms to touch him only to realize he had relaced her shift only enough to tighten the bonds on her arms. When he moved his kisses to her throat, she moaned with a mixture of frustration over her inability to touch him and a rapidly soaring passion. Gillyanne was astonished at how swiftly and fiercely Connor could stir her desire. He was a fire in her blood, an aching need she feared she would suffer all her life.

That thought was soon banished from her mind when Connor began to kiss the insides of her thighs. When he took those kisses a little higher, Gillyanne cried out a shocked protest. Connor grasped her by the hips, holding her steady when she tried to pull away, and soon, she did not want to. Blinding pleasure flooded her body with each stroke of his tongue. . . .

Books by Hannah Howell

ONLY FOR YOU

MY VALIANT KNIGHT

UNCONQUERED

WILD ROSES

A TASTE OF FIRE

HIGHLAND DESTINY

HIGHLAND HONOR

HIGHLAND PROMISE

A STOCKINGFUL OF JOY

HIGHLAND VOW

HIGHLAND KNIGHT

HIGHLAND HEARTS

HIGHLAND BRIDE

Published by Zebra Books

HIGHLAND BRIDE

Hannah Howell

ZEBRA BOOKS
KENSINGTON PUBLISHING CORP.
http://www.kensingtonbooks.com

In memory of Joyce Flaherty—the best of friends, the best of agents.

But if the while I think on thee, dear friend
All losses are restored and sorrows end.
—Shakespeare

Prologue

Scotland, 1465

"Sir Eric! Sir Eric!"

Sir Eric Murray sighed and turned to face the too thin man hurrying through the garden toward him. He had found himself a nice secluded spot in the castle garden, or so he had thought, in order to read the news from home. Although he liked Sir Donald well enough, he did not appreciate his rare moment of peace being so abruptly ended. As Sir Donald stumbled to a halt in front of him, Eric sat up straight on the shaded stone bench.

"I didnae ken ye had returned," Sir Donald said, using a small scrap of linen to dab at the sheen of sweat upon his narrow face. "The errand the king sent ye on was swiftly tended to, was it?"

"Aye," was all Eric replied, unsure of just how secret the king meant to keep the business and knowing how avid a gossip Sir Donald was.

"The king awaits ye. He doesnae ken ye have returned, either."

"Nay, I havenae told many. I ken I will be kept verra busy and wished for a moment of quiet to read the news from home."

"And is your bonny lady wife weel? And your children?"

"All weel, although I begin to feel a need to return and nay just for the love of them. My wee lass Gillyanne has taken it into her head to go and see her dower lands. My love isnae sure how long she can rein in our headstrong child or even if she should."

"Weel, now, there is a fine coincidence. 'Tis your daughter Gillyanne's dower lands the king wishes to discuss with you."

"I hadnae realized anyone kenned she had any. 'Tis something we have tried to keep quiet, at least as concerns the what and the where."

"Most of the court now kens the what and the where."

"How?"

Sir Donald swallowed nervously. It was just one word, but it had been spoken sharply and Sir Eric's expression was hard, almost threatening. "Weel, three knighted lairds have been pressing the king about that tower house. It borders all of their lands, yet they didnae ken exactly who held it. They tracked a hint of something to your clan, but your steward refused to answer their queries. The king demanded an answer of the mon and 'twas finally given. Then the king told the three lairds that the land was the dowry of your lass, that she was as yet unwed, and it seemed to him that they must now seek ye out." He took a hasty step back when Sir Eric suddenly stood up, every inch of his lean body taut with anger. "They are all landed knights and lairds, Sir Eric. I cannae see that ye would object to wedding your lass to any one of them."

"Oh, but I would object," Sir Eric said softly, coldly.

"I object most heartily. One, I wish my child to wed for love, as I did, as my brothers did, as many of our clan have. Two, I certainly dinnae wish men hungry for a piece of land trying to gain it through my wee Gillyanne. Are any of these knights still here?"

"Nay. They lingered for a few days after hearing who held the lands, but ye didnae return and so they left. Actually, one left quietly in the dark of night and the other two left swiftly the next morn. They are probably planning to seek ye out later, mayhap e'en court your lass."

"Aye, or they have hied away to see who can gain hold of my wee lass first and drag her afore a priest." Sir Eric started to stride out of the gardens, a wide-eyed Sir Donald stumbling along behind him. All Eric could think of was his tiny Gilly—so like her mother with her red-brown hair and faintly mismatched eyes—being dragged off and hurt by some fool who hungered for her land and the thought enraged him. "The king has unleashed a pack of wolves upon Gillyanne. I pray my wife has kept the lass locked up tight, and does so until I can get home."

Chapter One

"I dinnae think our mother was verra pleased about this, Gillyanne."

Gillyanne smiled at the handsome auburn-haired James who rode at her side. He was the brother of her heart, and even he knew that the woman he called his mother was actually his aunt. Soon he would claim his heritage, become laird of Dunncraig, but Gillyanne knew it would be only a distance of miles that would separate them, never one of heart or spirit. She also knew that he did not think she was completely wise in her decision to travel to her dower lands.

"And did ye have to bring those thrice-cursed cats?" he muttered.

"Aye. There may be rats there," she replied calmly.

She reached down to gently scratch the ears of her two cats, Ragged and Dirty. Ragged was a huge dark yellow tom who well fit his name, with one eye gone, one ear missing a bite-sized chunk, and numerous battle scars. Dirty was a sweet, delicate female, a mottled pat-ternless blend of black, grey, orange and white, who had not truly suited her name from the moment she had been rescued and cleaned. They traveled every-where with her in a special fur-lined leather basket that was firmly attached to her saddle. The three of them had not been separated in three years, not since the day she had found them where they had been cruelly tossed into a rat-infested dungeon cell at a neighboring keep. Both of them had been weak and bloodied, the cell littered with more dead and dying rats than she had had the stomach to count. They had both more than earned their keep since she had brought them home with her.

"Oh, aye." James nodded and reached out to briefly pet both cats, revealing that his harsh words were not heartfelt. " 'Tis nay like home at Dubhlinn. S'truth, Mither and I could gain little knowledge about your tower house save to learn that 'tis nay a ruin. Mither felt that the trouble was that the mon she traded mes-sages with didnae truly understand what she was asking of him or what she wished to hear. The mon thought safe; she thought clean. The mon thought protection; she thought comfort. She finally decided safe and pro-tected would suit us for now, that 'twas clear a woman's eye was needed."

" 'Tis because this used to be MacMillan land and 'tis a MacMillan mon who guards it. Mither doesnae ken him weel, save that my great-uncle MacMillan praises his worth, and the mon doesnae ken Mama. Weel, this visit should mend all of that."

"I but pray it is comfortable."

"If it has a bed, a bath, and food, I will be content for now. The comforts such as exist at Dubhlinn can come later."

"Aye, true enough." James eyed her curiously. "I am

nay sure I understand your stubborn need to come here, though.''

"I am nay sure I do, either." Gillyanne smiled at her cousin, then sighed and shrugged. " 'Tis mine. I can say no more than that. 'Tis mine and I wished to acquaint myself with it."

"In truth, I think I can understand that. I keep feeling drawn to my lands though I shallnae set my arse in the laird's seat for another year or more."

"Nay too much more," she said encouragingly.

"Nay, I think not. Dinnae think I resent or regret being held back. 'Tis best. I need seasoning, need more training, and have only just gained my spurs. Our cousin holds my place weel and I need to be able to fill his large boots. An untried laird will do my clan no good at all." He frowned a little. "I wonder how those who live upon your dower lands will feel when a wee lass comes to claim the prize."

"Mither wondered as weel and sought some assurances. It appears it willnae matter. 'Tis but a small keep with few people and Mither got the feeling they would welcome just about anyone. The only one they call the leader is an aging steward. They have all been left a wee bit uncertain of their future and would like it settled."

"That is in your favor then," agreed James. "Why do I think that ye are considering staying here?"

Gillyanne shrugged again, not surprised he had guessed her thoughts. She did indeed have the occasional thought about setting up her own household at Ald-dabhach. And, mayhap, she thought with a small smile, changing the name to something more interesting than *old measure of land*. There was a restlessness inside of her which she did not understand. She loved her family dearly, but they only seemed to make that restlessness worse. Perhaps, if she had her own lands to tend to, she would feel useful and that would sate the hunger gnawing at her insides.

Although she was reluctant to admit it, there was another reason she was finding it difficult at home. It tasted too much like envy, but she was finding it more and more difficult to be around so many happily married couples, to watch her cousins build their own families. Each new birth she attended was, for her, a blend of pleasure and increasing pain. She would be one and twenty soon and no man had ever looked at her with the slightest warmth. Several trips to court had not helped, had in fact been painful proof that men simply did not find her desirable, and all of her family's love and reassurances did not really ease the sting of that.

At times she grew angry with herself. She did not need a man to survive. Deep in her heart she knew she could have a full, happy life with no man at her side. But, right beside that knowledge was the fact that she ached for the passion, the love, and especially the children a husband could give her. Every time she watched one of her cousins with her children, watched the heated glances exchanged between husband and wife, she knew she did not *need* that to find some sort of happiness, but it did not stop her from *wanting* it all.

"If ye hide yourself away here, how will ye e'er find a husband?" James asked.

It took a moment but Gillyanne finally quelled the urge to kick her cousin off his horse. "I dinnae think that is a problem I need fret o'er, Cousin. If there is a match for me, and I have seen little proof that there is one, he can find me here as easily as he can at Dubhlinn or the king's court."

James grimaced and dragged his hand through his hair. "Ye sound as if ye are giving up. Elspeth and Avery were about your age when they found their husbands."

"Near, but still younger. I believe they also experienced the occasional twitch of interest from men ere they were married." She smiled at her cousin when he continued to frown. "Dinnae trouble yourself so. My cousins met their mates in unexpected places. Mayhap I will, too." Gillyanne broke through a line of trees and announced, "Ah, and there it looms. My keep and my lands."

Ald-dabhach had obviously consisted of little more than a peel tower at one time. Over the years two small wings had been added to the thick tower and it was now surrounded by a high, sturdy wall. Set upon a steeply inclined hill, it would be easily protected. The tiny village which sat in its shadow looked neat, the fields all around it were well tended or used to graze cattle and sheep. A small creek wound its way behind the keep, the setting sun making its waters sparkle and gleam. It was, Gillyanne decided, a rather pretty place, and she hoped it was as peaceful as it looked as she urged her mount toward its gates.

" 'Tis sturdy," James said as he stood next to Gillyanne on the walls of her keep after the evening meal.

Gillyanne laughed and nodded. "Verra sturdy."

There really was not much more to say about her dower property. It was clean, but had few of those gentlewomanly touches such as linen cloths for the tables in the great hall. This was not surprising since mostly men resided at Ald-dabhach. There were those women who slept within the keep, two older women married to men at arms, and one very shy girl of twelve, the cook's daughter. Sir George the steward was sixty if he was a day and had both poor eyesight and bad hearing. Most of the men at arms were in their middle years. Gillyanne had the distinct impression that Ald-dabhach had become a place where the MacMillans sent the weary and, she glanced down at one of the few young men at the keep limping toward the stables, the lame. It rather reconfirmed her opinion that it was a peaceful place. The five men who had traveled with her with an eye to

staying were young, strong, and had been greeted almost
as effusively as she had been.

"I think your men will stay," James said, "which will
please the maids here."

"Oh, aye. We did end up with a sudden rush of serving
maids for the evening meal. They must have been watching our arrival from the village."

"And ran straight here. Clearly, there is a shortage
of hale young men." James sighed. "I was rather hoping
the not so hale lads here had found mates because the
lasses were nay foolish enough to think such things as
a limp mattered. Now I must wonder if it was just because
there was no choice."

"With some, but others show more sense." She nodded toward the man with the limp just disappearing
into the stables. "I saw his wife and him together ere
she left to go to the village. The lass looks at him as if
he is the handsomest, strongest, bravest young mon e'er
born."

"So I may cast aside my moment of disillusionment."

"Aye, your hope in the goodness of people is
restored."

"Yours, of course, ne'er faltered."

"With some people it doesnae just falter, it trips and
falls flat on its face," she drawled and smiled when he
laughed.

James draped his arm around her shoulders and
kissed her cheek. "Ye see too much and see it too clearly
'tis all."

"I ken it." She stared out into the increasing dark.
"I can see the good of that. It can warn us, cannae it.
Elspeth says ye just have to learn when to be deaf to it,
but I am nay sure I will e'er have that useful skill. I can
ignore it all if the person is just, weel, ordinary, but if
there is aught about him to make me wary or curious,
'tis as if I want or e'en need to see what is there. Elspeth
mostly senses things, sees something in the eyes. Me? I

swear I can often *feel* what is there. Elspeth is verra good at guessing if one lies, senses fear or danger as it flares up. Me? Let us just say that, at times, a crowded room can be a torture."

"I hadnae realized it was that strong. It must be verra difficult to be constantly battered by everyone else's feelings."

"Not everyone's. I cannae always read you, nor most of my family. The worst one to catch a sniff of is hate. It feels appalling. Fear isnae so good, either, for a part of me kens 'tis nay mine own, but that fear occasionally deafens me to my own good sense. I have blindly fled places only to suddenly come to my senses. 'Tis then that I realize the fear is gone for I have left it with the person who truly felt it."

"And this is what Elspeth feels as weel?"

"A little. She says her skill is a more gentle thing, like a scent in the air she can put a name to."

" 'Tis glad I am I dinnae suffer from such *skills.* "

"Ye have your own special one, James," Gillyanne murmured and patted his hand where he had rested it upon the wall.

"Oh?" He eyed her with suspicion, not trusting her look of sweetness. "What is it?"

"Ye can send a lass to paradise. All the lasses say so." She giggled when he blushed even as he scowled at her.

"Cameron is right," James grumbled. "Ye werenae beaten enough as a child."

"Humph. As if Avery's big dark knight worries me. He has been muttering empty threats for nearly eight years."

"And ye enjoy every one."

"He has a true skill. One can only stand back and admire it." She grinned briefly when he laughed.

"Do ye sense much here, Gilly?" he asked quietly. "Anything I should fret o'er?"

"Nay, although I have learned nay to stare at every

person I meet. If I must be cursed with this skill, 'tis glad I am that my fither chose the Murray clan to be adopted by, a people who understand my gift since so many of them possess such gifts themselves." She rested her arms on the top of the rough stone wall and stared out over her lands. "At the moment, all I feel is a calm, a peace, a gentle contentment. There is also a sense of anticipation, of waiting, yet I cannae feel any fear in that. I feel as if I made the right decision in coming here. This place or mayhap just these lands, give me a sense of belonging."

"Your parents will be hurt if ye choose to stay."

Gillyanne sighed and nodded, acknowledging the one true regret she felt. "I ken it, but they will understand. In truth, I think that is one reason Mither tried so hard to stop me, or, at least, hold me at Dubhlinn 'til Fither returned. I dinnae want to leave them and, God's tears, I will probably continuously mourn the fact that I willnae be stumbling o'er kinsmen each time I turn around. I suffered some doubts as we rode here, but, once through those gates, I felt this was right. This is where I should be. I dinnae ken why or for how long, but, for now, this is where I should make my home."

"Then ye must stay. Ye must heed that calling. Ye wouldnae feel so without cause."

She leaned against his warmth and briefly smiled. James did not share in any of the odd gifts that seemed to run rampant in the Murray clan, for he was no real blood relation, either. His strengths were compassion and a sweetness of nature. He never questioned, however, never doubted or feared the gifts of others. In fact, James' complete lack of any gift was one of the things she found most endearing about him. That and the fact that she rarely sensed anything about the way he thought or felt. They were just two ordinary people when they were together and she did not think he would

ever understand why she found that to be such a comfort
at times.

"I am nay sure ye will find a mon here, though," he
continued. "We have had ample proof that there is a
lack of them."

"True," she replied, "but it doesnae matter. There
are enough to defend us all if the need arises."

"I wasnae talking about defenders, or someone to lift
heavy things, and ye ken it. Here is nay where ye will
meet your mate."

It was not easy, but Gillyanne resisted the urge to
strike him—hard. It was a severe reaction to what had
been a simple statement of fact. There were no men to
choose from here, and, according to Sir George, the
men from the three clans which encircled her lands
were not ones to pay a visit. Worse, Gillyanne had gotten
the strong feeling George was very thankful for that
oversight on the part of those lairds. Any visit by someone from one of those clans would certainly be treated
with trepidation and a great deal of wariness. No feud,
but no friendship, either. That meant a continuing pau-
city of men. Gillyanne hated to think that the peace,
the contentment, she felt was not from seeing her lands
and keep, but from accepting, deep in her heart, that
she would always be no more than Aunt Gilly, maiden
aunt Gilly, spinster aunt Gilly, dried up old stick Gilly.

"It doesnae matter," she finally said, not believing a
word of it. "I dinnae need a mon to be happy."

"Dinnae ye want bairns? Ye need a husband to get
yourself a few of them."

"Nay, just a lover." She almost laughed at James' look
of shock. "Or," she hurried on before he could sputter
any response, "I can train the lasses to be ladies of their
own lands and households. Or, I could collect some of
the forgotten children one is always seeing on the streets
of every town, village, and hamlet. There are many
bairns in dire need of love, care, and a home."

"True, but 'tis nay the same, is it."

"Nay, but 'twill do if naught else comes my way. Dinnae fret o'er me, James. I am capable of making my
own happiness, A future with a loving husband and
bairns would be best, but I can find joy in living without
such blessings. In truth, one reason I wished to leave
home was because I grew weary of trying to make people
believe me when I told them that. Their loving concern
began to become an irritation and that is nay what I
want."

"Sorry," James murmured. "I was doing the same,
wasnae I?"

"Some. I feared gagging on my own envy at times, as
weel, and that is nay any good. Though it hurts to be
apart from my family, if I am to remain a spinster, if
that is truly my fate, apart is probably for the best. I
would rather lead my own life than become too en-
snared in theirs. I would rather be visited than housed."

"Do ye truly believe they would treat ye unkindly,
Gilly?" James frowned at her with an odd mix of uncertainty and condemnation.

"Ne'er on purpose, James," she replied without hesitation. "Yet, they are all so content in their lives, with
their husbands and their bairns, they quite naturally
wish the same for me. So they introduce me to men,
drag me to court, sweetly try to clothe me better or
change the way I wear my hair." Gillyanne shrugged.
"I am twenty now, but, as the years pass, that prodding
may grow a little stronger, their worry more obvious.
Nay, 'tis best if there is some distance. They can cease
trying to find me a mate and I will no longer feel their
sad concern when none appears." She hooked her arm
through his and started down the steep, narrow steps
that led to the bailey below. "Come. Let us see what
our beds feel like. It has been a verra long day."

James said no more although Gillyanne got the feeling he wanted to. She suspected he wished to encourage

her, soothe her with flattery that somehow made her tiny, thin self sound bonny, but could not think of anything good enough. It was the same with the rest of her family and it was one reason she had begun to feel uncomfortable around them. Each time one of her family tried to boost her pride or sense of worth, she was painfully aware of why they felt the need to do so.

As she readied herself for bed, she idly planned a few improvements for her rather barren bedchamber. There was work for her to do here and she knew she could find satisfaction in that. She would make these lands her future, her life. Perhaps, if she and her family ceased looking so hard for her mate, he would finally come her way.

When she had to give a little hop to get up on the high bed, she sighed and scrambled beneath the covers. She suspected her size might have something to do with her lack of suitors. There really was not much of her, in height or in womanly curves. Men liked a little flesh on the bones of their women and she had almost none of that soft fullness they craved.

Her cats suddenly joined her on the bed, Dirty curling up against her chest and Ragged against her back, flanking her with their warmth. As she closed her eyes, she wished men could be as easily pleased as cats. A warm place to sleep, a little stroking, and a full belly and they were content. Her cats did not care if she had small breasts, a sometimes too sharp wit, and the skill to sense a lie, sometimes even before it was uttered. What she needed was a man of simple needs, one who could see past her lack of curves and her odd ways. In her dreams he existed, but Gillyanne feared that was the only place she would ever find him.

Chapter Two

"They be here."

Gillyanne glanced up at George before returning her attention to her meal and dropping the occasional piece of cheese to Ragged and Dirty who lurked beneath the table. She had been so occupied with thoughts on all she wanted to do in her new home, she had not even seen the man walk up to her. The man's thin face was drawn into its usual somber lines and Gillyanne sensed that he was worried. Since that was the feeling she had constantly had from him since her arrival two days ago, she did not allow it to alarm her. George seemed to savor being worried.

"Who are *they*, George?" she asked, teasing Dirty into standing on her hind legs to get the offered piece of chicken.

"The lairds," George replied.

"Which lairds?"

"The three that we ne'er see and dinnae wish to."

"Ah, those lairds."

"They will soon be kicking at our gates."

"And should I open those gates?"

George sighed heavily and shrugged his thin, rounding shoulders. "I have to wonder why they have come, m'lady, when they have ne'er done so before. Oh, they cross our land from time to time, but nay more. Sent messengers a wee while ago asking who held these lands and I told them 'twas the MacMillans. Ne'er heard a word after that, so I decided that news hadnae troubled them. So, I be asking meself, why now? Why come here now?"

"And a verra good question it is," Gillyanne said. "Since they are the only ones who can reply to that, I believe we must put the question directly to them."

"Let them in?"

There had been a definite squeak of fear in George's voice, but Gillyanne politely ignored it. "Only the three lairds—alone and without their weapons. If they but come to talk, that should be agreeable to them."

"Aye, a good plan."

"Get Sir James to stand with ye," she called after George who was already leaving to carry out her orders.

"Another good plan," he said even as he went out the door.

Approval felt nice, Gillyanne decided, but knew it would be fleeting. She suspected most of George's came from the fact that she was allowing only three men inside the walls, an easily overcome number. The man would soon realize that her plan left Ald-dabhach encircled by whatever men the lairds had brought with them.

Seeing young Mary entering the great hall, gracefully dodging the fleeing cats, Gillyanne instructed the girl to see that food and drink were set out for their guests. Within hours after arriving at Ald-dabhach, Gillyanne had seen that Mary showed true promise of becoming an excellent helper, despite being only twelve. Confident that her orders would be carried out swiftly and correctly, Gillyanne turned her thoughts to her uninvited guests.

It was almost impossible to make a plan before facing the three lairds since she, nor anyone else apparently, knew why they had come. Until she knew that, Gillyanne decided the best thing to do was to act the laird herself, to be regal and aloof, yet not so much so that she caused any offense. She sat up straight in the laird's chair, glanced down, and hoped that none of the lairds would notice that her feet did not quite touch the floor. When she heard the sound of people approaching the great hall, she stiffened her back and began to repeatedly remind herself that Ald-dabhach was hers.

James led in three men who were closely followed by two of her men at arms. George slipped in behind them all and tried to disappear into the shadows at the side of the doorway. The three men looked at her, blatantly searched the room for someone else, then turned their full attention back toward her. The two shorter men openly gaped at her while the tall man briefly, subtly, quirked one light brown brow at her.

"My lairds, I welcome ye to Ald-dabhach," Gillyanne said. "I am Lady Gillyanne Murray. Please, come and sit at my table. Food and drink will arrive."

The black-haired laird was the first to step forward and bow. "I am Sir Robert Dalglish, laird of Dunspier, the lands which border ye on the east and south." He sat down on her right, leaving space for James who was quick to take her place at his side.

The squarely built red-haired laird stepped forward next, his bow so curt as to border upon being an insult. "I am Sir David Goudie, laird of Aberwellen, the lands bordering ye on the west and the south." He sat down opposite Sir Robert, but kept his hard gaze fixed upon James.

Slowly the tall man strode forward, scowled briefly, then stiffly bowed. "I am Sir Connor MacEnroy of Deilcladach. I am laird of all the rest of the lands which surround you." He sat down on her left.

Mary, with her young brothers acting as pages, brought in the food and drink, giving Gillyanne a welcome moment to catch her breath. There was an unsettling mixture of wariness, tension, and belligerence emanating from the men and Gillyanne had to fight to keep it from affecting her. It told her, however, that these men were not here to simply welcome her to Alddabhach. She wanted to demand an immediate explanation, but knew that could easily make her look weak, could reveal her uneasiness. As she sipped her wine, she tried to draw strength from James, to imitate his calm.

Sir Robert did not seem such a bad fellow. His bow had been elegant, his words spoken politely, and, after his first look of surprise, his expression had become one of mild interest. Sir David made her wary. The man seemed to challenge her right to sit in the laird's chair. Gillyanne got the strong feeling that Sir David did not like the idea of a woman holding land, or anything else of value. Sir Robert was a courtier and Sir David was a somewhat brutish warrior. Gillyanne knew it was an extreme simplification, but it would still serve in helping her deal with each man until she could learn more.

The man seated on her left concerned her the most. Gillyanne could feel nothing when she fixed her attention upon the impressively large Sir Connor, nothing but the faintest hint of wariness directed toward the other two lairds. She was not even sure she was actually feeling that, but might simply be making a guess based upon the way he looked at the other two men. The man rarely looked her way.

He unsettled her yet Gillyanne was not sure if that was because of his size, her inability to feel anything when she concentrated on him, or, she inwardly sighed, his beauty. Sir Connor MacEnroy was tall, broad-shouldered, and possessed a lean muscular strength that gave his every movement grace. His hair was a rich golden hue and hung in thick waves past his shoulders. His features were the sort to make a woman sigh despite the large scar that ran from the corner of his left eye in a faint curve over one high cheekbone to just below his left ear and the slight irregularity in his long straight nose that revealed it had been broken at least once. There was a small scar on his strong jawline and another on his forehead. His gently curved eyebrows were several shades darker than his hair as were his long, thick lashes. The few glimpses she had gotten of his eyes had caused her heart to beat a little faster. She did not believe she had ever seen such a lovely blue in anyone's eyes. They were the color of bluebells, a flower she had always been fond of. A quick glance down at his hands revealed that they, too, were beautiful—strong, well-shaped, with long, graceful fingers. The scars on the backs of his hands told one that, despite his youth, he had long been a man of battle.

"So, ye claim Ald-dabhach, do ye?" Sir David asked, his tone of voice making the question sound very much like a demand.

"Aye, 'tis mine," Gillyanne replied sweetly. "My great-uncle gave it to me as my dower lands. 'Twas most kind of him."

"Dower lands are for a lass to give her husband. Are ye wed or betrothed?"

"Nay." It was an impertinent question and Gillyanne found it increasingly difficult to speak kindly. "My great-uncle assured me that I dinnae need a husband to lay claim to Ald-dabhach. These are *my* lands." When Sir David scowled at her and grunted, Gillyanne felt a strong urge to hit him, but James suddenly placed his hand over her clenched fist.

"Ye need a husband, lass," Sir David announced, "and that is why we have come here this day."

"To get me a husband?"

"Nay, no need to go searching. We will marry you."

"All of ye? I dinnae think the church will allow that." Gillyanne heard a soft grunt from her left, but decided not to take her gaze off Sir David in what would probably prove a vain effort to guess what Sir Connor's grunt meant.

"Nay. Ye will choose one of us."

The fact that Sir David responded as if her words were to be taken seriously almost made Gillyanne laugh. Sir Robert was looking at the man as if he could not decide whether to laugh or strike the fool. A quick glance at Sir Connor revealed that he was closely watching her now, although she dared not even try to guess why.

"And why should I do that?" Gillyanne asked.

"A lass cannae hold land on her own," Sir David said. "Ye need a mon to lead here."

"M'lady," Sir Robert said quickly, before Gillyanne could reply to Sir David's arrogant remarks, "my friend here may nay speak with the softest words, but there is some truth in what he says."

Gillyanne thought that if Sir Robert was trying to soothe her, he was doing a very poor job of it.

"These are nay peaceful times, m'lady," Sir Robert continued. "Each clan must strive to be as strong and as battle ready as possible. Clever and willing as ye may be, 'tis a job a mon is trained to."

"I ken it. 'Tis why I feel so secure here—as laird. Not only am I ably assisted by my cousin Sir James Drummond, laird of Dunncraig, and the men my fither Sir Eric Murray trained, but by Sir George, a verra experienced mon chosen by my great-uncle." Gillyanne folded her hands on the table and smiled widely at the three men. "And I am surrounded by three strong lairds whom Sir George assures me have ne'er troubled nor threatened us."

"M'lady," Sir Robert began.

"Leave it be, Robbie," snapped Sir David. " 'Tis fair clear that the lass refuses to see reason."

"Reason? Ye have said that I am in need of a husband and I have politely disagreed with ye," said Gillyanne. "Nay more, nay less."

"Dinnae play the fool. Ye ken that we want this land, want one of us to be holding it and nay some tiny lass given it as a gift from a fond kinsmon. Ye choose one of us as a husband or we will be doing the choosing for ye," Sir David said even as he stood up.

After a brief hesitation both Sir Robert and Sir Connor also stood and Gillyanne sighed with honest regret. "And so agree all of you? Ye all stand together?" When Sir Robert nodded in reply, she looked at Sir Connor. "Ye have said naught, Sir Connor. Do ye stand with these men, agree with all their plans for me and my lands?"

"They are fine lands, m'lady," Sir Connor replied, "and ones we have all coveted for a verra long while."

Gillyanne nearly cursed as the three men strode away, James quickly moving to escort them out of the gates and secure those gates firmly behind them. Two scant days at her keep and she was already at odds with three neighboring clans. That was a disastrously short period of time in which to end what appeared to have been years of peace. She quickly refilled her goblet with wine and had a long drink.

"I believe we may have a wee problem," James drawled as he strode back into the hall.

"Nay. Truly?" she murmured.

James gave her a mildly disgusted look as he sat down next to her and helped himself to some wine. "They want you."

"They want this land."

"We are doomed," said George as he emerged from the shadows by the door, walked to the head table, and slumped into the seat on Gillyanne's left. "There are a lot of men out there."

"A lot?" Gillyanne asked James.

"Aye, but I dinnae think they will come at us all at once," James replied.

"Nay? Why not?"

"Whilst they will nay stop one of the lairds from claiming you, none of the other lairds will help him do so. I believe they will each make a try upon their own."

"I wonder how they will decide who will go first."

"Draw lots, toss a coin, throw the dice?" James shrugged. "Does it matter?"

Gillyanne shook her head. "Nay. It seems great-uncle's gift isnae the blessing I thought it was."

"Ye have just received three offers of marriage." James laughed and ducked her half-hearted attempt to hit him.

"Why dinnae ye just accept one of them, m'lady?" asked George. "Each mon is a belted knight and a laird, and, though I cannae guess at what spurs a lass's choice, none of them appeared to be too hard on the eye. Young and strong, too. Good lands."

"I am sure each one is a fine mon," Gillyanne said, smiling at the distraught Sir George. "They dinnae want me, though, do they? They want this land. 'Tis clear they dinnae want to start a battle or e'en a feud by just grabbing what they crave, but they see in me a chance to take it without causing such trouble. And, if I had chosen one o' them, 'twould serve to keep them from fighting amongst themselves. I shall now become the prize in some game. Not exactly the chivalrous wooing of a lass's dreams."

"Few lasses get that."

"Sadly true." She sighed, and lightly drummed her fingers on the table. "Yet, I dinnae wish any blood to be spilled o'er this."

"Cannae see how that can be avoided if ye mean to make them fight for you."

"I do not believe it will be a hard fight in the beginning. They will wish to test our strength and skill first. Nor do I believe that they wish to see much damage done to Ald-dabhach and its people."

"Oh, nay. And, they must be careful nay to harm or kill you."

"It *would* be a little difficult to wed me and claim my lands if I am dead. That would also set them at odds with my great-uncle, something they appear reluctant to do. Nor would they want to anger my own clan. *I* am clearly not considered as great a threat. Odd, though, that they would risk angering my great-uncle by forcing a marriage down my throat."

James frowned and rubbed a hand over his chin. "Once they discovered this land was held by an unwed lass, they may weel have begun to fear that ye might soon wed someone, and someone with an eye to gain more land. The MacMillans have shown themselves to be peaceful neighbors if nay true allies. Whate'er mon ye might marry could easily prove to be far less amiable."

"With it being so peaceful here, I would have thought that these lairds would attempt to treaty first," Gillyanne said.

"It wasnae always peaceful here, m'lady," said George. "The fathers of those three lairds, and their fathers afore them, and afore that, too, were a bloodthirsty, covetous lot of men. Ald-dabhach suffered, too, but mostly from being crossed by raiding parties, and treated as a larder for all those fools. Treaties were made and broken time and time again. Betrayal was common. This land fair ran red with the blood of all three clans and some of ours as weel."

"What ended it all?" asked Gillyanne.

"The lairds' fathers killed each other off. There wasnae much left but scorched earth and far too many graves, though I think the MacEnroys suffered the most. Mere boys the lairds were, but they stepped out of the ruins and made a pact with each other. The wars and the slaughter would end with them. They didnae become dear and trusting friends, but they will nay fight each other. If one breaks the bond and attacks another, he will find himself facing the other two lairds. They willnae rush to aid each other if one must fight another enemy, but they willnae help that enemy, either."

"A peace, but not necessarily one of mutual aid."

"Exactly, m'lady, and so it has stood for near twelve years. There have been a few times when some crime was done one or some insult was given, but it didnae start a battle or a feud. The lairds met and thrashed out a solution."

"Weel, I suppose, if it really was that bad," began Gillyanne.

"M'lady, by the time the old lairds died, I was stunned that there was anyone left alive to pull himself out of the rubble those fools had left behind and start again."

"Ah. That does explain why they want no stranger to come here, wed me, and claim my dower lands."

Gillyanne sprawled more comfortably in the large chair and stared at the top of the thick wood table trying to sort through her tangled thoughts. What she needed to do was buy some time, time in which her father could arrive. Instinct told her he would hie to Ald-dabhach as soon as he was done with his errand for the king. Then he would turn his fine coaxing skills on the three lairds and untangle this mess. Until that happened, she had to somehow hold firm to Ald-dabhach and her maiden state and yet not get anyone on either side killed or injured. It was not an easy problem to solve.

"Ye are going to fight, arenae ye, lass," George said, looking very close to tears.

"Nay hard," she assured him. "I promise you. What I need is time. My fither will come soon and he can help to sort this tangle out. Those lairds will treaty with him, I expect."

"Aye," agreed James, "but we cannae be sure exactly when he will come."

"Which is why I wish to reassure George that I willnae fight hard and long. Nay, I but mean to drag my feet for a wee while, praying that Fither will ride to my rescue. Demeaning, but necessary. 'Tis just my luck that the first real difficulty I face here is one where a mon is required, an older, more powerful mon than ye, James," she added with a brief grin.

"So, we prepare ourselves to repel an attack or two."

"But gently, as I truly wish no real harm done to either side."

"Ah, then I shall toss pillows at them." He laughed and easily ducked another half-hearted attempt to swat him before growing serious again. "Trickery is needed, lass. We need clever ways to halt or divert any attack made against us."

"Do ye think the first attempt will come on the morrow?"

"I do. Those three want the matter settled as much as we wish to hold on until our fither arrives."

"Then I had better begin to brew my first surprise," Gillyanne said as she stood up.

"What will that be, m'lady?" George asked as he and James followed Gillyanne out of the great hall.

"Something that smells as wretched as I can make it smell and which will stick weel to whate'er it is poured upon. One doesnae have to hurt a mon to make him wish to flee, far and fast."

"But, if it will smell so bad they will run from it, willnae we be tormented as we brew it?"

"I fear there is always some price to pay for indulging in such battle tactics." Gillyanne laughed at the grimaces her two companions pulled. "It willnae be so bad. I will leave the worst stench to be added at the last moment. And, just remember, we will be able to walk away from it. The poor fools we tip it on will probably stink for days, e'en if they burn their clothes."

As Gillyanne led her companions onward, she found herself hoping that the MacEnroy laird would not be the first to attack and wondered why. He had seemed the most intent of the three and thus could prove to be the most dangerous. She shrugged aside her suddenly confused thoughts, telling herself that it was only that it seemed such a shame to desecrate such a beautiful figure of manhood with the eye-watering stench she was about to brew.

"How did ye end up being the third to go?" demanded Diarmot, crouching by his brother Connor who was seated beneath a tree. "Ye usually have better luck."

Connor kept his gaze fixed upon Ald-dabhach. " 'Tis lucky to be third."

"Lucky to give those two fools a first chance at the prize?"

"Aye, and a first chance to fail."

"Did the lass bring an army with her, then?"

"Half a dozen hale, weel trained men."

"That doesnae sound like enough."

"If they are as weel trained as she claimed, a half dozen men could hold that place for a wee while. So could a clever laird. And that lass is clever."

Diarmot sat down and looked toward the keep. "A clever lass can be a curse. Mayhap ye should let one of the others win."

"Nay. I want Ald-dabhach. The lands are rich, producing more than those who live here need. We have no such bounty at Deilcladach. Twould also give ye a place to guard and people to lead. Each one of the other lairds has something to give a brother or two. I have four brothers and not e'en a cottage to offer. Clever lass, or nay, there are many reasons to hope that the MacEnroys gain this land.''

"How do ye ken that the lass is clever? Ye didnae meet with her for verra long.''

"Long enough. Sir David thinks he needs but knock a few heads, march in, and drag the lass afore a priest. He has little respect for the men behind those walls and less for the lass. That is his folly. Sir Robert is not much better, although he has the wit to foresee some trouble in gaining the prize. I am nearly certain that they will both fail and so I will sit here and watch. I am particularly interested in what the lass will do and how high a cost she will ask of her people.''

Connor found his thoughts briefly fixing upon the tiny lady holding Ald-dabhach. There was something intriguing about her and her looks, although he would be hard pressed to say just what. Lady Gillyanne was tiny, might just reach his armpit if she stood up very straight, and her feminine curves were not much more than shadows of those held by so many other women. Her hair was neither red nor brown and her eyes were a mix of green and blue, one having more blue in it and the other having more green. Everything about her was dainty, from her long-fingered graceful hands to her small feet which he had noticed had not quite reached the floor. She was not a woman he would have thought to feel lustful about, yet he did, and that could prove to be a problem. He also had the feeling those odd but beautiful eyes saw a great deal more than most.

"So, we may be here a few days," Diarmot said, scattering Connor's idle musings about the lady he intended to claim.

"Aye. Best keep a guard on that priest," advised Connor. "He wasnae pleased to be dragged along and may try to slip away.''

"Agreed. I will have one of the lads take him to that wee church in the village and hold him there. I have the feeling that just capturing the lass willnae be enough to make the other two claim ye the winner."

"Nay. I must capture that wee lass, wed her, bed her, and get her back to Deilcladach as swiftly as possible."

"Since the lass obviously didnae want to have any of ye as her husband, she may have a complaint or two o'er such a hurried wedding and bedding."

Connor shrugged. "It will matter naught. I will have her *and* her fine lands. The game will be mine."

Chapter Three

"Here they come."

Gillyanne nearly echoed James' prayer of gratitude. Even with the heavily perfumed cloths tied over their noses the stench of what awaited the advancing army in buckets and pots all along the wall was hard to bear. She was astounded at the foulness of the brew she had made. It was so foul she was not sure the potion she had mixed to clean the pots and buckets would be strong enough. Gillyanne also suspected that, if she offered to mix a potion for anyone at Ald-dabhach after this, they would either flee or beg her on their knees not to do it.

"Which laird is it?" she asked George who stood on her left, well concealed behind the wall.

"Sir David," he replied after chancing a quick peek over the wall.

"Oh, good."

"Aye, that one deserves this curse we are about to pour on his head."

"I hope I made it sticky enough."

"Weel, young Peter spilled a wee bit on his shirt and it wouldnae come off with water or fierce rubbing."

"Did ye try my cleaning potion?"

"Aye, and it worked, but he had ripped his shirt off by then and was scrubbing at his arm."

"Oh." Gillyanne frowned. "The stench went right through the shirt onto his skin, did it?"

"It did, but that wasnae what troubled him. Said his skin was afire and he started pouring water o'er it."

"It burned him?" Gillyanne asked, her voice softened by horror.

"Nay. Once he started washing it away the feeling passed quick and the redness faded so swiftly 'twas most likely all his scrubbing that caused that." George rubbed at the grey stubble on his chin. "Just a wee hint of a rash."

Gillyanne slumped against the wall in relief. "Thank God. I dinnae wish to maim anyone. Still, mayhap we should be verra careful about pouring it o'er their heads. It could damage their eyes." She noticed that George gave her the same look of utter male disgust that James did.

"These lads coming at us arenae so verra concerned about us," James reminded her. "They certainly look weel prepared to do a wee bit of maiming and killing. *And* since they are down there and we are up here, 'tis somewhat impossible *not* to pour this wretched muck o'er their heads."

"I ken it. Just tell everyone to yell out 'ware your eyes' before they throw the stuff down." When George and James passed that order along, Gillyanne was not surprised to hear a few groans and chuckles over such womanly softness. "I hope someone here can get a goodly amount of this muck on that fool," she added when Sir David rode close to the walls.

Sir David Goudie irritated Gillyanne like a nettle rash. He was full of his own self-importance. She felt certain he was one of those men who felt women were useful in only one way and that he would be doing the world a great service by ousting her from her rule at Ald-dabhach. Gillyanne would love to lock him in a room with the females of her family for a few days of torment and education.

"So, if all else fails and ye are forced to accept one of the lairds as your husband, I wager he willnae be the one," drawled James.

"That oaf? I think not."

"Lady Gillyanne," bellowed Sir David, "are ye prepared to surrender to me?"

"Why should I do that?" she yelled back.

"Because I have a cursed army before your walls!"

"They will certainly feel cursed in a moment," she murmured, causing James and George to laugh; then called down to Sir David. "My walls are verra tall and thick, Sir David, and, in all truth, 'tisnae such a verra big army."

"Ye would risk the lives of your people just to cling to your maidenhood?"

"And this land. But, my maidenhood is verra dear to me as weel. In fact, I think I may become a nun and these lands could be the dowry I bring to the church."

"O'er my dead body!"

" 'Tis a shame I am too soft of heart to take up that challenge," Gillyanne muttered then, when she saw Sir David signal his men to begin the attack, she called out, "Now, men! Ere they loose a single arrow!"

"Ware your eyes!" called many voices all at once.

Gillyanne was pleased with how swiftly she was obeyed. She might be a tiny female, but the people of Ald-dabhach showed no hesitation in accepting her as their laird. It probably helped that the men she had brought with her readily accepted her right to command, but that knowledge did not lessen the heady feeling of the moment by very much.

As the vile potion was tossed over the walls there was a stunned silence amongst the men below. Gillyanne wondered if the silence was born of terror, the men fearing it was boiling oil or the like, or if the stench had rendered them all mute. Then the howling and curses began. Looking down, she felt a distinct pang of sympathy for a lot of the men were retching. Her people had scattered the foul brew far and wide. She caught sight of several odd objects sailing through the air to hit the men who had not been very close to the walls. Gillyanne cheered with the others on the wall as several struck Sir David.

"What were those things?" she asked Sir George.

"Some of the lads thought to pour the stuff into a pig's bladder and the like so that it could be tossed farther out from the walls," George replied. "Tested it with some water first. Works fine, doesnae it."

"Verra fine indeed. How many pigs were sacrificed for the cause?"

"Nay so many. They used a lot of the innards, ye ken, nay just the bladders. Best ye nay look now, m'lady. Some of the Goudies are tearing off their clothes."

"Aye, there are a lot of bare bums fleeing o'er the hills. Shame they left their clothes behind for it keeps the stench a wee bit too close to us for my liking."

"I can send a lad or two out to put them in a pile and set them afire. I dinnae think there will be much risk to that. They will be mucking up our river, though."

" 'Tis flowing swiftly so whate'er gets into it should run by us fast enough."

"Do ye think the next laird will come at us soon?"

"Nay," James replied. "In the morning. They appear to be doing this in a verra direct manner. Approach, ask Gilly to surrender, then attack. Today is Sir David's chance. The others will wait to see if he tries again."

"Ah, so ye think they have each been given a day," said Gillyanne.

"Aye. One day to try their luck. We will keep the watch strong upon the walls, but I truly believe we will see naught happen until the morrow."

"Ye dinnae think Sir David will be back?"

"He may want to try again, but he will have a verra hard time pulling his men back to these walls when their eyes are still watering from that smell."

"Then let us retire to a sweeter smelling place and plan our next move."

"Do ye think she poured boiling oil on them?" Diarmot asked Connor as they watched the disorderly rout of Sir David's men.

"I cannae feel she would be so brutal," replied Connor, smiling faintly when he saw that an increasing number of the Goudies were naked. "If she had poured that evil on them some of them would be nay more than staggering torches, yet, e'en though many seem near desperate to get their clothes off, I see no smoke."

A soft breeze curled around them as they stood on the small rise. Connor's eyes widened even as Diarmot cursed and clapped a hand over his nose. He swiftly did the same, noticing that every one of his small army was covering or pinching his nose and trying to back away from the smell drifting toward them.

"She dumped the contents of the privy pits on them," Diarmot said.

"If the privy pits of Ald-dabhach smell like that no one would stay within its walls," Connor murmured, noticing that, after the first shock, the stench was faint enough to be endured.

"Addled eggs," one man said, daring a faint sniff.

"Nay, 'tis pig muck," said another.

"I still think 'tis the privy pits," said Diarmot.

"And I think 'tis all of it." Connor shook his head.

"The lass must have found every foul smelling thing she could and made herself an evil brew. And, by the way the men are tossing aside their clothes, I suspect it was made to stick fast."

It was admirably clever, Connor mused. She had routed her enemy ere they had struck a single blow. It was a thoroughly bloodless victory. Connor had felt that Lady Gillyanne would wish no harm to her own people and he was pleased to have been proven right. It was now apparent that she would also try hard not to spill the blood of the very men trying to steal her lands.

"Do ye think Sir David will try again?" asked Diarmot. "He has until sunset today. Hours left."

"He may wish to, but, nay, I think this battle is o'er. His men willnae wish to risk a second dousing. And, by the look of it, near half of them are naked. 'Tis said we used to fight naked, but I suspect his men will want new clothes first."

Diarmot laughed then frowned, casting an uneasy look toward the walls of Ald-dabhach. "Do ye think she has any more of that evil brew? Mayhap e'en enough to fend off two more attacks?"

"I doubt it. We will ken the answer to that on the morrow when Sir Robert and his men approach those walls. I suspect they will do so verra, verra cautiously. Sir Robert may not have nurtured the same depth of scorn for the lady as Sir David did, but he foresaw no difficulty in winning. 'Twas why he was so angry o'er losing the chance to go first. I believe he will act with more respect for her now."

"Ye suspected her cunning, didnae ye."

Connor nodded. "In truth, I willnae be too surprised if we are all routed on the first try."

"Weel, I will pray that our defeat is a far sweeter smelling one."

*   *   *

Gillyanne crossed her arms and studied the two separate piles of herbs on the head table in the great hall. The second routing of the enemy was not going to be so easy. There were too many things that could go wrong with her plans. Yet, she felt almost desperate to win against Sir Robert if he was to be the next one at her gates. Although she could not say exactly why, she dreaded the thought that he might win and drag her to the altar. He was a handsome man and had seemed courteous, yet everything inside her recoiled at the thought of wedding him.

"So, do we make them miserable," James asked, pointing to one pile of herbs, "or happy?" He pointed to the other.

"I dinnae ken." Gillyanne sighed. "If the wind should turn against us . . ."

"I swear to ye, m'lady, at this time of the year it willnae," George said. "It always comes off the river behind us."

"So the smoke should blow out and away." She rubbed her fingers over her temple.

"Of course, 'twill also blow toward the other two lairds and their men."

" 'Twill serve them right. They shouldnae be sitting out there thinking of how to take what is mine."

"Oh, aye, there is that."

"And, 'twill nay bother them much for it will be much weakened ere it reaches them."

"So? Kind or mean?" James just grinned when Gillyanne stuck her tongue out at him.

"I think we will be kind. 'Tis nay that I doubt your word, George, but fate and the weather might turn against me and the wind send the smoke back at us. One ye must breathe in and it will calm ye, eventually put ye to sleep. The other can be a bother if it simply gets on your skin.''

"Then, aye, let us be kind,'' agreed James. "If the smoke drifts our way, a thick rag o'er our noses might prove protection enough.''

"True. We will make sure everyone has one at the ready.''

"The other problem is how to get the enemy to stand still near the fires we will build. They are sure to suspect some trickery when they see the fires there. After all, 'twill be morning so we cannae say they are watch fires.''

"Oh, aye, we can—if we set them ere the sun rises. Do we have enough wood, George?''

George nodded. "We do, but 'twill sore deplete our supply. No matter. We can collect more.''

"We still havenae come up with a way to make the fools dawdle near these fires,'' James reminded her. "Ye ken there is one way, dinnae ye, but I willnae press ye to do it.''

"Aye, I do ken a way.'' Gillyanne shook her head. "I have ne'er understood why it affects people as it does, but it would work, and thus I would be a fool not to use it.''

"Use what?'' asked George.

"She will sing to the next laird and his men,'' replied James.

"Weel, lass, I am sure ye have a bonny wee voice, but . . .'' George stuttered to a halt when James held up his hand.

"Sing a wee song for George, lass,'' James said.

Gillyanne sighed, clasped her hands together in front of her skirts, and sang as short a song as she could recall. The silence which greeted the end of her song did not really surprise her; it was a common reaction. She blushed a little when she glanced around to see that George was not the only one listening to her, nor the only one wiping a tear away.

"It was a happy song," Gillyanne muttered.

"Oh, aye, it was," said George and he sniffed. "Purely joyous."

James laughed softly and kissed Gillyanne on the cheek. "Ye cannae hear it as we do, lass. And, 'tis probably just as weel for ye might ne'er finish a song and that would be a grievous thing. 'Tis a sound that caresses the ear, and stirs the soul. Ye were blessed by the angels and I think we can all hear their touch when ye sing."

"Now I *am* embarrassed," she whispered, covering her burning cheeks with her hands.

"Just dinnae be so shy ye canne sing to our enemies on the morrow."

"I think I will tell all the lads to stop up their ear-holes," said George.

James nodded. "A good idea. We dinnae want them so caught up in her singing they dinnae notice if the wind changes or if the laird guesses our trickery ere it has routed him. We certainly dinnae want to fall prey to our own wiles." He winked at Gillyanne then asked, "How will this work, lass?"

"We have to get the herb into the fire. The smoke from it will soothe the men, make them act as if they are caught in a dream. Enough of it and they will doze, or get so dreamy some of our men can creep up on them and knock them o'er the head. I had thought of binding some to arrows and shooting the arrows into the fires. That willnae work for, once an arrow is loosed from the walls, 'twill be thought that we have attacked. I dinnae think e'en my singing will make men ignore a sudden flurry of arrows coming their way."

"True. Mayhap we could just toss the packets in."

"It would still draw attention, I think, and 'twould be best if they dinnae grow suspicious about the fires."

"We can post a lad at each fire," said George.

"Will that be safe?" asked Gillyanne.

"Safe enough. No one will think it strange that some

lads tend the watchfires. Only a fool leaves a fire unwatched. Then, when the lads see the enemy approaching, they toss in the packets and get themselves behind the walls."

James nodded. "And their swift retreat will be witnessed so none will think it odd that they didnae pause to douse the fires."

"Odd, but having so many good solutions to each problem come so quickly makes me a little uneasy," murmured Gillyanne.

"Ye fret too much, Gilly." James studied the pile of herbs. "It doesnae look like much."

" 'Tis certainly enough to gentle that army. I am just nay sure it will make the smoke strong enough to put them all to sleep."

"We have more," George said.

Gillyanne stared at the pile of herbs that, if properly brewed, could knock down a whole army, then looked at George. "Why?"

"Ah, weel, the lady in the village, Old Hilda, collects the herbs when the time is right whether we need them or nay. Then she prepares them here. That particular flower grows verra freely around here. We have a small keg full of that herb dried and ground. Old Hilda is paid for each collection, ye ken. Nay much, but she doesnae wish to give that up just because we havenae used what she prepared last time. She also has the right to come and get a wee bit from here if she has a need and I think she likes the idea of there being such a large bounty for her to pluck her choices from."

"Fetch it up, George. We will be sure to leave something behind as there is naught else as good as this to ease one's pain," she assured George as she helped him bag the herb she was not going to use. "We can make some packets for the lads to toss into the fire as weel as a few for us to throw in if we think the enemy needs a stronger dosing."

"M'lady, if all goes weel and we leave our enemy asleep upon the ground, what do we do with them then?"

"Weel, if none of the laird's men are able to move, we shall slip out and strip them of their arms."

"Oh, dear. I think that, when these men take a second try at us, they willnae be so kind nor so easy to fool."

"I fear the same, but I pray my fither will have arrived by then. If he hasnae, weel, as I told ye before, I willnae allow anyone to be hurt just to save me from an unwanted trip to the altar."

"Are ye prepared to surrender to me, Lady Gillyanne?"

Gillyanne stared down at Sir Robert who looked quite handsome on his great black gelding. The wind was her friend today, she mused, blowing gently and in such a way as to hold the increasingly thick smoke from the fires close to Sir Robert and his men. It was wafting around them in such a way they could not help but breathe it in and the occasional cough she heard was proof enough of that.

Taking a deep breath, she stepped up on the wall, James quickly grabbing her by the ankles to steady her. James had insisted that she dress in her best gold and ivory gown and leave her hair undone. The way Sir Robert's men were staring up at her told her James had been right in thinking it would catch the eye almost as much as her singing would catch their minds and hearts. She just prayed the smoke would swiftly catch hold of their wits.

"Nay, Sir Robert, I think not," she called back.

"Why do ye stand up there? Do ye think to draw me close enough to the walls to douse me with some of that stinking brew?"

"Oh, nay, sir. We used it all on Sir David yesterday. One should always be thorough."

"Of course. Weel, get off that wall. I wouldnae want ye wounded or killed during the attack."

He shook his head as if to clear it. Gillyanne noticed several of his men were smiling and a few had even sat down. The smoke from the burning herbs was already doing its work.

"All this fighting for the right to claim my wee, pale hand in marriage reminds me of a song I once heard," she said, smiling down at Sir Robert, amused at how he smiled back, then shook his head again. " 'Tis one I heard whilst in France. Do ye ken French, sir?"

"I think so. Surely I must. *Maman* was French, ye ken."

"He sounds drunk," James said.

"I suspect he feels it, too," Gillyanne replied then began to sing.

Gillyanne put her heart into her singing, choosing songs that moved her, ones whose tale or poetry stirred her blood. She had just finished her fifth song, a heart-rending one of love lost, when James told her to stop. Even as he helped her down from the wall she glanced down at Sir Robert and his men. Most of them were sprawled out on the ground right below the castle. A few had wandered away and had either fallen down or were still wandering, lost in their dreams.

"In truth, James, I simply cannae believe it worked," Gillyanne said.

"Neither can I," he said and laughed before kissing her on the cheek. "Come, let us get them disarmed."

"Aye. Those fires are nearly out and I dinnae ken how long they will remain unconscious."

"One left."

"Aye." Gillyanne looked toward the MacEnroy camp, a tall figure barely visible amongst the trees. "That one willnae be as easy to knock down."

* * *

"She has killed them all," whispered Diarmot in shock.

"Nay." Connor shook his head in disgust when one of Sir Robert's men staggered up to cling to one of his and tell the shocked man what a lovely fellow he was. " 'Tis some potion to make them senseless. Blind with happiness," he looked at a man who knelt on the field below screaming at the heavens, "or trapped in their own dreams. She is fortunate none of Sir Robert's men held secret any dangerous madness."

"But they didnae eat or drink anything."

" 'Twas in the smoke. When some briefly blew our way did ye nay feel a sense of . . ." Connor groped for the appropriate word.

"Peace? Pleasure in all I could see?"

"Exactly. That smoke and her voice. They trapped poor Sir Robert and his men as weel as a spider's web traps a fly."

"Ah, aye, that singing. We nearly lost Old Nigel because he wandered closer, drawn toward that voice. If 'twas such a delight from here, 'tis nay wonder Robert and his men stood there enraptured until that smoke felled them." He pointed toward Ald-dabhach as the gates opened. "Now they will kill him."

Connor held up his hand to stop his men from moving forward, thinking they were about to witness the cold-hearted murder of helpless men. "Nay. Look. They but take the weapons. Heed me. This lass wants no bloodshed. It would have been far easier for her and her men to just shoot the Goudies or the Dalglishes. Instead, she must be spending hours plotting these elaborate schemes to rout her enemy without spilling a drop of blood. And, she has done so twice now."

"I can understand disarming Sir Robert and his men, but why are they stripping them?" asked Diarmot.

"A little added humiliation, I suspect. She should be careful. Few men take weel to humiliation, especially when delivered by such wee female hands. Sir David can be heard ranting long into the night. I suspect Sir Robert will soon echo him."

"They will be watching closely to see what she does to you."

"Aye." Connor studied the collection of men sprawled on the ground before Ald-dabhach, most of them naked. Even Robert's horse looked almost asleep as he was tugged inside the walls. "They will be eager to watch my defeat."

Diarmot's eyes widened just a little. "Ye *expect* to be defeated by the wench."

"I believe I do. If naught else, how can one predict or protect oneself against such trickery? A stench that clings to a mon and smoke that steals a mon's senses? Aye, I suspect she will have a trick to play upon us as weel."

"Ye are verra calm for a mon facing humiliation."

"I will look upon it as part of my strategy, as naught more than a necessary step toward winning the prize I seek."

"Ah, I see, a strategy. Verra wise. Just what is this strategy?"

"That e'en a lass as clever as Lady Gillyanne Murray has to run out of tricks sometime."

Chapter Four

The red hint of dawn was lightening the sky as Connor stood watching Ald-dabhach. He had not lied to Diarmot when he had told his brother he would accept the humiliation this small woman would probably deal out as part of his strategy. That did not mean he liked the idea or that he faced it with any hint of calm. This was not really battle, but an intricate game and it would take time for him to learn the rules. It irritated him that he could not guess what she might do next so he could not avoid or end the threat he faced. He told himself he should be heartily relieved that she did not wish any bloodshed for, otherwise, he would be walking over the graves of the Goudies and the Dalglishes just to face his own death.

"Connor," Diarmot called softly as he approached his brother, "Knobby has returned and he has something to tell you."

Looking at the tall young man who was so thin all his joints seemed far too prominent thus earning him his name, Connor waited silently for the report. The game had begun. He was sure of it.

"People have been fleeing Ald-dabhach for the last hour or more, laird," Knobby said, his voice surprisingly deep and resonant for a man with such a thin chest.

"Are ye certain they are fleeing?" Connor asked.

"What else would they be doing?"

"Playing a game," Connor muttered, certain of his opinion, yet not sure how this trick would work. How could she expect to defeat him and his men if she was all alone? "Tell me exactly what ye saw? Slowly and precisely."

"At first 'twas a slow business. One or two people at a time with a bit of a wait between. Then more and more. They are all carrying things. They are definitely fleeing the place, like rats from a sinking ship. I suspect they fear this tussle will get bloody soon and they want nay part of dying just because a lass willnae choose one of ye as her husband."

It made perfect sense. Lady Gillyanne had been presented with three very eligible lairds to choose from. Why would the people of Ald-dabhach wish to shed even one drop of their blood because she refused to marry? Lady Gillyanne might call herself their laird, but they could well see her as no more than a lass who had been given a piece of property by a doting kinsman. Why should they be any more accepting of a wee lass as a laird than battle-trained knights like Robert and David? Connor had to wonder why he felt so suspicious.

"Did her own men leave, too?" he asked. "Or that cousin of hers?"

"Nay. I didnae see any of them."

"They *would* stay with her," said Diarmot.

"Of course they would," murmured Connor. "Six men. One wee lass."

"E'en they have to see that they cannae hold that place with so few."

"And since she has shown that she doesnae wish any blood spilled, they probably willnae e'en try." He put his hands on his hips and scowled at the keep he so coveted. "Once they ken all the others have gone, they will probably let us walk right in."

"Aye, so why do ye look as if ye dinnae believe your own good fortune?"

"Because I dinnae. It all seems so right, so reasonable, yet I doubt the truth of it all. After all, the people of Ald-dabhach stood by her when Sir David and then Sir Robert rode forth to try and take the prize. Why should they turn their backs on her now?"

Diarmot shrugged. "Because they ken ye are the better fighter?"

"That would please me but I dinnae think so."

"Because she has run out of tricks and they might have actually had to fight us?"

"Possibly. Yet, I smell a trap." He grimaced and rubbed the back of his neck. "Curse her and her games. I feel certain this is a trick yet I must go forward. 'Tis my turn to try for the prize and, by now, she has undoubtedly figured out that we each have only one day. Armed with that knowledge, she can simply outwait me and then I lose anyway."

"So ye ken she has set a trap, but ye will walk into it?"

"I can see no other choice to make. At least we can go in certain we willnae pay with our lives."

"True, and that is some comfort."

"Tell everyone to take only one weapon. We may find ourselves disarmed as was done to Robert and his men and I dinnae want us to return to our camp to set here with no arms at all."

"I will pass the word. And, I think I will find some braies or a breechclout, something to cover my nether regions. I noticed when Robert and his men were stripped such things were left on those men who wore them. I would just as soon nay be left to walk back to camp with naught to cover my tender parts."

Connor grimaced as he was left alone again and thought of the fine linen breeches he wore beneath his clothes. If they were exposed, he hoped everyone who saw them would think they were some rich laird's affectation. He did not want the world and its mother to know he wore them to protect skin far too sensitive to wool and other rough cloth. It just did not seem a manly affliction to suffer from. He did find some comfort from that embarrassment in the knowledge that two of his brothers suffered the same delicacy.

By the time the sun had fully appeared in the sky, Connor was ready. His men look as resigned as he felt, even the few he had decided to leave behind to guard their remaining arms and the horses. Connor could see the Goudie and Dalglish men lined up to watch them. He hoped they would not be too entertained as he moved forward, his men falling silently into step behind him.

"He is headed this way," announced James as he strode into the great hall, followed by the five Murray men. "He and his men are on foot."

"Ah, afraid I will steal his horse as I stole Sir Robert's," Gillyanne said as she made herself comfortable in the laird's chair.

"Ye didnae steal that horse. 'Tis spoils of war."

"Weel, I think I will return it when this is all over."

"Why? 'Tis a fine horse."

"I ken it, but Sir Robert is obviously verra fond of the beast. He was still demanding its return when his men dragged him away." Gillyanne grinned. "Ne'er had a naked mon yell at me." She giggled when her men laughed but quickly grew serious again. "Do ye think Sir Connor will step into this trap?"

James nodded. "What choice does he have? This is his day, his turn. He has to do something."

"Do ye think the mon suspects something?"

"If he has any wits, he does. As I said, he has no choice. 'Tis his turn and he has to ken that we could just outwait him." He looked over the table heavily laden with bread, cheese, wine, and every sweet treat the cook could produce. "Are ye sure about this?"

"Nay." Gillyanne smiled and shrugged when he frowned at her. "There was a risk with my other plots, too."

"Nay as big a one. The others didnae get within grabbing distance of you."

"True, but there are six armed men here to, er, dim his urge to grab. And such a feast spread out to greet him and his men. After a few days of camp fare, what mon could resist all of this?" There was a half-hearted murmur of agreement from James and the others. "Aye, there are risks, but there is also a good chance that it will work."

"I ken it. He will be wary of the food and drink, unless he is a complete fool."

"And I dinnae believe he is which is why I shall join them in this meal."

James cursed softly. " 'Tis a part of your great plan that I truly hate. Just dinnae eat or drink too much. A runt like ye could put herself to sleep for days."

Gillyanne crossed her arms and glared at the chuckling men then tensed. "I believe I hear George's tremulous tones."

"So, he has walked right into the lion's den," James murmured as he took his place next to Gillyanne's chair and the five Murray men lined up behind her.

"As ye have said—what choice did he have?"

When Sir Connor and his men followed George into the great hall, Gillyanne felt the pace of her pulse increase. She suspected it was not all due to the dangerous game she was about to play. Sir Connor MacEnroy was an impressive figure of a man. Gillyanne doubted any woman alive could look at him and not feel a tickle of appreciation. He was big, strong, and beautiful, a Viking of old come to full life. She shook aside her fancies and smiled a greeting at him, ignoring the suspicious way he looked over the bounty on the table.

"Expecting me, were ye?" Connor asked as he sat in the chair to her right.

"Once I realized I was alone," she began.

"Nay completely alone." Connor briefly looked over the six young men standing guard over her then met her far too innocent gaze. "I could just take ye and walk out of here."

"I dinnae think my men would like that."

"But ye have shown that ye want no blood spilled."

"And I dinnae, yet when one is pressed hard to the wall . . ." She shrugged then smiled and, with a graceful motion of her hand, indicated the food and drink set out for him and his men. "Can we nay break bread together and discuss this sad business calmly?" She decided the cynical, faintly amused look he gave her, one brow raised, could easily prove irritating.

"After what ye did to the others, why should I trust any food or drink offered by ye?"

"Of course. I understand."

Gillyanne was proud of the touch of hurt she had put into her voice. She filled her goblet with wine from one of the jugs then placed a wide assortment of food upon her plate. This time she could eat and drink without fear. Untainted food had been strategically placed amongst the rest specifically for this moment and the half-full jug of wine she had poured from was also clear. If she was fortunate, the men would eat and drink enough to put them out cold before she was forced to down any of the tainted food and drink. Meeting

Connor's intense stare, she took a deep drink of the wine and ate a honey cake.

Connor inwardly grimaced when his men took her actions as a sign that all was well, sat down, and began to help themselves to the wine and food. He did not believe her little show proved much of anything, but continued open mistrust could become an insult. The six well-armed men at her back might react badly to that and he really did not want to have to kill them. He decided he would eat, but would go lightly on the wine.

"What do ye wish to discuss?" he asked as he spread honey on a thick slab of bread. "I have taken Ald-dabhach, have I not? Therefore, it and ye are now mine." He felt the odd urge to smile at the look of irritation she cast over his men when many of them grunted an agreement to his bold statement.

"Weel, to be precise," Gillyanne said in a firm but pleasant voice, "ye have nay *taken* Ald-dabhach. We have *allowed* ye to come inside."

"I could put an end to that fine distinction quickly enough." He held up his hand when her men tensed, their hands moving to their swords. "I willnae. I but point out a wee truth. One I suspect ye were aware of ere ye let us inside."

"Since ye were invited in, I rather hoped ye would hold to the rules of courtesy and hospitality."

"Did ye? How sweetly trusting of ye." Unable to resist, he helped himself to a few of the sweets set out in front of him. "Why continue to resist? Ye will have to accept one of us if ye truly wish no blood spilled."

"Mayhap I have no wish to marry."

"If ye mean to spin that tale about going to a nunnery, dinnae bother. I dinnae believe it any more than David did."

When he put a few cakes on her plate, she inwardly cursed, for they were tainted ones. Her reprieve was obviously at an end. However, since she had already eaten several things, she suspected she could delicately nibble at these and not rouse any suspicion. The way the MacEnroys were devouring the food and drink she did not think she would have to wait too much longer to savor yet another victory.

"Eat up, lass," Connor drawled. "Ye could use a wee bit of meat on your bones."

"If ye mean to convince me that wedding one of ye is in my best interest, a little flattery wouldnae be amiss," she snapped, not only stung by his words, but annoyed that she had just devoured a small cake in the midst of her anger.

" 'Tis wooing ye seek, is it? Why? At the end of it the mon still gets what he first sought, the coin or the land that comes with the bride."

She nearly gaped at him. Gillyanne could not be sure if he really believed what he said or if he was trying to goad her. It irritated her to acknowledge there was some truth to his cynical words, but she had never heard anyone say such things. That this man might not believe in any of the things her clan held dear troubled her more than she cared to admit or thought it should. Try as she did, she could get no sense of how the man felt or thought. Reaching out to him, she felt as though she threw herself against a solid wall, and she was not sure she could blame that on the beginning effects of the herbs hidden in the food.

"If that is how ye feel, why trouble yourself? And, why are the three of you so intent upon this nonsense anyway? I have no interest in stirring up trouble, am perfectly content to keep all as it has been for years."

"Ye are an unwed lass. Aye, when we sought the holder of this land after rumor said it was nay longer held by the laird of the MacMillans, we sought a treaty or e'en a chance to buy the lands. When the king told us it was an unwed lass, we had to agree with our liege's opinion that the best solution was for one of us to marry the lass. There is e'er the chance ye could wed another mon, isnae there, and one who wouldnae be so peaceful, might e'en cast a covetous eye on another laird's lands."

Connor leaned back in his chair wondering why he felt almost compelled to be so honest. " 'Tisnae nonsense to want to end the chance an enemy might slip into one's midst. I decided I am eight and twenty, of an age to be wed, and these are good lands. I would prefer it if ye would choose me, but I would accept any one of the other lairds as laird here. What I dinnae understand is your hesitation. Each one of us is young, strong, nay too ugly, can give ye bairns and offer protection, are lairds of our own lands and nay poor. I would have thought a lass would have little complaint about such a bountiful choice. That has me wondering why ye are playing these games, especially when ye dinnae wish to have a real battle o'er it all. Ye buy time. Why?"

"Time for my fither to come and sort ye fools out," she snapped, thinking that she had never heard anyone describe a reason to marry so coldly, without even one small hint of interest in the woman he would have to marry.

"I see. And ye dinnae think he would approve of the choices offered?"

"Nay," she said and was not surprised at his look of disbelief for it had been evident in the tone of his question. "My fither wouldnae like the way ye are all interested in the lands and nay in me. We Murrays believe a mon and a lass should choose their own mate and for love, nay for money or land."

When his snort of disbelief turned into a jaw-cracking yawn, Connor frowned. He felt a brief twinge of alarm when he looked at his men and saw that they were all fighting to stay awake. As he turned an accusing look upon Lady Gillyanne he caught her yawning and saw that she looked very sleepy as well. Connor felt a sudden urge to laugh and told himself it was a result of whatever

potion she had given them. The occasional thump he
heard told him that his men were rapidly succumbing,
and, after a brief look at the wine he had drunk so
sparingly, he looked at the food and shook his head.

"Ye poisoned the food," he said.

"Nay poisoned. Just something to make ye all sleep."
Gillyanne yawned again. "After all, I wouldnae poison
myself, would I?"

"True. Yet, considering all ye ate, why is such a wee
lass like ye still awake?"

"The first foods I chose were nay tainted."

Diarmot laughed. "At least we had a grand last meal,"
he said and dropped his head down on his crossed arms.

"I wish ye wouldnae speak as if I have murdered all
of ye," grumbled Gillyanne. "I am but giving ye a wee
nap."

"And will soon take our weapons and our clothes,"
Connor said. "I suspect your people didnae really flee
here, either."

"Nay. They have been slipping back inside the walls
e'er since ye arrived."

"Clever lass," he said as he stood up, even as he
wondered why he was doing so.

"I would sit down, sir. Ye willnae have quite so far to
fall that way."

Connor felt Sir James place his hands on his shoulders
and allowed the man to push him back down into his
seat. He was losing his grip on conciousness very quickly
and none of his men were sensible. There was really no
point in even trying to wriggle free of the trap.

"I can appreciate the cunning here, lass," he told
Gillyanne, idly thinking that he sounded drunk.

"Thank ye."

"The others, weel, though they might appreciate the
skill of the game, they willnae be as forgiving as I am."
A little surprised that he had managed to complete that

warning, Connor allowed the encroaching blackness to take him down into its folds.

"I began to think he would ne'er fall down," muttered Gillyanne as she bathed her face with cool water from the bowl George held out to her and felt a little of the herb's effects fade away. "He certainly ate enough."

James nodded. "But he didnae drink much wine. Didnae trust it, I suspect."

"Ha! Fooled him. He wasnae surprised, was he."

"Nay. He expected ye to do something. He probably held only a wee hope that he would uncover the trick ere ye played it out." He smiled faintly at a yawning Gillyanne. "Are ye going to have a wee nap, too?"

"I think not. It would have happened by now. George, there isnae much food or wine left, but ye best see to its disposal." Gillyanne looked at the sleeping MacEnroys. "Weel, best we finish this game."

"Ye dinnae think they will be asleep for long?" James asked as he and the Murray men began to collect the MacEnroys' weapons.

" 'Tis difficult to say. I was careful to go lightly with my brew for too much can put one into a sleep that can last forever. 'Tis best if we dinnae take too much time in ending this game."

The MacEnroys were soon stripped of their clothes and tossed into carts. Gillyanne glanced over their snoring captives and smiled faintly. Nearly every one of them had either braies or some sort of loin covering beneath their clothes. Then her gaze fixed upon the sprawled form of Sir Connor. It seemed unfair that he could still be so handsome when dressed only in some odd linen breeches.

"Such a modest group," drawled James as he moved to stand beside her. " 'Tis evident they planned weel for the possibility of defeat. None of them had more than one weapon and then there is this obvious attempt to make sure they werenae left completely naked. Odd things the laird has on."

"My cousin used to wear something like that," said George as he shuffled up to peer into the cart. "He couldnae abide certain cloth next to his skin. Itched like hellfire and caused a furious rash. Wool was the worst."

"Ah, aye." Gillyanne refused to look at James for fear they would both start laughing at the thought of this huge laird having delicate skin, and she did not really wish to be unkind. "Acts upon the skin like nettles."

"Aye, so my cousin said, though he was sorely troubled by it. Said it wasnae monly."

Gillyanne shook her head. "Foolish. Many people are troubled in such ways by common things. With me, 'tis strawberries. Ye would ne'er think this giant unmonly, would ye?" George shook his head rather vehemently. "Weel, carry them away, lads."

"How far, m'lady?" asked George.

"Nay too far," she replied. "A mile or two. Just far enough to add to their confusion when they wake and give them a long enough walk back to their camp to pinch their feet." She watched as the men drove the carts out of the bailey using a well-hidden rear entrance.

"If ye have to choose, 'twill be that one, will it?" asked James.

"He certainly is a handsome fool. Makes one think of Vikings, the Northmen of the old tales."

"An honest mon, I think."

"He certainly didnae hesitate to say what he thought."

"Gillyanne, I am willing to fight," James stuttered to a halt when Gillyanne shook her head. "Ye deserve better than to be dragged afore a priest because ye have lands one of these fools covets."

"I do, but naught better has shown itself in nearly one and twenty years, has it? That matters little. I willnae have anyone hurt or killed o'er this. After all, James, they offer honorable marriage. Sir Connor wasnae really boasting when he listed all that makes these three lairds acceptable choices for husbands. I was more than willing to use trickery to play these bloodless games, to buy time in the hope that Fither would come and help me out of this tangle. But, if the fighting turns real, I *will* put an end to it and ye swore to accept my decision.''

"Aye, I did," he snapped, "but I didnae swear to like it. Curse it, Gillyanne, ye cannae think it will be a marriage in name only.''

"Nay. I suspect it will be consummated. A lost maidenhead isnae a fatal wound. And, just think, mayhap I will finally discover what lusting is all about," she added and hurried back inside the keep before James could make any response.

"Curse it, where *are* we?"

Diarmot's muttered words made Connor wince. Cautiously, he opened his eyes, the bright sunlight aggravating the throbbing in his head. Slowly he raised himself into a sitting position and looked around. Most of the men were sitting up and, he noted, those who had bothered to don some underwrappings still wore them, as he did.

"I believe we are about a mile or two north of our camp," Connor replied.

"We have to walk?" Diarmot indulged in a full minute of highly creative cursing. "If I e'er meet the mon who raised that wench, I will beat him—soundly and often.''

"She certainly is a wily wee lass," muttered Knobby, holding his head in his hands.

"Why drag us out here?"

As he eased himself up on to his feet, Connor replied, "To make certain we cannae try a second time to get her.''

"Oh." Diarmot staggered a little as he stood up. "Aye, most of the day will be gone by the time we get back to our camp. Do ye really think that tiny lass is the one thinking up all these tricks?"

"I suspect she has the able assistance of her cousin, but, aye, these plots and tricks are of her devising."

"Are ye sure ye want to marry her?" asked Diarmot as he fell into step beside Connor who started them all on the walk back to their camp.

"I want those lands." Connor realized that, although he had begun this venture reluctant to take a wife, that reluctance was gone, but Diarmot did not need to know that. "And such a clever, devious wit could be a boon."

"Or a wretched curse. She is verra small."

"Aye, nay much bigger than a child, but woman enough to wed, bed, and breed. At least I can be assured I will have children with all their wits about them."

"And then some. Ye ken, there will be a real battle now. Ye may not want it, but Sir Robert and Sir David will be eager to avenge their humiliation at her hands."

Connor nodded. "They may not be thinking of the damage they could do to the prize they seek."

"Do ye think the lass will ken the danger?"

"I did try to warn her before I took my wee nap." Connor thought the problem over for a moment. "Aye, she will ken it. If she still wishes no blood shed, she will have to act to stop the onslaught."

"So, she will finally pick a husband?"

"Will she? That would seem to be her only choice. Yet, with this lass, we probably shouldnae be surprised if she uncovers another one."

Chapter Five

Decisions, decisions, Gillyanne mused as she stared up at the ceiling of the great hall. She idly stroked the two cats crowded into the laird's chair with her as she struggled to plot her next move. When she had first arrived at Ald-dabhach she had thought her biggest decisions would be such things as whether or not she could get someone to clean years of accumulated smoke and dust from the ceiling she was now staring at. It certainly needed it. Instead, she was faced with a decision that could affect her entire future. She had thought that problem all settled when she had finally made the move to Ald-dabhach.

But, nay, she thought crossly. She who had never even been briefly wooed now had three lairds pounding at her gates trying to get her to marry one of them. She was little more than the quill needed to sign the deeds. Gillyanne was not sure, but she thought that was even more insulting than being thoroughly ignored by men.

Still, she had defeated each one of them once and felt some pride in that achievement. She had also humiliated each one, and, although Gillyanne felt they had deserved it, she suspected she would soon pay for that. Men did not deal well with humiliation, especially when it was inflicted upon them by a tiny female.

They willnae be as forgiving as I am. Sir Connor's warning refused to be banished from her mind. In truth, she was a little surprised he had been so amiable about it all. Since she seemed unable to read the man in even the smallest way, she had decided he was a hard man, probably very proud and very stubborn. His remarks about marriage implied he held many of those very annoying man-is-master views. That sort tended to take humiliation hard. Yet, he had prepared for his defeat, had even seemed to appreciate how she had accomplished it, and there had even been the smallest hint of amusement in him. Strangely enough, even though she could not understand him at all, and despite the few unflattering things she had surmised about him from his wrong-headed opinions, she trusted his word that he was forgiving about what she had done. She also believed he was right to say the others would not be.

Which meant that a real battle was soon to come, she thought with a sigh, and she had no more tricks or plots. The peace this land had enjoyed for so long would be torn away. People would be hurt, even killed. All they had built would be damaged or destroyed. And for what?, she had to ask herself. Because she did not want to marry one of three very eligible lairds? Because she did not want to lose control of her dower lands? Because she cherished her virginity so much she was not willing to sacrifice it to buy time for her father to come and help her out of this mess? Although it was grossly unfair that she was being forced to accept such things, not one was worth risking people's lives for. That was a cold hard truth she simply could not ignore.

"Is the answer ye seek written up there?"

Gillyanne smiled faintly when James sat down on her

right. "If it is, 'tis weel hidden by the dirt." She sighed. "If those fools lurking outside the gates are preparing to really fight, then there really is only one answer, isnae there?"

"I certainly havenae thought of another and, believe me, I have thought o'er the problem so hard and continuously my head aches." He shook his head. "It galls me, and 'tis a fair hard blow to my monly pride, but the only one who can solve this in your favor is our father. He is the only one who has the power to stop this, not only because he is your father, but he is close to the king."

"Who apparently set these hounds upon my trail."

James grimaced. "To most 'twas a verra reasonable solution he offered to the problem. Few fathers would object to the selection offered and they did present their offers first. 'Tis we Murrays who are seen as odd with our insistence upon choice." He smiled faintly. "There are many who would say ye now have more choice than most lasses get."

"I ken it. I certainly wouldnae get any sympathy if I complained to someone outside our clan." She sighed. "The people here have some sympathy, but nay much. I think they understand why I would nay wish to give up my lands to men who dinnae e'en try to woo me, but they also see three fine lairds prepared to marry me. Nay ugly, nay old, nay weak, nay poor. In truth, each one is just what many a maiden wishes for. Once I made it clear I wished no blood spilled o'er this, the people of Ald-dabhach were willing to help me hold the fools back for a wee while. They helped me gain three days' reprieve. I really cannae ask them for more. If these men now mean to truly fight, I must end this game."

"We should have an answer to what they plan to do ere the night is o'er."

"Oh? How so?"

"We sent a lad out to see what he could see, mayhap e'en to creep close enough to hear a wee word or two. No need to look so worried. E'en George felt sure 'twas safe enough, that the worst which might happen is he will be captured and we will ken nay more than we do now. Aye, if the lairds plan a battle, people will suffer, but George was confident they wouldnae hurt the lad if they caught him. After all, if they had wished to simply battle their way through the gates without a care to lands or people, they would have done so at the start."

"True. I hope he arrives soon. Something tells me I best get a sound night's sleep, that 'twould be wise to be weel rested on the morrow. After all, if one is facing a great change in one's life and fortune, 'twould be rude to yawn one's way through it."

Connor leaned against a tree, his arms crossed on his chest, and frowned at the other two lairds. David and Robert were letting their anger rule them. If they unleashed that upon Ald-dabhach there would not be much left to claim. They could easily wound or kill the woman they sought to marry. It was true that being defeated and somewhat humiliated by one tiny woman was a bitter potion to swallow, but Connor did not think it was worth destroying the very prize they sought. The woman did, after all, have every right to defend herself and her lands by any means she could. They would all do the same.

"Do ye think they will be much calmer by the morning?" Diarmot asked as he moved to stand closer to Connor.

"Nay," replied Connor, careful to speak quietly so as not to be overheard. "They feel their wee monhoods have been threatened. They think more of retribution than of gaining hold of the lass and her lands."

"Mayhap ye could convince them to let ye go first,

toss dice for it as ye did before. If the gates of the keep need to be kicked down, I think ye would do it with the least cost to Ald-dabhach and its people.''

"They willnae approach singly again for fear of yet another defeat." Connor shook his head. "If David suffered yet another defeat at Lady Gillyanne's tiny hands, I wouldnae be surprised to see him begin to froth at the mouth and rip out his hair. He willnae chance it."

"I ne'er thought this would be so difficult."

"Nay? We are dealing with a woman."

Diarmot briefly smiled. "True. And, yet, how many lasses have three lairds asking for her hand?"

"Ah, but 'twas nay really her hand we asked for, but her lands, and the lass has some pride. 'Tis a lass's place to wed and, if she has lands, to give them into the rule of her husband. Howbeit, mayhap we should have at least attempted some wooing."

"Have ye e'er wooed a lass?"

"Nay, but how difficult could it be? A few kisses, a few sweet words. I think I could have done it."

"I think Robert could have done it better. 'Tis best it didnae come to that. Ye would have lost that game."

Connor supposed there was some truth in what Diarmot said, yet he still felt a little insulted. He had had women. Not many, it was true, but that was probably because he did not leave Deilcladach very often. There were some women there who were always willing to bed down with him. The rare times he had traveled somewhere else, he had enjoyed the favors of a few women, answered a few welcoming smiles.

Thinking about that for a moment, he realized responding to a woman's lusty invitation was not really wooing. Neither was tumbling with one of the whores around Deilcladach. Then he decided it was not worth worrying about. Soon he would either wed Lady Gillyanne or he would not. One did not have to woo a wife and it was wise if one did not woo another man's wife.

"Weel, are ye with us or nay?" demanded Sir David.

Pulling his attention back to the matter of attacking Ald-dabhach, Connor looked at Sir David. The man was so angry, so eager to make someone pay for his humiliation, Connor was not sure he could talk any sense into the fool. Sir David was also still a little rank which, unfortunately, probably acted as a continuous reminder of what the tiny Lady Gillyanne had done to him. It looked as if the only one who could stop any blood from being spilled on the morrow was the lady herself. Since she would have to marry one of them to do it, Connor was not completely sure there would be any reprieve for Ald-dabhach or its people.

"And what happens if the lady herself is hurt or killed in the attack?" Connor asked.

"Then all will be as it was."

"Ye dinnae think the MacMillans or the Murrays or her cousin's clan the Drummonds might be angered?"

"The woman started this fight. I refuse to go home like a whipped cur, driven off by some half-grown lass. So, are ye with us or nay?"

"I am with ye, if only because, at the moment, I seem to be the only one who would like to see the lass live long enough to marry one of us."

"Oh, dear," Gillyanne murmured as George led the youth he had sent to spy on the lairds into the great hall. "George looks worried."

"George always looks worried," James murmured and sipped his wine.

"I have discovered that he has many different levels of being worried. This looks to be a particularly strong worry. The lad doesnae look too happy, either." She smiled at George and the youth. "Sit down, George, and ye, Duncan, is it not?" She poured them each some wine as they sat down and the five Murray men moved closer to her end of the table.

"Aye, m'lady, 'tis Duncan. I am wee Mary's uncle."

She allowed George and Duncan to have a drink before asking, "And what have ye learned, Duncan?"

"I was verra lucky, m'lady," Duncan replied. "I got close enough to hear things and all three lairds had gathered together."

"That was most kind of them. I assume they are nay too pleased with me."

"Weel, nay, they arenae. Sir Robert and Sir David are verra angry, though Sir David is the worst."

"That doesnae surprise me."

"Sir Robert didnae argue with anything the mon said so 'tis most certain he agrees with a lot of it. They are planning to attack us on the morrow, m'lady."

Gillyanne sighed. "I feared as much. Nay one at a time, either, I suppose."

"Nay. Sir David says they will join together to kick down our gates and decide which one gets ye afterward."

"If I am still alive after the onslaught. Ye havenae mentioned Sir Connor."

Duncan hastily swallowed another drink of wine. "He didnae say much, m'lady. Stood there frowning at the other two and passing a word or two with his brother. When Sir David finally demanded to ken if Sir Connor was with them or nay, he finally spoke out. He did mention that a full, hard attack could put ye at risk. Sir David felt that would just put all back as it was. Sir Connor asked if the fool didnae think that that might annoy your kinsmen, but Sir David said ye had started this and he wasnae about to slink home with his tail atween his legs. Then Sir Connor said he was with them but only because he seemed to be the only mon there who would like to see ye live long enough to marry one of them."

Even though Sir Connor would be with the attacking army, his hesitation was strangely comforting. It was true that she would do none of them any good if, by the time she was dragged before a priest, it was only to be given last rites. Still, it was one mark in the man's favor that he was not joining the chorus that was screaming for her blood.

" 'Tis clear my time has run out," Gillyanne said. "I did suspect this outcome yet I had hoped there would be some time ere they reached the decision to fight. A need to come to terms between themselves, mayhap one last attempt to get me to do as they wish, and other such things that might have given me a day or two or e'en more."

"From what I saw and heard, m'lady, two of those lairds are too angry to talk o'er anything, e'en the best way to attack."

"They mean to simply charge the walls?" asked James.

"Aye, though I am nay sure how many MacEnroys will do that. Their laird didnae like the idea, but the Goudies and the Dalglishes dinnae have much respect for our fighting skills." Duncan briefly smiled. "Sir Connor said we didnae need much skill to fill a bunch of charging fools with arrows. Said they didnae need to bring a scaling ladder for he suspected they could soon just pile up the dead and climb o'er them. I tried to stay to hear more, but some of the men started wandering too close to where I was hiding. Ere I slipped away, though, 'twas fair clear that Sir Connor wasnae going to be heeded. Sir David leads and Sir Robert stands with him, so Sir Connor must follow."

"But nay too close," said James; then he looked at Gillyanne. "Gilly, let us. . . ."

"Nay." She smiled faintly at the disgruntled looks on the faces of James and the five Murray men. "I have no doubts about your fighting skills or e'en the ability of those within Ald-dabhach to defend their home," she

added with a nod to George and Duncan. "This isnae
something to fight o'er, to spill blood o'er."

"They are forcing ye into marriage."

"At the suggestion of the king himself." She nodded
at the grimaces that briefly contorted each man's face.
"And, once blood is spilled by the ones outside our
walls, it could mark the end of the long peace. 'Tis the
same if blood is spilled by any of us within these walls.
That becomes an insult to the MacMillans, the Murrays,
and the Drummonds. And all their allies. Instead of a
small argument between those three fools and me, this
could grow into a long-lasting, widespread, painfully
bloody feud."

"Saints' tears," muttered James as he rubbed his
hands over his face.

"Exactly. And for what? Because I willnae pick one
of three lairds for a husband?" She shook her head.
"Nay. That would be madness. I dinnae want to marry
any of these men, nor do they plan to woo me into
changing my mind, but I will pick one and put an end
to this. I promised I wouldnae let this come to a bloodletting and I hold to that."

"But ye will be wed to a mon ye didnae choose."

Although she could understand James' distress and
distaste over the situation, she did think he was beginning to be annoyingly repetitive. "By blatant and weel
witnessed coercion." She nodded when the men's eyes
widened with sudden understanding. "When my fither
finally arrives, he will mend this. No one else can, not
e'en ye, James. We have argued that truth already—
several times. True, I may nay enjoy myself for a while,
but naught will happen to me that is so verra terrible.
I dinnae think it will e'en hurt what small chance I
might have of eventually finding a husband of my own
choice. And, who can say? Mayhap the one I choose will
prove to be the one I wish to keep." Gillyanne suddenly

noticed Mary lurking in the doorway. "Is something wrong, Mary?"

"Nay, m'lady," Mary replied as she took a few steps into the hall, "I but wished to see that my uncle was safe."

"Weel, come here then and have a good look. We are nay saying anything ye cannae hear."

She smiled faintly when the young girl hurried over to her nearly as young uncle and embraced him. Duncan blushed, looking both pleased and a little embarrassed by his niece's concern. Although she had not been at Ald-dabhach very long, Gillyanne had quickly seen that the people here were as closely bonded as the Murrays. If any one of them was hurt or killed, they would all grieve. She could not do that to them, not simply because she had no wish to marry a stranger. Gillyanne knew she could survive even a bad marriage, and one she was almost certain she could escape in the end.

"Mary, ye are a woman," Gillyanne bit back a smile when the girl stood up very straight and nodded, "so, tell me, if ye faced the choice that I do, which mon would ye pick?"

"Nay Sir David Goudie," she replied with no hesitation. "I am nay saying the mon is bad, but I think he would soon make ye wish ye had stood firm and fought." She blushed faintly when she added, "I think he is one of those men who feels a lass is in her rightful place only when she has a mon's boot on her neck."

"Ye are a clear-eyed lass," said James. "All good reasons for Gillyanne not to choose that fool, and from those verra reasons would soon grow one more."

"What?" Gillyanne asked when James paused to grin at her.

"The fact that ye would try to kill the fool within days of the wedding."

"Within hours," she said and joined the others in a brief moment of welcome laughter before looking back at Mary. "I agree. Sir David would be a poor choice. I thought so from the start. Sir Robert Dalglish?"

Mary frowned and lightly bit her lip. "I am nay sure about him, m'lady. When he came here with the others he seemed to be a gentlemon and he is a handsome mon. Yet, when he realized what ye had done to him and his men and that ye had taken his horse, he acted much like Sir David. And, the things he screamed at you were things no true gentlemon should e'er say. Nay, mayhap ne'er e'en think. So, I cannae say. I just," she shrugged, "dinnae *feel* sure about him."

"Your thoughts echo many of mine about the mon. Which leaves us with Sir Connor MacEnroy."

"Aye, m'lady, and if ye were choosing a mon for his appearance, he should certainly be your first choice."

"True." It was hard not to laugh at the way the men rolled their eyes. "He looks just like one would think the old marauding Northmen must have looked."

"Oh, aye. A huge Viking indeed. He accepted the trick ye played upon him with calm and dignity, unlike the others. I have ne'er heard anything bad about the mon. I *have* heard tales of how fine a laird he is, pulling his clan up from the mire years ago and making them all prosper e'en though he was nay more than a lad himself. 'Tis a fine tale. I think, e'en if he didnae look so fine and strong, I would choose him. At least he has shown that he can control his temper."

Gillyanne nodded even as she mused that she would be willing to wager that Sir Connor not only controlled his temper, but nearly every other emotion. It could be that he did such a thing when he faced a battle or felt threatened. If, however, she had difficulty sensing anything about the man because there simply was not anything to sense, even a brief marriage to the man could prove difficult. Then, too, Sir Connor could be like James in that he possessed some strange unseen armor that prevented people like her from seeing too much. Gillyanne could not believe that a man who had pulled his clan out of the ruin made by years of feuding did not have a very big heart indeed.

She suddenly looked at the men who were all watching her. "And ye, gentlemen, do ye agree with wee Mary?" They all nodded. "Then Sir Connor is the one I shall bless with my own wee self. On the morrow, ere the army begins to gather, Sir James and I will go out to the lairds and I will tell them of my decision."

James frowned. "Would it nay be better if ye called them to ye here?"

"Aye, but after what I have done o'er the last three days, I dinnae believe they will agree to that."

"Nay, probably not. Yet, it could be dangerous."

"How? They wish to marry me to get these lands. I think the worst that can happen is they might start fighting amongst themselves and we will be forced to flee ere we are caught in the middle. Also, if I go to them, it may just keep any of their men from settling themselves inside these walls. Once in, they would be verra hard to oust."

"But this keep is what they seek to grab through marriage to you," said the youngest of the Murray men.

"True, Iain," Gillyanne replied, "but I believe I can keep the mon waiting on taking full possession for a while. After all, he will hold the laird to all of this anyway. I am nay sure why, but I believe the first thing my chosen husband will wish to do is wed me and get me shut up behind the walls of his own keep as swiftly as he can."

"Because he doesnae trust the other two lairds," said James.

"Not completely. That much I did sense when they were all here. I dinnae think a feud will start, but I suspect they may consider trying to snatch away the *prize*. So, the rest of ye are to shut the gates and keep them shut unless I tell ye to open them—nay matter what happens. Or James does. If naught else, my fither will be seeking some answers when he gets here and ye are best placed to answer them. And, James, ye will ride back to Dubhlinn to tell the ones there just in case Fither goes there first. Then I should like it if ye would come to me at Deilcladach, bringing whatever I might be forced to leave behind."

There were several moments of hearty argument, but Gillyanne finally got the agreements she sought. James and the Murray men had come to Ald-dabhach to protect her and felt they had failed. She could not seem to convince them otherwise. Fortunately, her plans made sense and, despite their bruised pride, they had to accede to her wishes. All too soon she found herself alone with a scowling James.

"This is how it must be, James," she said gently. "Ye ken that, dinnae ye?"

"My head does. The rest of me rages against it. And I really dinnae wish to give our mither this news."

"Aye. After poor Sorcha was raped, beaten nigh unto death, then joined a nunery, Fither feared for our mither's health. Of course, there was no need. She is stronger than she looks. Then I was taken hostage by Cameron MacAlpin along with cousin Avery. That turned out weel for Avery as she loves her dark knight, but Mither was wracked with worry. Now this. I think she will begin to fear she has caused some curse to be set against her daughters."

"And Fither will be enraged. Not only for what has been done to you, but for the worry it shall bring to our mither."

"Make her understand that I am fine, that I am mostly irritated, and that I willnae be harmed."

"And is that the truth?"

Gillyanne thought about it for a moment and nodded. "Aye. 'Tis the truth. I cannae sense anything about Sir

Connor. He is as closed to me as ye are, more so, I think. Yet, although that worries me a little, I believe it also intrigues me. Then, when I search deep into my heart, I find no fear of the mon. Aye, I shall be set in the bed of a mon I dinnae ken much about, but, when I try to worry o'er that, a little voice in my head reminds me that he is a bonny, bonny mon."

James laughed and shook his head. "Ye have spent too much time with our rogue of a cousin Payton." Then he grew serious. "I will tell Mither what ye said. If Fither is there, I will tell the tale from the safety of a few feet away."

"He wouldnae hurt you," Gillyanne protested even though she heard the hint of dark humor in his voice.

"I ken it, but his anger will be so strong I may be knocked o'er by it."

"Aye, but e'en at his angriest, Fither will ken that 'tis best if this is solved with words, nay swords. He will also ken that a coerced marriage may be set aside, and, unlike these three lairds, he has the king's ear." She shrugged. "And, who can say? Mayhap when I gain the chance to walk away, I willnae want to. At least I ken, without doubt, that I will get that choice in the end. Verra few lasses do. This need not be forever."

"And that is why ye are able to do it, isnae it?"

"In part. I truly feel no fear of the mon. When I say those vows, I will mean them, yet, in my heart will rest the certain and verra comforting knowledge that, if there proves to be no hope of a good and true marriage, I can just walk away."

"Will ye tell Sir Connor that?"

"I will warn him about Fither, but instinct tells me the mon willnae heed what I say."

James slowly smiled. "The poor fool. Fither will come as a great surprise to him. And, I think, so will you."

"Without a doubt, Cousin. He thinks he need but

wed me, claim my dower lands, and all will be as it should. 'Twill be interesting to see how long it takes him to see that naught which occurs with a Murray lass can e'er be so simple.''

Chapter Six

"The lass has left the safety of the keep and has but one mon with her," cried Sir David as he started to mount his horse.

"What are ye doing?" demanded Connor, grabbing the reins of Sir David's horse to stop the man.

"I am going to go and grab the lass."

"She is coming to us under a sign of truce with no one but her own cousin at her side. Ye must honor that."

"I must, must I?"

"Aye, David," said Robert, "ye must. The king himself kens we have come here. 'Twould be wise to walk a verra careful path."

After a brief hesitation, David dismounted and Connor breathed a silent sigh of relief. He suspected David acted out of the somewhat blind fury he felt toward the small woman walking toward them. There was always the chance Robert had seen an opportunity to grab the prize for himself as well. Connor would not be surprised to learn that, despite Sir Robert's tactful words, that man was also a little suspicious.

"My lairds," said Gillyanne as she paused a few feet away, "I wish to treaty with you. Ye do notice this wee flag of truce we carry, aye?"

"Aye," said Connor, her words revealing that she had watched the little struggle with Sir David and guessed its meaning. "We are ready to talk."

"And, if we cannae come to some agreement, I will be allowed to return to the keep with my cousin."

"Agreed. Ye will be allowed to go back and prepare for battle," said David, glaring at her.

Gillyanne met the man's glare with a faint smile. "I am hoping to avoid the need to watch ye hurl yourself against my walls in some futile but verra monly display of fury."

Sir David took a threatening step toward her, but Sir Robert grabbed him by the arm and held him back. Gillyanne could see that Sir David was straining at the reins of whatever agreements the lairds had made amongst themselves. The man could prove to be a problem in the future which, Gillyanne decided, was another good reason to choose Sir Connor. She sensed Sir Connor would be able to deal with the somewhat brutish fellow while Sir Robert appeared to be on far closer terms with the man. In some subtle way, it was those two men against Sir Connor. When her father came to her rescue David and Robert would ally themselves with each other, she was certain of it. Just as she was certain they would both leave Sir Connor to face her father all alone.

"I would ask that ye wait until my fither arrives," she said, looking at Sir Connor.

Connor crossed his arms over his chest and steadily met her look. "Why should we do that?"

"To discuss the matter of marriage to me with my fither as is right and proper."

"Again—why? The king himself has set us upon this path. We have our liege's approval."

"But the king didnae talk this o'er with my fither ere he set ye after me. My fither willnae be pleased about this and 'tis something ye would be wise to think about."

"Ye cannae believe your father can argue a king's decision," said David, his tone one of deeply felt contempt.

Seeing how the lady's eyes narrowed in anger, Connor quickly spoke up. "Whether your father can change the king's mind or nay, simply doesnae matter. We will settle this now. Any displeasure your father suffers can be dealt with later."

It was obvious not one of the men believed her father would or could, in any way, go against a king's wishes. They treated the king's suggestion of this solution to their problem as if it were a royal command and Gillyanne knew that was their mistake. She also knew nothing she could say would convince them of that.

"So be it," she muttered and sighed with an even mixture of irritation and resignation. "When this foolishness began, I swore I wouldnae allow any blood to be spilled o'er it."

"Ye have changed your mind?" Sir Connor asked.

"Nay," Gillyanne replied. "I will end this now. I choose Sir Connor MacEnroy as the laird I will take as my husband."

There was a heavy moment of silence in which Gillyanne easily sensed the other two lairds' anger over her choice. Connor then nodded, stepped forward, and grabbed her by the hand. James tensed, but Gillyanne stopped any move he might make with one abrupt slashing gesture of her hand. She was startled, however, when Sir Connor began to stride toward the tiny church barely visible from where they stood, dragging her along behind him. James and the others hurried to follow.

"What are ye doing?" she snapped, fighting not to stumble as he pulled her along.

"Taking ye to the priest," Connor answered.

"Ye brought a priest with you?"

"Aye, and he isnae pleased to have been kept waiting for four days."

His tone of voice indicated that was all her fault and Gillyanne suppressed a fierce urge to kick him in his far too attractive backside. "Ye are just going to drag me off and marry me? Shouldnae we plan a feast or something?" When he briefly glanced at her over his shoulder, one brow raised, Gillyanne decided that it was indeed an irritating gesture.

"I believe ye should understand why I feel disinclined to dine at your table again."

"A lass should be allowed some way to mark such a day."

"Ye have had it. Three days of turning back three armies, defeating three lairds, and all with naught but a bruise or two—and those were inflicted upon us, by you. Few lasses can lay claim to such a feat."

Gillyanne could hardly argue with that. She had not anticipated this immediate saying of the vows, however. Now she was heartily glad she had settled everything before leaving the keep as she suspected she would not be returning to it any time soon. As he tugged her down to kneel beside him in front of a plump, extremely cross-looking priest, she hoped he would not consummate the marriage with such speed.

Barely had the last of the vows been spoken when Connor stood up and Gillyanne was yanked back onto her feet. Connor pulled her into his arms with an equally abrupt movement, actually lifting her off her feet. Gillyanne was about to protest the way he was acting when he kissed her. His lips were warm, soft, and tempting. She felt almost entombed in strong, clean man yet was not intimidated, did in fact find it very pleasant. Just as she felt an intriguing warmth begin to seep into her blood he released her, and, still dragging her along by the hand, started out of the church. Stunned, Gillyanne felt only a flicker of shock when the priest was offered help in getting home and refused it in a highly unpriestly manner.

"Where are ye taking her?" demanded James, stepping in front of Connor and stopping the man's march back to his camp.

"I am taking my wife to Deilcladach," replied Connor.

"Are ye nay going to take hold of Ald-dabhach?" asked Robert when he caught up to them.

"I have hold of it." Connor tugged Gillyanne close to his side. "Right here. 'Tis enough for now."

"Curse ye," snapped James, "ye cannae just grab her, wed her, and drag her off."

"Nay? Why not?" Connor stepped around James and strode on toward his camp.

Glancing over her shoulder, Gillyanne could see that James' rarely seen, but glorious temper, was rapidly rising. "Dinnae fret o'er this, James. Ye have things ye must do." She was relieved when he nodded curtly and strode back to the keep.

"What must he do?" asked Connor as he reached his saddled horse and mounted.

"He must be sure my family has the whole tale," she replied as she was swiftly, but gently, pulled up to sit behind him. "Ye refuse to see the trouble ye court, but it will soon be kicking at the gates of Deilcladach. Calling your keep the Devil's Shore isnae enough to keep my fither away, either. In truth, when he comes, ye may just think that the Devil himself has indeed arrived."

" 'Tis good for a lass to have such faith in her father."

Gillyanne had no chance to respond to that. Connor issued a few curt commands to his men, a few equally curt farewells to Sir David and Sir Robert and kicked

his horse into a gallop. As she wrapped her arms around
his trim waist and hung on tightly, she glanced back at
the camp they were rapidly leaving. Most of his men
were following, but a few lingered to clear away what
might have been left behind. Instinct told Gillyanne
those men were also there to keep an eye on Robert
and David, to make sure those men left Ald-dabhach.
It was yet more proof that these three lairds were allied
through necessity and not through mutual trust or
liking.

Although she had expected this course of events, she
had not anticipated the extreme haste. It felt more like
a kidnapping than a wedding. She had only the clothes
she wore and it would be many days before James could
bring her things to Deilcladach. This was not the wedding she had always dreamed of.

In an attempt to keep her spirits up, she tried to recall
all that was good about the arrangement. Ald-dabhach
and its people were safe. Her father would come after
her and would rescue her, if she still needed to be
rescued. Even if she had been forced to choose Connor,
he was, in many ways, a fine choice. A lass could certainly
find few so fine of looks or strong of build. The kiss at
the church had not been very intimate or long, but it
had shown some promise of passion. As she rested her
cheek against his broad back, she decided there was
hope of something pleasant coming from this wretched
tangle.

Connor made a very male noise of satisfaction and
rolled off Gillyanne. She stared up at the roof of the
tiny cottage and wondered which she felt more inclined
to do—scream or cry. After barely two hours of riding,
he had stopped at a tiny cottage, pleasantly forced the
aging couple there to leave, and dragged her to a pallet
by the peat fire. His kisses had stilled her protests. His

caresses had melted her bones. Then, suddenly, he was inside her. The passion he had stirred within her had dimmed for a moment, dampened by such an abrupt, if nearly painless end of her maiden state. She had just begun to feel it flare to life again when Connor had found his own satisfaction and left her. Left her aching and unsatisfied, she thought in angry wonder. Once he had taken her maidenhead and she had neither screamed nor wept, he had obviously ceased to care about what she felt or needed.

Gillyanne glanced down at herself and carefully pulled her skirts down. He had not even fully removed their clothing. She was just relacing her bodice when he sprang to his feet and straightened his clothes. For a brief moment, as he gently helped her to her feet, she thought there might be a moment of tenderness, a soft kiss or a touch, but he simply stood there and looked at her, a hint of a frown curving his beautiful mouth.

"Did I hurt ye?" he asked.

"Nay," she began to reply.

"Good." He patted her on the back and started out the door. " 'Tis time to finish the journey home."

Gillyanne stared after him and wished she had some thick cudgel to beat him with. She could not say she had been raped or abused, but she certainly had not been made love to. There was a faint soreness between her legs, but it was made inconsequential by the deep, nagging ache of unfulfilled passion. The fact that it had all begun so wonderfully, with such promise, made that even harder to bear. Muttering every curse she knew, she found some water, hastily cleaned herself, yanked on her braies, and left the cottage. She was too angry to be embarrassed by the fact that all of Connor's men and the old couple had been standing around outside waiting for Connor to consummate his marriage.

Intending to vent some of the anger growing inside her, she marched up to Connor only to find him and

Diarmot scowling at two fair-haired youths who were just dismounting in front of them. It would have been impossible to know the smaller of the two was blond except that a few wisps of hair had escaped the unusually large hat he wore. Gillyanne stepped closer to Connor. The brief look he gave her told her all too plainly that he had forgotten her for a moment. She silently cursed some more and wondered now much longer she would be able to control her temper.

"Wife," Connor said, "meet my brother Andrew and my sister Fiona. My wife Gillyanne."

It was not easy to hide her surprise over the revelation that the smaller of the pair was female, but Gillyanne smiled and nodded a greeting.

"Why have ye come?" Connor demanded of the pair.

"We began to wonder what had happened to ye," replied Andrew. "When ye left, ye didnae think ye would be gone for more than a day or two."

Connor was almost certain he heard Gillyanne mutter something that sounded very much like arrogant swine, but he had to ignore it, keeping his stern gaze fixed upon his siblings. "I told ye to stay at Deilcladach."

"But we were worried about ye and Diarmot," protested Fiona.

"There was no need to worry," Connor said. "Now there is. Ye disobeyed my orders."

The wary looks on Andrew and Fiona's faces made it all too clear that Connor was a man who expected his orders to be obeyed. Gillyanne got the feeling, however, that punishment would be little more than suffering his disapproval. That the pair clearly thought that bad enough said a lot about the close bonds of the family.

Andrew nervously cleared his throat. "Weel, since ye are unharmed and obviously won the prize, Fiona and I will go back to Deilcladach now."

"Ye will ride with us," Connor said. " 'Tis nay safe for the two of ye to be riding o'er these lands by yourselves."

Another dire breach of conduct, Gillyanne mused, as she watched the shoulders of the pair slump a little. Despite the fact that Fiona appeared to be staring at her feet, Gillyanne suddenly realized the girl was studying her very closely. She sensed no anger or wariness, just a strong curiosity. It occurred to Gillyanne that Fiona might not be dressed as a lad simply for this unapproved ride. Before she could consider that possibility any further, however, Connor grabbed her by the hand and pulled her to his horse.

Her cousins would never believe this, Gillyanne thought, as she was settled behind him and they started to ride. She was not sure she did. There was a small part of her that wondered if it was all some strange dream. A hasty wedding, a hasty retreat, an annoyingly public and hasty bedding, and a little more hasty retreating. It was all almost funny.

"Why do ye wear a mon's clothing?" asked Connor.

Confused, Gillyanne glanced down at her gown. "Ye ken many men who wear gowns, do ye?"

"I mean the braies ye wear under your skirts."

"A lot of women in my family wear braies."

"Ye willnae."

She was more than ready to indulge in an argument over that blunt command, but he spurred the horse into a gallop. Although Gillyanne knew she could still make herself heard, she decided to save that quarrel for later. One could not have a good, satisfying argument while trying to stay in the saddle of a rapidly moving horse. It did strike her as a typically annoying male thing to do for Connor to tell her she could not wear one small, insignificant male garment while his sister galloped over the countryside dressed as a lad.

And that was a puzzle, Gillyanne decided. Every instinct she had told her Fiona often dressed as a lad, might even do so all the time. Considering the history of the MacEnroys over the past dozen years there was the possibility Fiona had been raised much like another brother. Gillyanne felt no real shock or outrage over that, but Fiona would now be becoming a woman or was very near that age. It would explain the intense curiosity the girl revealed. She inwardly shrugged. There would be time later to sort out the puzzle of Fiona.

Fixing a glare upon her husband's broad back, Gillyanne knew there were several puzzles she would have to solve. The man himself was a very intricate puzzle indeed. Of immediate importance to her, however, was how such a beautiful man could be such a poor lover. One thing she had hoped to gain from this tangle was a taste of passion. Well, he had given her a taste, but he had left her hungry. If that was his usual way in bed, Gillyanne suspected she would soon be praying long and hard for her father to come and rescue her.

It was another several hours' ride before they reached Deilcladach. Gillyanne had tried to get a good look at the keep as they approached it, but it proved difficult to see around her very large husband. For a man who probably did not have one extra pinch of meat on him, Connor proved to be a sizable obstacle. What she did notice was that his lands did not appear to be as rich as Ald-dabhach's. Ald-dabhach could easily produce more than it needed while this land looked as if it would barely supply enough to feed the people who lived on it, and that only in the best of years. That would explain Connor's deep interest in getting his hands on her lands.

Immediately noticeable amongst the people greeting Connor and his men were two tall, fair-haired youths. Connor, Andrew, and Diarmot moved to greet them and Gillyanne frowned as the five men were immediately surrounded by many of the clan. It was obvious these were two more brothers. It was also increasingly obvious that she had either been forgotten or was expected to attend to herself. She was just wondering if she could dismount from Connor's massive horse with any semblance of grace when Fiona paused by the horse and stared up at her. The girl had lovely violet eyes, Gillyanne noticed, and experienced a fleeting twinge of envy.

"My other brothers," Fiona said, pointing to the two young men Connor was greeting. "Angus and Antony. Andrew is eighteen, Angus is twenty, and Antony is two and twenty. Close in age and in almost every other way. We call them Angus, Nanty, and Drew."

Fiona did not wait for a response, but hurried away to join her brothers. Angus, Nanty, and Drew were all about the same height, had the same dark golden hair, and were lean of build. Gillyanne suspected it would be a while before she could easily tell them apart.

A moment later she gaped as everyone disappeared into the keep, leaving her still sitting upon Connor's horse. Gillyanne wondered if this was what some wives complained about, the cessation of the man's courtly ways once the vows were said. Since Connor had yet to display any courtly ways, she doubted it was that simple. She stared down at the ground and wondered if she should slide down out of the saddle or hop down. Getting down was suddenly very important because she was eager to chase her husband down and kick him—repeatedly.

"Do ye need help, m'lady?"

Gillyanne looked at the tall, too thin man standing by the horse. "Who are ye?"

"They call me Knobby, m'lady."

"A little unkind."

"Nay, 'tisnae meant so. My name is Iain and there are eight Iains here so 'tis less confusing to call us all something else."

"Ah, of course." She decided to ignore the gleam of laughter in his dark eyes. "I believe I could use some help descending from this mountain as it appears my overgrown oaf of a husband has forgotten me."

"Och, nay, m'lady," Knobby protested even as he helped her down. "He was telling everyone how he had brought home the prize."

The prize, Gillyanne thought, and wondered if anyone would take notice if she hurled herself to the ground and had a kicking, screaming fit of fury. It would be a childish thing to do, but it might prove satisfying. Glancing down at her dusty, wrinkled gown, she decided it would not endure such abuse, not if it was to last until James brought her clothes.

"Ye certainly are a wee one, arenae ye," murmured Knobby.

Gillyanne gave him what she hoped was her best scowl, even as she began to think there was no such creature as a short male MacEnroy. "If ye wish to see your next saint's day, it might be wise to keep that opinion to yourself."

"Ah, as ye wish. Strange, I hadnae noticed that ye have red hair."

"That is because I dinnae. 'Tis brown," she muttered as she brushed off her skirts.

"Nay, m'lady, with the sun on it, 'tis red. And, I hadnae guessed that ye have green eyes, either."

"I shall tell ye a secret, Knobby. When my eyes are this color, 'tis wise to tread verra warily around me." She nodded when he took a small step away from her. "Now, where has everyone disappeared to?"

"To the great hall, m'lady. 'Tis a feast they will be having to celebrate the laird's victory and safe return."

"How nice," she said between tightly gritted teeth.

This was far more than she ought to be asked to bear, Gillyanne thought as she stared at the hard-packed ground of the inner bailey. She finally had a husband, and still she was ignored. Hand in hand with her anger was hurt and the two emotions fed on each other, strengthening each other, until she felt nearly ill with emotion. Gillyanne slowly began to count, fighting to grasp some control of her runaway feelings. If she went after Connor now, she feared she would make such an utter ranting fool of herself, the MacEnroys would probably think she was a mad woman and lock her up.

"Er, m'lady?" Knobby called, his voice softened with unease. "What are ye doing?"

"Counting," she replied, feeling a brief urge to weep and using her anger to ruthlessly quell it.

"Counting what?" Knobby frowned as he studied the ground she stared at.

Gillyanne took a deep breath and slowly unclenched her fists. "I am just counting. My cousin Avery says that ye can often get your temper under control if ye just count verra slowly."

"Is it working?"

"Nay. Instead of just counting and calming down, I find I am counting all the ways I can hurt and torture that fool I have just married."

She saw color flood his narrow face and wondered if she had just angered the man. After all she had heard about the MacEnroys, there was a good chance his clansmen held him in very high regard indeed. A moment later, she realized the man was not furious; he was struggling mightily not to burst into open laughter. Gillyanne sighed in resignation. It seemed that, if men did not ignore her, they found her amusing. It was no wonder that any hint of vanity she might have once had had withered and died long ago.

"I believe I am ready to go to the great hall now," she said.

"Aye, and 'tis best if ye hurry," Knobby said in a slightly choked voice. "The food will disappear verra fast."

As she walked toward the tall iron-banded doors of the keep, Gillyanne idly wondered if Knobby was so thin because he was slow to get to the table. She glanced over her shoulder and was not really surprised to see

him nearly bent over with laughter as he led Connor's
horse to the stables. It would amuse a man to hear
someone as small as she was threaten a great tree of a
man like Connor. Of course, those men were only the
ones who had never met a Murray woman.

After using nearly all of her strength just to open
the heavy doors and get inside, Gillyanne followed the
sounds of many voices to the great hall. She stood in
the doorway and looked around. Her husband sat in a
big chair at the head of a long table centered amongst
all the others. It was obvious he was regaling his clan
with tales of all that had happened at Ald-dabhach, the
men who had been with him readily adding their views
on it all. Not one of them noticed that the woman who
had brought them this bounty was not seated next to
her husband.

Some of the anger she had managed to tamp down
surged to life again as she saw that there was not even
a place set for her at the table. She took a few deep,
slow breaths to restore her calm then strode into the
great hall. First she would grab something to eat and
drink, and then she intended to have a few words with
her new husband. The lands he was so pleased to hold
were her dower lands. If she left, if the marriage was
ended, he would lose those lands. That gave Gillyanne
some small measure of power and she intended to use
it.

Chapter Seven

It was almost impossible to get her food past the hard knot of fury in her throat, but Gillyanne tried. She reminded herself that this was no love match. Connor had wanted her keep and lands and she had wanted to stop any bloodshed over them. Passion had not brought them together. The unwary disclosures of the king had set them on this path. That, and the greed of men. Connor had simply appeared to be the best choice out of three fools. Gillyanne could not believe she had been so utterly wrong.

All that good sense did little to ease her growing rage as she covertly watched Connor nearly smile at the fulsome maid Meg. The way the woman so openly fondled him was quite bad enough. The occasional triumphant glances Meg sent her way were far, far worse. The only place most women wielded any power was within the household itself and Meg's confident, contemptuous looks told Gillyanne that she might never gain that prize.

Gillyanne took a long drink of the thick, tart wine

and tried to wash the bitter taste of humiliation from her mouth. It was hard, hard to accept that she was little more than a deed to this man, and very hard to accept that he had obviously forgotten her from the moment he had gotten her safely behind his gates. She would have had to dismount by herself if not for Knobby's aid, had had to trail after him, his family, and his men long after they strode off to the great hall, and had even had to fight for a place at the large table as well as for a share of the food. Such callous disregard was probably for the best, she tried to convince herself. She had married the man in the hope of buying time, time in which her family could come and extract her from this mess. It should not matter what happened now as long as she was not harmed, but it did.

What Gillyanne could not understand was why it hurt and why she could not convince herself that all she suffered was badly stung pride, just as in the past when she had been ignored by men. This man was, after all, *her* husband. They had been wed by a priest and the marriage had been duly consummated. Not painfully, true, but, as far as she was concerned, hastily and not very well. Gillyanne was still completely astonished that such a beautiful man could be such a poor lover. But then, she mused sourly, perhaps he had not been at his best because he had considered the act no more than the signing of a deed. The fact that he obviously intended to give Meg some of his best, if he had any, made Gillyanne grind her teeth.

Meg moved to stand behind Connor, draping her plump arms around his neck and nearly enfolding his head in her ample bosom. Connor briefly laughed and the lusty chuckle acted upon Gillyanne like spark to tinder. She cursed and surged to her feet, ignoring the sudden silence as she strode to her husband's chair.

"Best move those," she hissed at Meg as she placed her hands on Meg's full breasts and shoved the woman back. "I have need of my husband's ears for the moment."

"Ye overstep, lass," Connor said quietly, but he was a little astonished at the fury he could see on her small face and the way her anger enlivened her wide, faintly mismatched eyes, making them an interesting shade of green.

"Nay *lass*. *Wife*. Recall me? The woman whose tower house and lands ye so covet? The one ye dragged afore a priest and so ineptly bedded?" She ignored the loud unified gasp of his men and family, interested only in the flush of anger that colored his high-boned cheeks and savoring it.

"A husband has the right to beat his wife."

"Try it. Ye refuse to see the trouble ye have tempted by what ye have done, but 'tis there, fool, and will soon be clamoring loudly at your gates. 'Twill land on ye tenfold if my fither sees but one wee bruise on me. Ye tempt that rage e'en now by treating me with so little respect."

"A mon has a right to his pleasures." He struggled to hide his surprise over the vicious curse she spat at him

"Does he now." She straightened up. "Then surely it must follow that so does a woman."

" 'Ware, lass."

Gillyanne ignored him. She knew the cold fury in his voice should make her hesitate, but she, too, was furious, too furious to be cautious. After a quick look around, she grabbed Connor's brother Diarmot by the arm and yanked him to his feet, as surprised as he looked at her surge of strength. Gillyanne started to drag him out of the great hall, a little piqued by the look of utter horror on his handsome face.

"Jesu, lass, ye will get me killed," Diarmot stuttered, too shocked to fight her pull, and too concerned with keeping an eye on his brother who was slowly rising from his chair.

"Nay, not you," Gillyanne replied, refusing to look back at the man she could hear rapidly approaching. "Me, aye, mayhap, but nay you. He might knock ye around a wee bit, but from what little I have seen thus far, ye must be used to that."

She released a soft cry of surprise when Diarmot was suddenly ripped from her side. Gillyanne got one brief glimpse of the young man sliding across the floor on his backside before a strong arm circled her waist. Connor carried her out of the great hall like a sack of grain, that one strong arm all the hold he needed. Gillyanne briefly considered sinking her teeth in his thigh, but her hair was in the way. She also decided it might not be wise to further aggravate him.

After stomping up the narrow stairs, he kicked open a heavy door and tossed her onto a wide bed. Gillyanne scrambled to her feet just to see him start toward the door. Cursing softly, she leaped off the bed, raced by him, and slammed the door shut. She stood in front of it, arms crossed over her chest, and glared up at him. Although she was not sure what she wanted from him, it was certainly not to be left in a bedchamber while he returned to fondling Meg.

"Move, lass," Connor ordered.

"The name is Gillyanne," she snapped. "And I will-nae allow ye to return to your adulterous rutting."

Connor stared at her, torn between anger and a sudden urge to laugh. She was little, delicate, barely reached his armpit, yet faced him as if they were equals. Other than his sister Fiona, no woman had ever cursed him, insulted him, or scolded him. He frowned. Women were supposed to be docile, to heed a man's word, especially highborn lasses. Connor began to wonder just what sort of family Gillyanne had been raised in that she had obviously been allowed to ignore that truth.

"Your husband has ordered ye to move," he said.

"Och, so now ye recall that ye are a husband. Does this mean that ye will start to treat me like a wife?"

"Curse ye, I *am* treating ye like a wife."

Gillyanne blinked, her anger vanishing beneath a wave of confusion. The way Connor said those words told her he meant them, wholeheartedly. That made no sense.

"Are ye now. Might I ask just how ye believe a wife should be treated?" Gillyanne asked a little too sweetly.

"He certainly doesnae let her rut with another mon. Any fruit of your wee body will be mine and mine alone."

"It would have been close. Diarmot is your brother after all." She found the look of shock upon his face utterly satisfying. "Now, how do ye believe a wife should be treated?"

Deciding she had to have been jesting about Diarmot, Connor replied, "Gently."

She frowned when he said no more. "And?"

"He is to see that she is weel fed."

"Oh? Then mayhap the husband might pause a moment to see that she has a seat at the table and a full plate before her ere he turns his attention to playing with his whore."

He had to concede he had failed there. "I am nay used to a wife yet. And her name is Meg."

Her name is Meg the Mutilated if she does not cease her games, Gillyanne thought, but just drawled, "How nice for her. Next?"

"A husband is to see that she is weel clothed or at least warmly dressed."

Gillyanne simply glanced down at her dirty, wrinkled gown, then looked back at him, one brow raised.

"We have only just arrived here. I dinnae carry ladies' gowns about with me and there was nay time to collect yours ere we left Ald-dabhach."

He was beginning to sound defensive and Gillyanne thought that a hopeful sign. "Fine. Next?"

"A lady is to be gently bedded and carefully tended 'til she carries a child."

"Ye make me sound like a thrice-cursed garden."

Connor was very sure ladies were not supposed to curse, but decided to ignore that for now. "Ladies must be treated with care and respect for their modesty. A mon reserves his rougher passions for maids like Meg. Such things would shock a lady."

"What pig muck." She ignored his look of surprise. "Who told ye such utter nonsense?"

"My uncle Sir Neil MacEnroy. He is an expert in the ways of gentle-born ladies."

"Is he now?" she muttered, making no attempt to hide her scorn. "Kens all the ladies, does he, that he can speak with such assurance?"

Forced to consider the matter as he searched for an answer, Connor realized he had none. He was not sure when or where his uncle had met any ladies. The man rarely spoke of any. That was not something he was about to admit to the angry little female standing before him, however.

"He taught me all I ken," Connor said and was sure the fleeting look he glimpsed upon her face was one of utter derision.

"Your uncle was taught differently from me," Gillyanne said as, confident he would not try to walk away now, she moved to sit on the bed. "He was right about food and clothing and a place to live."

"Ah, a place to live. I have given ye that." He was pleased that he had done one thing correctly.

"Aye." She decided not to point out that he had dragged her from a perfectly good place to live to bring her here. "But, as a gentle-bred lady myself, I must take exception to what else he said."

"A lass doesnae argue with a mon. His word is law."

Gillyanne stared at Connor, cursing her continued inablity to read him in any way. She did not really want to think him dimwitted enough to believe such nonsense. He was sorely in need of education. His uncle, she mused, was sorely in need of a sound beating.

"This lass argues," she said.

"I have begun to notice that."

She looked utterly adorable sitting on the edge of his great bed, her small feet several inches off the floor. Connor felt desire stir and tried to tamp it down. It was not easy when he could all too clearly recall the beauty of her lithe body and the warm, tight feel of her when he had been inside her. He had seeded her as is a husband's duty, but he had been left wanting. The restraint he had practiced had stolen some of the pleasure from the bedding. That was why he had turned to Meg, yet, he had to admit, Meg had not sparked his lust at all. That could prove to be a problem for, if he did not satisfy those heartier urges elsewhere, he might try to satisfy them with his wife and she was a lady. She was also so small, so delicate, he feared he could easily hurt her.

"This argumentative lass is telling ye that a husband doesnae go sniffing about another woman's skirts. That is adultery. That is a sin."

"Then there are a lot of sinners in this world."

"Too many, but that doesnae make it right. Such things may be winked at in this world, but will nay be winked at in the next."

"A mon has some hearty desires, lass, which need a lot of feeding. A lady cannae tolerate it. That is what lasses like Meg were made for."

"Bollocks."

"A lady shouldnae use such crude language."

"Keep speaking such utter nonsense and ye will soon see just how crude I can get." She sighed and flopped back on the bed. "Oh, go and rut with your whore. I

dinnae ken why I should care. Ye werenae verra good
at it anyway.'' Gillyanne was not surprised when he suddenly loomed over her for, deciding that reasoning with
him was not gaining her anything, she thought goading
him might work. He certainly looked thoroughly
goaded now.

"I was verra good," he snapped. "I took your maidenhead with barely a wince from ye. I didnae hurt ye."

"Nay, ye didnae. Didnae give me much pleasure,
either."

He was staring at her as if she was the oddest creature
he had ever met. She stared back, but got nothing, no
sense at all of his thoughts and feelings. It was frustrat-
ing, but she began to get the sinking feeling it was
definitely one of the reasons she had chosen him.

"Ladies dinnae want pleasure, cannae feel it. They
expect their mon to take such crudities to his leman."

Gillyanne propped herself up on her elbows, bringing
her face so close to his as he leaned over her that their
noses almost touched. She was feeling heartily cheated.
Circumstances had forced her into marriage with this
beautiful man and she had thought she might at least,
finally, taste some of that pleasure which put such a
sparkle in her cousins' eyes. Instead she got a man who
treated her as if she would break beneath a passionate
caress. There had been such promise in those first few
kisses, and she was determined to see if that promise
could be fulfilled. If not, well, she would let him go his
way, and she would wait for rescue. She ignored the
whisper in her mind which told her she would never
be able to follow that plan. That made no sense at all.

"I shall make a bargain with ye," she said. "Show me
these rough pleasures, these hearty desires. Treat me
just as if I was your leman, nay your wife. If I cannae
abide it, I will trouble ye no more about your whore. I
will make but one rule—dinnae shame me by parading
your lovers afore my eyes and your people. Ye do that

and ye leave me exposed to the scorn of your clan. That I willnae tolerate, nay quietly. So, come, show me what I am supposed to be so revolted by."

Connor straightened up and reached for the laces on his doublet. He was tempted to accept her bargain. He wanted to give her the fullness of the desire he felt for her, wanted to see if he could bring the warmth of desire into her beautiful eyes. He wanted to touch every silken inch of her without worrying she would be shocked, wanted to kiss her perfect little belly hole, feast on her raspberry colored nipples, and kiss her slender white thighs. It startled him a little, but he even wanted to kiss those soft reddish brown curls between those beautiful legs, something he had heard about, but had never felt the urge to try.

And why not, he decided as he began to remove his doublet. It might frighten or disgust her, but she had given him permission to indulge himself at least this once. Unless she swooned or started to fight him, he would heartily indulge himself. If, afterward, they returned to a genteel, occasional seeding of her womb, he would at least have one memory to cherish. The way her eyes started to widen as he shed his clothes made him wonder if her courage was already fading.

Gillyanne felt increasingly hot as her husband took off his clothes. She had seen very little of him before. He was all smooth, golden skin and lean, hard muscle. A thin line of hair began below his navel, thickened around his groin, and dusted every inch of his long muscular legs. He was beautiful and very manly, she mused as she looked at his groin again. It was probably a good thing she had not had a clear view of him before the consummation of their marriage. If she had seen the size of what he had intended to put inside her, she doubted she would have been quite so sanguine about it all as she had been. She had not seen many manhoods in her time, and most had been in what her cousin

Avery laughingly called the *bored* position. She was sure, however, that Connor was particularly well blessed in that area and he was most certainly not bored.

"Afraid?" he asked as he tugged her to her feet and began to remove her clothes.

"Nay, I was just noticing that ye are, er, nay *bored,*" she murmured, trying not to be too discomforted by the amount of light in the room as he undressed her.

"What do ye mean?"

"My cousin Avery calls a monhood at rest one that is in the *bored* position."

"Just how many have ye seen?" he demanded, pausing in the unlacing of her chemise to scowl at her.

"Weel, I dinnae go about trying to peep at any mon's," she said, vaguely insulted by his unspoken accusation. "But, in a crowded keep and with a multitude of male cousins and brothers, a lass does glimpse one now and again. Avery gave a name to the various . . . weel, positions it can take. There is *bored, a wee bit interested,* and *not bored at all.*"

"Lasses shouldnae be looking at monhoods and they shouldnae be naming them things."

"So many rules," she murmured. "I best tell Avery to cease calling her husband's Sir Draigon, I suppose."

He tossed her chemise aside and stared at her linen braies as he fought the urge to laugh. It was a puzzle how she kept doing that for he was not a man much given to laughter. Except for the occasional brief chuckle, he could not recall the last time he had really laughed. It was not the sort of thing a laird should do. If he went about grinning and laughing, he would soon lose control of his people. It was strength which held them all together.

"Ye are still wearing those braies," he said.

"Aye, I am, and I mean to keep doing so."

"They are a mon's clothes."

"And 'tis just like a mon to protect his nether regions

whilst expecting a lass to endure the cold and risk chafe whilst riding. And, no matter how careful and modest a lass is, some fool will be trying to peek under her skirts. Weel, what is under my skirts is for no eyes but mine and my husband's. So, dinnae think ye will get me to stop wearing them.''

The mere thought that some man might catch a fleeting glimpse of her treasures was enough to make Connor decide that braies were really not such a bad thing for a lass to wear. He unlaced them and, the moment they fell to her feet, he picked her up and set her on his bed. She looked unsettlingly small lying there in his big bed. Delicate and easily bruised.

Gillyanne felt herself blush beneath his steady gaze. When he frowned, her embarrassment changed to unease. She knew she was small, but so were most of the women in her family and their men seemed well pleased. One quick glance at his stout manhood told her that Connor's frown was certainly not born of a lack of interest.

"Are ye just going to look at it or do ye mean to use it?" she finally drawled, unable to bear that unwavering stare for another moment.

"Use it," Connor replied and he sprawled on top of her.

She murmured in delight when he gave her another one of those kisses which held so much promise. Gillyanne wrapped her arms around his neck and held him close. He was big, warm, and heavy, but she enjoyed the feel of his body against hers. At the first tease of his tongue against her lips, she parted them. As he stroked the inside of her mouth, she felt that delicious tingling warmth begin to flow through her veins, and that strange yet delightful tightening low in her belly was back. Now she would know what it was all about, would learn what put that look in lovers' eyes that could make even her blush.

Connor could feel those beautiful nipples harden against his chest as he kissed Gillyanne. He wanted to take immediate, greedy advantage of that, but firmly told himself to go slowly. It was not simply because, despite exposing her to the less genteel side of passion, he wanted to try to avoid completely disgusting her so that they might be able to do this again. He was not sure why, but he wanted to do more with Gillyanne than he did with women like Meg, more than a little mutual touching, some kisses, then pounding away until he spilled his seed. And that last, he thought, almost smiling as he kissed her long beautiful throat on his way toward those lovely breasts he so craved, was the very best thing about having a wife. He did not have to pull away at the last moment, spending himself outside in the cold. If, along with the pleasure of staying warm and snug inside her when he found his release, he could have Gillyanne like some of the loving, too, he might actually find something approaching contentment.

When he inched his way down to her breasts, he propped huimself up on his elbows and covered them with his hands. They nestled into his palms as if they belonged there. Partly because of his size, he had always chosen bigger women to bed, fulsome, heavy-breasted lasses, yet he did not think he had ever felt anything as perfect as holding Gillyanne's small, firm breasts and feeling her nipples brushing against his palms as she breathed. He slid his hands to the sides of her breasts, and, after a moment of enjoying the sight of those dark pink nipples so hard and inviting, he slowly licked each one. The soft cry Gillyanne gave made him hesitate, dismayed that he had shocked her so quickly. Then he felt her arch closer, rub herself against him, and tremble. He did it again and her reaction was much the same. Pure astonishment gripped him when he realized that she was heatedly appreciative of the caresses. Then he shook himself free of that surprise and proceeded to feast upon her, licking, nibbling, and suckling until he had to grip her firmly by one slim hip to still her movements against him.

Knowing he was close to losing control, he kissed his way down her belly. Even as he kissed her navel, tickling it with his tongue, he slid his hand between her legs. Only his firm grip upon her kept her from bowing up right off the bed. This time he knew what her reaction meant for he could feel it beneath his fingers as he stroked her, could feel the heat and damp welcome of her. He pressed his face into her stomach, fighting the urge to kiss her there, right on those pretty curls. It was too soon. Instead, he satisfied himself by breathing deeply, savoring the smell of her clean skin and the warm musk of feminine arousal.

It was almost too much and he lifted himself up. Even as she clamped her slim, strong legs around him as if to keep him from escaping, he eased into her. The tight, hot feel of her made him groan. She spoke his name, her voice thick and shaking with the force of her need, and he felt the last of his control snap. As he began to move, every inch of her slender, clinging body encouraging him not to temper his thrusts, he kissed her and tasted her wild greed. He felt her release grip her and plunged deep inside her, shuddering from the force of his own. The way her body seemed to drink of his, the way her nails grazed the skin of his back, and even the way she drummed her small heels against his backside, only added to the intensity of his pleasure. Finally, he collapsed against her, keeping just enough of his wits about him to fall slightly to the side, his face buried in the pillow.

Gillyanne began to stroke Connor as she slowly came to her senses. She murmured in regret when he softened and slipped free of her body. This was what it was supposed to be like, she mused as she rubbed her feet up and down the hair-roughened skin of his strong calves.

Now she fully understood all those long glances and soft sighs. She was just not sure what this meant for her and now was a poor time to try to sort it all out. She had to be certain Connor now understood that he did not have to take his *rougher* passions elsewhere.

"I am still alive," she said, meaning to jest but not really surprised to hear a touch of wonder in her voice.

"I think I am, too," he muttered, sneaking a look at her and feeling disgustingly pleased with himself over the lingering flush of pleasure he could see upon her face.

"And I wasnae disgusted at all."

"Nay, ye werenae, only that was just a wee taste of what a mon's hearty loving is like."

"Only a wee taste?"

"Aye. I may yet do something to disgust you."

"Humph. Just go ahead and try."

He intended to, Connor thought, and actually grinned into the pillow. It was hard for him to accept that his uncle had been wrong. It was easier to decide that Gillyanne was a rare find, but one in a thousand. Perhaps her family had raised her to see no wrong in enjoying the loving with her husband. A lot of questions filled his head, but he bit back every one. For whatever reasons, Gillyanne enjoyed lovemaking, freely and wildly. Her cries of pleasure had been sweet and true.

And loud, he thought, and did smile a little. He would not be surprised if everyone at Deilcladach had heard her cries. Only a fool would question such a gift and Connor MacEnroy was no fool.

Chapter Eight

Connor opened his eyes and studied the breast his nose was touching. It was a lovely breast—pale, silken soft, firm, and inviting. It was his little wife's breast. He briefly savored a strong sense of possession. No other man could kiss that breast, tease that raspberry tinted nipple to hardness, or feel that delicate, perfectly shaped breast warm his palm. At least, not without risking a long and intensely painful death, he mused, and then wondered why the mere thought of another man touching Gillyanne should make his innards twist with rage. Having a wife was not the simple matter he had first thought it would be. Of course, it could be just this particular wife, he decided, as he circled that pretty nipple with his finger and felt Gillyanne twitch. He was just about to kiss that breast when someone pounded on the door.

"God's tears," he muttered and looked up to see Gillyanne watching him, noting that her eyes were cloudy with sleep and budding desire.

" 'Tis morning," Gillyanne murmured and clutched

the sheet to her chest as Connor sat up, forcing her to do the same if she was to remain covered.

He nodded. "A fine time for a tussle." He scowled at the door. "But, I see, nay this morning. What?" he bellowed as the pounding continued.

"Uncle Neil is here," Diarmot bellowed in reply. "He wants to see you. Now."

"Tell him I am begetting my heir."

"Told him. He isnae pleased ye got married without telling him. Wants to see the wife."

"Keep him fed. I will be down in a few minutes." Cursing his uncle all the while, Connor washed, dressed, and headed out of the room, calling back over his shoulder, "Best ye hurry down to the great hall."

Gillyanne did not even have the chance to reply before he was gone. She flopped back on the pillows. That was a somewhat abrupt and rude awakening, she mused. A flicker of hurt, even insult, came to life in her heart, but she quickly smothered it. She could hardly expect the man to turn into some sweet-tongued courtier after but one night of loving. Connor was as new to the art of being a husband as she was to being a wife. He was going to need a lot of training.

She climbed out of bed to begin her morning ablutions. There were other things she could not be sure of, she realized. Despite the gloriously passionate night they had just shared, Gillyanne could not feel certain she had changed any of Connor's strange attitudes concerning the treatment of wives, nor that he would be faithful now. In truth, all she had proven to him was that at least one gentle-born lady could handle what he called a man's rougher passions. That was not exactly a large step forward.

There was also the fact she had entered into their marriage simply to end a battle, to gain time for her father to rescue her. As she started to don her sadly worn clothes, she shook her head and scolded herself about lying to herself. Those reasons had been there, but so had a strong lusty attraction for Connor, even a greed to finally grab a chance to learn how passion tasted. What she had done was snatch an opportunity to see if that attraction meant Connor was the mate of her heart and, if he was, could she make him share in that feeling. And, if not, she had the chance to get her father to help free her.

"And, until that is all decided," she muttered as she tied back her hair with a strip of leather and started to leave for the great hall, "I shall behave as if this marriage is built on firm ground, as sacred as the vows spoken and as unbreakable." Suddenly, she recalled that Uncle Neil was the fool who had filled Connor's head with all those alarming notions about women, and she moved a little faster. It was not wise to leave her husband alone with that particular man for too long.

"Uncle Neil," Connor said as he strode into the great hall. "Weel met."

As he went to his seat and had a scowling Meg pour him a tankard of goat's milk, Connor studied his uncle. The greying man was filling his tankard with ale despite the early hour. Connor had always known that his uncle drank too much, yet, for some reason, it was a truth that struck him particularly hard this morning. He also wondered where the man had been which allowed him to join them to break his fast. Neil looked as if he had suffered through a particularly rough night, yet instinct told Connor the man had not ridden hard or far. And, just where had Neil heard that he was married if not from Diarmot?

"So, ye got yourself married, lad," Neil said, looking little pleased by the news. "Why?"

"Diarmot did not tell you?" It troubled Connor that he should suddenly feel so conflicted about his uncle,

should suddenly feel any need at all to question the
man who had been such a guiding force since the deaths
of his parents.

"The lad just said ye was upstairs with the wench
when I asked where ye and the wife were."

"How did ye ken I e'en had a wife?"

"Near everyone twixt here and Edinburgh kens ye
now have a wife, lad. Three belted knights and lairds
making fools of themselves trying to grab one lass is the
sort of tale that travels fast."

Connor wondered why he felt so dissatisfied with that
answer then shrugged aside his doubts. News could
indeed skip over the heather and hills with astounding
speed. And, no matter which direction his uncle had
come from, he would have traveled over lands where
near every man, woman, and child would have heard
the whole story.

"I won the game, secured the prize, and now Ald-
dabhach is under my rule," Connor said with some
pride.

"Thought the lass chose you."

"She did, but only after each one of us had tried and
failed to take Ald-dabhach and showed signs that we
were prepared to try again, harder and, mayhap, with
less care about the land and its people. She is a crafty
wee lass, but soft of heart. She wanted no bloodshed.
Once her trickery failed to send us on our way, she
decided to quit the game."

" 'Twas nay trickery," Gillyanne protested as she
entered the hall in time to hear Connor's words. " 'Twas
strategy."

Neil looked at Gillyanne and scowled. "God's toes,
lad, couldnae ye have waited 'til she grew a wee bit?"

As Gillyanne made her way to the seat next to Connor,
she decided it would not be wise to pause by her husband's uncle and clout the man offside the head. "I
am done growing."

"Och, ye didnae do a verra good job of it. And by the looks of the rags she wears, she be a poor lass as weel."

"She brought Ald-dabhach to the marriage, Uncle," Connor said, hiding a sudden anger he felt over his uncle's blunt and somewhat unkind words. "Naught else is needed. And, her cousin will soon bring her things here to her. There was no time to collect them and I felt it best to get her secured here."

"Ye think the others will try to take her from ye?"

"I believe they might, aye."

"So, the fighting will begin all over again."

That alarmed Gillyanne and she tried to concentrate on the porridge and bread a young boy had just set before her. She had surrendered and allowed herself to be married in order to prevent bloodshed. It was appalling to think that, by saving the people of Ald-dabhach, she may well have started anew an old feud.

"Nay," Connor said firmly. "They may try some trickery, mayhap e'en a kidnapping, but there will be no resurrecting the old feuds and hatreds. Robert and David dinnae want that any more than I do. All three of us spent our youths doing naught but cleaning up the mess our fathers left behind. We are weary of it."

Meg arrived to set a plate of bread before Connor. The woman rubbed up against him and cast him such a sultry look that Gillyanne felt a sudden craving to bury her eating knife in the woman's heaving bosom. Connor leaned away from Meg and waved her off. Gillyanne nearly choked on her porridge when he gave her a brief wink, but then she frowned. If the oaf thought he ought to be praised for obeying vows given before God, he had better think again.

"Shouldnae be so cool to your leman, Connor," advised Neil. "The lasses have their ways of making a mon pay."

"Meg is nay longer my leman."

"Ah, got a new one? Who? Jenny? A fine, buxom lass, that one."

"I am a wedded mon now, Uncle."

Connor was still not sure he agreed with or even believed a lot of what Gillyanne had said last night, save for one thing. It *was* wrong to flaunt his mistress before her and his clan. It would indeed rob her of all respect, making it hard if not impossible for her to take her place as the lady of Deilcladach. That could not be allowed. And, if Gillyanne continued to accept and return his passion as she had during the night, he really saw no need to take a mistress. He was a lusty man, but he had never really craved a continuous, ever-changing assortment of women. All he required was that the lass be warm and willing and Gillyanne showed great promise of being both. He glanced at his little wife and was not really surprised to see her glaring at his uncle, although she tried hard to hide it. It was a little inconsiderate of his uncle to mention such things in front of her.

"What has being a wedded mon got to do with taking a leman?" asked Neil, filling his tankard yet again.

"If Connor trots after other mares now, 'tis adultery, and I believe that is a sin," murmured Gillyanne.

"A mon needs a warm, willing lass now and again." When Gillyanne softly snorted in obvious contempt of his opinion, he demanded, "Just who are ye, lass?"

"Gillyanne Murray of Dubhlinn, daughter of Sir Eric Murray and Lady Bethia."

"Sir Eric Murray?" Neil stared at her for a moment then looked at Connor in alarm. "He is a king's mon."

If the man's name alone made his uncle look so uneasy, Connor began to think Gillyanne's warnings about what her father would do might not be such empty threats. It was, of course, completely unacceptable for a wife to threaten her husband and he was going to have to explain that to her, but first it might be wise to get her to tell him a little more about her father. He had assumed that there would eventually be an angry father to treaty with, perhaps even a small bride price to be paid to soothe the man's annoyance, but his uncle's reaction to the man's name signified it would, or could, be far more than that. He did not need another laird to watch out for.

"The king himself directed us to Ald-dabhach and its maiden," said Connor. "In truth, the king was the one who suggested that one of us marrying the lass was the best way to stop all our fretting o'er those lands."

"Ah, weel, that should help ye. I suspect Sir Eric will have been told all that ere he charges o'er here seeking his bairn."

Gillyanne spread some thick honey on a slice of bread and slowly ate it as she studied Connor's uncle. He was the man who had shaped far too many of Connor's attitudes. If the way he was swilling ale at such an early hour was any indication, he was also a drunk. The gossip he began to relate slowly revealed a subtle but deep-set contempt and mistrust of women. There was something about the man that made her very uneasy and she could not blame all of that feeling upon those two flaws. She sensed in the man a deep guilt and anger which he could not drown with all the drink he so recklessly poured down his throat. Sir Neil MacEnroy was a man with secrets, she decided. Dark, ugly secrets he was terrified someone might uproot. Gillyanne was tempted to dig them out, but, after a brief glance at Connor, she was not sure that would be kind. She decided to simply watch the man closely to see if he really was the danger she now felt he was. If he was, then all consideration for Connor's feelings and all fears of hurting her marriage with unwanted revelations would have to be cast aside.

Her attention was caught when Neil began to relate some court gossip which she suspected he did on purpose. It did not surprise her to hear her cousin Payton's name followed by a long recitation of his affairs and she inwardly winced. Then Neil spoke of her father and, after only two short tales indicating that he walked the same lecherous path as Payton, anger brought Gillyanne to her feet.

"Ye insult my fither, sir," she said.

"Insult?" Neil looked at her in astonishment. "I but tell the lad of what a fine lusty mon your father is."

"He is a fine mon and I suspect he is lusty, but the gossip which sets him in the beds of other women is naught but lies. My fither is no adulterer."

"Now, lass, ye being his bairn, ye just dinnae wish to see the truth."

"I ken weel the truth," she interrupted him. "My fither would *never* betray my mither." She clenched her hands into tight fists and ached to hit the man when he rolled his eyes. "He loves her. If that carries no weight with ye, then closely heed what else he says. He freely admits to being much akin to my cousin Payton whilst still in his youth, but nay now. As he says, he spoke vows afore God and he feels retribution for breaking those is nay worth risking just for a rutting with some wench. Fither also says that, if naught else, Mither is the woman who risked her verra life to give him bairns, who tends his hearth and comfort, and who will stand by him e'en when he is old, scarred, and crooked. For all that, he can at least be faithful. So, if ye dinnae believe in his finer sentiments, ye can heed his practicality. I will nay hear any more ill talk about him."

With a nod to Connor, Gillyanne did not wait to be formally excused, but strode out of the great hall. Her proud exit was slightly marred by the need to elbow her way through the knot of Connor's five siblings crowded in the doorway. As she passed through them, she briefly met Fiona's gaze and decided she needed to do something about the girl. First, however, she intended to vent

her anger by giving Connor's bedchamber a thorough
cleaning.

"The lass ye wed doesnae understand the ways of the
world," Neil said, nodding a greeting to the rest of his
nephews and his niece.

"Mayhap not," agreed Connor, "but I think she
understands her own family verra weel."

"Are ye taking her side?"

"I dinnae see a *side* in all of this, Uncle."

"The lass certainly looked furious," murmured Diarmot as he sat down next to his uncle and reached for
the bread.

"I was but entertaining Connor with some tales I
heard at court," said Neil. "The lass is just too sensitive,
doesnae like hearing how men behave."

"She said naught when ye told me of the lusty adven-
tures of her cousin," Connor reminded his uncle.
" 'Twas the tales ye told of her father that made her
angry."

" 'Twas naught but the truth I was telling. Foolish
bairn just doesnae want to think her father behaves like
other men."

Connor did not wish to argue with his uncle over
this yet felt a strong need to defend Gillyanne's anger.
"Weel, whether that is true or nay, it was a wee bit
unkind to repeat such tales about her father. We both
ken that much of the gossip one hears, especially that
whispered about at court, is nay true."

Neil studied Connor for a moment then said, "Ye
dinnae believe the gossip about her father is true."

" 'Tis nay my place to believe it or nay. Yet, the lass
believes in all she said, and so fiercely, it must have been
bred somewhere. The words she claimed her father
said also have the ring of truth. As *she* said, heed the
practicality if not the sentiment. So, nay, I am inclined

to believe it all lies, mayhap lies intended to hurt the mon so close to the king that he inspires jealousy. E'en if all true, 'tis still nay the sort of tales to repeat to the mon's own daughter.''

"Connor has the right of it, I think, Uncle," Diarmot said. "Lady Gillyanne has a fair amount of pride in her father. Ye can hear it in how she speaks his name. Aye, and in the way she thinks just mentioning the mon's name to Connor is as good as wielding a club. To be fair, no one really likes to hear bad about their father. Handsome mon, is he?''

"The lasses think so," grumbled Neil. "He and that cousin of hers. They both have the women fair to tripping o'er each other to lure them into their beds. 'Tis the cousin ye hear the most about. The men, or most of them, seem torn atween liking and respecting the lad and wishing he would suffer some gross, disfiguring injury, for they hate his ease with the lasses. The women speak of the youth as if he is all that is beautiful and good in a mon." Neil made a harsh noise of disgust and took a drink.

As his brothers pressed for more tales, Connor sat back in his chair and tried to sort out his feelings. He had actually argued with his uncle over something concerning his wife, however mildly. It might be that it was exactly what a husband should do, yet it carried the taint of softness. He would have to guard against that sort of thing more vigilantly, especially, he mused as he watched Fiona slip away, since little Gillyanne apparently had a true skill at gaining allies.

"What are ye doing?"

Gillyanne looked up from the hearth she was scrubbing, a little surprised to see young Fiona seated in a chair watching her. Since first setting eyes on Connor's sister, she had seen the glint of curiosity in Fiona's lovely violet eyes, yet this was the first time Fiona had really approached her. Gillyanne wished she knew if it was because Fiona wanted to learn from her or if the younger girl simply found her an odd creature demanding of further study. It was hard to get any exact sense of what the young girl felt. That tight guard on one's feelings was obviously a MacEnroy trait.

"I am cleaning the laird's bedchamber," Gillyanne replied then glanced behind her to see the plump maid Joan rolling up the carpet on Connor's side of the bed. "Nay, Joan, take the draperies, tapestries, and bed linens—hangings and all—first. Oh, and have one of the women come up with some more water and whate'er else may be needed to scrub this floor."

"This is Meg's job," Fiona said and quirked one brow in a perfect imitation of Connor when both Gillyanne and Joan snorted softly in amusement heavily weighted with derision. "Meg does whate'er she wishes to, true enough, but 'tis really her place to do the cleaning."

" 'Tis verra clear that she has no intention of doing it. I dinnae ken how she could abide staying in this room, although I did notice that the bed was clean." Gillyanne stared at Connor's bed, thought of him tangling beneath the sheets with another woman, and wanted to burn it.

"Meg was ne'er in that bed. None of Connor's women have been. Not that he has had so verra many. He is verra particular about that bed. I was surprised to hear ye were in it, but then ye are his wife and verra clean. He has the linens changed every week." Fiona frowned. "I am nay sure when mine were last cleaned."

"I shall tend to your room next then. Come, help me put the mattresses o'er the window sill so that they might air," Gillyanne said as soon as Joan left. "Then, as they are put back onto the bed, I have found herbs to sprinkle between each layer."

"To make the bed smell pretty?" Fiona asked as she

moved to help Gillyanne carry each mattress to a narrow window and force it to drape over the sill, half in and half out.

"That is some of it. The herbs will also hold back the damp and the bugs."

"I would ne'er have thought Connor had any bugs in his bed."

"None that I noticed, but the herbs will insure that they ne'er steal into that warm nest. We can flip this mattress o'er in an hour or two and let the other side air. I suspect Connor's liking for clean linens has helped to keep the bedding fresh."

"I think Connor is so particular about his bed because we spent so many years in damp, filthy hovels as we rebuilt this keep."

Gillyanne nodded with approval when Joan returned to take the rugs away for a hearty beating. The woman brought along her young cousin Mairi armed with a broom, a bucket, and something to scrub the floor with. She idly wondered if Connor would even notice the changes made by a thorough scrubbing then inwardly sighed. He might, but she doubted he would say anything. She returned to scrubbing the hearth and sternly told herself she needed no approval or praise from her husband. The quiet satisfaction of a job well done should be enough.

"Is there anything I can do?" Fiona asked a little timidly.

"Ye could take one of those rags and, using the water from one of the buckets, wash the walls. Are ye sure ye wish to, though?"

"Aye, tedious as it sounds. I am a woman now and I finally faced a hard truth. I cannae be a warrior, nay as my brothers are. My fate is to wed a mon and give him bairns. 'Tis good I ken how to fight at my mon's side, but he will also expect me to ken how to keep his hearth." Fiona started to wash the walls.

"Ye have been taught none of the womanly arts?"

"What would Connor, my uncle, or my brothers ken about a lady's ways? Dinnae mishear me. I have no complaints about how I have been raised. Connor did the best he could when, as little more than a lad himself, he was left with an infant girl to care for and so much to be rebuilt. 'Tis for him, too, that I now wish to learn a lady's ways. I willnae shame him, myself, or my husband with my ignorance."

"Although many of my kin would howl with laughter o'er me teaching a lass the ways of a lady, I shall do my best."

They all worked quietly for a while, but the moment Mairi left, Fiona said, "I suppose I shall have to learn to wear a dress."

Gillyanne laughed. "Aye, I fear ye will. When my cousin James brings me my clothes, I can give ye one of mine." She quickly looked Fiona over. "Twill need only a wee bit of fitting. Now, I have heard some tales of all that happened here, all the fighting and the death, but could ye tell me the whole of the tale as we work?"

Fiona took a deep breath and began the long dark tale of years of battle, destruction, and death. When Mairi returned to polish the wood, she occasionally added to the sad story. As the horror of it all was told, Gillyanne began to understand what forces had made the man Connor was today.

At barely fifteen Connor had seen the brutal slaughter of much of his clan, including his parents. The lands had been devastated, leaving little food or shelter for the shattered remnants of the clan he was made laird of. There followed years of hardship as he led the rebuilding and protected his siblings and clan. It was an accomplishment to be proud of, but Gillyanne had to nod in agreement when Fiona said she felt Connor still suffered some guilt over not fighting and dying at his father's side.

It explained **so** very much. The burden placed upon Connor's young shoulders would have broken many another, but he had steeled himself to do what was needed. Gillyanne now knew why she could sense so little of his feelings. They were buried deep within him, rigidly caged by years of discipline and the struggle to survive. There had been no time, no room, for the softer emotions. She suspected his intense need to appear the strong leader his battered clan required was another reason he had so fiercely subdued feelings such as joy, tenderness, and anything else he feared might carry the taint of weakness. Now, even though all was peaceful, and all but the loved ones lost had been restored, he still clung to that hard man.

And it was going to take an awful lot to crack that shell, Gillyanne thought with a sigh. After so many years she could not even be certain there was any joy or softness left inside Connor. He still clung to the need to protect all those under his rule, no matter what the cost to himself. Gillyanne wanted to believe that a man who made love to a woman as Connor had to her had to have some remnants of the softer emotions inside of him, yet she also understood that it could be no more than lust behind those stirring kisses. She faced a hard battle if she was to find in her marriage any of the beauty or joy her cousins had found in theirs. What chilled her blood was the fear that she did not know how to win such a battle, nor if she had the right weapons.

Chapter Nine

"She didnae bring the hot water up again."

Gillyanne glared at the empty tub and told herself Fiona did not deserve to feel the lash of her simmering anger. After five days of nights filled with passion and days spent ignored by her husband, Gillyanne had come up with a plan. It was mostly an extension of what she was already doing in taking on the role of the lady of Deilcladach. Unfortunately, cleaning the place properly was taking a lot longer than she had anticipated and Connor had not really noticed much yet. So, she had tried to think of all the small comforts a wife could give her husband. One of those had been to have a nice hot bath ready for him at the end of the day. That decision had been made three days ago and she had yet been able to enact it.

The problem was that it was Meg's duty to bring the water to the laird's chamber. Gillyanne had expected some trouble when she had discovered that, but never this blatant disobedience. And, this time, she refused to do it herself or have someone else do it. If nothing else, it was unfair to ask the other women to help do work Meg should be doing. They had plenty of their own to do. In Joan's case, it was rather unkind for most of the women knew that, while Joan did Meg's work, Meg was probably bedding Joan's husband. Meg's utter disregard for any order given by the laird's wife was also weakening Gillyanne's position in the keep, more so than did uncle Neil's open contempt and dislike. If the women Gillyanne dealt with were not so understanding and Meg was not so heartily disliked, she suspected she would be little more than a jest to the people of Deilcladach.

"Just why do ye want a hot bath brought up here each night?" asked Fiona.

"I am verra tired of being almost completely ignored by my husband every day," Gillyanne replied.

"And ye think a bath will change that?"

"Nay, 'tis nay just the bath. Although, I like a hot bath at the end of the day and I believe Connor does as weel." Gillyanne sat down on the bed next to Fiona. "Connor calls me wife and shares his bed with me yet this isnae really a marriage yet. We share verra little else. Aye, he now holds the seat next to his for me at the evening meal, but he talks mostly to your brothers, your uncle, and his men. I thought to make my mark by cleaning this place, but I begin to think Connor is one of those men who willnae realize what has changed until the whole place gleams and that willnae be any time soon."

"Och, nay." Fiona shook her head. "I hadnae realized how filthy the place was until we scrubbed my bed-chamber clean."

"I have seen filthier. There was cleaning done here, but nay enough, and nay often. Not for several years, I suspect."

"Ah, weel, several years ago Meg became the one who gave the orders to the women."

"Oh. One of those clever monly decisions." Gillyanne suddenly frowned. "She has been Connor's leman for that long?"

"At that time she was my uncle Neil's. I think she has been with each of my brothers as weel." Fiona shrugged. "Ye were explaining why the bath is so important to ye."

" 'Tis one of those small comforts a wife can give her husband. I thought that, if I filled his life with a few of those, he would soon notice me outside of the bed. And, if he bathes here ere he dines, he will have to spend a wee bit of time with me, time that might include some talking so that we may learn about each other. He just might get used to it."

"Aye, or he just might take ye to bed *afore* he dines."

Gillyanne sighed and nodded. "There is that possibility, but he could still grow accustomed to bathing in the comfort of his own chambers and, mayhap, to being helped at his bath by a woman."

"He is already being helped by a woman." Fiona gasped and clapped her hand over her mouth.

"Let me guess," Gillyanne stood up, clenching her hands into tight little fists. "Meg."

"And Jenny and Peg," Fiona said, watching Gillyanne warily.

"The three sluts of Deilcladach. 'Tis no wonder Meg wouldnae get me the water. She has the perfect opportunity to seduce Connor back into her bed at the end of every cursed day. Weel, nay more," she snapped and strode out of her bedchamber.

"I dinnae think ye ought to go to the bathing shed," Fiona warned as she hurried after Gillyanne. "There will be naked men there."

"I have seen a naked mon before."

Fiona inwardly cursed her loose tongue as she followed Gillyanne. She was not exactly sure what her brother's wife expected of him, but had known that

Gillyanne would not like him getting his back scrubbed by Meg. A squawk of surprise and protest escaped her when, as she trailed Gillyanne through the kitchens, Joan grabbed her by the arm

"Ye told her, didnae ye?" Joan sounded more resigned than annoyed.

"I didnae mean to. It just leaped out of my mouth," Fiona replied.

"She certainly looked furious."

"Aye, which is why I have to go with her."

"Wheesht, to protect that bawd Meg? What for?"

"Depending upon what she finds, it may not be just Meg she sets after. And, she is such a wee lass, e'en if she just goes after Meg, she could be hurt."

Joan smiled as she released Fiona. "Oh, if it comes to a battle atween those two, I think I would be wagering my coin on her ladyship. Aye, I would indeed."

Fiona left Joan and the other women, wondering why they were all laughing. Instinct told her Gillyanne could probably take care of herself, but that confidence did little to still her worry. She had not wanted to admit it in front of Joan and the other women, but Fiona was a little concerned about how her brother might react to being confronted by an angry wife in front of his men. Seeing that Gillyanne was almost to the door of the bathing hut, Fiona ran to catch her up. Her heart told her this marriage could be good for Connor and she was increasingly afraid that he was going to fail at it in some way, perhaps even badly enough to drive Gillyanne away.

Gillyanne cursed softly as she neared the bathing house and heard the laughter of men and women. She did not fully believe Connor was bedding down with Meg again, but her inability to sense what the man felt or thought stole her confidence in her own opinions.

If she was being played for a fool, she wanted to know it.

She admitted to herself that it was more than a fear of Connor's faithlessness which spurred her temper. The passion she and Connor shared, as well as the vows she had spoken, compelled her to try and make her marriage more than heated lovemaking at night and tending the man's keep all day. After a great deal of thought, she had finally come up with a plan and Meg was ruining it before it had even been tested. It was far past time that she and Meg had a confrontation.

The sight which greeted her inside the bathing house brought Gillyanne to an abrupt halt and had her clenching her fists so tightly her nails were sinking into her palms. She was only faintly aware of the other men, most of them naked, and that moment when they suddenly noticed her, grew still, then scrambled into the tubs. All her attention was fixed upon her tall, beautiful husband. He was not yet naked. He stood there in his fine linen breeches. Right in front of him stood a coyly smiling Meg, her hands untying the laces on those breeches. Gillyanne tried to decide which one of them she would kill first.

Connor was just about to unlace his breeches when Knobby began to relate an amusing tale about the blacksmith and his wife. He paid little attention to Meg when she sidled up close to him and pushed his hands aside, taking over the chore of unlacing him. Then Knobby grew abruptly quiet, his eyes growing so wide Connor suspected it had to sting. Before he could ask what was wrong, all the men started to leap into the tubs, even the ones who still wore braies or breechclouts. A few men grabbed drying cloths and wrapped themselves up in them, looking remarkably like outraged maidens. The hairs on the back of Connor's neck rose uncomfortably as he slowly looked in the direction where all his men were staring.

The moment he saw Gillyanne standing there, her eyes green with fury and a worried Fiona at her side, Connor became painfully aware of Meg's fingers brushing against his skin as she finished unlacing him. He told himself he was doing nothing wrong yet shoved Meg away and clutched the now open front of his breeches. It astonished him that he had to bite his lip to stop a flood of excuses and explanations. He had done nothing wrong, he reminded himself, yet he still felt as if he had erred in some way.

Then he realized what his wife would have seen before his men had all scrambled to cover themselves. "Ye shouldnae be here," he said, hurriedly relacing his breeches. "There are naked men here."

"I have seen naked men before," she snapped.

"Weel, ye werenae married then. This is no place for a woman."

"There are women here now."

"Ah, aye, weel, they have seen all of us, havenae they?"

"And sampled ye too, I suspect."

The way his men nearly gaped at him told Connor that sudden tingle of heat he felt in his face was indeed a blush. He felt embarrassed and just a little ashamed yet he did not understand why. After all, he had not even known Gillyanne when he had been enjoying the freely offered favors of Meg, Jenny, and Peg. He had had every right to indulge himself. Then he inwardly grimaced. It *was* awkward to have three women he had bedded all lined up in front of his new wife. When he realized those three women were giving his wife smug, insolent looks, he glared at them so fiercely even Meg moved away.

"Now I understand why ye wouldnae bring me the hot water I requested," Gillyanne said, glaring at Meg who was twining herself around a burly man wrapped in a large drying cloth.

"She wouldnae bring ye the water for your bath?"

Connor sincerely hoped he was not going to be dragged into the middle of some female quarrel yet he could not really stand by and allow Meg to be disrespectful to his wife.

"Actually, it was *your* bath I tried to have prepared. I had thought ye might like to have your bath in the comfort of your own chambers with your wife to assist you. 'Tis one of those many things wives should do for their husbands."

"It is?" Connor thought he might enjoy that.

"Aye, but 'tis clear that ye enjoy this monly gathering." Gillyanne noticed that Meg was caressing the man she was with, her pale hand beneath his draping, and the man was beginning to respond with evident interest. "Meg, do ye think ye might rein in your bawd's ways until Fiona isnae here? She kens ye are a whore, but she is a wee bit young to see ye behave so." She then recognized the man. "And ye are Malcolm, Joan's *husband*. Ye should be thoroughly ashamed of yourself."

"A mon has his needs," Malcolm protested, although he did try to move away from Meg's grasp.

"Oh? I see. Joan refuses ye her bed," Gillyanne said, knowing full well the woman did not. "If she denies ye your husbandly rights then I suppose she deserves the deep, painful humiliation she suffers kenning that ye rut with Meg and that all here ken it."

"All?" croaked Malcolm.

Gillyanne ignored him, idly wondering how the man could be so stupid as to think only a few knew of his faithlessness. "And, 'tis probably a just punishment that Joan not only do her own work, but that left undone by the woman ye betray her with. Aye, each time she does Meg's chores because Meg is probably busy rutting with you, Joan should be properly chastised for failing ye as a wife. Harsh justice, but necessary, I suppose."

Malcolm looked positively ill and Gillyanne was pleased. She looked at Connor who was frowning at

Malcolm. When he finally met her gaze, however, the frown had faded and, for one brief moment, there was a gleam of amusement sparkling in his lovely eyes. Her anger had cooled a little and she decided now was probably not the best time to vent her displeasure with Meg or Connor. Gillyanne suspected she had made it clear enough already.

"Weel, since here is where ye choose to bathe, I shall leave ye to enjoy it," she said, pleased with the sweetness of her tone.

"Och, weel, aye." Despite the camaraderie of the bathing house, Connor had to admit that bathing with his wife held far more attraction than sharing a big wooden vat with other naked men while three whores scrubbed their backs and occasionally frolicked with one of the men.

Gillyanne turned to leave then looked back at Connor, her expression one of gentle sorrow with a hint of repentance. "I ken 'tis verra wrong, so I feel I must confess. Being such a sensitive, gently bred lady, I fear I will find it verra difficult to touch those parts of ye touched by another woman." She gave a delicate shudder. "Aye, it could be many a long night ere I could banish the sordid, painful image from my poor, tormented mind." She gave him a fleeting, teary smile, grabbed Fiona by the hand, and walked away.

"Ye certainly do have a way with words," said Fiona, staring at Gillyanne in amused awe.

"My mither says 'tis a gift from my fither." Gillyanne sighed as they approached the keep. "Dinnae tell Joan about Malcolm."

"He looked near to emptying his belly."

"Aye, but a mon's guilt and shame can be such fleeting things. He may e'en try to make amends, but it too could be fleeting. I just cannae believe the fool didnae think that his wife kenned it all. Do men think we women ne'er speak to each other?"

Fiona grimaced. "The men dinnae notice, but those three women do seem to think that spreading their thighs for the men of Deilcladach makes them important. Not only do they boast about having bedded another woman's mon, but they havenae done their share of the work for a verra long time. They wait upon my brothers and that blinds those fools to how little those women actually do. I think e'en they ken that Connor wouldnae be pleased to learn how they neglect their share of the work." Fiona looked at Gillyanne. "Do ye think Connor will come to have his bath in your bedchamber now?"

"I dinnae ken, but I intend to have one myself."

"So, ye didnae get pummeled," Joan said as Gillyanne strode into the kitchens, "and since ye arenae covered in blood, I suspect ye didnae pummel anyone yourself."

"Nay, though the temptation was there," replied Gillyanne.

"I would have thought the temptation would be seeing all those MacEnroy men naked," said Mairi and sighed.

Gillyanne laughed. " 'Tis sorry I am I didnae take too much notice ere they all scurried to cover themselves."

"We filled the bath for you," said Joan. "E'en if the laird doesnae join ye, I thought ye might be wanting one."

"Thank ye, Joan, I do." As Gillyanne started out of the kitchens she suddenly recalled which of the MacEnroy men Mairi had shown a hint of interest in. "I believe I may have seen more than I thought for an image or two does linger in my mind. Knobby."

"Ye saw Knobby naked?" asked Mairi, her eagerness to hear about it far too evident.

"Must have for I was just thinking of how he is as long and thin without his clothes as he appears with them on. Weel, except for one place. And, there, oh

my, he certainly is *long*, but he isnae *thin*. Nay, not thin
at all."

For a moment all the women in the kitchen silently
contemplated young Knobby, obviously trying to envi-
sion the plain, too thin man possessing something many
women would heartily appreciate. Then they all glanced
at each other and laughed. Mairi sighed again, looking
a little forlorn.

"Now I understand why Jenny is always after him and
complains so because he doesnae succumb to her wiles
verra often. I just wish he didnae succumb at all." Mairi
shrugged. "Still, he is just a mon."

"True, but if he shows some restraint when he isnae
betrothed or wedded, nay e'en wooing a lass, he is better
behaved than most men. What I see here is a lass who
wants a lad but is too shy to let him ken it and a lad
who probably doesnae think any lass would be interested
in him."

"And so it will have to be the lass who girds her timid
loins and takes the first bold step," said Joan, starting
an argument between the two cousins.

"I think I will stay and listen to this," said Fiona.
" 'Tis an old argument, but I dinnae want to miss the
moment when Mairi finally agrees with Joan. And, who
kens, Connor might come up to have that bath ye told
him about."

Gillyanne headed to her bedchamber and her waiting
bath. She was not all that sure Connor would show up.
In a way, it was not really other women she needed to
worry about, but the men of Deilcladach. Connor, his
brothers, and the other men were as tightly bonded a
group of men as she had ever seen. It was understandable, she supposed, as they had all been boys when the
feuding had stopped, mere youths faced with all the
responsibilities of grown men as well as the daunting
task of rebuilding. Boys forced to protect women and
children, to keep them all fed and sheltered. The ties

were strong and Gillyanne feared she would never be
able to find a place for herself. Even sadder was the
growing knowledge that she not only wanted to, she
needed to.

"I think my wee wife just threatened me," Connor
finally said after watching Gillyanne disappear into the
keep.

"Oh, aye," agreed Knobby as he waved Jenny away
and tended to his own bath. "Ye stay here to be bathed
by these lasses and 'twill be a cold bed ye rest in tonight
and mayhap a few nights after that. 'Twas verra clear."

"A wife shouldnae threaten her husband."

"Laird, your wife found ye down here with your
leman's hands on your breeches and two other lasses
ye have bedded down with standing by. Now, I dinnae
ken all that much about women. Dinnae think any of
us do since we spent most of the last twelve years rebuilding and just staying alive. Yet, I think I can see why the
lass was angry to catch ye bathing, attended by three
women ye have rutted with, and her all prepared to give
ye a nice private bath afore the fire. I am thinking ye
are lucky all she did was threaten ye with chilling your
bed."

Connor frowned in mild surprise when most of the
men muttered in agreement. "So, ye all think I should
bow to her blackmail."

"Weel, ye could go, get your bath, and sternly lecture
her on speaking so disrespectfully to her husband."

A smile briefly curved his lips when the men laughed.
He obviously had their approval for following Gillyanne
and would lose no stature in their eyes by bending in
this. As he reached for his clothes, Meg stepped up
to him, and caressed his back. Connor stared at her,
suddenly recalling a few other things Gillyanne had said.

"If your wee wife is fool enough to turn from ye, ye

ken where to come for some warmth," Meg said, tensing with obvious insult when he stepped away from her touch.

"I am a wedded mon. For now, I mean to hold to vows spoken. My wee wife has given me no reason to do otherwise." Connor looked at Malcolm who stood slumped against the wall. "In truth, I believe 'tis past time I make another rule. I cannae and willnae try to control the morals of my clan. So long as the rules ye break are nay mine and dinnae affect the safety or prosperity of Deilcladach, then 'tis upon your own soul. Howbeit, it appears some of my people are being hurt and that I cannae allow. So, within these walls, ye women willnae bed down with the wedded men. I ken 'tis nay all your doing, but ye will now learn to say nay once in a while. If ye must rut with a wedded mon, ye will do it elsewhere and ye will at least attempt to maintain some discretion."

Connor heard no objection from his men, did in fact see many nods of approval and agreement. "And, one more thing. Ye women can consider this a warning, a verra strong warning. Spreading your legs for the men isnae considered your work. It seems ye have begun to think your freely offered skills make ye far more important than ye are. Ye *will* do your share of the work. I dinnae allow the men to set aside duty or work for pleasure. I certainly willnae allow the women to do so. Ye all have tasks to do and ye will do them or ye will leave Deilcladach." He fixed a hard gaze upon Meg who looked furious. "And ye will do as Lady Gillyanne commands. She is my wife, the lady of Deilcladach, and thus can demand your respect and obedience."

He was not surprised when Meg simply walked away, obviously too furious to argue or even speak.

"Ye had best watch her," advised Knobby as he stepped out of his bath, tugged the cloth Jenny was trying to dry him with out of her hands, and began to dry himself off.

"Do ye really think that is necessary?" Connor tugged on his clothes, realizing that, if he lingered here too much longer, he could lose all chance of having a bath.

Knobby moved closer, Diarmot quickly moving to join them. "Laird, Meg will cause ye trouble. She already has in small ways. She has bedded down with your uncle, ye, and your brothers. O'er the last few years she has grown arrogant. 'Tis clear she has been treating your wife, the lady of this keep, with utter disrespect."

"That does prove that she thinks herself far more important than she is, but how does that make her a possible danger?"

"I dinnae ken." Knobby grimaced and rubbed one long, slender hand over his chin. "All I do ken is that she has taken to acting as if she is the lady of this keep, ruling it o'er the other women who dinnae complain because she was either sharing your bed or that of one of your kinsmen. When ye wed and decided to try and hold to your vows, ye took away some of Meg's power. Today ye took away near all of it. Once the women hear what ye said today, they willnae bow to Meg's commands or demands, nor silently do her work. They will treat her as what she truly is—nay more than a baseborn lass who cannae keep her legs closed. Meg will be enraged about that."

"Ye have ne'er bedded down with her, have ye?" Diarmot said, looking at Knobby in some surprise.

"Nay. My mother and my sister often spoke of the wench. I kenned how ill she treated the other women." Knobby shrugged. "Just felt it would be like a slap in the face to my kinswomen. Aye, I weaken now and again, and have a wee rut with Jenny, but I wish I wouldnae. She and Peg follow Meg. And, weel, to tell the truth, I can ne'er fully forget that I am sticking my precious pintle into a well-used vessel."

Diarmot grimaced. "I believe *I* shall try hard to forget that. Curse ye for putting that image into my head."

"I will watch her," Connor said. "If she causes trouble, I will send her away. She can do her whoring in the village or e'en in a wee hut in the wood. Now, since I have given up my bath here, I best hie myself to my bedchamber or I shall lose the chance to have one there."

Diarmot crossed his arms on his chest and watched his brother walk away. "What do ye think, Knobby?"

Knobby frowned. "About Meg?"

"Nay, though ye are right in your warning. Meg does indeed bear watching and I intend to do so. Nay too sure of what real trouble she could cause, but Meg is a mean spirited whore who thinks too much of herself. Nay, I speak of my brother's wee wife."

"I think she is a good lass. Wee Fiona likes her."

"Och, aye, and she will be good for my sister. I am thinking she might be verra good for Connor, too."

"Could be, if he will let her. He is a fine laird and a good friend, but . . ." Knobby hesitated.

"But he has carried the weight of rebuilding and keeping us all safe for so long it has fair to crushed all the life out of him." Diarmot smiled faintly when Knobby nodded. "When the lass is around, I can see a flicker of life in him, e'en a gleam of laughter now and then. She is spirited, opinionated, and far too clever. She challenges him at every turn. My uncle doesnae like her."

"Nay, he wouldnae. Connor listens to her. Sir Neil is nay longer the only one he heeds."

"And that too is a good thing. I have ne'er felt the confidence and trust in that mon that Connor has. It always seemed to me that he could have helped us far more than he did. He did little more than come round now and then to fill our heads with his opinions. I dinnae think he has e'er done any actual work here.

No matter. It would be good if Gillyanne could make Connor see our uncle more clearly, but 'tis more important for him to learn how to truly live again. I think that lass is the one who could do it.''

"As I said—if he lets her. There is e'er the chance that, if she starts to reach those parts of him he has buried because he felt he had to to survive, he could just turn away from her."

"Then, my friend, ye and I shall have to watch out for that so that we can move quickly and block his retreat."

Chapter Ten

Gillyanne draped her arms over the side of the tub and stared at her knees which barely broke the surface of the water in the deep round tub. She had to accept the truth. If she was not already in love with Connor, she was only a heartbeat or two away from it. A woman did not feel as she had upon seeing Meg touching Connor so intimately unless her heart was involved. There had been anger, at both Connor and Meg, but there had also been hurt. The possibility that Connor was still bedding Meg had twisted her heart. That had only eased when she had realized that, despite Meg's bold efforts, Connor was holding to his vows, but the image was still seared upon her mind and knotting her insides.

A part of her was pleased that she was finally experiencing such things as passion and love, but another part was dismayed. She was tumbling into love with a man who gave her very little of himself. Even worse was the fact that she could think of no way to pull more than passion from the man. Connor was not like other men, even men who had been hardened by life's disappointments. His feelings were so deeply buried, Gillyanne feared they were beyond saving.

He was not dead to all feeling, but he revealed only hints of emotion. A gleam of amusement, a hint of a smile, a flicker of anger. It was as if his need to be strong, to protect his family and clan, had crushed all other emotion, had soundly beaten those other feelings into submission and still held them there. Gillyanne knew she could not survive with just glimpses, hints, and flickers of emotion. She did not expect Connor to become some sweet-tongued, soft-hearted fool for her, but she needed more than passion. Her heart was involved now and she needed to hold some small part of his.

She suddenly snorted in disgust with herself. She did not want a small part of Connor's heart, she wanted it all. It seemed only fair since she was giving him everything. She wanted what her cousin Elspeth had with her husband Cormac, and what her cousin Avery had found with Cameron, or, at least, something approaching that. At the moment, however, she would settle for any tiny sign that she was reaching him, was making a crack in that armor which encased his emotions. Just a small crack, one she could wriggle into and keep wriggling into, until, one day, Connor woke up and realized she was there, deep in his heart, and that he wanted her to stay there. That would take time, though, so she had to think hard on what to tell her father when he arrived.

The sound of the door to the bedchamber opening abruptly yanked Gillyanne from her thoughts. She cursed softly in surprise, crossed her arms over her breasts, and bent her legs up toward her body to shield her nakedness. It eased her embarrassment only a little when Connor strode into the room. The look he gave her as he shut the door made her far too aware of her nudity.

"Ah, good, I havenae missed the chance for a bath," he said as he began to undress.

"Ye havenae had one yet?" Gillyanne was astonished at how swiftly Connor removed his clothes.

"Nay." He tossed aside the last of his clothes and stepped over to the tub, almost smiling for Gillyanne looked adorable all curled up in an attempt to maintain some modesty. "I decided I needed to come and lecture my wife."

"Lecture me?"

"Aye. A wife shouldnae threaten her husband." He stepped into the tub.

Gillyanne wondered how such a large tub could suddenly seem crowded as he sat down. "I didnae threaten ye."

"Nay? It sounded like a threat to me."

"It was naught but a confession of simple fact." She was so surprised when Connor chuckled that she limply allowed him to tug one arm away from her breasts and press a washing cloth into her hand.

"Weel, except for that one wee place," he pointed to the spot just below his navel, "I remain untouched."

Even though a soft voice in her head told her it was a mistake, Gillyanne looked at the spot he pointed at. It was not that patch of skin her gaze became fixed upon, however, but the long, hard proof that Connor was interested in far more than a bath. She thought it odd that an appendage she had always found mildly amusing should now cause her blood to heat and her pulse to race. And make her feel so compelled to touch him, she mused, even as she reached out.

Connor murmured his pleasure as her long fingers curled around him. Her touch set his blood afire and her increasing boldness pleased him. For a moment he closed his eyes and savored her still hesitant touch. It was not long before he realized that, unless he put a stop to such play, there would be little bathing done, and he reluctantly pulled her hand away.

He was unable to suppress a grin as he gently tugged on her hand which still held the washing rag and she turned a faintly glazed look upon him. "Bath first, then play. The playing was making me forget the need for a bath." Connor decided the unusually high spirits he was feeling were understandable, for what man would not be cheered by such a warm look in his wife's eyes.

Gillyanne shook free of at least some of desire's haze and began to bathe her husband. It was not just the sight of his fine body that disordered her thoughts, but the way he was acting. He had chuckled and grinned. She quickly told herself not to let her hopes rise too high, not to see this unusual good humor as some sign that she was already reaching him. It could be no more than a natural, manly response to being bathed by a naked woman in the comfort of his bedchamber and knowing that, once the bath was done, he could heartily indulge himself with that woman. And, she mused a little crossly, his vanity was probably stoked by her inability to hide how much pleasure she took in his form.

"Husband," she gasped in shock when he cradled her breasts in his hands, teasing the already hardened tips with his thumbs. "Ye said ye needed to bathe."

"I am washing you." He was still occasionally amazed that he could be so stirred by what many men would consider a sad lack of bosom.

"I have already bathed."

"Aye? Then why are ye still in the tub?"

"I was having myself a wee sulk." He gave her a look that indicated he thought her a strange little creature and she sighed. " 'Tis something my mother does. Every now and then she goes to her room to have what she calls a good sulk."

"Your mother does that often?"

"Nay, and she says she doesnae do it near as often

as she used to before my father found her and loved her." Deciding it would be easier to wash his back and hair from outside the tub, she slipped free of his grasp, stepped out, and quickly wrapped a large drying cloth around herself.

"Ye missed a few places," he said and reached for her.

She eluded his grasp, stepped behind him, and immediately began to wash his hair. "Now, to finish my tale. Mither says that, e'en when one has a good life, sometimes there can be a sadness or a day when naught goes as it should. Days when ye have to swallow words ye really want to say, when ye have an argument, and other such small troubles. When she can make the time, she steals away to her bedchamber and broods o'er all these wrongs, sometimes cries, sometimes curses, but, most of all, has a good sulk. Eventually, Fither wanders up and coaxes her out of it." Gillyanne laughed softly. "Sometimes that can take a while for she says his coaxing ways are the verra best part of her sulking."

"It still sounds an odd thing to do. Do ye do this often?"

"Nay often. I may look like Mither, but I have Fither's temper. Unfortunately, I dinnae have his control. If something goes wrong for me, I just want to curse it or hit it. Howbeit, ladies cannae always do that. Sometimes they must bite their tongues, act sweet or be calm when all others are angry and upset. 'Tis then that the art of proper sulking can be useful. It does help some to ken that ye can slip away and wallow in it all; it gives ye the strength to get through the time of trouble." Realizing she was done washing his hair and was now just playing with it, a far too revealing action, Gillyanne rinsed his hair and began to wash his back.

"Mither says it can work as weel when 'tis more a grieving than a sulk," Gillyanne continued, hoping that, if she talked of herself and her family, Connor may soon do a little of the same. "It helped when my sister Sorcha was raped, repeatedly, and beaten nearly to death. Mither had to be strong and calm to help poor Sorcha and she said kenning that she could slip away to her chambers for a wee while now and again to scream, weep, or tear at her hair, was a great help."

"What happened to the ones who hurt your sister?" Connor wondered if the answer to that question would tell him something important about Gillyanne's father, a man he would soon meet.

" 'Twas an old enemy of Fither's and two of his comrades. They had captured Sorcha and my cousin Elspeth, Sir Balfour Murray's daughter. Fither and my uncles, Balfour and Nigel, hunted them down, reaching them ere they could do to Elspeth what they had done to Sorcha. They sent the girls home first with most of the men and, when Fither came home much later, he told Mither the men were dead and she said, 'Thank ye, Husband.' I ne'er asked how they were killed, yet there was such a chilling look upon Fither's face, I did fret o'er the matter now and again. Especially since, whene'er the incident was mentioned, that look would briefly return."

Connor waited a moment for her to continue. Since she had finished scrubbing his back, he got out of the tub, and started to dry himself off. He suddenly needed to know exactly what punishment her father meted out to those men. He no longer wondered if the truth would be important; he was certain.

"And ye found out what was done, didnae ye?" he finally asked.

Gillyanne nodded and replied in a slightly hushed voice. "My cousin Payton finally told me years ago. They castrated the men, then gave them each a belly wound. Then they took them to a place where the wolves still roamed and left them there, staying only long enough to see a pack of the beasts arrive, drawn by the scent of blood, and begin the execution.''

"And ye thought it too harsh?" Connor thought it a beautifully creative justice.

"I did for a wee bit. 'Twas hard to believe three men who didnae e'en like to give their bairns a light swat upon their bums could be so brutal. Payton brought me to my senses with three hard facts. These men had hurt Fither's bairn, and had intended to hurt his niece. Both girls look just like their mothers and Fither and my uncles had to be deeply moved by that image, too. If left to live, that mon would have remained a threat to us all. Payton said the look I occasionally saw on Fither's face was when he recalled the viciousness of his act and it faded when Fither next recalled why he had been driven to behave so.''

"Your cousin is right. I think I may have been e'en more vicious had such a crime been done to my sister. Another hard truth is that your father was probably drowning in rage at himself and guilt for he had failed to protect his bairn.''

A man who would soon be kicking at *his* gates, Connor mused. He had not raped or beaten Gillyanne, had e'en married her. It was easy to see why the man might be enraged, however. This might not be a simple matter of a few hot words, some negotiations, and, mayhap, a bride price. Then he saw the way Gillyanne stared at his body as he idly rubbed the drying cloth over himself. Not only did the heated appreciation in her eyes stir his blood, but it told him she would help soothe her father's rage. And, he reminded himself, Gillyanne had already proven that she wanted no blood spilled over this.

"Shouldnae a wife dry her husband after she has gotten him all wet from bathing him?" Connor asked, offering her the drying cloth.

Gillyanne almost grunted as she took the cloth and

began to dry him off, then feared she might have spent too much time around the MacEnroys already. She quickly lost all interest in anything other than slowly rubbing that cloth over Connor's big, strong body. The man did not appear to have any modesty, but, at times like this, Gillyanne was rather glad of that flaw.

In the short time they had been lovers, she had slowly grown bolder, refusing to allow the fear that she might do something he did not like to hold her back. Thus, she had already discovered a few places where Connor loved to be touched. Other than the obvious, she thought, forcing herself to ignore the bold appendage that seemed to demand her attention. As she caressingly dried him off, she glanced up at his face. His eyes were closed and there was the hint of a smile upon his handsome face. When it came to lovemaking and passion, Connor was unusually open and free.

It was as Gillyanne rubbed dry his long legs that she recalled something her cousin Elspeth had once told her. When asked, her cousin Avery had blushingly agreed with Elspeth's startling revelation. At the time she had thought it a rather odd thing to do, but, now, with Connor's manhood within kissing reach, it did not seem so strange at all. Deciding faint heart ne'er won bold laird, she dropped the drying cloth, placed her hands on his lean hips, and kissed the stout proof of his desire for her. Connor's whole body jerked and then he trembled. Gillyanne decided to read that as a sign of interest and licked him.

Connor was stunned when he felt Gillyanne's soft lips touch his staff. He stared down at her as she ran her hot, wet tongue slowly up the full length of him. Shuddering from the ferocity of the pleasure which ripped through his body, he threaded the fingers of one visibly shaking hand through her thick, damp hair and tipped her head back. A touch of wariness began to dim the soft look of desire on her face and he was briefly sorry for that.

"What are ye doing?" The moment he spoke, Connor decided it was a stupid thing to say.

"I would have thought it was rather obvious," Gillyanne drawled, intrigued by the way the flush of passion upon his high cheekbones somewhat contradicted the stern line of his mouth and the glint of uncertainty in his eyes.

"This is what wives do for husbands? 'Tis nay just some whore's trick?" The few times he had heard of such a delight, a well-paid whore had been the one giving it.

"My cousin Elspeth told me her husband liked it and, curious creature that I am, I asked my cousin Avery if 'twas the same with her mon. She said aye. Neither of them are whores and their husbands would be eager to end the life of anyone who called them one. But, if ye wish me to cease . . ." she began.

"Ah, weel, nay. If 'tis a thing a wife can do for a husband, ye may proceed."

She gave him a faintly amused look as he loosened his grip on her hair. Connor shuddered when she licked him again. This could prove to be more delight than he could endure, he mused, as the touch of her soft lips and the heated caress of her tongue soon had him clenching his fists at his side. When she took him into the warmth of her mouth, he fought to maintain the steely control he had so perfected over the years, but it was no use. Thread by taut thread it snapped until he groaned, fell to his knees, and pushed Gillyanne onto her back. With visibly shaking hands, he yanked away the drying cloth she had wrapped around herself and fell upon her.

Gillyanne gasped then laughed softly when she was suddenly tossed onto her back. It had been deeply arousing to love Connor that way, to feel that big, strong body tremble beneath her hands. He set upon her with such feverish intensity, she suspected she ought to be

afraid, but she met and equaled his ferocity. When he
roughly thrust into her ready body, she knew he had lost
all control. Gillyanne also knew that she would probably
find a bruise or two on her far too delicate skin later,
but she did not care. Wrapping herself tightly around
him, Gillyanne's last clear thought was that any man
who could get so wildly passionate had to have other
strong emotions tucked inside him, and she intended
to ferret out each and every one.

Connor remained sprawled on top of Gillyanne, half
on his sheepskin rug, half on her. His face was pressed
against the side of her neck as he fought to regain his
senses. He had lost all control. That in and of itself was
alarming, even more so was the fact that he had inflicted
that wildness upon his tiny, delicate wife. Beneath the
hand he placed over her breast he could feel her heartbeat, feel the steady rise and fall of her chest as she
breathed. He had not killed her. Chancing a peek at
her cheek, he saw no sign of tears, so he had probably
not hurt her. She was not trying to flee his grasp so he
had to assume he had not terrified her when he had
fallen on her like some maddened, ravenous beast. Gillyanne, however, was splayed out beneath him like some
broken doll and was not moving.

"Gillyanne?" he called softly.

"Mmmm?" Gillyanne roused herself just enough to
lazily run her fingers up and down Connor's spine.

He had not knocked her unconcious, either, he
thought with an inner sigh of relief. Now the trick would
be in getting away from Gillyanne without his utter loss
of control being mentioned. Forcing his heavily sated
body to move, he gave her a light slap upon the hip
and leaped to his feet. He nearly smiled at the cross
look she gave him before she scrambled to grab the
drying cloth he had tossed aside and wrap herself in it.

"Best we hurry on down to the great hall or those fools will have eaten all the food," he said as he started to pull on some clean clothes.

By the time Gillyanne got to her feet, Connor was dressed. He yanked her into his arms for a brief kiss, then left as he ordered her again to hurry. Gillyanne sighed and, after a quick wash, began to dress. She was going to have to teach that man that a little tenderness, a kiss and an embrace, after such passionate lovemaking could be most enjoyable.

She was surprised to find Connor, Diarmot, and Knobby all standing at the bottom of the stairs when she finally started on her way to the great hall. "Is something wrong?" she asked, even as she noticed the three brothers she had yet to sort out lurking behind Diarmot.

"Your cousin is here," replied Connor.

"Oh, good," cried Gillyanne as she ran down the last few steps and headed toward the massive doors leading to the bailey. "He will have brought me my things and have some news from home."

Connor grabbed her by the hand and pulled her to his side. "He has two other men, weel armed men, with him."

"Of course he does. Only a complete fool would travel these lands without some protection."

Sound reasoning in a woman could be irritating, Connor decided. "He can leave your things at the gates and ride away."

Gillyanne wondered how one moment she could be so desperate for this man's touch and, in the next, want to clout him on the ear. "He accepted this marriage and has come as a friend. He probably wishes to stay a few days to assure himself that I am being treated weel."

"Ye are being treated weel. He can accept my word on that."

"Why? He doesnae ken who ye are, had ne'er e'en

heard of ye until ye came kicking at the gates of my keep."

Connor almost idly wondered if his little wife would ever accept something he said simply because he, her husband and laird, had said it. "Nanty, ye and Angus, and Drew go bring our uninvited guests in, and, if they wish to clean up ere they eat, show them where." He looked at Gillyanne. "The two men with Sir James can fill their bellies and stay the night, but they leave come the dawn. Your cousin can abide here for a wee while if he feels he must." He started pulling her toward the great hall. "We will await your cousin in here."

"But, James will have my clothes and I should like to change this gown," she protested as she hurried to keep pace with him.

"Ye can abide it for one more night."

It was not long before a smiling James strode into the great hall. Seeing the basket he carried in his hands, Gillyanne cried out with joy. He was only a step away from her when her cats leaped out of the basket onto her lap.

"Cats?" Connor nodded a greeting to James as the man sat down next to Diarmot, across from Gillyanne.

"Aye," Gillyanne said, giggling at the way her pets licked her chin. "Ragged and Dirty." She pointed to each as she named it. "If ye have any vermin here, these two will soon hunt them down."

Connor grunted softly, staring at the cats as he began to eat. "The dogs will eat them."

Gillyanne gasped then frowned. "Ye dinnae have any dogs."

"I can get some."

Although she felt sure he was jesting, she hugged her cats. The brief glint of amusement she saw in his eyes and the way Diarmot grinned eased the last of her anxiety. Her husband had an odd sense of humor, Gillyanne mused, as she turned to introduce her cats to Fiona who sat down beside her. It was going to be a challenge to figure it out.

Shaking his head over the way Fiona joined Gillyanne in fawning over the cats, Connor looked at James. He could not think of one thing he distrusted or disliked about the man, yet he was reluctant to have him at Deilcladach. Sir James Drummond was a handsome devil and very close to Gillyanne. That did trouble Connor and he frowned. That had the taste of jealousy and that, too, troubled Connor. Such emotion could be a weakness, could even be used against him.

"So kind of ye to invite me to stay," James drawled.

"Ye can see that she is hale and unbruised," Connor said, "so ye need not make it a verra long visit."

James laughed. "Oh, aye, I think I will bide here for a while. Until all is settled the lass should have some kin at hand."

" 'Tis all settled now. She is my wife. The marriage has been consummated—thoroughly."

"But ye dinnae have her father's blessing."

"Gillyanne is nearly one and twenty. She doesnae need his approval." He frowned when James just shrugged. "He will come here."

"Och, aye, as quickly as he can."

"With an army?"

"Not at first. I have been to Dubhlinn and assured Mither that Gillyanne is safe. Fither will wish to talk first."

Connor nodded, hiding his relief. "As his daughter did, the mon willnae wish blood spilled o'er this."

"Dinnae think 'tis ye or your people he will fret o'er. He kens that, in any battle, nay matter how quickly won, some of his people will be hurt or killed so he picks his battles verra carefully. Fither is a good mon, gentle e'en, usually even of temper, favoring wit o'er strength, and he has a verra keen wit. His temper is rarely seen, but, when it is stirred, 'tis glorious and hot. And naught can rouse it faster and hotter than harm done to his family."

"I willnae hurt Gillyanne."

"Nay, not physically," James murmured, studying Connor closely as he sipped his wine. "Ye are a hard mon, Sir Connor MacEnroy, hard to the bone, I am thinking."

"I have had to be," Connor said and wondered why he felt any need to defend what he was, what he had made himself be for his clan's sake.

"Gillyanne is a soft woman, free of spirit, open of heart, full of life. A passionate, loving, giving soul. A hard mon like ye could hurt her in many ways without lifting a hand and, sadly, ne'er ken ye have done so. So, aye, I will bide awhile to see that all goes weel. Ye see, Sir Connor, ye may have buried all the softness within yourself, but I willnae let ye smother it all in my wee cousin."

Connor understood James' words. He was just not sure he understood what the man meant. Now was not the time to sort it out, however, so he forced his thoughts away from Gillyanne, away from the strangely unsettling thought that he could hurt her.

"Ye are her cousin, so why do ye call her parents mother and father?" Connor asked, seeking some understanding of the obviously close bond between James and Gillyanne.

"Ah, weel, her mother is my aunt. I am the child of Lady Bethia's twin sister. When my parents were murdered, Lady Bethia saved me from a like fate. 'Tis during that time she met Sir Eric. I was a barely weaned bairn. Sir Eric gained guardianship of me from the king and he and my aunt took me in, raising me as one of their own. As soon as I was of an age to understand, they told me the whole truth, but they were and are my parents and their children my siblings. The truth of who I was didnae change that. We use the word cousin if only to explain why I am a Drummond and the others are Murrays, but they are my true and only family, my parents, my brothers and sisters. If I wasnae a laird with a clan awaiting me to take my place, I would be a Murray. In truth, neither Gillyanne nor I, nor any of our siblings are Murrays by blood for Sir Eric was a foster son who, for a while, thought himself a Murray bastard. After he discovered exactly who he was, he chose to remain a Murray."

For a brief moment, Connor felt the sting of envy. It was clear these Murrays were willing to help ones in danger or in need. There had been no one like that at hand when he and his siblings had found themselves alone, homeless, and facing starvation. In truth, he suddenly thought as he glanced down the table at his scowling uncle who was refilling his tankard, even the only adult kinsman left alive had done little more than wander by now and then to pontificate. It was a traitorous thought, but, now that it had slipped into his mind, Connor could not shake it away.

Following the direction of Connor's gaze, James murmured, "Ye should watch that mon. He doesnae like my cousin."

"That mon is my uncle," Connor said, but with no hint of anger and then he sighed. "Ye are right. He doesnae." He looked at Gillyanne, watching her briefly look at Neil, her expression one of wary annoyance. "Gillyanne isnae too fond of him, either."

"One thing ye should ken about your wee wife—if she reveals an unease about someone, heed it."

" 'Tis just annoyance with some of the things my uncle says."

"Then she would give him the sharp side of her tongue, nay more. Believe this or nay, but Gillyanne *feels* things about people we cannae. 'Tis as if she can read their hearts." James grimaced and raked his hand through his hair. " 'Tis hard to explain, but, 'tis as if

Gillyanne can see and feel what others feel. And now ye think us both mad.''

"Nay. I have heard of such a skill." Connor suddenly felt almost naked. "She can do this with everyone?"

"Nay. She can rarely guess what I feel and she said trying to read you is like hurling herself against a wall. All I say is, heed Gillyanne if she has difficulty with someone. She apparently has a problem with your uncle. Find out what and why ere ye shrug it aside."

Connor nodded, but wondered if he really would heed James in this particular matter. Suddenly he was having traitorous thoughts about Neil. He did not really want his new wife's opinions to add to that change in his feelings about the man. Later, he told himself. He would sort out his own troubled thoughts first, and then see to hers.

Chapter Eleven

It was one of the hardest things Gillyanne felt she had ever done, but she walked away from Sir Neil Mac-Enroy. She did not strike him as she ached to. She did not respond to his verbal poison, to his taunts and insults, though the words burned on her tongue. In truth, she needed to put some distance between herself and Connor's uncle, and not just because she feared upsetting Connor by getting into a screaming brawl with one of the few of his elder kinsmen who had survived the long, bloody feud.

Nay, she mused as she grabbed a basket and made her way out of the keep. It was a pure relief to get away from Sir Neil despite how heavily the unsaid words sat in her belly. The man stank of bitterness and anger. And fear, fear that the dark, writhing secrets he held within him would slither out. Every time she had to be near him, the turmoil of his spirit reached out to try and pull her into its quagmire. It made her feel ill and agitated. It also made her increasingly tempted to demand that he give up those secrets.

That, she knew, would be a mistake. Gillyanne was almost certain that Neil did not want to be saved by a confession. Neil MacEnroy's secrets were the sort which could tear the heart and soul out of a person. They would devastate his family, who had already suffered enough in their young lives. Gillyanne could only pray that she was wrong in feeling he was not innocent of that slaughter, that somehow he had had a hand in the feuding, at least in those last few blood-soaked years of it. Connor and his brothers may have been heeding and admiring a man who had helped destroy all they had known and was, quite possibly, not all that pleased that so many had survived. It was all too chilling, too desperately sad, to think about.

"Sorry I am late," said Fiona as she ran up beside Gillyanne.

Gillyanne smiled at the girl. "Are ye sure ye were nay just dragging your wee feet?"

"Nay, not this time." Fiona grinned when Gillyanne laughed. "This is one lesson about being a lady of the keep that I think I might like. Kenning about herbs and healing sounds interesting and verra useful. Weel met, Knobby," she said as that man strode up behind them. "Are ye late, too?"

"I dinnae think so," Knobby replied. "I think m'lady is a wee bit early."

"Aye, I fear I am." Gillyanne grimaced. "I fear I was fleeing the urge to bash Sir Neil o'er the head with a cudgel." She nodded a greeting to Joan's husband Malcolm who was guarding the gates they walked through.

"Uncle doesnae seem to like you, Gilly, and I dinnae understand why," Fiona muttered, looking both embarrassed and annoyed. " 'Tis as if he doesnae want Connor to be wed at all, which makes no sense. I ken he doesnae like the lasses. He barely e'en speaks to me and it has gotten worse since I began to leave my cap off." She shyly tugged at the thick golden braid which hung down her back. "Yet, 'tis the laird's duty to wed, if naught else, and ye brought some fine lands with ye when ye came."

That she had been married for those lands was not something Gillyanne really wanted to be reminded of, but she did not say so to Fiona. Neither could she tell the girl that her uncle had secrets and that Gillyanne began to think Neil was afraid she would uncover them. She was heartily glad to hear that Neil barely acknowledged Fiona. At least there was one MacEnroy whose head had not been filled with Neil's particular poison, his tainted words of wisdom.

"Mayhap the mon had grown fond of it being just him and the lads whene'er he stayed here," Gillyanne finally replied. "And, as ye say, he doesnae like the lasses so he probably sees marriage as a curse."

"Aye, there is that. And how is your plan working? Has displaying your wifely skills softened Connor at all?"

Gillyanne cast a nervous glance over her shoulder at a widely grinning Knobby. "It has only been a week, Fiona."

"Dinnae fret, m'lady," Knobby said. "Unless ye talk of murdering the laird in his sleep, I willnae be telling him anything." He rubbed a hand over his chin as he moved up to walk beside Gillyanne as they entered the wood. "The laird is a hard mon."

"Like rock."

"He has had to be, m'lady, and it has served us weel. There wernae many males e'en as old as he was. Too many of the older lads died with the men."

" 'Tis too sad to think on. How did ye survive?"

"I was fighting at my father's side, my two older brothers already dead, when the old laird saw that we couldnae win. The old laird ordered every lad beneath the age of eighteen years to flee. Och, we protested, but he ordered us again, telling us it was now our duty to help and protect the women and children, to make sure the MacEnroys didnae fade to dust on that black day. My father just looked at me and told me to go, to save my mother and sister. By then there were nay that many of us left, but almost all did as they were ordered to.''

She could sense the same guilt in Knobby that she had guessed Connor felt. ''Ye only need to look around to ken that it was the right decision, the best thing to do. The MacEnroys would have been naught but a memory if ye hadnae. And, the women and bairns did need ye.''

''Most times I ken that truth. Now and then I wish I could have stayed at my father's side and avenged the deaths of my brothers.''

''Ye wouldnae have avenged them. Ye would have just died. And think on your father. He had seen two of his bairns die and kenned that, if ye stayed, he might have to watch ye die, too.''

''I was sixteen, m'lady. More mon than bairn.''

''Ah, Knobby, I suspect, at that moment, ye were more bairn than mon to your father. My father treats my brothers as the men they are, or nearly are. Yet, if they were caught in a battle that couldnae be won, he would probably make them run. As your father probably did, he would look at them and suddenly think that it was but yesterday he watched them take their first steps, but yesterday when their voices first grew deeper. He would think of all they hadnae done yet. Your poor father had already seen two of his children die and the thought that ye would soon join them was probably a torment. Ye gave him peace when ye left. Ye gave him hope that the MacEnroys would not become little more than a verse in some troubadour's song. Ye gave him hope that his wife and daughter would have someone to help them survive. And, mayhap, he thought of your mother, too, of how it would tear at her mother's heart to have to bury all of her sons, so he gave ye back to her. Nay, your duty that day was to survive, to help your mother and sister, to help rebuild them a home and a clan to belong to." He was looking at her so intently that she decided she was pontificating too much, blushed a little, and looked away. "Sometimes 'tis harder to survive."

After a long moment of silence, Knobby said, " Ye are right. I ne'er thought on it so hard or so deep. Now that I do, I ken that ye are right. 'Twas our duty and 'tis naught to be ashamed of. 'Tis hard to recall it sometimes since so many of those first years were spent hiding and just trying to stay alive. And, I did give my father peace when I left. I could see it there upon his face although I chose to recall only the grief."

"Too much grief," she whispered, able to imagine it, and wishing she was not. "No grown men survived?"

"No MacEnroys who fought at the keep. Some villagers and crofters who had fled and stayed hidden. Lads, bairns, women, and a few of the aged or lame who couldnae fight. Ye must have noticed how few of the older women have a mon."

"Aye, a lot of widows."

"Some returned to their families. Those born and bred here had nowhere else to go."

"And they all looked to Connor," she said, stopping to look around and seeing several plants she could use.

"And he but fifteen. That is why he is so, weel, hard. But, the past shouldnae rule him now. We have rebuilt. The boys are truly men now and the feud is o'er. Despite those troubles, he did used to be a proper laddie, high spirited and ready to laugh. That lad can ne'er be reborn, but there are those of us who think the laird would be the better for it if he loosened a few of the chains he has wrapped his soul in."

"Aye, he would be. One just has to hope those chains havenae choked that free-spirited lad to death." She shook her head. "Enough of this dark talk. Fiona, time to learn about herbs and healing."

"We could use someone with a healing skill," Knobby said as he leaned against a tree. "Ye have some, m'lady?"

"Some," Gillyanne replied. "My aunt Maldie and her daughter Elspeth are weel kenned for their healing skills. All the Murray women train under them. Some of us are better than others."

"Mayhap ye ought to brew up a love potion for Connor," said Fiona.

"There is no such thing."

"Wheesht, of course there is. 'Tis one of the things the lasses go to the wise women to get."

"And throw away coin better spent elsewhere. The few receipts for love potions that I have e'er seen are more apt to kill the poor mon. And, if there was such a beast, how often would ye have to give it to the poor mon? Once a day, once a week, once a month? I think e'en the dullest wit would soon question why his lady was making him drink so many potions. Ye would also have to be careful when and where ye fed it to him."

"Ah, because he might espy another lass and fall in love with her. 'Twould have to be a private place then. Like here."

"It might serve, but it could still all go terribly wrong. He could drink the potion, but, when finished, not look right at ye first. Nay, he might glance to the left or the right, and, the next thing ye ken, he is proposing marriage to a newt."

The moment they all stopped laughing, Gillyanne began to teach Fiona about herbs, plants, and healing. It had been interesting to have such a serious talk with Knobby. Each day she gained more knowledge about the MacEnroys, about the tragedy that had formed them, and about Connor. Sadly, very little of that knowledge came from Connor. All her display of wifely skills seemed to be getting her was more lovemaking. She was not surprised that the baths led to lovemaking for, after all, he or both of them were naked. It had surprised

her a little when she had taken him some food and
drink two days ago while he was out in the fields and he
had tumbled her behind a hedgerow. Connor seemed to
think that her various attempts to accustom him to the
comforts of a wife were an invitation to lovemaking.

Not that that was such a bad thing, she mused,
savoring a tingle of heated memory. Passion could help
her push her way into his heart. They still shared little
more than that, however, even after a fortnight of marriage. She could swear he had scared himself with that
brief moment of good humor and their wild lovemaking
after the first bath, for he had become as remote as she
had ever seen him for two full days. Fortunately, that
had eased but, if he was to take three steps back for
each one taken forward, she would never reach him. It
was heartbreaking and Gillyanne wished she could talk
to some of the women in her family. That was impossible
at the moment, however, which left her completely on
her own and she had no confidence in her ability to
woo and win a man, especially one like Connor.

Fiona drew her attention and Gillyanne was glad of
it. She had far too much time to fret over her marriage
as it was. Once she was certain Fiona recognized the
type of moss she wanted, Gillyanne allowed the girl to
skip off to look for more. Fiona was honest in her wish
to learn the ways of a lady, but Gillyanne knew she had
to lead the girl along one slow step at a time. The girl
had enjoyed the freedom of behaving like a young boy
for far too long to suddenly have her days filled with
learning the often tedious ways of being the lady of the
keep.

Espying a particularly rare plant that had many uses,
Gillyanne moved to collect it only to find her skirts held
firm by the brambles she had tried to cross through. As
she softly cursed, a chuckling Knobby moved to help
her. Just as he released the last piece of her skirts, Gillyanne saw something move behind him. She lifted her

head to see what it was and opened her mouth to cry
out a warning, but was too late. A heavily bearded man
brought the hilt of his sword down hard on Knobby's
head, and he sprawled unconscious at her feet with
barely a grunt.

"You!" she gasped as several other men appeared and
one, tall handsome man was immediately recognizable.

Sir Robert bowed slightly. "Aye. Me. Shall we go,
m'lady?"

For one brief moment, Gillyanne thought of screaming for help, then discarded that plan. It would only
bring Fiona into this trap. She next considered fighting,
trying to escape, and looked at the half dozen big men
with Sir Robert. It might be possible to elude capture
for a while, but too much resistance would probably
gain her nothing but bruises and the noise would also
bring Fiona running. Inwardly cursing the dowry that
had brought her all this annoying attention, she held
out her hand and let Sir Robert lead her away.

Fiona remained concealed in the leaves and shrubs
for many minutes after Sir Robert took Gillyanne away.
Returning with an armful of moss, Fiona had heard the
harness jingle of several horses and known Gillyanne
and Knobby were no longer alone. Instinct had sent
her hurrying to hide, and hard-learned skills had helped
her creep up unseen to watch Knobby fall to a blow,
and Gilly be kidnapped.

The question now was what to do next. She quelled
the urge to run after Gillyanne. One small woman-child
could not help her. Her next thought was to race to
Deilcladach and tell Connor what had happened. Then
she looked at Knobby. She could not leave the man
alone and hurt. He might rouse quickly with no more
than a badly aching head, but such wounds could be
unpredictable. Unconscious, poor Knobby had no way

to protect himself from any danger, man or beast. Sighing, Fiona cautiously left her hiding place and went to help Knobby.

After struggling to pull him free of the brambles and turn him on his back, she studied him for a moment. It was not going to be easy to get him back to Deilcladach, but she could not just sit and wait until he woke up. Fiona undid his cloak, then used her own to tie him to his. It made a poor litter, but it would have to do, she decided as she grabbed one end and started to drag him along. She had only gone a few feet when she started praying she would meet with someone soon. Knobby was the thinnest person she had ever known, but Fiona began to think that his bones must be made of solid lead.

She had just decided that she could not pull Knobby along one more inch when Colin the swineherd and his son appeared pulling a cart full of kindling. They emptied the cart and put Knobby into it. It was not a good fit, but it was better than her poor litter. Leaving them to bring Knobby along, Fiona raced for Deilcladach. As she ran, she prayed Connor was close at hand, prayed Gillyanne would be alright, and prayed, very hard, that this would not start the feuding again.

Connor poured the bucket of cold water over his head to rinse away the sweat raised by sword practice. He shook off the excess water, ignoring the protests of James and Diarmot as they were splashed with it. He was just about to hurl a few friendly insults about their fighting skills at them when he saw Fiona race into the bailey. She stopped and frantically looked around. Connor, with James and Diarmot at his heels, was already running toward her when she saw him.

"Gillyanne," she gasped as he reached her side, but she had to pause to catch her breath.

"Easy, lass," Connor said, putting a supporting arm around her thin shoulders and feeling her tremble. "Slow, deep breaths." He nodded his approval when Andrew arrived with a wet rag and gently bathed Fiona's face and hands. "Calm yourself and then we can talk."

As he gently rubbed Fiona's arm and waited for her to calm, Connor fought to calm himself as well. Fiona had gone with Gillyanne to learn about the collecting of healing plants. Knobby had chosen to go with them. It was obvious something had happened to both Gillyanne and Knobby. Danger had drawn near to his clan, touched it, and harmed two of his people. That could not be allowed.

Although he was worried about Knobby, he realized his feelings were a great deal fiercer concerning Gillyanne. Knobby had been with him through the dark years of rebirth and struggle. They had grieved together, gone cold and hungry together, pulled each other from the depths of hopelessness, and conquered it all—together. He was not surprised at the depth of his concern for the man's safety. With Gillyanne it was far more than concern, far more than worry, it was a bone-chilling fear.

That made no sense to him. He had only known the woman for a few weeks. In her slim arms, he had found the sweetest, hottest passion he had ever tasted, but that did not explain this chilling dread that he had lost her. She was his wife, someone he needed to beget legitimate heirs, and, in Gillyanne's case, to gain a fine piece of land. It was his duty to take care of her, protect her, and breed her. It was acceptable for him to feel concern for her safety, and, perhaps, suffer some guilt over his failure to protect her. It was *not* acceptable to be so utterly terrified that he might never see her again.

He would have to sort out that puzzle later, he decided when he saw that Fiona had calmed down enough to speak clearly. "Where is Knobby?" he asked, forcibly resisiting the urge to demand what had happened to Gillyanne.

"Colin the swineherd and his son are bringing him in their wee cart," Fiona replied. "He was knocked o'er the head. I tried to drag him home, but he is heavier than he looks."

· "Did ye see what happened?"

"Nay all of it. I had gone to collect moss and was returning when I heard horses. I hid and crept up to them as close as I could. It looked as if Knobby had been helping Gillyanne get free of some brambles and 'tis how they crept up on him and knocked him out. Mayhap that is for the best as he would have fought them and might have been hurt verra badly or e'en killed."

"Who was it, Fiona?"

"The Dalglish clan. Sir Robert himself was there."

That surprised Connor for, although he had expected some trouble from Sir David, he had not really considered Sir Robert a threat. "And she went with them?"

Fiona nodded. "She didnae want to. She stood there in the brambles glaring at the fool, looking verra fierce as she can do. I got the feeling she was thinking hard and she kept glancing in the direction I had gone. Then she cursed and let him take her. I think she feared anything she did would bring me running and she didnae want that."

"Why would he take her?" asked Diarmot, frowning in confusion. "She is wed to ye, Connor. Her lands are now yours. 'Twas all understood and agreed to ere we e'en rode to Ald-dabhach. Win the lass, win the lands, and no trouble o'er it. The marriage has been consummated. It cannae be set aside, so what can the fool gain?"

"Actually, the marriage can be set aside," James said quietly, drawing all eyes to him. "She wasnae willing. She was coerced."

"She said 'aye'," Connor said, but a knot of unease began to tighten in his chest.

"Only after three attacks and the threat of a fourth."

Connor was suddenly all too aware of the fact that many women found Robert attractive, enjoyed his courtier's skills. "So, he means to seduce my wife into leaving me and marrying him."

"Mayhap he will seek to ransom her," said Diarmot. "Get at least a part of the land he lost when she chose you."

"Mayhap he will just bed the wench thinking ye wouldnae want her back," said Neil as he pushed himself into the circle around Fiona. "Then he will woo her and take all those lands. Ye cannae accept this insult, lad. This will start the feuding again and 'tis all that fool lass's fault."

"One more word old mon, and I will be closing that nasty mouth of yours with my fist," James snapped, before turning a hard glare upon Connor. "He willnae be able to seduce her. Is he a mon who would rape a lass?"

"I have ne'er heard that said of him," replied Connor. "A skilled seducer who is a wee bit too fond of other men's wives and virgins. I cannae promise he willnae force her to his bed, but he will certainly try to lure her there."

"Then there is time. No mon can seduce a Murray lass unless she chooses to be seduced."

"He has a fine skill and the lasses think him handsome."

"And Gillyanne considers herself a wedded woman."

"As if that e'er troubled a lass," muttered Neil, then he looked at Connor. "Are ye so hungry for that land ye will take back a shamed wife?"

Connor stopped James' advance on Neil by placing one hand on the younger man's chest and then he frowned at his uncle. "Ye have no reason to speak ill of Gillyanne yet ye have chosen to do so since the day she arrived. Guard your words, Uncle, for this is the last time I will stop this lad from seeking retribution." He inwardly sighed when Neil stared at him in shock and anger. "And unless there is more to this than Robert trying to steal a prize he lost fair and square, there will be no feuding."

"And if he *has* hurt her?" asked James.

"Then I will make it a feud of but two—him and me. Revenge and retribution exacted in a fair fight. If he has seduced her . . ."

"He cannae." James almost smiled at the fleeting look of doubt and uncertainty on Connor's face. "Ye dinnae ken our family or ye would understand and believe me. Gillyanne considers herself your wife, bound by vows given before God. She willnae break those. And, there isnae a sweet word or seductive gesture he can try that she willnae scoff at, willnae recognize for the false flattery it is. There are a lot of bonny lads in our family, ones weel versed in the wooing of women. Gillyanne kens every trick and lie a mon like that will try. There is also the simple fact that, if she had felt any interest in the mon, she would have chosen him, wouldnae she?"

Connor found that reminder deeply comforting, which worried him a little. It indicated that he could well feel more for Gillyanne than possessiveness or an understandable husbandly concern. It also hinted that he was losing the battle to keep her at some distance, to think of her only as *the wife*, the woman who would give him children and keep his home. Such a growing weakness explained why, despite his talk of negotiation and preventing any resumption of the feud, he ached to lay waste to Robert's lands and cut the man into many very small pieces.

"Let us cease talking and go get her," said Fiona.

"Ye will stay here," ordered Connor.

"But . . ."

"Nay. Ye and Drew will stay here." Connor ignored Drew's swift protest. "Ye ken weel that I ne'er take all of ye away at the same time."

All complaints stopped at this reminder of one of his firmest rules and Connor turned his attention to Knobby's arrival. He thanked Colin and his son for their help and looked at his friend. Knobby was awake, but very pale. Connor carefully helped him to sit up in the cart.

"I didnae see anything," Knobby began, his voice hoarse with pain.

"Fiona did. Sir Robert took Gillyanne," Connor told him.

"Do we go after her now?"

"Some of us. Ye will stay here. 'Twould be good to have ye at my side, but I think 'twill be a while ere ye can sit a horse."

"Aye. What can that fool be thinking of?"

"We cannae decide. It seems there is a way to end this marriage. Coercion can be claimed," he explained in response to Knobby's look of surprise. "If Robert can sway her, she may turn to him and get her father to end her marriage to me."

"She willnae." Knobby fixed Connor with a stern look. "She willnae end the marriage for the sake of that mon."

There was meaning beneath Knobby's words, the hint of a warning, but Connor had no time to ask his friend to be clearer. Joan and Mairi arrived to fret over Knobby. James, Diarmot, Nanty, and Angus all moved closer, tensely awaiting the command to ride. Connor moved to mount the horses that had been brought to them, silently bidding the others to do the same. Connor noticed that his uncle made no move to join them, simply stood beside Meg, each of them wearing the same look of fury.

"What is your plan then, laird?" asked Knobby, pausing by Connor's mount as Joan and Mairi helped him to the keep.

"Why, I go to pay a call upon Sir Robert Dalglish," Connor replied.

Knobby rolled his eyes. "Do ye mean to go knock upon his gates and say, *Please, sir, may I have my wife back?*"

Connor slowly grinned. "Aye, something like that," he replied even as he kicked his mount into a gallop.

Chapter Twelve

Robert was beginning to lose his charm, Gillyanne mused as she chewed on a honey cake and glanced around his great hall. It was a lot grander than Connor's with its fine tapestries, chairs, and candles. The man either had more wealth than Connor or he spent more of what he did gain on his own comforts than Connor did.

The increasing note of irritation in Robert's voice told Gillyanne that it might be time to stop ignoring him. Despite all his efforts to flatter and woo her, she had not spoken one word to the man since her capture. She could almost smell the anger in him. Men truly did hate it when a woman ignored them, she mused, and gave Robert a cold look as he refilled her goblet with wine.

"Ye are a fool," she said and sipped her wine as he looked at her in surprise which rapidly changed to a hastily hidden fury.

"Och, aye? Would a fool ken that ye can end your marriage to Connor?" he asked.

Gillyanne was not pleased that he had obviously figured out that she did have some opportunity to get out of this tangle. An escape plan was no good if it was known and it was highly possible that he would tell Connor. On the other hand, she could not understand why it should matter to him or prompt him to kidnap her.

"Mayhap," she murmured. "Of what interest could that be to you?"

"Ye can change your mind, alter the choice ye have made."

"Oh? Ye think I would slip free of Connor and then bind myself to ye? Is that what all this insipid flattery and eyelash fluttering is for? To try to seduce me away from Connor?"

"Ye cannae tell me ye wish to stay wed to the mon," Robert snapped.

"If I seek to end a marriage forced upon me because three idiots seek my lands, why, in God's sweet name, would I then turn about and enter into yet another marriage with yet another one of those fools?"

"Connor may be a fine laird and warrior, but I doubt he makes a verra fine husband. The mon feels naught. He is hard and cold. His only interest is his clan, making it strong, and keeping it strong."

The man was jealous of Connor, Gillyanne realized, although not because of her and her dowry. She doubted it was a strong enough feeling to cause Robert to renew the old, bloody, and destructive feud, however. As she studied him she sensed another, uglier, emotion in the man. He was trying to woo her, but he did not want her. Nay, if she guessed right, Robert was nearly revolted by the thought of taking Connor's *leavings*. The feeling was so strong, it was as if he had spoken it aloud.

"Connor may be all ye say, but far better a cold, hard mon than one whose stomach fair turns at the thought of wedding and bedding a lass Connor has lain with," she said quietly, and the way he paled told her she had read him well.

"Twill be as if ye are a widow," he muttered and took a deep drink of wine.

"I would quickly become one if I married you."

"Nay, Connor works the hardest of us all to keep the old feud from returning."

"He is also a verra possessive mon. As ye have said, he lives for his clan. As his wife, I am now one of his clan and ye have caused me distress."

"I havenae hurt ye."

"Nay. Ye did hurt Knobby, though. That may annoy Connor a wee bit. And this will certainly annoy my clan and all their allies. Let me see, for this one act of blind greed, ye could find yourself facing Connor, the Murrays, the MacMillans, the Armstrongs of Aigballa, Sir Cameron MacAlpin and his clan, the Drummonds and the Kircaldys. Mayhap a few others if needed for I have a verra large family and many a good marriage was made."

"Curse it, woman, I offer marriage and nay dishonor or harm. 'Tis nay a cause for war."

Gillyanne shrugged. "If I wish to return to being laird of my own lands, unburdened by husbands I dinnae want, it could cause a wee bit of trouble. My family doesnae take it weel when one of their lasses is made to do something she doesnae wish to do. 'Tis tradition to allow us to choose our own mates, ye ken."

"No one lets a lass choose."

"My clan does."

"M'lady," Robert said, reaching out to take her hand in his, "ye dinnae love Connor nor would ye have chosen him under any other circumstances. The mon ignores ye most of the time and cavorts with the whores at his keep. His own uncle insults ye at every turning yet Connor does naught to defend ye. Ye work hard to make that rough keep more civilized and he ne'er notices or thanks ye. Is that truly what ye wish? Ye deserve far more. I can give ye more.''

It stung to hear her marriage described so, especially since so much of what Robert said was true. Pushing aside the hurt and sorrow those words roused, Gillyanne concentrated on the fact that Robert knew far too much about what went on behind the walls of Deilcladach. He obviously had a spy right inside Connor's home.

"Just how do ye ken so much?" she demanded.

Robert opened his mouth to speak, but was abruptly distracted when a loud rythmic thudding began to echo in the great hall. "What in God's holy name is that?"

Gillyanne smiled faintly. "Mayhap 'tis my husband come tirling at the pin. And a good strong knock upon the door it is, too."

"Nay, he couldnae get here so quickly. Your guard was unconscious. And, he didnae see any of us so could- nae tell anyone who took you."

"But Fiona wasnae knocked down and probably saw everything. Forgot about her, didnae ye?"

"My laird," cried a man as he stumbled into the great hall, " 'tis the MacEnroys!"

Robert cursed as he ran his fingers through his hair. "And ye are letting them beat down my gates?"

"But, we dinnae fight with the MacEnroys. Ye want us to start now?"

For one heart-chilling moment, Robert said nothing. Gillyanne feared he would choose battle. She and her lands would cause a renewal of a deadly feud. It was an appalling thought yet she did not know what to say or do to stop it. In the short time she had been at his keep, it had been easy to see that the Dalglish clan had probably not suffered as severely as the MacEnroys, so Robert might not be as driven to keep the peace as Connor was. All she could do was pray that Robert would choose peace despite his greed for her land.

"Nay, we willnae fight," Robert snapped, his frustration and anger clear to hear in his voice. "Let the fool in before he destroys my gates." He glared at Gillyanne when his man hurried away. "I dinnae suppose ye will change your mind."

"What about? Giving up one unwanted husband for another?" She frowned as if she actually considered the matter then shook her head. "Nay, I think not."

"I begin to think Connor deserves you."

"Thank ye."

"It wasnae a compliment."

"Nay? Pardon. My mistake. Ah, I believe I hear the gentle pitter-patter of my husband's boots."

Robert was staring at her as if she was the oddest creature he had ever met and one he would dearly like to strangle. Gillyanne idly wondered what it was about her that kept putting that look in a man's eyes. She had not even really displayed her particular skill, her one insight easily explained away as a lucky guess. Connor's abrupt and rather impressive entrance into the great hall distracted her from that puzzle.

"Greetings, husband," she said, giving him a faint smile then nodding at Diarmot, James, Angus, and Nanty who stood firm behind him.

"Wife," Connor said, studying her intently for a moment before turning his attention to Robert.

Connor was relieved to see that Gillyanne looked well except for a slight disarray obviously caused by the swift flight to Robert's keep. He did wonder, however, why he still felt strongly inclined to spit Sir Robert on the end of his sword. Possessiveness, he told himself. A simple, uncomplicated, manly sense of possession. Gillyanne was his and no man took what was his. He would probably feel much the same way if Robert had stolen his horse. Or nearly so. His mood somewhat improved, he found he could see Robert more clearly, the haze of fury thinning a little.

"Ye will nay fight to keep what ye have stolen?" he asked Robert.

"Will ye fight hard to get her back?" Robert asked instead of replying directly to Connor's cold words.

"She is *my* wife."

Gillyanne almost winced, then told herself she was a fool to be stung by his unemotional statement of possession. This was hardly the time Connor would choose to boldly avow his undying love for her. For a brief moment, she savored the image of him doing just that, then forced herself to banish the dream. Connor was not the sort of man to do such a thing even if he felt such a depth of emotion and it was also far too early in the game for him to do so.

"I *could* ransom her," Robert murmured.

"And I could challenge you, fight you, and leave ye bleeding in the dirt."

"Mayhap. That would start the feuding again."

"Nay, for 'twould be an honorable battle between two knights. A challenge made, a challenge accepted. What made ye do this? We were all agreed ere we set out for Ald-dabhach that we would accept her choice."

"Her mind can be changed and I believed she might be ready to do so."

"Why?"

Robert shrugged and hid his expression by taking a sip of wine. "Rumor."

"More than rumor," Gillyanne said. "The mon kens too much, Connor. He has eyes and ears inside Deilcladach."

"Come here, wife." Connor nodded when, after a brief, frowning hesitation, Gillyanne moved to his side. "Who is your spy, Robert?"

"I have placed no spy within Deilcladach," Robert replied.

"Then who has decided to become one?"

"Does it truly matter? She undoubtedly knew I would not use the information to harm ye or your people."

"Meg," Gillyanne muttered and heard Diarmot, James, Angus, and Nanty echo her.

Connor agreed with his companions, but said nothing, just continued to stare at Robert. "Ye dinnae think stealing my wife and trying to claim her lands would hurt me and my clan?"

"Pardon," Gillyanne snapped, glaring at her husband. "He only stole me. I dinnae see Ald-dabhach strapped to my back, do ye? He took *me*. Just *me*."

"I believe I am aware of that," Connor drawled, and tried to hide a sudden tickle of amusement as he looked at her belligerent little face. "Mayhap ye should go and wait by the horses. My companions can take ye. Then Robert and I can talk mon to mon without worrying that we might say something that will bruise your tender feelings."

Gillyanne had just taken a deep breath in preparation of searing her husband's ears with a few harsh words, when James and Diarmot each grabbed her by an arm. They hurried her out of the great hall, Nanty and Angus right behind them. She resented being shooed away like some troublesome child, but decided it might be best if she did not hear any more about her cursed lands. It would only annoy her more.

"Ye handled that weel," said Robert as soon as he and Connor were alone, sarcasm weighting his every word.

"How I deal with my wife is none of your concern," Connor said coldly. "Nothing that occurs within my keep is. Ye have allowed the rantings of a jealous bitch to lead ye close to disaster."

"So, ye *would* have fought for her, wouldnae ye?"

"She is my wife, a MacEnroy now," was all Connor would say.

"And ye need those lands."

"Aye. That is no secret. The bounty there will give my clan a bulwark against starvation. She will give me heirs, might e'en now be carrying my son." He noticed Robert grimace even though the expression was a fleeting one. "I dinnae think ye wish my cuckoo in your nest."

"I would have waited to marry her until I was sure she wasnae breeding."

Connor moved closer to Robert and, almost idly, pointed his sword at the man's throat. Robert's eyes widened and Connor knew the man was heartily cursing himself for not keeping even one of his men by his side. It would be disastrous to even wound the man yet Connor silently admitted he still felt a slight urge to do so.

"Did ye touch her?" Connor demanded.

"Nay," Robert replied, pressing himself back into his chair. "In truth, she had only just begun to speak with me. And then it was only to heap insult upon my wooing and threaten me with ye and all of her kin."

It was surprisingly hard to subdue a grin as Connor sheathed his sword. He felt both relieved and amused. It was easy to see Gillyanne responding to Robert's charm with the sharp edge of her tongue.

"Will I be having trouble from Sir David next?" Connor asked as he helped himself to some wine.

"Nay. I havenae told him what I have learned and see no reason to confide in him now. It may all be the truth, but it has proven useless. In truth, David doesnae really want her. She badly bruised his pride."

"Ye dinnae really want her, either, do ye?"

Robert grimaced and ran a hand through his hair. "I would prefer a more biddable wife."

"Weel, when ye decide 'tis time for ye to woo one, I suggest ye avoid any lass named Murray. If but half of what the lass tells me is true, ye willnae find one of those amongst that clan. And, I suggest ye be more particular

about whose words ye heed. A lover cast aside will play
his or her own game with little thought to the consequences for you."

"So, ye tossed aside your leman to please your new
bride. I should have considered that. Yet, what she said
had the ring of truth, considering the mon ye are and
all."

That piqued Connor's curiosity, but he resisted the
urge to demand Robert explain himself. "If that fulsome
adder hisses in your ear again, I would pay her no heed
at all. She will nay longer be privy to anything that occurs
within my walls."

"Ah, so the cast aside lover is soon to be cast out."

"Ye would do the same."

"Aye, I would. In truth, I would be far harsher in my
punishment of such a betrayal."

"She has her uses. She will just have to employ them
from a wee bothy on the moors from now on."

"Since ye have been so kind as to offer me advice,"
Robert drawled, "allow me to return the favor. There
is more than one adder in your nest, my laird."

Connor tensed and carefully set down his empty goblet. "Who?"

"Nay, I willnae be giving ye a name. I have no real
proof and I will make no accusations without it. 'Tis
nay your brothers nor your wife nor that fool Knobby.
How is he, anyway?"

"Cursing ye with each throb in his head." In an
attempt to calm himself and subdue the urge to shake
a name out of Robert, Connor told the man how Fiona
had brought Knobby back, thus stealing the time Robert
had hoped to use to woo Gillyanne.

"The lass is a MacEnroy to the bone," Robert murmured and shook his head. " 'Tisnae her, either."

" 'Tis good to ken who it isnae. 'Twould be better to
ken who it is."

"Aye, but ye must lance that boil without my help. I

willnae brand a mon a traitor without proof. I warn ye only because I ken enough to feel it justified. Watch your back. Every snake eventually exposes itself to the sunlight.''

Connor nodded, repeated his warning to Robert, and left to take his wife home. He felt a bit of a fool and it was an uncomfortable feeling. Despite his wise advice to Robert about cast aside lovers, he had been surprised by Meg's betrayal. He had ignored the woman's sullen attitude and the way Meg had tried to make things difficult for Gillyanne, but, even if he had not, he doubted he would have guessed how far the woman would go to try to rid herself of a rival.

Where he decided he had erred was in scorning Meg's high opinion of herself and her lofty sense of her own importance. When he had set her aside and ordered her to do her share of work, he had taken away the power she had stolen for herself, reduced her from someone the women of Deilcladach had had to bow to to just a whore. It should have occurred to him that she would make someone pay for that, that she would thus see Gillyanne as an enemy and try to be rid of her. Connor promised himself that he would begin to pay more heed to what the women of Deilcladach did and said.

But first, he thought with a sigh as he saw how his little wife glared at him, he was obviously going to have to hear a few things his wife had to say. Thwarting her attempt to ride with James, he tossed Gillyanne into his saddle and mounted behind her. As they rode away from Sir Robert's fine keep, Gillyanne kept herself so straight and taut in the saddle, Connor knew she would have an uncomfortable ride home. It was clear that she did not like the way he had spoken of her lands yet she had been fully aware of the reasons for their marriage. Vanity, he supposed. It probably stung to be constantly reminded of that fact. She could not know that, if a ransom had been demanded, he would have used some, if not all, of her lands to free her. Since that confession would carry the taint of some of the feelings he was battling with, Connor decided he would keep it to himself. He did not wish to reveal that weakness to anyone.

"Weel, your fine new lands are now safe," Gillyanne muttered, then cursed herself for voicing her hurt and insult.

"Aye," he replied calmly, briefly smiling over her sulky tone. "And all in time for ye to give me my bath."

Gillyanne briefly savored the vision of pushing Connor out of the saddle and then riding over his prone body a few dozen times. "I think I am too weary from my ordeal to indulge ye tonight."

Connor suspected she was referring to far more than the bath he so enjoyed. "Ah, too bad. I have worked up a wee sweat riding to your rescue."

"Are ye saying that, if I dinnae pamper ye with your bath, ye will come to bed stinking of a long, hard ride?"

"Aye." He saw her small hands clench into tight little fists and idly wondered if she would use them on him.

"Fine then. I will give ye your cursed bath. I suspect it will be prepared shortly after we arrive at Deilcladach, anyway."

He made a show of sniffing her. "Ye could do with a wash, too."

She punched his thigh, but knew the soft grunt he made was one of surprise, not pain. Gillyanne doubted she could hurt that well-muscled tree trunk he called his leg. A sensible part of her knew he was teasing her, goading her on purpose, but the bruised part of her that had been forced to accept her lack of allure for men was stung by his mild insults. She had to remind herself that he had forced her to sit close to him, that he was idly nuzzling her hair and stroking her stomach, before she could banish that hurt. It was foolish not to be able to accept simple teasing. She firmly told herself to be pleased that he had softened enough to indulge in such play.

"I will bathe whilst ye are booting Meg out of Deilcladach," she said and tried not to tense as she waited for his response.

Connor bit back a chuckle. He was sure Gillyanne did not think she was sharing his favors with Meg, but could understand how she would not like to have to see the woman every day. It would be interesting, however, to hear why she felt he should banish the woman. After all, Meg had not participated in Gillyanne's capture. The woman had simply given private information to an ally.

"I am going to toss the woman out, am I?"

"She betrayed you, told Sir Robert about what went on inside your keep, and, I suspect, where and when I would be outside the walls."

Although Robert had not said so, Connor had deduced that for himself. There was no denying that Meg wanted Gillyanne gone from Deilcladach. He knew he should count himself lucky that Meg had gone to an ally and not an enemy.

"I considered just warning her not to try such games again. Meg probably didnae think I would find out her part in it all."

"Probably not. In truth, I suspect if ye scold her, she will act all contrite, beg forgiveness whilst weeping buckets of tears, and vow on her dead mother's grave ne'er to do it again. 'Twill be a lie. As soon as she feels ye are lulled by her penitent attitude, she will try something else. 'Twas bad enough that ye pushed her out of your bed, but ye made that rule about not bedding husbands which was something she used to keep some women under her boot heel. And then ye demanded she do the work she was supposed to, immediately stealing all the power she had once wielded. Ye turned her back into what she really was and is, a mere maid and a whore. Ye must pay for that insult and, since it happened after I married you, Meg sees me as the cause of it all. She is furious with ye, but she loathes me."

"And 'tis nay jealousy which causes ye to speak so? Nay just a wish to see my former lover gone from your sight?"

"Of course I would like to see her gone, her and her two fellow whores. If I had had lovers ere we wed, I doubt ye would wish to have to deal with them each and every day." Gillyanne interpreted his harsh grunt as agreement. "Meg is more than a thorn in my side, however, and ye ken it. If she is allowed to get away with this betrayal, she will think herself free to try again. And she will. She wants revenge. I am nay sure ye are in any real danger, but I think I might be, and I curse myself for a fool for nay realizing it."

"She will be gone," he said. "I was but curious as to why ye would believe she needed to be banished."

Gillyanne grunted then inwardly cursed. She hoped she had not revealed any of the bone deep jealousy she felt for Meg and, to a lesser degree, the other two women Connor had bedded. The man was far too arrogant already. He certainly did not need to think he held his wife's heart in the palm of his big hand, which, to Gillyanne's dismay, she suspected he did. Until she had some hint from him that she stirred more than his lust and sense of possession, she intended to guard her own feelings. If this marriage failed, she would be hurt, but she refused to be humbled. If he did not know all she felt for him, he would not know just how deeply his lack of love cut her. It would be a small salve to her pride, but it might be all she had left.

The moment they rode through the gates of Deilcladach, Gillyanne felt Connor tense. He was preparing himself to be the stern laird, she realized. What little softness she might pull from him at other times, such as when they were alone, swiftly vanished when he had

to face his clan as their laird. Although she could understand it, it tasted too much like defeat for all her hopes.
After all, she could not separate him from his clan,
could not stop him from being their laird. All she could
hope for was that she could teach him that he could
be both a loving husband and a strong, respected laird.
It would not be an easy lesson to teach.

He dismounted, then helped her down. "See to the
readying of our bath, wife."

Although a part of her wished to see Meg's shame
and banishment, Gillyanne would not allow herself to
indulge it. She hurried into the keep, pausing only to
check on Knobby and Fiona before going to prepare
Connor's bath. There was a small chance she could gain
something by being there to offer comfort and ease
after such a trying chore. She was sure it was one of those
things that made a man appreciate a wife. Although
she ached for affection, she decided she could find
satisfaction in Connor's appreciation. It was a small step,
but at least it would be one in the right direction.

Chapter Thirteen

Connor grinned when he stepped into his bedchamber and saw Gillyanne standing naked by the tub. She squealed and quickly got into the tub. As he started to shed his clothes, he realized just how much he enjoyed these baths, did in fact look forward to them at the end of the day. After facing the possibility of losing her to Robert and facing a betrayal within his own clan, he was especially eager for it. There was a danger lurking in that eagerness, but, for the moment, he decided to ignore it. Meg's screeches of fury were still ringing in his ears and he wanted to replace them with Gillyanne's cries of passion. Or, rather, her bellow of delight, he thought, and grinned again as he climbed into the tub.

"What are ye grinning about?" Gillyanne asked, a little disappointed that he was not in a dour mood which she could now improve with her wifely skills. The man was not cooperating at all with her plans.

"I was just contemplating deafening myself with your cries of passion," he drawled as she started to wash his feet.

"Are ye saying that I am loud?" She was not sure if she was insulted or just appalled at the thought of being loud enough to be overheard.

"Ye fair bring the stone walls down around us."

"There are some things a mon shouldnae tease his wife about." Gillyanne scrubbed his arms, a little annoyed when her vigorous scrubbing did not invoke so much as a faint wince. "He might wish to consider the possibility that he could embarrass his poor, modest wife so deeply she willnae dare to even breathe, to utter e'en the faintest of whimpers, despite all his best efforts."

"A telling point, wife," he muttered as she washed his hair.

"I rather thought so." She carefully rinsed his hair then briskly washed his back.

Connor took the washing cloth from Gillyanne's hand. "Of course, some men might see that as a challenge."

"Oh, dear."

Gillyanne stared up at the ceiling, enjoying the weight of her husband's body, and decided that the man had a true skill with a washing rag. She just hoped the bed dried out before it was time to retire for the night. Sadly, she also had to confess that she had proven little challenge for Connor. Gillyanne was not sure exactly what noise she had made, but strongly suspected it had been loud, which probably gratified the big oaf. All she could do was pray no one would be rude enough to mention if they had heard her.

"What happened with Meg?" she asked Connor, seeking to avert her thoughts from how she may have embarrassed herself.

"Ah, aye, Meg." He nuzzled Gillyanne's neck. "She tried to deny it all, then tried to beg forgiveness. I told her that allowing her to live was all the forgiveness she was going to get."

"And she didnae understand that at all, did she?"

"Nay, the ungrateful wretch. She cursed me and cursed you."

Connor sat up and stretched. He realized he could think on the sordid confrontation with Meg without anger now. Sensual satisfaction thrummed through his veins, keeping that anger away. He kissed Gillyanne, got out of bed, and began to get dressed. The way his people had stood firm behind him as he had banished Meg also helped his mood.

" 'Twas just to banish her," Gillyanne said as she quickly tugged on her shift. " 'Twas also verra merciful. Many another laird would have done far more than just tell her to leave."

"Robert said he wouldnae be so kind. She seemed to have far more possessions than she ought when she left, so, I suspect, she added thievery to her crimes. I had planned to set her in some crude hovel, but she is in a cottage in the village. It allowed me to gently suggest that Jenny and Peg may wish to join her there. Without Meg's arrogance to protect them from the other women, I believe they will go to her."

"Do ye think they helped her, were part of the betrayal?"

"I think they kenned what game she played and didnae warn me. 'Tis nearly as bad. And, I decided 'twas an unkindness to the lasses who work so hard and are virtuous to allow whores to wander so freely and openly about the keep."

"Joan will be pleased."

"Aye, though Malcolm seems much chastened. Nay, 'tis best to clean house. Those women can do their business in the village. Knobby told me Mairi says 'tis the way of it in most places."

"Mairi has traveled?"

"She and her mother came to us from another clan. Mairi's father had died and her mother was being plagued to wed a mon she couldnae abide, so she left. Sadly, they arrived but days before the killing, seeking Joan's mother, a kinswoman. Joan's mother was killed and Mairi's mother sorely wounded, leaving her so frail she died a few years later."

"So many young ones left alone," Gillyanne murmured as she finished dressing.

"I think our youth turned in our favor in the end."

"Aye, possibly."

Connor shook off the sadness such memories always brought, grabbed Gillyanne by the hand, and headed for the great hall. Since everyone at Deilcladach knew the tale, most of them intimately acquainted with the grief and the hardship that followed, he had spoken of it very little. Now, each time he told Gillyanne another tale of those troubled times, he realized the worst of his grief had passed. The only strong feeling that lingered was an angry regret that there had been no one he could wreak vengeance on. The ones responsible had killed each other off.

As he and Gillyanne entered the great hall, Connor was a little surprised to find everyone ready and waiting. It was something that was becoming increasingly common. He sat down and helped himself to some food as the others quickly took their places at the tables. It was not until he was halfway through his meal that he realized there had been no way everyone could have known he was about to come down to the great hall. The meal was not served at precisely the same time every evening, although lately he had begun to suspect that his wife was trying to arrange it so. Neither had any bell been rung to call everyone to the table.

"How is it ye were all waiting and the food was set out?" he asked Diarmot, his curiosity finally getting the better of him. "I heard no bell rung, or the like."

"Dinnae need a bell," Diarmot replied. "We just wait for the bellow."

"The bellow?"

"Aye, the bellow. Once we hear that, we ken ye will be down to eat within the half hour. Most often, 'tis about fifteen minutes."

Gillyanne felt as if her cheeks were on fire, her blush was so deep and hot. A brief attempt to convince herself that Diarmot could not possibly be referring to what she thought he was was killed by the looks of amusement on the faces of the men. She groaned and rested her forehead on the table, resisting the urge to bang her head on the hard wood a few times.

She was just starting to pray that the floor would open up and swallow her, taking her away from this humiliation, when a strange noise to her right caught her attention. Then the feeling of joyful amazement came to her from many of the ones sitting around the table. Slowly, she lifted her head and looked at Connor. It took her a full minute to realize he was laughing. It was a rich yet boyish sound. Her delight over that quickly began to fade as, one by one, the others at the table began to join in. The pleasure she felt at seeing Connor laugh was quickly smothered by renewed embarrassment.

"A clarion call to sup," Connor said in a choked voice, and started to laugh again.

"We havenae rung the bell since ye started taking your bath in your chambers," Diarmot said and collapsed into laughter that closely resembled giggles.

Anger started to creep up through her embarrassment and Gillyanne snapped, " 'Tis nay that loud."

"Nay?" James cried. "Lass, ye could bring down the walls of Jericho." He started laughing so hard he had to clutch at Knobby to stay in his seat.

"Ye are all behaving like children." Gillyanne stood up and collected her plate and goblet. "I shall eat in the kitchens." As she strode away, she noticed Fiona stopped giggling long enough to grab her food and follow her. "Unruly boys, the whole lot of them."

Upon entering the kitchens, Gillyanne cursed softly then sighed. Joan, Mairi, and the two kitchen maids were giggling so hard there were tears in their eyes. Feeling extremely ill-used, Gillyanne sat at the table only to realize that her appetite had fled. She was wondering if she should force herself to eat when Joan sent the kitchen maids to wait on the men and she and Mairi sat down across from her and Fiona. Both women looked sympathetic, but still far too amused for Gillyanne's liking.

"M'lady," Joan said, her voice husky from laughter, "they dinnae do this to shame or hurt you."

" 'Tis such a private matter," Gillyanne muttered.

"Men dinnae always think so." Joan clasped her hands to her chest and looked torn between laughing some more and weeping. "Oh, lass, the laird was laughing. Laughing! I havenae heard the like since before the killings."

"I dinnae think I have e'er heard my brother laugh," said Fiona.

"Weel, aye, that certainly delighted me," admitted Gillyanne. "Unfortunately, the oafs were quick to remind me just what they were all laughing about. 'Tis so humiliating. And, I suppose I just hate to be reminded of how loud I can be. 'Tis a curse."

"Oh, nay, m'lady," protested Joan. "Old Nigel told us how he heard ye singing e'en though he would have thought himself too far away. He also told us 'twas the voice of an angel, that it pulled at him so strongly, he had to be held back. Ye were blessed with that voice. I but hope to hear it some day."

"It does seem as if my singing is appreciated. Yet, curse it three times, whilst singing loud and true may be fine, I am also loud when I am angry, sometimes loud when I am happy, and now it appears I can call men to a meal when my rogue of a husband gives me pleasure.''

"Aye, and I promise ye that beneath that laughter rides envy.'' Joan nodded when Gillyanne frowned with uncertainty. "What mon wouldnae want to pleasure his woman so weel she rattles the stones with her cries? I wouldnae be surprised if monly pride that he can do so, and now all ken it, is part of the reason Connor laughed so freely. 'Tis the way of men to feel pride in their rutting skills, e'en those fools who dinnae have any.''

"Connor yells, too," Fiona said. "Truly. It may not be as clear as yours, but one doesnae have to listen too hard to hear him.''

That was somewhat comforting to know, but Gillyanne still sighed and shook her head. " 'Twill be hard to look them all in the eyes now that I ken they all ken my private business.''

"M'lady, the moment ye began to give the laird his bath in that bedchamber, we all kenned what would happen,'' Joan said. "Only a fool would think two lusty young people could bathe together innocently.''

"Oh, of course. And I am foolish to think men ought to understand my sensibilities. *They* have none. I think I shall make an effort to mute myself.''

"That would just present Connor with a challenge.''

Recalling the lovemaking that had caused that much talked about bellow, Gillyanne smiled slowly and winked at Joan. "Aye, that it might.'' She joined the others in an enjoyable bout of the giggles.

"Hope we havenae hurt the lass's feelings,'' Diarmot said when everyone finally finished laughing.

"I think she was just cross,'' Connor murmured,

frowning toward the kitchens. "Why would she be angry?"

"Women dinnae like their private business talked about," said James. "Gilly was probably embarrassed to learn everyone kenned what the two of ye were doing. If Mither kenned what I have just done, she would kick me to Stirling and back."

"We are married. E'en if we werenae, when a mon and a woman go into a bedchamber and shut the door, every fool kens what they are doing. She must ken that."

"Of course she does. She also kens that it can be a noisy romp and thus isnae as secretive as ye may wish it to be. Wheesht, when Fither has been away for a wee while, he and Mither near race up the stairs and have, on occasion, been heard to be knocking o'er the furniture. Then there is the occasional bit of clothing found in the solar or some other room that must be discreetly returned." James rolled his eyes. "And, when our cousins Avery and Elspeth visit with their husbands, the sounds one hears when walking by the bedchambers," he shook his head, "ye would think ye were in some brothel for lusty sailors. E'en food disappears. And, 'tis sore difficult to keep one's tongue in one's mouth when ye hear the maids complaining about how difficult it is to get honey off the linen. *But,* ye *ne'er* speak of it. Weel, we arenae supposed to, though teasing does occur. Infuriates the lasses every time, too."

Connor stared at James in stunned silence. He simply could not conceive of the sort of life the man described. It was true that his siblings and he had occasionally indulged in rough play, but there was little time for such frivolity. Even before the killings, the only real foolishness or laughter had come when, due to their youth, he and other children had briefly forgotten that they were in a constant state of war. The Murrays sounded happy, secure, and Connor realized he felt a twinge of envy.

"Honey? Why would there be honey on the linens?" he asked, seeking a diversion from his dark thoughts.

James laughed, glanced around to be certain there were no women close at hand, and proceeded to tell the men of the delights one could reap from playing with one's food. Connor realized there was a great deal about bedsports that he had never learned. He would have all his fingernails ripped out before he would admit it, however. It was some comfort to see, by the expressions on the faces of the other men, that he was not the only one suffering from ignorance. They were all a rather unworldly lot, he realized. James was easily prodded into telling more by the younger men, the older ones listening closely while acting as if this was all very old news.

It was late, time to seek their beds, when Connor realized his wife had not returned. He looked for Gillyanne in the kitchens, but only one of the little kitchen maids was there finishing her work. As he started toward his bedchamber, Connor wondered if Gillyanne had been deeply hurt by the laughter. He found it a great source of pride that he could make his little wife bellow like a warrior leading a charge, but ladies could be sensitive and protective of their modesty. If she was honestly hurt, perhaps feeling shamed, he would have to try and soothe her, and Connor doubted he had such skill. Yet, if hurt and outrage threatened the fullness of the passion he and Gillyanne shared, he suspected he could find some. It had not been easy, but he had finally accepted that he found joy and contentment in Gillyanne's arms. Since it would be seen as lustiness by others, he felt he could heartily indulge himself yet not appear weak. He had no intention of losing that now.

He suddenly thought of the laughter he had indulged in. It had felt good, refreshing. Connor knew he had briefly shocked his people with such levity, had seen that on their faces, but it had been quickly accepted.

Even welcomed, he realized with surprise. Neither had he seen any lessening of respect, any weakening in his position as their laird. He had no intention of becoming some jovial fool, but Connor decided it might not hurt to enjoy the occasional laugh or reveal his amusement. In truth, having retasted the pleasure of sharing a laugh, he doubted he would be able to resist another taste now and again.

Connor breathed a sigh of relief when he entered his bedchamber and found Gillyanne in his bed. At least she was not hiding from him. Although, he mused with a smile as he stripped off his clothes, there was not much of her to see above the bedclothes. After a quick wash, he slid into bed and pulled her into his arms. Her eyes remained closed, but, if she was trying to pretend she was asleep, she was doing a very poor job of it.

"Are ye sulking, lass?" he asked, stroking her back and frowning when he realized a linen shift was keeping him from enjoying the feel of her soft skin.

"Why should I sulk?" she muttered, trying to ignore the beauty of the strong chest she was pressed against. "Such deep embarrassment and humiliation is worth nay more than a wince or two, aye? Why, I only thought of sinking into a deep hole and pulling the earth o'er my head for a moment or two."

Connor pressed his lips against the side of her neck, hiding his expression. He knew now was not the time to follow his decision to more openly reveal his amusement. The lass did have a way of speaking that made him want to laugh, though, and that had been true from the beginning. Connor realized he was looking forward to sharing a laugh with her on occasion.

"No one meant to shame ye, lass."

"I didnae say shame. I feel no shame. 'Twas just embarrassing, deeply so." She sighed, feeling a renewed sting of embarrassment and knowing it would take a while to get over that. " 'Tis a private matter between us."

"Gilly, we are wed. The moment we seek privacy, everyone kens what we are doing. 'Tis exactly what they would be doing or what they wish they could be doing."

"Aye, I ken it, but they shouldnae talk about it, for sweet Mary's sake. Men might like to slap each other on the back and boast about it and, aye, women talk amongst themselves, but 'tis nay something to speak so publicly about."

Connor was not sure what to say. He did not really consider the teasing amongst those at their table tonight as anything more than a jest shared amongst family. Since he had laughed and was actually feeling rather smug, rather pleased that everyone knew he could make his wife yell with pleasure, his sympathy for her bruised feelings was faint.

"So, I have come to a decision," she said.

Not sure he liked the sound of that, Connor pulled back to eye her warily. "And what would that be?"

"That I am going to become more genteel. Aye, they all may ken what we are doing up here, but I will no longer amuse them with noises. Nay, I willnae be calling the fools into sup any more."

Gillyanne was not surprised when his eyes narrowed. His manly pride had scented a challenge, just as she had suspected it would. She would undoubtedly suffer some discomfort before she could accept, then ignore, the fact that others heard her and Connor make love, but she did not intend to allow it to last for long. The sharing of passion was still the only time she felt she was reaching Connor, penetrating his hard shell, if only for a little while. She would not let a few crude jests force her to pull away from that. In truth, she was not sure she could. She craved the pleasure Connor gave her far too much to let anything interfere with it.

Connor pushed her onto her back. At first he thought

she had donned the very modest sleep shift because she had gone to bed alone and was cold. Now he realized it was all part of her plan to become more genteel. She might even think to try and become what his uncle had said most wellborn lasses were in the bedchamber. That he would not allow. He had spent long,torturous days before accepting the fact that he lost himself in the passion they shared and that he looked forward to these times of intimacy in their bedchamber. No attack of maidenly modesty would be allowed to rob him of that.

"What is this?" he asked, plucking at the laces on her shift until they started to come undone.

" 'Tis what a genteel wife would wear to bed," Gillyanne replied.

"Aye? I am to just fumble my way around it, am I?"

She gasped when he suddenly grabbed the shoulders of the shift and yanked them down until her breasts were bared. Her arms were also pinned to her sides, not painfully so, but it would take a lot of wriggling to get them free. Gillyanne felt no fear, knew deep in her heart that Connor would never hurt her. What she did feel was intrigued and just a little aroused. She had turned into quite a wanton, she thought with an inner, slightly rueful, smile.

He kissed her and Gillyanne let the sensual magic of that kiss flow through her. The feel of his broad chest pressed against her breasts was enough to make them ache. Gillyanne tried to move her arms to touch him only to realize he had relaced her shift enough to tighten the bonds on her arms. When he moved his kisses to her throat, she moaned with a mixture of frustration over her inability to touch him and a rapidly soaring passion.

"Connor, I cannae move," she protested, surprised she could even speak for his kisses had reached her breasts.

"Genteel ladies dinnae move." Using his fingers and

tongue, he stroked her nipples into a tempting hardness. "Genteel ladies are supposed to just lie there like silent martyrs and let their wedded husbands have their will of their bodies."

"I dinnae think that is quite right."

She wanted to argue some more, but Connor drew the tip of her breast deep into his mouth. With each suckle he pulled all thought from her head and stole all ability for coherent speech. Gillyanne was still astonished at how swiftly and fiercely Connor could stir her desire. He was a fire in her blood, an aching need she feared she would suffer all her life. And, she did fear it, for there was still a good chance that their marriage would prove to be an utter failure.

Even that concern was banished from her mind when Connor began to kiss the insides of her thighs. When he took those kisses a little higher, his lips then his tongue touching the heated softness between her legs, Gillyanne cried out a shocked protest. Connor grasped her by the hips, holding her steady when she tried to pull away, and, soon, she did not want to. Blinding pleasure flooded her body with each stroke of his tongue.

The only thought left in Gillyanne's head was that she had to move, she had to touch him. A part of her mind was aware that the strain upon her arms was a little painful, but, then, she heard cloth rip, and she was free. She could not believe it when she heard and felt Connor laugh as she buried her fingers in his thick hair. A moment later Gillyanne knew she was reaching her peak and she struggled to speak.

"Now, Connor," she commanded. "Please, now!"

"Nay, wife. This way. Let go and give it to me."

Gillyanne could not hold back. Her release tore through her. She was still shuddering from the force of it when Connor began to send her soaring all over again. This time when she called to him he did not hesitate, fiercely joining their bodies. She clung to his strong body as he drove them both to the heights.

It was difficult to know how much time had passed before Gillyanne felt able to even move, let alone speak. She idly stroked Connor's hip, enjoying the feel of his weight upon her and his warm breath against her neck. A part of her was a little appalled at how wantonly she had responded to such a deep intimacy, but she easily smothered the feeling. Connor was her husband, and if what they shared was enjoyable to both of them, she would not fret over it.

"I bellowed again, didnae I?" Knowing full well that she had, it was more of a statement than a question.

"Aye, twice," Connor replied, male satisfaction weighing his words. "My ears are still ringing."

"Arrogant beast."

"Mayhap I should go down and see if any of those fools have staggered out of their beds expecting a meal to be set out."

Gillyanne found she was able to giggle at the image. "Weel, go on then."

"Nay, I cannae move." He yawned and sleepily kissed her neck. "Ye wrung all the strength right out of me."

"I am feeling a wee bit weak myself."

"Good, then I have done my duty as your husband and may now seek my rest."

Although Gillyanne smiled at his teasing, she suffered a faint pang of disappointment as well. After such blinding passion, after a joining of such beautiful unity, she would prefer loving words to teasing ones. She swallowed the urge to try and pull a few out of him. Such things had to be given freely. What worried her was that she would never hear them, that despite the perfection of the desire they shared, Connor would keep all else locked tightly within himself. Gillyanne pressed her lips to his hair and wondered just how long she should wait for those soft words before she began to look the fool.

Chapter Fourteen

"What are ye doing?"

Gillyanne sighed with resignation as she sat up in response to that stirringly familiar deep voice behind her. She wondered how Connor always seemed to catch her at her worst. It was true that the herb garden she was laboring over looked neat, attractive, and rich in new growth. Unfortunately, it was also true that she looked as if she had wallowed in the mud. When he moved to stand in front of her, she was pleased to see him almost grinning for it revealed a loosening of the tight reins he kept on himself. Obviously that bout of laughter two nights ago had freed his sense of humor. Gillyanne just wished the change was not so often gained at her expense.

"I am resurrecting your herb garden," she replied.

"We had an herb garden?" Connor frowned as he looked around, thinking it a lot of work for his delicate wife.

"Aye, although there was little more left than a plot of weeds with a few herbs tangled up in them. 'Twas the herbs and the remnants of a stone path between the plots that told me one used to be here. I found some seed still stored in a small chest in the kitchens as weel." She pointed to a tangle of weeds and vines near the wall. "I think there used to be a kitchen garden o'er there. Fiona and I plan to begin uncovering its secrets on the morrow if the weather holds fine."

"I dinnae recall such things, but I was only a lad when the destruction came, and young lads care little about gardens."

She nodded. "And most of the older women died, that knowledge dying with them." Gillyanne frowned for he suddenly looked at her with a tense gravity that was a little worrying. "Is something wrong?"

"Your father is here."

"Here? In the keep?" She scrambled to her feet, her excitement quickly dimmed by dismay as she recalled how dirty she was.

"Nay. He is outside our gates with a dozen armed men."

"Oh, dear."

"He demands to speak with you."

"Not you?"

"Nay, at least not yet. I made him swear that he would-nae hold ye or try to take ye away."

Gillyanne grimaced, suspecting her father had found that a galling, bitter oath to take. "So, I am to go and speak with him?"

"Aye, when ye swear that ye willnae try to flee with him."

"I swear it."

She met his hard stare calmly. Connor did not need to know all the reasons behind her ready agreement. Now was simply not the time to run home with her father. She was still Connor's wife. She was also still willing to make this marriage a good one. It was too early to give up the fight. There was also the simple matter that leaving on her own or being taken away by her kinsmen could cause more trouble than it was worth. She was Connor's wife by the laws of the church and Scotland and one did not interfere with those laws without stirring up controversy.

When Connor nodded and reached for her, she hastily backed up a step. "Tell my fither I will be out to speak to him in fifteen minutes. I must clean away some of this dirt. Twould be best to greet him looking as good as I am able."

Connor watched her dash into the keep and started to return to the walls to speak with her angry father. Even though he had not discussed the matter with Gillyanne, he had not forgotten what James had told him, that there was a way Gillyanne could end their marriage. If James knew it, then Sir Eric Murray did as well, which was why the man had not been immediately welcomed into Deilcladach. Unfortunately, the man had not left, had remained adamant in his wish to see his daughter. Even James' assurances that Gillyanne was fine had not swayed Sir Eric. Making both father and daughter swear that she would remain at Deilcladach was the only compromise Connor could think of, but he was not happy with it.

"I think that mon would be mightily pleased to gut ye," murmured Knobby after Connor had loudly relayed Gillyanne's message to her father from the top of his walls.

Watching the way Sir Eric paced in front of his men, Connor nodded. "I can see where the lass gets her temper."

"Odd, but I expected him to be bigger."

"The way she uses his name to threaten people would surely make one think him a giant. Mayhap he is bigger when seen up close."

"Ye are nay going out there, are ye?" Knobby protested, only to have to hurry to catch up with Connor as his laird climbed down from the walls.

"I willnae lurk close at hand. 'Tis best if father and daughter can talk privately. I just want to be a presence."

Gillyanne ran through the gates of Deilcladach and all the way to her father's open arms. She did not really need any comforting, but it felt good to be held by her father again. When he finally set her slightly away from him, she stood patiently while he looked her over. The conversation they were about to have would undoubtedly be uncomfortable at times and she was in no hurry to begin it.

"Ye havenae been harmed," Sir Eric said, only the faint hint of a question in his voice.

"Nay, Fither," she replied. "Sir Connor would ne'er hurt me."

"Tell me what happened."

"Ye didnae stop at Dubhlinn and get this tale from Mither? I sent James to tell her."

"She told me. Now, I want ye to tell me."

She grimaced, but began to tell the story. Gillyanne took particular care in relating how she had repelled the first three attempts to capture her and was pleased to see her father smile. His rage at Connor could not have that tight a hold on him if he could find some amusement in her tale. She hurried over the part of the story that included the wedding, bedding, and flight to Deilcladach. The sharp look in her father's eyes told her she had not fooled him at all.

"Was it consummated?"

"Aye, Fither," she replied, staring at her boots to hide her blush.

"Is that him o'er there betwixt us and the gates?"

Gillyanne glanced behind her, surprised that Connor

had come outside the walls. "Aye. The tall one to the front of the others."

"And just who are those others lumped up behind the fool?"

"His brothers Diarmot, Drew, Nanty, and Angus, his sister Fiona, and his right-hand mon Knobby, whose real name is Iain."

"There is a lass in that lump?"

"Aye, the smallest one. She is barely thirteen."

Eric rubbed his chin. "There is a reason that she looks like one of the lads?"

"Her brothers raised her."

"Ah." Eric looked from Connor to Gillyanne and back again a few times, before bluntly asking, "Ye swear he doesnae hurt ye? He is a big lad."

"Oh, aye." She blushed furiously, not needing her father's quirked brow to tell her she had revealed some of her lust in those two words. "I swear to ye, Fither, Connor would ne'er hurt me."

"I have spoken to the king." He smiled faintly when she sent him a faintly worried look. "I was at my most charming. He was e'en a little apologetic. 'Tis all in my hands. He willnae take back what was seen by all as his permission, but if I choose to end this, he will accept that and support my decision. Do ye wish this ended?"

"Nay," Gillyanne said, a little surprised at how quickly that word had sprung to her lips for she had been undecided for so long. "Not yet. The marriage was by priest and it has been consummated. Shouldnae I at least try to make it a good marraige?"

"Aye, ye should. Do ye love the brute?"

Gillyanne grimaced. "There is a good chance that I might. Some days I do, other days I am nay so sure."

"And why is it such a difficult thing to decide? Do ye sense something false about the mon?"

"Nay. In truth, I can sense verra little about what Connor feels or thinks. When I try to reach out to him,

I feel as if I have run into a wall. Yet, I dinnae believe there is a false bone in the oaf's overgrown body. That comes from observation o'er the last few weeks." She sighed, briefly sent a longing glance toward Connor, then met her father's curious gaze. "He is a hard mon, a tightly controlled mon."

"What have ye learned about him?"

Gillyanne related the tale of Connor's life. She could feel her father soften toward her husband as she spoke, and a gleam of respect entered his eyes. There was no doubt in her mind that, if she could make her marriage to Connor work, her father would readily accept him as part of the family, and not simply because she was married to him. Fortunately, her father would also understand that, even if a man was all that seemed good to other men, it did not necessarily mean he would make a good husband.

"I believe I understand," murmured Eric, studying the tall laird whose scowl deepened the longer he and Gillyanne talked. "A life like that and the need to lead whilst still little more than a beardless lad could strangle all the softness right out of a mon."

"Exactly." Gillyanne crossed her arms beneath her breasts. "He has honor, courage, strength, and a deep sense of responsibility." She could feel a blush sting her cheeks but forced herself to be honest. "We share a passion. His uncle set some strange ideas about gently bred ladies into his head, but Connor had the wit to heed another opinion. For one thing, he was prepared to see that he neither needed a mistress, nor was it particularly wise to have one."

"Oh, I suspect he was." Eric shook his head and briefly laughed. "Ye havenae told me anything bad yet, lass."

"As ye said, all the softness has apparently been crushed out of him. I dinnae ask that he become some courtier spouting poetry and flatteries. All I ask for is some ... weel, emotion, some hint that he feels something for me besides passion."

"Ye want him to love you."

"Aye, I do. At the moment, I would settle for some hint that I have reached his heart, that I have stirred more than his desire. Ah, Fither, he laughed two nights ago, and it shocked everyone. One of the women was near to crying, she was so moved to hear it. Fortunately, his people had the sense to quickly adapt to this wonder thus nay making Connor uncomfortable."

"One small step at a time."

Gillyanne nodded. "I willnae stay in a marriage where my husband willnae or cannae give anything of himself. I am willing, however, to remain his wife until I either get what I need to make me stay, or ken that he just doesnae have it to give, at least to me, and finally walk away."

Eric put an arm around her shoulders and kissed her forehead. "Ye want to try and make a good marriage, but ye also need to ken that ye willnae be trapped in a cold one."

"Aye, Fither. I ken it will fair tear my heart to pieces if I have to leave, but, if I cannae make a place for myself in his heart, 'twill hurt me far more and for far longer if I stay."

"Ye are wise to see that, my Gilly. Your mother gave me softness enough when we first wed, yet it really wasnae enough. I was in some torment for months ere we confessed what truly dwelt in our hearts. The mere thought of years of nay kenning or of gaining only wee pieces of her affection fair chills my blood. I would ne'er leave ye to that fate. There is a way out."

"I ken it. Coercion?" Her father nodded. "I wasnae really willing. Aye, I chose him out of the three and I said the vows, but only after three attacks and the promise, or rather threat, of a fourth and united one. That will serve?"

"It will." Eric looked toward Connor and nearly smiled. "He grows impatient."

It certainly looked as if Connor was closer than he had been a few moments ago. "I swore I would return."

"James, m'lad," Eric said, causing James who had lurked a few feet behind Gillyanne to step closer, "Do ye stay here?"

"Aye, unless ye have need of me." James watched Gillyanne move away to confront her scowling husband. "He is uneasy."

"We both vowed she would stay. Mayhap he isnae as untouched as she thinks."

" 'Tis difficult to say, but, aye, I would be willing to wager that she has touched his heart. The question is whether or not he will ever let Gillyanne ken it or e'er let himself accept that truth. God's tears, there is also the chance that, if he does ken he is softening to her, he will do his utter best to kill the feeling. I believe he sees such emotions as weaknesses and he willnae allow himself to have one, other than his clan, that is."

"So, ye think it a good plan for her to try and win him?"

" 'Tis certainly amusing at times." James exchanged a brief grin with Sir Eric. "Aye, she should try. Gilly loves him. I am sure of it. If this is to end, she needs to ken she did all she was able to to win the mon's heart. It all rests upon just how deeply he has buried his emotions and his willingness to let them be pulled free again."

"She will have time. E'en with good reason to end a marriage, 'tis nay something that can be done quickly." Eric crossed his arms on his chest and almost smiled. "I believe I am about to meet my newest son by marriage."

"Connor," Gillyanne said as she confronted her husband, "why are ye lurking about out here?"

"I just wanted to see your father up close," he replied. "He isnae a verra big mon, is he?"

"Big enough, and one doesnae have to be some hulking, great giant to wield a sword weel." She crossed her arms over her chest. "Just wanted to see him, hmm? Foolish me to e'en wonder, for a wee moment, that ye might think Fither or I couldnae keep our word."

"Aye, foolish you." Connor watched her closely. "Ye were talking for a long time."

"Had a lot to say. After all, when the mon rode away to serve his king, I was bedded down safely in my wee chaste bed, then, suddenly, I claim my place as laird of Ald-dabhach, repel three attacks upon my keep, am dragged before a priest . . ."

"Ye werenae dragged," Connor drawled.

Gillyanne ignored his interruption, ". . . am tossed, all unprepared, into the rough waters of marriage, and shut up behind the thick walls of Deilcladach. Fither was naturally a little curious."

"Are ye through?"

"I believe that was all."

"Good, now ye can introduce me to your father."

"I am nay sure I ought to bring the two of ye too close together," she murmured even as Connor started toward her father, pulling her along with him. "He isnae too happy with you."

"Mayhap not, but I dinnae think he will be waving his sword about, here and now."

When they stopped in front of Sir Eric, Connor was surprised at how slender and short the man was. Sir Eric's person did not hold much threat for Connor. In the man's eyes, however, Connor could see the danger. There lay the truth that, despite his slender elegance and handsome looks, this man would make a deadly enemy. Here was the skill and wit which handily compensated for any lack of height or bulk. This was a man he could learn from, skills he had already seen James display.

"Fither, this is Sir Connor MacEnroy, laird of Deilcladach, and my husband," Gillyanne said, the way the two men stared at each other starting to make her uneasy. "Connor, this is my fither, Sir Eric Murray, laird of Dubhlinn." Although the bow each man gave the other was brief, there was no hint of insult to be seen in either, and she breathed an inner sigh of relief.

Eric glanced over Connor's shoulder. "I fear that my men may grow nervous and wary if that odd clump of people who shadows you shuffles any closer."

"Back up," Connor snapped, not even looking to see if he was obeyed.

It was not easy, but Eric resisted the urge to grin at the way the group stumbled back. "Ye should have come to me first."

"As a lass of twenty with her own lands, I didnae think she needed her father's permission to wed."

"Nay, but *ye* did."

"Fither," Gillyanne murmured, worried about the tension between the two men, but both men ignored her.

"And, ye willnae give it to me now, will ye?" said Connor, reaching out to take Gillyanne's hand back in his.

"Nay, not yet, laddie." Eric looked at their joined hands then at his daughter. "I will come again as soon as I am able."

"Do ye return to Dubhlinn first?" Gillyanne asked, stepping toward her father only to be firmly held back by Connor.

"Aye. Your mother is anxious to hear what I have learned. She may come with me when next I visit."

"If ye come as kinsmen, ye will be welcomed at Deilcladach." Connor ignored the kick on the leg Gillyanne gave him.

"Fair enough."

When her father stepped close enough to kiss her cheek, Gillyanne had to fight Connor's pull on her to receive that kiss. The moment her father straightened up, Connor yanked her back against his side. One would think she was trysting with a lover rather than saying farewell to her father, Gillyanne thought crossly. Connor bowed a farewell before pulling her back toward Deilcladach.

Gillyanne turned as much as she could to wave farewell to her father and frowned when she saw that James was still standing with him. "James? Do ye leave with Fither?" she asked, needing to speak loudly as Connor continued to drag her to his keep.

"Nay, I will be along in a moment," James yelled back, laughing softly at the way Gillyanne was so obviously scolding her husband as he dragged her along. "She will be fine, Fither," James then reassured Eric.

"Aye, I ken it," Eric said and smiled faintly. "I think the lass is far closer to her goal than she kens. Yet, as ye say, the fool may fight the feelings that now cause him to rush her back behind his walls for fear that I might pull her away from him. Gillyanne will, of course, see such actions as nay more than the fool keeping hold of the lands he covets." Eric shook his head before abruptly asking, "Does he ken her skill?"

"Since she cannae use it against him, nay, I dinnae think so. I have mentioned it and it didnae cause any unease."

"Has he kinship with a mon called Sir Neil MacEnroy?"

James' eyes widened. "Aye, Sir Neil is his uncle. Gillyanne doesnae like him, but, then he isnae too friendly and nay fond of women."

"Watch him. I have but met the mon a few times and, although I havenae Gillyanne's skills, the mon gave me a verra bad feeling." Eric briefly clasped the younger

man on the shoulder. "Ye dinnae mind lingering here
'til I can return?"

"Nay, there are things I can show these men. They
are good, dinnae mistake me, but they are mostly lads
who have trained themselves."

Eric nodded. "And, so, they may have a trick or two
ye could learn as weel."

"They do. If the wishes of others count, Gillyanne
will remain. Save for that uncle and the keep's whores,
every mon, woman, and bairn wants our Gilly for their
lady. The whores recently moved to the village and I
will watch the uncle. Since I also intend to try to push
that big fool in the right direction, I have plenty to keep
me busy. Godspeed, Fither." James laughed when, as
Eric and his men rode away, they all drew their swords
to salute Gillyanne who waved at them from the walls.

"They salute her as if she is a warrior," grumbled
Neil, and stomped away before anyone could respond.

Connor frowned slightly as he watched his uncle
climb down from the walls. Neil had not softened toward
Gillyanne at all, had, in fact, gotten angrier and more
derisive with each passing day. Not sure what he could
do about it, Connor turned his attention to his wife who
was leaning over the wall waving her father out of sight.

"That fool lass is going to tumble right o'er the wall,"
Connor muttered as he started toward her.

"Why was your uncle so annoyed by that salute?"
asked Knobby as he followed Connor. "Wheesht, the
lass held off three attacks without spilling a drop of
blood and only surrendered to protect her people.
Deserves a wee salute from her kinsmen."

"My uncle isnae happy about this marriage. I dinnae
ken why he dislikes Gillyanne. It could be that he dislikes
women, sees them as good for but one purpose. He has
ne'er spoken weel of gentle-bred ladies, either. Mayhap

he holds that against her, too. Soon I will have to speak to him. Gillyanne doesnae deserve his poison."

"Nay, she doesnae. What ails the mon?"

"I dinnae ken. I have ne'er heard him be so foul of temper and mouth before."

"Before it was just ye, the lads, and the whores. A wife changes things."

"True." Connor took the last few steps toward Gillyanne a little faster. "Unless that wee wife falls out of the keep." He grasped her around the waist and pulled her back from the walls. "One strong breeze from behind, lass, and ye will be naught but a spot upon the ground. The mon cannae see ye any longer."

"I ken it," Gillyanne said and, when Connor released her, brushed down her skirts. "What was your uncle so cross about?"

Briefly, Connor considered lying, but the way Gillyanne watched him told him she would guess his game. "He didnae like ye getting the sort of salute given to a great warrior."

Gillyanne rolled her eyes as she headed to the narrow steps running down the inside of the wall and leading into the bailey. "That mon doesnae think a lass ought to get anything save a rutting or a knock offside the head," she muttered, and briefly grinned back at Knobby when that man laughed. "I dinnae think I have e'er met such an ill-tempered soul."

Neil was a great deal more than ill-tempered, but Gillyanne had still seen no real need to tell Connor any more than that. Since Connor was so close to his uncle, her *feelings* were simply not enough to accuse or condemn the man. The fact that Neil seemed to have made it his crusade to make her life miserable, and all knew it, telling Connor what she felt could all too easily be viewed as a shallow attempt to banish someone who irritated her. She needed hard proof that Neil was not the friend and helpful elder Connor thought he was.

It would come soon, Gillyanne thought with a mixture of sorrow for Connor's impending pain, and satisfaction that yet another of her *feelings* would be proven accurate. Either the ale and wine he drank could no longer restrain the turmoil within Neil or she had somehow stirred it all up, but the secrets Neil kept were churning inside him with the strength of a flooded river. Gillyanne wondered if Neil knew she could sense the truth about him, that she could read those dark secrets and lies he kept inside, and that was why he was so vicious toward her. That could make him dangerous. A man who held such secrets, and for so long, might be willing to do just about anything to stop them from being exposed to the light.

The fear and unease she had originally sensed in the man was being pushed aside by fury and loathing, both aimed directly at her. Even if she could not tell Connor, Gillyanne decided it might be wise to talk to someone and soon. She was willing to do a lot to spare Connor's feelings, but presenting an easy, unguarded target to a man who might well wish to bury her alongside the secrets he held close, was not one of them.

That thought lingered in her mind and so she was very pleased to see James when he joined her in the herb garden she had returned to work in. "Fither wished ye to stay with me?" she asked him as he stood there surveying her handiwork.

"Nay, not directly," James replied, "but he was most pleased that I chose to stay."

"Connor willnae hurt me. I thought I had made Fither see that."

"He saw it. He also trusts in your instincts about such matters. Nay, he was just pleased ye wouldnae be left alone, without e'en one kinsmon, only two bone lazy cats." He met her admonishing glance with a grin, but quickly grew serious again. "He told me to watch Sir Neil closely."

"Fither kens who Sir Neil is? He has met the mon before?" Gillyanne suspected a meeting would have been all it was for her father would never have the patience or need to deal with a man like Sir Neil.

"Briefly, at court. He bemoaned the fact that he lacks your skill, but he said the mon bore watching. Ye think so, too, dinnae ye."

Gillyanne nodded. "I do. The mon fair crawls with guilt and anger. That anger, and now a goodly dose of loathing, is aimed at me. I think he kens I can see the truth of his black heart and twisted soul."

"And ye think he may attempt to blind ye to it?"

"Aye. Blind me and then bury me—verra deeply."

Chapter Fifteen

"Are ye sure Fiona needs to ken how to dance?" asked Joan as she sat down at the laird's table in the empty great hall.

" 'Tis one of those things all gentle-born lasses are expected to learn," Gillyanne replied.

In the two months since Gillyanne had arrived at Deilcladach, Fiona had begun to look more and more like a young woman. She had yet to show herself outside the bedchamber in a gown, still feeling too awkward. Yet, with her thick fair hair barely restrained by a wide leather tie and her shirts softened by embroidery, Fiona no longer looked nor completely acted like a boy. Gillyanne had noticed many a look of surprise, even interest, in the gazes of the young men of Deilcladach. It was understandable for Fiona was a very lovely girl and would undoubtedly be a stirringly beautiful woman.

"I think I might like dancing," Fiona said. " 'Tis sadly true that many of the things a lady must learn are nay so verra interesting or fun, such as needlework. Yet," she smiled faintly and touched the embroidered flowers on her shirt, " 'tis pretty. The healing arts, the herbs and potions, are verra interesting."

"And ye show a true skill, a sharp instinct that is invaluable," said Gillyanne. "If ye truly have an abiding interest in such things, mayhap ye could visit with my Aunt Maldie or my cousin Elspeth. They are truly skilled healing women." Even if she and Connor parted, Gillyanne suspected she could arrange something like that for Fiona.

"I think I would like that."

"A good healer is certainly something Deilcladach needs," agreed Joan and Mairi nodded as she sat down beside her cousin.

"Weel, I truly believe Fiona will be a verra good one indeed." Gillyanne gave the blushing girl a smile.

"Ye are verra good," said Fiona.

"Good enough. I told ye, all the Murray lasses train under Aunt Maldie whom e'en the mighty Douglases have turned to on occasion. What makes a really skilled healer, however, is a keen eye for what ails a person, a sense of which herb or potion is best, and e'en how to try something new. I think 'tis strong in ye, Fiona. I can oftimes sense where the pain is, or, sadly, near smell death's cold touch, but, I swear, Aunt Maldie can but walk into a room, sniff the air, look at ye for a wee moment, and then ken just what ye need. My senses are nay that keen, but, I think, with training, Fiona's could be."

"Can ye really sense a person's pain or when they are dying?" Fiona asked as she helped Gillyanne move a chair.

Gillyanne inwardly grimaced as she surveyed the space she had cleared to be sure it was enough. She had said too much, but she could not take the words back now. Glancing at the three women, she saw only curiosity, no fear, so decided to be honest. Instinct told her these three would not turn away from her, and it might help to have someone beside James who knew of her odd gift and, she prayed, believed in it. The time might come when she needed a MacEnroy to heed her.

"Aye, I can." Gillyanne sighed and shook her head. "E'en though I am nay a Murray by blood, I seem to have one of those *gifts* that run rampant in the clan. Aunt Maldie does have great skill and knowledge, but she also has the gift of healing. And, she can feel what her husband feels, especially his passion. My cousin Elspeth is like that, too. She took one look at Cormac Armstrong and kenned he was her mate though she was but nine. Animals are drawn to her, e'en the wild ones allowing her to tend a wound. My uncle Nigel has a strong sense of when danger approaches, says he can almost smell it in the air. His daughter Avery is the same. There are others, too. Me, I can feel what others feel. Not all. Others, weel, 'tis nigh on a torment to be near them for I can feel so much. 'Tis as if some people are but a book I can read."

"Can ye do that with us?" asked Joan.

"A wee bit. When I first met ye, I kenned ye were troubled, a trouble of the heart that pained ye. I quickly kenned that Mairi was pining for someone." She grinned when Mairi blushed then grimaced. "In Fiona, I sensed a curiosity. What proves helpful to me, and did then, was that I sensed none of the bad emotions. No anger, jealousy, or mistrust. So, I didnae seek more."

"Can ye guess Connor's feelings?" asked Fiona.

"Nay, hardly at all. As I told my fither, to try to sense anything Connor feels or thinks is like hurling myself against a verra thick wall. In truth, the feelings I can sense best are the ones ye would consider the bad ones—fear, pain, hate, such as that."

"They are the strongest, I suspect."

"Aye, and I think when people feel such emotion, it fills them more, controls them more, than, say, simple contentment." The way Fiona stared at Gillyanne so hard for a moment made her wonder if she had erred in being so truthful.

"What do ye feel when ye are near my uncle?" Fiona suddenly asked.

"I try not to get too close to your uncle," Gillyanne murmured. "Werenae we going to teach ye how to dance?"

"Gillyanne, I really wish to ken what ye feel about my uncle. Ye need nay fear I willnae take it weel. I have no affection for the mon. He has none for me. Often, I feel he forgets I am e'en here. I am but a useless lass, ye ken. I dinnae like the way Connor heeds near everything the mon says, or used to. Oftimes I fear 'tis just jealousy that makes me dislike Uncle Neil. 'Twould be nice to ken that it isnae just that. Ye need nay fear we will repeat anything ye say." Fiona looked at Joan and Mairi, who both nodded their agreement.

"Ah, me. Weel, he hates women." She smiled at the way all three women rolled their eyes. "No skill needed to ken that, eh? I dinnae like him near me because I sense he is seething with anger and fear. He has secrets, dark ones, ones he tries to drown with all that drink he pours down his gullet. There are lies hidden there."

"Ye can sense lies?"

" 'Tis said no one can lie to my cousin Elspeth. 'Tis nay the lie or what the lie is,but a feeling one gets from someone who tells a lie, or, in your uncle's case, tries to hide ones told. 'Tis often easy to tell a person is lying and ye need no great skill to see it. Most people have a way to hide it. A faint blush, an unwillingness to meet your eyes as they speak the lie, or, a certain nervous gesture such as tugging on one's hair. If ye ken a person weel enough, have watched them closely, ye can usually guess when they lie. My cousin Payton doesnae lie much at all, but, when he does, he tugs on his ear. He still cannae understand how I and my cousins always catch him out and, of course, we will ne'er tell him."

Fiona laughed softly, then sighed as she grew serious again. "Sadly, I must agree with all ye have said about my uncle." Joan and Mairi murmured their agreement as well. "There is something, weel, verra wrong with my uncle. I dinnae think Diarmot is verra fond of the mon, either. I have ne'er heard anyone say that the mon has e'er done anything save come round now and again and fill Connor's head with his advice. He has his own lands yet he doesnae appear to have given us any food or coin to help us and he ne'er took any of us to live with him after the killings."

That news stunned Gillyanne. If nothing else, Neil should have sheltered the youngest of the children until there was adequate shelter and food for them all at Deilcladach. "Are ye certain?"

"As certain as I can be without asking everyone directly." Fiona glanced at Joan and Mairi who shook their heads. "No dispute from there, I see. So, he comes, eats, drinks copiously, deafens us with his wisdom, and leaves. Ye would think our uncle, our father's own brother, would occasionally at least work up a wee sweat helping six orphaned children, wouldnae ye?"

"Aye, ye would." Gillyanne knew what Fiona was telling her was important, but it was also far beyond her understanding. "That is news that requires a long, hard think, and I dinnae believe I want to do that right now. Later. I shall set my mind to it, later, and tell ye what conclusions I reach. Now we dance."

"We have no music."

"I shall sing. Softly."

"Ye can sing loudly, if ye wish. We dinnae mind."

"Er, nay. I dinnae wish to draw attention to myself."

Gillyanne sang a tune suited to teach Fiona a slow, stately dance. For a while, she struggled to instruct the younger girl, ignoring the way Fiona paid less and less attention. Joan and Mairi, who had claimed an interest in learning how to dance something more than a rough

jig or reel, made no pretense at all of following her
direction. The way they stood and stared at her began
to embarrass Gillyanne. When Fiona stopped almost
completely, the dancing lesson reduced to Gillyanne
forcibly placing Fiona where she should be, Gillyanne
stopped singing and shook her head.

"Ye were nay paying attention," she gently scolded.

"I was. Weel, to your singing," Fiona said.

"That is verra kind, but . . ."

"Ye sing like an angel."

"Aye, just like Old Nigel said," murmured Joan and
sighed, Mairi echoing the sound.

"This isnae going to work," Gillaynne said. "Mayhap
we can try it without my singing."

"Ye cannae dance without music," Fiona protested.

"I was the only one dancing."

"Fair enough. I swear, I will pay close heed this time.
'Twas just the shock of hearing such a sound coming
out of ye. Now that I ken what ye sound like, I can
appreciate your beautiful singing and follow your
instruction, too. I swear it."

Gillyanne studied her serious face for a moment, then
looked at Joan and Mairi, who quickly nodded their
agreement with Fiona's vow. "If ye are sure, we can try
again. I dinnae want to be dragging ye about again."

"Ye willnae. Come, please, Gillyanne. I truly want to
learn."

Nodding, Gillyanne proceeded to sing. The lesson
began hesitantly enough for her to doubt the strength
of the promises made. Then, as if they also recalled
their promises, the three women began to pay more
attention. By the time they had finished one stumbling
round of the dance, Gillyanne was feeling hopeful. Then
she heard a noise, turned, and found the doors to the
great hall now wide open and crowded with people. She
blushed and closed her eyes.

"What are all ye fools doing here?" bellowed a voice Gillyanne had no trouble recognizing.

"We were listening to the singing," mumbled a bulky red-haired man who quickly disappeared from the doorway.

Connor elbowed his way through the crowd in the doorway, most of the men quickly fleeing. He hoped they were returning to the practice field they had all just slipped away from. One moment his men had been training hard, the next he and Knobby had paused in their swordplay to find themselves alone. The moment the sound of sword striking sword was stilled, Connor heard the singing. With every step he had taken toward the keep, he had forced himself not to be seduced by the sound of her voice. It worked, for the most part, but he had to gently clout Knobby offside the head several times to knock some sense back into the man.

It was not hard to understand what infected his men. Gillyanne had been blessed with a voice that was clear and sweet. And that beautiful sound could carry far, the strength of her voice astounding when one saw how tiny the woman was who made it. It was enthralling, intoxicating. With willpower, however, one could listen to the beauty yet not lose all one's wits. Since he felt it would be a sin to silence her singing, he was going to have to teach his people the sensible way to listen to her.

He frowned at the four females in his great hall. "What are ye doing?"

"I was teaching Fiona, Mairi, and Joan how to dance," Gillyanne replied.

"Why does Fiona need to learn to dance?"

" 'Tis one of those things a lady must learn, Connor," replied Fiona.

"It seems a great waste of time."

"Weel, aye, ofttimes it is," Gillyanne agreed. "In truth, Fiona may ne'er need the skill. On the other hand, if she goes to some great house, or e'en to court, she will have use of it, could e'en look poorly against other lasses if she doesnae have any skills in the dances."

Connor opened his mouth to say there was little chance any MacEnroy would be invited to any grand keep or the king's court, then shut it. Now that he was married to Gillyanne, he was no longer one of three small, unheralded lairds living in lands remote enough to escape the attention of most people. He did not know all of her connections, but each new tale she told made him increasingly certain that her kinsmen were neither unheralded nor remote from the world. Fiona could well find herself thrust into a world he had never been a part of and knew little about.

"Ye must do it here?" he asked, fearing he faced hours of constantly forcing his men back to work.

"I thought we would be private. Mayhap to that field outside the walls? 'Twould be private in most ways, but we could still be seen."

His first thought was to deny her. Then he realized there was no need to do so except for his own fears. Robert would not try to grab her again and the man had assured him that David had no interest in even trying. There had been no reports of strangers or thieves in the area. Since someone might question why he had said nay when all looked safe, he decided to let her go despite the unease he felt. She would not go outside the walls alone, however.

"Ye can go, but Knobby and Diarmot will go with ye. Your cousin as weel, if he wishes."

"That isnae verra private," she protested, but only gently, for she knew such a guard was common for the ladies of the keep.

"Private enough."

Within moments, Gillyanne, Fiona, Joan, and Mairi were walking toward a softly grassed field with Knobby, Diarmot, and James walking behind them. A part of

Gillyanne was disgruntled over her quick surrender to Connor's commands, but good sense helped keep that ill feeling from growing. No Murray man would allow his lady out unguarded. It was hardly fair to be annoyed with Connor for doing something her family would heartily approve of.

"Here is a good spot," Gillyanne announced, stopping in the middle of the small field and looking around.

"It should be easy enough to keep an eye on ye here," said James. "Diarmot and I will walk the edges."

"Actually, James, I was hoping ye would sing."

"Ah, sweet, ye must nay let the avid appreciation of others silence that fine voice."

Gillyanne grimaced. " 'Tis embarrassing, but that isnae why I asked ye to sing. 'Tis nay easy to teach a dance and sing the tune one dances to at the same time. If ye sing the tune I need, I can lead the dance. Once the steps are learned, I can sing as we practice."

"Diarmot and I will walk the ground," Knobby said. "Try to nay squawk too loudly." He laughed and easily avoided James' half-hearted attempt to swat him. "We shouldnae be long."

As the still chuckling Diarmot and Knobby walked away, Gillyanne looked at her grinning cousin and realized James had made some good friends at Deilcladach. It did not surprise her for James was a very likable young man. She just hoped her decision about Connor, if it resulted in the end of her marriage, would not also end his friendships. Soon to be a laird himself, he could use all the friends and allies he could gather.

After discussing what she wanted to teach Fiona, Gillyanne and James agreed on the songs he would sing. He began to sing the first song and Gillyanne started to instruct her small group in the steps of the dance. It went a lot more smoothly. James had a lovely, clear voice, but it did not have the same effect upon the dancers as hers had. After a brief moment of silent appreciation, the women finally paid full attention to her, and Gillyanne was pleased to see a natural grace in all three women. It would make teaching them the dances easier, even a pleasure.

Amidst a great deal of laughter, Gillyanne pulled Diarmot and Knobby into the lessons after they returned. Gillyanne subtlety made certain Knobby and Mairi were paired and shared a conspiratorial wink with Joan as the two blushing young people stumbled their way through the dance. She hoped this short time of forced proximity would allow the shy Mairi to convey her interest in Knobby, and the uncertain Knobby to see it and act upon it.

"I dinnae think I am verra good at this," Knobby said as he stumbled to a halt, then sent a friendly scowl toward a chuckling James.

"No one is at the beginning," Gillyanne assured him. "When James learned to dance we offered to tie a pillow to his backside because he fell on it so often."

"Cruel woman," James protested, but he laughed along with the others. "What finally saved me from continued humiliation, Knobby, was that I made myself think of it as sword fighting. I told myself I wasnae trying to learn some prancing steps to impress a lass; I was learning a new, deadly way to fight."

Gillyanne was about to say that was the most foolish thing she had ever heard when she saw the looks on Diarmot's and Knobby's faces. It obviously made perfect sense to the men. If it helped them learn to dance, then she supposed it was useful. Gillyanne just wished their expressions had not altered to suit their thoughts, becoming hard and intense. They certainly did not look like men given a perfect chance to flirt with a lass. As the dance began again, Gillyanne faced a highly amused Joan and knew the woman was fighting laughter as hard as she was.

* * *

"What is Diarmot doing?" asked Angus as he joined Connor on the walls and followed his gaze toward the group in the field.

"I believe he is learning how to dance," replied Connor.

"Why would he want to do that?"

"My wife says 'tis something expected of the highborn. It seems 'tis done at some keeps and at court."

"I have ne'er seen dancing at the earl of Dinnock's keep."

"Nay, but we have only been there twice and neither time was a festive occasion. Gillyanne and James have both been to court, and, I suspect, have been at much grander entertainments than we have."

"Oh." Angus frowned at the scene in the field. "Do ye think we all ought to learn?"

Connor shrugged. "Perhaps. I was standing here thinking that, some day, ye lads will marry. I now have something to offer Diarmot as a living, as my mon at Ald-dabhach, but I have naught for the rest of you."

"We dinnae need anything, Connor."

"I ken it and 'tis good ye could be content with living here or at Ald-dabhach, but then I saw that ye, Drew, and Nanty might be able to gain land through marriage as I did. To find the lasses with coin or land, ye will have to go to keeps like the earl's or e'en the king's court. Ye will also have to show weel against lads who have more to offer than a bonny face and good blood."

Angus nodded. "A wee bit of refinement, a few courtly skills."

"Exactly. Ye have all been blessed with strong bodies and looks the lasses seem to like. Add a wee touch of the courtier, which the lasses also seem to like, and ye could make a good marriage."

"Is that what ye plan for Fiona? Have ye a mon already in mind for the lass?"

"I fear I didnae realize how near she was to being a woman, so, nay, I havenae chosen anyone," replied Connor. "As I stood here watching her, I recalled many a thing my wee wife told me and I think I will let Fiona choose for herself."

"Nay. Truly?"

"Aye, truly. I will keep a watch on who courts her and hold the right to try to stop what I might see as a bad marriage, but who she weds will be her choice. I want her happiness more than I want gain from her marriage. If she gains these skills, the ways most weel-bred ladies learn from birth, it will give her a wider choice. Instinct tells me that, when Fiona is of an age to wed, Gillyanne's family will help see that the lass gets to the places that will give her good choices and a lot of them."

Angus grinned and winked at his older brother. "I was thinking your wee wife's family would offer we unwed lads a wider choice of bonny lasses to woo."

Connor chuckled. "By the time the lass gets through listing all the names of her kin by blood or by marriage, it does seem as if she is related to half of Scotland. When I sought this bride, my eye was set on Ald-dabhach. Now I realize there was e'en more to gain than the land. We have many a new ally, Angus. Aye, they may not be large powerful clans like the Campbells or the Douglases, but we are nay longer alone. I may need to soothe a few angry feelings, but the bond is now there, strengthening *us* ."

"Sweet Mary, of course. I ne'er thought of it. And, aye, recalling how angry her father looked, ye will have to do some soothing. After all, if James spoke true, this marriage of yours could be ended."

"Gillyanne wouldnae end our marriage," Connor said with far more confidence than he really felt.

"Ye tell me how it would be a good idea to learn a courtier's ways to woo a dowered lass, yet ye dinnae follow your own advice."

"What do ye mean?"

"I mean, ye might try wooing your wife a wee bit, more than making her bellow with pleasure. Ye are a hard, solemn fellow, Connor, and," he looked at the dancers in the field, "your wee wife is full of the joy of life. She has had the freedom to enjoy all the things we ne'er have, from dancing to simple jests amongst kin. She needs warmth, Connor. I think she has been fair surrounded by it for her whole life."

"Do ye expect me to become some simpering flatterer?"

"Och, nay. I dinnae think ye could be that nay matter how hard ye tried. All I say is that ye ken she has a way to escape you, so ye should look close at what ye need to do to make her wish to stay. I dinnae think Gillyanne would want ye to be something ye arenae and dinnae want to be. But, would it really be so hard to say a kind word now and then, to talk to her outside the bedchamber, or tell her she looks bonny? Isnae she worth a little effort?"

Connor stared at the dancers in the field and considered Angus' words. It would appear that the threat to his marriage was well known to his family, that James' words had been heard and considered. Gillyanne had a bolthole and his family was obviously worried that he would push her to take it.

The problem was, he was not sure he knew how to woo Gillyanne or even if he should. According to his uncle, he was doing all a man should do for his wife— housing her, clothing her, feeding her, and breeding her. Although it felt disloyal, Connor had to admit that he was beginning to see that his uncle was not really the worldly expert he claimed to be. In truth, the last time his uncle had pontificated on what a wife was due and how to treat her, Connor had found himself thinking that the man might as well have been advising him on the care of a horse.

His biggest concern about trying to woo Gillyanne, about showing her some softness or care, was that a little could too easily become a lot. If he opened the door to his heart even a little, she could slip right inside. Connor feared she may have already done so, but, by keeping some distance between them, he could shore up his defenses during the day.

However, the threat that his marriage could be ended was a real one. Angus was just one of several who had felt compelled to advise him, had noticed that he needed to do something more if he wished to keep his wife. If he was cautious, he suspected he could do a few things without exposing himself too much. He had noticed how much cleaner and more comfortable his keep was now, and it would cost him little to compliment or thank her for that. He complimented and praised his men on jobs well done; it would not appear weak of him to do the same for his wife. As he considered the matter, he was able to think of other compliments that could be given without making him look soft or like some lovesick fool.

Just as he opened his mouth to tell Angus of his decision, his full attention was caught by the people in the field. They had all stopped and were staring at Gillyanne. A heartbeat later, she slowly collapsed. Connor heard himself bellow out a strange agonized cry even as he raced down from the walls.

Chapter Sixteen

The arrow came out of nowhere. Gillyanne felt something slam into her back, pushing her toward Diarmot who now faced her in the dance. She steadied herself and watched all the color fade from his face. James had ceased to sing. The others had all stopped as if turned to stone and stared at her in shock. Just as the pain struck, she saw everyone start to move. Knobby hurled Mairi to the ground, shielding her with his body. Joan did the same with Fiona. Diarmot reached for her and Gillyanne heard a strange noise come from the keep, like some animal in pain, as she felt all the strength seep out of her legs. She had almost completely collapsed upon the ground when Diarmot pushed her flat onto her stomach and shielded her with his body. Gillyanne looked to her side and met James' worried gaze.

"I have something in my back, dinnae I?" she said to James.

"Aye, an arrow," he replied even as he searched the surrounding wood for some sign of their enemy.

"Where is it?"

"High on your left shoulder."

"Shouldnae be mortal then. What was that noise?"

"What noise?"

"A roar of some kind. Sounded like a wounded bull."

"I think it may have been your husband." James looked toward the keep. "He is racing this way with near half the keep at his heels."

"Oh, dear, this will make him cross," she whispered and gave into the blackness that had been creeping up on her.

Connor fell to his knees beside Gillyanne as his men spread out to search the surrounding wood. Even as he had raced to her side, he had seen enough to know his men would find no army. He would try to decide what that meant later. For now, the sight of that arrow sticking out of Gillyanne's slim back held all his attention. He reached to pull it out.

"Nay," cried Fiona and she scrambled out from beneath Joan just in time to grab Connor's wrist and halt his move.

"The arrow must be removed," Connor said.

"Aye, but nay that way. We must push it through, cut off the head, then yank it out."

"That will be an agony!"

"Aye, but if ye pull it out as ye were about to, most times ye can do far more damage." Fiona touched Gillyanne's cheek with trembling fingers. "She explained it all to me. We must get her back to the keep where the herbs, water, and clean linens are."

Despite the sorrow and fear that made Fiona's voice tremble, Connor heard enough confidence in what she said to accept her word. He also heard no protest from James. As gently and carefully as he was able, he lifted Gillyanne into his arms and stood up.

"Connor," protested Diarmot even as, he too, stood up—"Is it safe?"

"Aye," replied Connor as he strode toward the keep

as fast as he dared, not wishing to add to Gillyanne's pain with the bouncing a hard run would cause. "There is no army or raiding party in the wood."

"Jesu. 'Twas murder."

"An attempt. Only an *attempt*," Connor snapped, refusing to consider any possibility other than Gillyanne's swift recovery.

Nothing more was said as they all retreated to the keep. Connor took Gillyanne to their bedchamber. Fiona was pale as the cleanest linen, but her hands and voice were steady as she snapped out orders. He held Gillyanne as the arrow was removed, feeling his belly clench as she screamed despite her unconsciousness.

"Save the arrow," he ordered and stepped out of the room to speak to one of the men who had already returned from searching the wood.

Connor was not surprised to hear that the only signs found were of one man and they had been impossible to follow. He stared at the crossbow the man gave him and had to fight the urge to immediately throw it in the fire. It might help them find the one who had tried to murder his wife. It was a weapon not many would own. After dismissing the man, Connor stepped back inside the bedchamber and set the crossbow down next to the arrow.

He watched in something close to amazement as his sister worked. Joan, Mairi, and even James responded to Fiona's commands without question or hesitation. It was apparent that Fiona had not only learned her lessons about healing, but had a true skill. Despite the cold fear he felt for Gillyanne, Connor experienced a sense of pride over the woman Fiona was becoming.

When Fiona had done all she could, she dismissed Joan and Mairi. She washed up and sank into a chair James set by the bed. After one long look at Gillyanne, Fiona covered her face with her hands. Connor moved to her side and stroked her hair.

"Ye did weel, lass," he said. "I am proud of ye."

"*This* I ken," she said as she lifted her head and wiped the tears from her cheeks. "I but pray she doesnae get an infection for we had only just begun the lessons on how to treat that."

"Ne'er fear, lass," James said. "We can always send for my aunt Maldie or cousin Elspeth. And, Gillyanne is stronger than she looks. A verra fast healer is our Gilly."

Fiona nodded, clearly taking heart from James' words. "Oh, Connor, who would try to kill our Gilly?"

"That is something I would dearly like to ken," muttered James.

"As would I," said Connor. "We have the weapons. They can help us find the bastard."

"Do ye think it was a Goudie or a Dalglish?" asked Fiona.

"Nay, but I will search amongst them."

"Weel, Robert did kidnap her, try to steal her from ye."

"True, but he didnae hurt her. I ken that Gillyanne lashed him hard with the sharp side of her tongue, but he didnae touch her. He also returned her without a fight. Robert had been led to believe he could alter the choice she had made. That is all he sought. He also assured me that I didnae need to worry about Sir David causing me any trouble. Nay, this wasnae ordered by either of them, but that doesnae mean there isnae some rogue in their midst who took Gillyanne's choice as a personal insult."

"I think it was someone closer," said James. "Someone near enough to watch and wait for a perfect chance to strike."

"Which would make the killer one of my own," Connor said quietly, unable to dispute the logic of James' reasoning.

"Aye, for a stranger lurking about would soon be

noticed. That would include any enemies ye might have as weel as any who might seek to hurt the Murrays. E'en if the Goudie and Dalglish clansmen are nay your enemies, I would think one of them lingering in the area would also be noticed."

"I ken it."

"But, why?" Fiona asked. "Why try to kill Gillyanne?"

"A good question, lass." Connor brushed his fingers over Fiona's pale cheek, finally seeing that his young sister had grown very close to his wife. "If I can find an answer to it, I think I can find the bastard who tried to kill Gillyanne. The why would point to the who, ye see. Sadly, I cannae think of any reason at all for someone to want to hurt Gillyanne. It cannae stop me from having an heir. I already have four and no one has tried to kill our brothers. No one can gain her lands. They would come to me or be returned to her own kinsmen. She hasnae spurned any lover." Connor glanced at James who shook his head. "So, it cannae be jealousy. Every reason I can think of just doesnae make sense when applied to her."

"Ye have spurned a lover," Fiona said quietly. "One who has already tried to make trouble between ye and Gilly."

"Meg? She was angry, but angry enough to lurk about, weapon in hand? Where would she get a crossbow and what could she have thought to gain e'en had she succeeded?"

"Your bed would be empty again," James said, but he sounded uncertain.

"Aye, but I wouldnae fill it with a whore who had betrayed me as Meg did," replied Connor. "And she kens it."

"Hate and anger," said Fiona, nodding when both men looked at her. "Meg had a verra good life here. She did no work and was the laird's woman. She had power o'er the other women, too. 'Tis all gone now.

She ne'er liked Gillyanne and I wouldnae be surprised if the woman hates her now. May hate ye as weel, Connor. Why do ye look so uncertain?'' she demanded when both men just frowned at her. ''Ye dinnae think a woman can hate strongly enough to want to kill someone? Or, do ye find it hard to think any woman could kill another? Mayhap she didnae do it herself, but I suspect she has the skills to seduce some fool into doing it for her.''

''I willnae ignore the chance that it is her,'' Connor assured Fiona. ''I ignored her before and she betrayed me. I am nay fool enough to ignore her again. Howbeit, first I will talk to Sir Robert and Sir David. Sir Robert warned me that there was another I should watch for, aside from Meg, but wouldnae tell me who. Mayhap now he will. 'Tis also proof that, sometimes, one's friends and allies ken more than ye do.''

''Go then,'' Fiona said. ''I can watch Gillyanne and Joan and Mairi will help. Ye can do naught here but wait.''

''I will stay,'' said James. ''If anything happens that Fiona cannae deal with, I can hie to my kinsmen and get help.''

Connor did not want to leave, yet he knew he should. It could be a long wait before they knew whether Gillyanne would worsen or improve. In that time, her attacker could easily flee beyond their reach. Unless word of what had happened and what he sought was quickly spread, people would forget what they had seen or heard, things that could prove important. There were dozens of reasons to set out on the trail of Gillyanne's attacker right now, but he ached to stay at her side.

''Find me if anything goes wrong,'' he commanded and forced himself to leave after shoving the crossbow and the arrow into a sack.

''How fares Gillyanne?'' demanded Diarmot as he and Knobby met Connor at the bottom of the stairs.

''Resting,'' replied Connor. ''The arrow has been

removed, the wound cleaned, stitched, and bound. Fiona watches o'er her.''

"Fiona?" Diarmot frowned up the stairs, his expression one of uncertainty.

"If ye could have seen her making e'en Sir James leap to her command, seen the calm yet swift way she worked, ye would realize our wee sister shows promise of being a most excellent healer. All we must fear is infection, for Fiona freely adnmits she kens little about that yet, having only just begun her lessons in it. Sir James comes from a clan with reknowned healing women and he showed no doubt in our Fiona. Joan and Mairi will also help.''

"But ye willnae stay at your wife's bedside?"

There was no condemnation in Diarmot's tone, only curiosity, so Connor replied calmly, "If I wait too long to hunt down the coward who did this, he could slip my grasp forever. So, nay, I go ahunting. First, we speak with our allies." He strode out of the keep and headed for the stables, Diarmot and Knobby close behind.

"I cannae believe it was one of them," said Knobby. "They would gain naught but a renewal of the feud we have all worked long and hard to bury—verra deeply."

"Aye, I ken it, but they ken things. Leastwise, Robert does. When I rescued him from Gillyanne," he exchanged a brief grin with his two companions, "he said things meant to warn me. He wouldnae be precise for he said he couldnae accuse anyone when all he had was little more than rumor. If naught else, he can tell me those cursed rumors and suspicions now.''

"Nay, I willnae give ye a name," protested Robert, warily watching a coldly furious Connor pace near his chair in the great hall. "Ye want someone dead, Connor, and I willnae give ye a victim when I have nay proof of his guilt.''

"Curse it, Robbie," Connor slammed his fist down on the table, "if I dinnae catch the bastard who did this, he could try again, and next time he might succeed."

"Ye dinnae think he has this time?" Robert asked quietly.

"Nay. The wound was high and quickly tended to. If there is no fever or putrefaction, Gillyanne will be fine. Her cousin claims she is stronger than she looks."

"Humph. That wee lass is finely honed steel and her tongue is sharper than any sword. God's bones, that makes ye smile? I dinnae think I have e'er seen ye do so, nay for longer than I can recall. Weel, mayhap some men like a spirited wife."

"Irritating as it can be at times, 'tis a mettle I wish bred into my bairns." He almost smiled again at the arrested look that briefly touched Robert's face then quickly grew serious again. "I would like the lass to live long enough to give me some."

"As do I," Robert assured him. "I have learned something of her kinsmen and it can only benefit me if one of my allies has close blood ties to them. It may gall me at times to ride your tail to gain, but I am nay such a fool as to let pride stop me."

"I havenae given her kinsmen's influence much thought."

"Nay, ye wouldnae."

"Robbie, *I want a name!*"

Robert shook his head. "Nay. I will tell ye this, however. Look to your whore."

"I dinnae have a whore," snapped Connor. "I have nay need of one. I have a wife now." Connor felt as surprised as Robert looked at his fierce declaration for he realized he meant it; he wanted no other woman.

"Meg betrayed ye once," Robert said. "Did ye think her anger would end because ye kicked her out of Deil-cladach?"

Connor tossed the sack with the weapons onto the

table. " 'Twas a crossbow, Robbie. A mon's weapon. I ken Meg weel enough to feel sure she wouldnae have the strength to use it nor the knowledge. And, 'tis nay a weapon easily found.'' He was keenly disappointed when Robert looked at the weapons and clearly did not recognize them.

"I didnae say she did it. Connor, 'tis said your wee wife can see into a person's soul, that she can read a mon like a book. 'Tis said she can look at a person and ken all of his secrets.'' Robert shrugged. "At first I ignored the whispers. She is a stranger, an outsider, despite having married you. Such people always have others whispering about them. Then, when she was here . . .''

"What?'' demanded Connor when Robert fell silent. "What happened?''

"She saw something in me that I ken weel could neither be seen upon my face nor heard in my words.'' He shook his head. "The lass stared at me for a moment then told me exactly what lay in my heart. And then I kenned the whispers were true.''

"What did she see?''

"Ye dinnae deny her skill, do ye.''

"Her cousin told me she has a skill at, weel, sensing things and that I should heed any warning she gives me about a person.'' Connor frowned. "I cannae believe he told many people this. How could such whispers begin?''

"From the ones ye have angered. And, one who has many a secret to hide, the sorts of secrets one would kill to keep hidden. Aye, if one kens she senses the secrets are there, 'tis but a short leap to believing she can see what they are. She kenned mine. I was at my most charming.'' He smiled when Connor scowled. "Your wife kenned it was all false, that beneath my flattery and wooing was an ugly truth—I couldnae stomach the thought of bedding a lass ye had bedded. Och, dinnae look offended. 'Tisnae like I fear ye are diseased or the like. Nay, 'tis just pride, mayhap vanity. Mayhap I dinnae wish to hear any comparisons made. Although, I havenae heard it said that ye are any great lover.''

Connor placed a hand upon his chest and smiled faintly. "I can make my wife bellow."

"Aye, he can," agreed a grinning Knobby. "Bellow fit to shake the walls."

"How indiscreet." Robert laughed softly and shook his head, but quickly grew serious again. "Someone fears your wee wife's skills, fears she will expose truths he prefers to keep buried. That someone is the one ye want. And, I say, look to Meg, for those who share a grievance, and an enemy, real or nay, ofttimes stick together."

"I will speak to Sir David then go to Meg," Connor said, infuriated that Robert still refused to utter any names, but knowing nothing would get the man to change his mind.

"David didnae have anything to do with this."

"I ken it. Howbeit, if ye have seen and heard things I havenae, mayhap he has, too."

"True, yet dinnae get too angry if he doesnae ken that he can help ye. David isnae verra keen-witted. If he has heard or seen something, he may simply nay realize that it is important."

Connor nodded, knowing Robert was right. David was a strong fighter, a warrior of unquestionable strength and courage. He could also choke on his own pride and be dimwitted enough at times to make one ache to kick him. Nevertheless, he would talk to the man. Gillyanne's life was threatened. He could not ignore any chance of discovering *who* threatened her. Connor also knew that, if David had a name or two to put forth, the man would not hesitate to do so. David would not concern himself with the consequences for doing so, either; would probably not even consider the possibility that he might give out the wrong name.

With Robert's good wishes for Gillyanne still ringing in his ears, Connor headed toward Sir David's keep. He rode hard, eager to talk to those he needed to as swiftly as possible so that he could return to Deilcladach. The danger of Gillyanne's wound, the threat of fever or infection, was something he could not push from his thoughts. He had to keep up a vigorous search for the one who had attacked her, but he also knew he had to keep as close a watch on her as he was able.

She had become important to him, Connor realized. Very important. When the threat to her was banished, he knew he would have to look closely at what he felt and what he would do about it. Somehow he was going to have to find a way to give Gillyane enough to make her want to stay with him, yet not let the feelings she stirred within him weaken him in any way. The strength and survival of his clan had to be the most important thing to him and for that he had to keep *himself* strong. Even more important, he had to *appear* strong, in complete control, and with no weaknesses, physically or emotionally. At the moment, however, such deep thinking and careful strategy were beyond him. He was afraid for Gillyanne and filled with rage at the one who had hurt her.

Sir David had to be knocked down twice before he realized Connor did not appreciate hearing any comment that even hinted at an insult to Gillyanne. The man was clearly still angry over the defeat he had suferred at Gillyanne's small hands. It was far past time the man ceased to sulk about it.

"Enough, Connor," grumbled David as he sat down at the laird's table in his great hall and poured himself an ale. "Sit. Drink." He nodded when Connor sat down and helped himself to an ale. "I will hold my tongue, though 'tis cursed hard. The lass embarrassed me."

"She embarrassed all of us and 'tis mostly our own fault," Connor said.

"And how did ye come to that conclusion?"

"We were arrogant, thought defeating a wee lass would be something we could do with our eyes closed."

"Mayhap," David grudgingly agreed. "Cannae blame a mon for being annoyed. I wouldnae try to kill the lass because of it, though."

"I ken it. Ye wouldnae creep through the shadows to kill anyone, let alone a wee lass. Nay, what I seek now is information. Robbie has heard things, has suspicions, but willnae give me names."

David nodded. "He has talked to me of it a wee bit, but wouldnae tell me any names, either. Robbie is a cautious mon, ye ken. Needs more proof, always more proof. Will ne'er accept rumor as enough e'en if it fair deafens a person. I am nay so precise which is why he wouldnae tell me. Kenned I would see naught wrong with telling you, e'en if he had advised against it." David shrugged. " 'Tis nay such a bad thing. Rumor isnae always set in truth. After all, I have heard a few about your wee wife."

"Such as what? The same as what Robbie has heard?"

"Dinnae ken. The whispers I have heard say your wee wife can see into a mon's soul. She can tell what secrets a mon hides in his heart. Men dinnae like that sort of thing. Tisnae a good thing to have whispered about one. It can make people start to think on the devil and witches. Ye might want to silence that nonsense. Unless, of course, 'tis true."

Connor inwardly cursed, but replied clamly, "Gillyanne has no magic, just a keen eye, mayhap a more, weel, sensitive nature. She may e'en have a keener ear. A mon cannae hide everything. He gives away things in how he acts, looks, or speaks. Most of us dinnae see it unless 'tis clear and strong. My wife just needs a whisper of it. As I said, no magic, no devil, just a useful skill. If she kenned *what* the secrets were, that would be magic. Just kenning a mon is hiding something isnae.''

''Aye, ye are right. Sounds a verra fine skill to have.'' David frowned and rubbed his chin, wincing faintly as his hand passed over one of the bruises Connor had given him. ''Still, the rumors started somewhere. Ye have to wonder where and why.''

''Robbie told me to talk to my leman Meg.''

''Why do ye have a leman? Ye have a wife now.''

It was hard, but Connor hid his surprise over David's shock and the distinct condemnation in his voice. Connor forced himself not to look at Diarmot or Knobby, knowing their expressions might cause him to actually laugh. The very last man he would have expected such an attitude from was David. The man had bedded most of the lasses on his lands and had bred a horde of bastards.

''Nay, I dinnae have a leman now. Howbeit, e'en though I put Meg out of my bed when I married, it was a while ere I was forced by Meg's betrayal to put her out of Deilcladach. She was angry and could think to avenge herself by causing trouble for Gillyanne. Meg would have needed some mon as an ally, however, to try and kill my wife, for Meg couldnae shoot a crossbow, nor would she have such a weapon, nor would she have kenned where to get one.''

''Weel, this Meg may not have shot the arrow, but 'tis clear to me she sought to see your wife dead. Accusing a lass of being a witch, e'en gently through rumors, could mean that lass's death, couldnae it?''

David's unusually astute observation kept Connor silent and deep in thought all the way back to his lands. Robert had called the rumors about Gillyanne common of the things said about strangers, but David was right. They were dangerous whispers, the sort that got people killed. That concerned him, but what concerned him even more was that, yet again, something private, something not known by everyone at Deilcladach, had been spread about outside its walls. What tied his insides into aching knots was the certainty that Meg had not known of Gillyanne's skills before she had been ordered out of Deilcladach. Someone had told her after she had left and, out of those people who knew, only one had been to see Meg in her cottage.

"I will go alone to speak to Meg," he told Diarmot and Knobby.

"But, if she is a part of this . . ." began Diarmot.

"Then she will pay. I can defend myself against her, not that I think e'en she is fool enough to strike out at me when all the village will have seen me go to her cottage." Connor stared at the village. "I willnae be long."

"Good. Be quick. And careful."

As he rode to Meg's cottage, Connor fought the conclusions that kept forming in his mind. They were traitorous, ungrateful, even painful. Unfortunately, they also answered far too many questions. Once at the cottage, Connor wanted to turn his mount back toward Deilcladach and hie for home. Inside could lie a truth that could tear him apart. He stiffened his spine as he dismounted. Telling himself a painful truth was better than more lies and a continued threat to Gillyanne, he stepped into the cottage.

The smell of blood weighted the air. Cautiously, drawing his sword as quietly as he could, Connor began to search the cottage. He stopped abruptly, and cursed over the sight that met him in the bedchamber at the top of the narrow stairs. His uncle was sprawled across the tangled sheets of a bed, a tankard still clutched in his hand as he stared sightlessly at the thick beams in the roof. The man's body was covered in blood. Someone had stabbed Neil many times, the final, and probably the truly mortal wound, was a direct blow to the heart. And Connor saw that that death blow had been struck with his own dagger.

Connor tossed his sword onto the bed next to his uncle. There would be no answers now, he mused as he closed the man's eyes, at least not the ones he now craved. He pulled his dagger from the man's chest, straightened up, and stilled as he felt three sword tips touch his back.

"I really didnae think ye would be fool enough to come back for your knife," said a deep voice Connor recognized as belonging to Peter MacDonal, the earl of Dinnock's sergeant of arms.

"I didnae kill the mon," Connor said, not really surprised when his claim of innocence did not stop the earl's men from disarming him and tying his hands behind his back.

"Ye can tell your tale to the earl."

As he was led out of the cottage, Connor caught sight of Knobby's sister and mother. He curtly told them what was happening and ordered them to tell his brothers and Knobby. Then he calmly allowed the earl's men to lead him away, knowing he had no other reasonable choice.

Chapter Seventeen

There was a chill in the air of the great hall of Dinnock. Connor suspected a lot of it came from the cold-eyed man he now faced. It was the earl's duty to deal out justice in his lands, but it was well known that the man did not appreciate being bothered by such troubles. Worse, the man took great pride in his cleanliness and appearance. After having spent much of the day in the saddle, riding hard after the truth, Connor would not be surprised if his muddied appearance, even the smell of sweat and horse that clung to him, offended his liege lord. Neither offense would help his cause, no matter what excuse was offered for unwillingly disturbing the earl's peace and probably his nose.

"Did ye get like that trying to flee my men?" asked the earl

"Nay, m'laird. I didnae fight your men at all," replied Connor. "I fear my sad state was caused by riding near all the day long as I sought the villian who tried to kill my wife."

"Is she dead?" Lord Dunstan MacDonal frowned, looking honestly worried.

"Nay, not when I left to begin my search."

"Good. We dinnae need the cursed Murrays or any of her other kinsmen coming round seeking retribution. So, ye killed Sir Neil because he tried to murder your new wife."

"I didnae kill my uncle." Although the insinuation that he would kill an aging, unarmed, quite possibly drunken, man was an insult, Connor fought the anger rising inside him. "If naught else, I needed him alive. I had questions only he could answer."

"Your dagger was found stuck into the mon's heart." The earl looked at the dagger that had been set upon the table in front of him and lightly drew his long finger over the ornate Celtic designs drawn into the handle. "E'en I recall this weapon from one of your rare visits here. 'Tis verra fine work and verra old."

"It has been passed down from father to son, laird to laird, since the first MacEnroy claimed the lands of Deilcladach."

"A piece ye wouldst take great care of."

"Aye. I kept it in my chambers, bringing it out only for important occasions, such as when I came here. 'Tis too valuable, one of the few pieces of my history to have survived the destruction wrought in the feuding, to be used as a common dagger. The fact that I bring it out so rarely is, undoubtedly, why I didnae ken it had been stolen."

Lord Dunstan studied him carefully, still lightly stroking the dagger handle. "Ye would have us believe it was stolen?"

"Aye." Connor knew that, question by question, the earl was going to try hard to lead him into a confession. He could only pray that the truth would be enough to keep him out of any trap the earl might set.

"And ye just happened to be at the cottage at that precise moment."

"Aye. I had already been to talk to Sir Robert Dalglish and Sir David Goudie. What they told me sent me to speak with the woman who lives there. I had also planned to speak with my uncle, but I hadnae thought to find him there."

"Nay at the cottage of your leman, certainly."

Connor decided he would advise his sons to be more restrained, more discreet, in the venting of their fleshly hungers. His past was proving to be far more of a complication to his present than those moments of fleeting pleasure had been worth. It began to look as if one particular piece of the past could easily get him hanged.

"Meg *was* my leman, m'laird," Connor replied. "I put her aside when I married the Lady Gillyanne Murray."

The earl nodded. "Your wife objected to your leman being so close at hand so ye set the woman up in that cottage."

"Aye, my wife objected to me bedding another, but she gave me sound reasons for that objection. She also showed me that I had no need for Meg's rough skills. I *chose* to set the woman aside. The moment the woman was nay longer my lover other problems came to my attention. Meg did no work, caused dissension and unhappiness amongst the rest of the women, was openly contemptuous of and disrespectful to my lady wife, and, finally, betrayed me."

"We were told that ye blamed the woman for Sir Robert's rash actions toward your wife." He frowned at Connor. "Ye told us nothing, yet kidnapping a laird's wife is a serious crime."

"Ye have probably heard the tale of how I came to be married." The earl nodded and Connor was pleased he would not be pressed to relate that complicated and somewhat embarrassing story. "Meg told Sir Robert the private doings of my keep and kin to make him believe

my wife's choice could be altered. There is a way my wife
and her kin could end the marriage. Robbie thought to
woo my wife into discarding me and marrying him. He
didnae hurt my wife and he didnae fight me when I
came to take her back. I felt it was but an error of
judgment that could be kept between us.''

" 'Twould be a fine thing if other lairds could solve
their problems with such calm reason,'' murmured the
earl.

"We ken all too weel the high cost of doing otherwise,
m'laird.''

"Of course. Yet the woman relayed but a wee piece
of gossip. Nay such a great betrayal.''

"She purposely went to Sir Robert and told him
exactly what was needed to cause trouble for my wife.
Aye, Sir Robert is an ally and the trouble proved to be
a wee one. That doesnae lessen the crime. Meg told
someone outside of Deilcladach our private business
simply to gain something for herself or for revenge. I
saw no reason to give her a second chance, to risk her
telling some enemy e'en more important secrets. I was
going to cast her out into some hovel, but decided an
empty cottage in the village was better for I could send
her two cohorts with her. After all, they had kenned
what game Meg was playing, but kept silent, giving their
loyalty to her rather than to their laird.''

"I would have been harsher in my punishment, if
what ye say is true. Peter, give Sir Connor some wine,''
the earl ordered his second in command. "I have more
to ask him. We would nay wish his voice to dry up, would
we.''

Connor accepted the drink of wine despite having to
be fed it sip by sip by Peter, as his hands remained
bound. The greatest problem with being accused of
something, Connor decided, was the need to prove he
was the one speaking the truth. It angered him to have
his every word doubted, yet he had to suppress that

fury. The earl had two tales he had to weigh the truth of, one against the other, and he did not know Connor well enough to know he would not lie. He did wonder, however, when and how the earl would decide which tale was the truth. It was hard to believe the earl would accept the word of a common whore over that of any laird, yet the man was obviously giving Meg's tale some serious consideration. Connor wished Gillyanne was at his side for he was suddenly certain there was something the older man knew that he did not, something that made the man give Meg's tale far more consideration than it warranted. Gillyanne might sniff it out, while he simply began to feel more and more uneasy, as if he was trapped in some game he did not know all the rules of.

"So, Sir Connor," Lord Dunstan said as soon as Connor finished the wine, "your explanations have the ring of truth, yet I have three women who tell the tale in a verra different way."

"Three whores," Connor said calmly, although he inwardly cursed the fact that he was fighting the word of three women instead of just one as he knew it made his fight more difficult. "Three lasses I tossed out of Deilcladach where they were verra comfortable. Three lasses who now have to work for the verra food they need to eat which they ne'er had to do before."

"Something to consider," the earl said and nodded as he thought it over.

"Might I ken exactly what tale was told? 'Tis evident the women blame me for the murder of my uncle, but did they tell ye why I did it?"

"Because ye finally learned the truth about the mon."

"The truth?" Connor tensed, his unease becoming a taut fear, yet he was not sure why he felt that way.

"The women claim ye were angry to discover your uncle was bedding your leman."

"He had had her before I did." Connor managed a

casual shrug. "I was done with her. He was welcome to take her back."

"They claim ye became angry and there was a vicious argument. Since your uncle was drunk, he didnae watch his words verra carefully. He expressed his dislike of your wife, but it was his revelation about the past which made ye strike out at him. When the women told me what the mon was guilty of, I confess I felt he weel deserved his fate. Yet, it was my place to judge his guilt, nay yours. Neither can I allow the murder of peers. 'Twould have been best if ye had challenged him instead. An honorable mon-to-mon battle to settle old wrongs. This was murder."

"I didnae murder my uncle," Connor repeated, but knew his declarations of innocence were not going to be heeded.

"Come, lad, I do understand what made ye do it. The mon was a base traitor. He kept that deadly feud alive, poisoned every attempt to settle it. I kenned he had courted your mother, but she was given to the laird, your father. Truth is, I always felt it was her own choice, though your uncle spoke of it as having been forced upon her by her parents. I kenned he remained bitter, but I ne'er guessed it had deepened so, had become such a murderous hatred.

"The feud was clearly taking too long to do what he wanted. 'Tis the only explanation for such a gross betrayal of one's own blood. To stir up his own brother's enemies with such lies and then to help them get round the defenses of Deilcladach? He had to have kenned that his treachery could easily kill many more than his brother. He put his entire family under the sword. Mayhap he had grown to hate your mother as weel." The earl shrugged. " 'Tis said some scorned love can verra easily become a deep hate. I doubt he gave ye and the other children much thought 'til he found ye had survived. Mayhap he thought ye would leave or die off in the hard times that followed for he certainly gave ye no help. He obviously didnae care if he was laird or ye wouldnae be standing here. It must have seemed such a God-given boon to him to have all who kenned what he had done slaughtered on that bloody day."

Lord Dunstan fixed his sharp dark gaze on Connor. " 'Twas justice, but it may be difficult to mark it so. Tell me the truth, lad, and I will work hard to free you. I would do it now save that the king himself has been demanding the end to such bloodletting, to taking justice into one's own hands. I cannae be seen to condone such murder and I willnae fight on your behalf if ye refuse to tell me the truth."

Connor was amazed he was still standing. Every word the earl had spoken had felt like a hard blow to the stomach. He wanted to bellow out a denial, but the words would not come. Since Gillyanne had arrived at Deilcladach, Connor knew he had wavered in his complete, blind trust of his uncle, had begun to see the man more clearly, and not liked what he saw. This horrifying tale explained so much Connor knew it was the truth, and it cut him so deeply he was surprised he was not bleeding.

Beneath that pain was a deep, burgeoning shame. He had been a complete fool, had clung too tightly to the blindness of youth, the sort youth often had concerning an elder kinsman. He had allowed the killer of his parents into his home, into his life, into the lives of the others Neil's treachery had left orphaned or widowed. All the time Connor had worked to be a strong laird, to rebuild his homes and lands, he had embraced the very man who had brought Deilcladach to ruin. If that final, devastating attack had not sated the man's need for revenge, Connor knew he could easily have been welcoming death into his clan. He had given his uncle vast opportunity to kill them all. Although that had not happened, Connor knew it was still a failure, one of such huge proportions he did not believe he had any right to call himself a laird.

Now was the time to defend himself, to explain that he had known none of this, but how could he explain his ignorance? What few scattered words did stumble through his mind sounded too much like the pathetic lies and excuses of a guilty man. Neither could he find the wit to speak clearly and he doubted the earl would sit patiently while he struggled to overcome all the emotions tearing through.

"I didnae kill my uncle," was all he could say and Connor knew he sounded cold, distant, revealing none of his shock or pain.

"Ah, lad, I had hoped ye could trust me," said the earl.

"I do, m'laird."

"Not enough. I shall give ye time to think o'er what ye wish to tell me. Peter will secure ye in a small tower room from which there is no escape. After a few days, we will speak again."

Connor knew he should heartily thank this man for the reprieve, but was only able to make himself bow before Peter led him away. The tower room he was placed in was small, but not harsh. Before his bonds were cut, a tray of food and wine was placed in the room, water for washing was left, and the fire was lit, extra wood stacked beside it. He stood, unable to move or speak, as his hands were freed and the men left the room.

Left alone to think, Connor mused with a curse, as he sprawled on his back on the surprisingly comfortable bed. He did not want to think. He did not want to contemplate the gross betrayal of a man he had trusted, cared for, and respected for years. Even in death, he thought, his uncle's twisted sense of revenge reached out to ruin his life. He could hang for the death of a man who deserved to die, a man whose hands had been soaked in the blood of his own brother and many of his own clan.

Even if he escaped or had his name cleared, how could he return to Deilcladach as its laird? His failure was too great. Connor placed his hands over his eyes, not surprised to feel tears. It was, perhaps, a good time to grieve, to weep for those who had died because of one man's jealousies, and for his own blind failure to see that truth. Weak though he thought it, Connor hoped allowing that weakness free rein for a little while would clear his head. When next he stood before the earl, he would need all his wits and a plan.

"Laird," Peter said when he returned to stand before the earl, "I am nay sure Sir Connor is guilty."

"Nay?" The earl tested the weight of Sir Connor's dagger in his hand. "Would ye nay kill the mon who nearly brought about the complete destruction of your clan, your family, and your lands?"

"Aye, and probably as slowly and painfully as I could. But, weel, I dinnae think he kenned it all until ye told him." Peter shook his head. "He said naught. He repeated his claim of innocence much as a child repeats a lesson. When we took him to the tower room, I got the feeling he was stunned, mindlessly so. He acted like a mon who had been knocked o'er the head by a rock yet lacked the wit to fall down. 'Tis difficult to explain."

"Ye didnae do so badly. I believe I shall send a message to the king."

"Because ye think Sir Connor is guilty?"

"He had cause, 'twas his weapon, and three women, whores though they be, claim he did it. It should be simple, yet 'tis not. I cannae believe Sir Connor would kill a mon like that. From all I have heard, I dinnae think he would act so foolishly nor allow himself to be so consumed by rage. Something isnae right here, and so I shall tell the king. He must be informed that one of his knights is dead, but I willnae accuse anyone of the crime yet."

"Ah, of course. Shall I take it for you?"

The earl nodded and stood up. "Aye, and 'twill be ready to go as soon as I can write the wretched thing. And, I want the king's response to be brought to me by a Murray. There is usually one of them lurking about in the king's court."

"Why do ye wish to bring a Murray here?"

"Sir Connor has married one of their women. There is a chance that marriage can be set aside, but, for now, Sir Connor is one of them. They will want to ken what is happening. And, if this Murray woman is anything like the others, she may weel show up here demanding her husband. 'Twould be a help if one of her kinsmen is here, too."

"Nay, surely no lass would come here demanding anything of ye?"

"Ye obviously havenae met a Murray lass."

Diarmot wiped his sweaty palms on his jupon as he waited for the guard to unlock the door of Connor's prison. He could not believe what was happening. One moment he was watching Connor leave to speak to Meg, the next he had the nearly incoherent mother of Knobby telling him his uncle was dead and that the earl's men had dragged Connor to Dinnock to answer to the charge of murder. He had not slept at all, pacing his room, his mind crowded with questions, waiting for daybreak so that he could ride to Dinnock. The earl himself had not been much more informative, but at least he was allowing him to see Connor. Even as Diarmot had expressed his gratitude for that kindness, he had been stripped of all his weapons and led away.

The moment Diarmot stepped into the room the door

was shut and barred behind him. It took him a minute to be able to see clearly, the room being only faintly lit by a small fire. When he finally saw Connor sprawled in a chair near the fire, Diarmot felt his uneasiness grow. There was nary a bruise on his brother yet Connor looked as if he had been beaten into a stupor.

"What in sweet Mary's name is going on?" Diarmot demanded, unsettled by the dead look in his brother's eyes.

"I have been accused of the murder of Sir Neil Mac-Enroy," Connor replied.

"Ye would ne'er kill our uncle."

"After what I have learned, aye, I would have gutted the swine without hesitation." Connor finished his drink, refilled his tankard, and asked, "Wine?"

Diarmot pulled up a stool to sit in front of Connor and helped himself to some of the wine in a large jug Connor held out. There had been a cold rage behind Connor's words. It was as if all affection for their uncle had been abruptly, brutally killed. He just hoped he could get Connor to tell him everything despite the very odd mood he was in. It was not going to be easy to get Connor free of this tangle. It would be impossible without every piece of information Connor might have.

"Your dagger was found buried in Uncle Neil's heart," Diarmot said.

"Aye, and it hasnae been put to such good use in many a generation. I wish I had been the one to put it there."

"Why, Connor? Why would ye wish to kill a mon ye have always revered, and why say he deserved to die?"

Connor rested his head against the back of his chair, took a long drink, and then closed his eyes. In a flat, emotionless voice, he told Diarmot the ugly truth about Sir Neil MacEnroy. When he was done, the silence was so heavy, Connor could almost feel it pressing in on him. He looked at Diarmot, not surprised to see his brother was pale and shaken.

"Jesu, and we let that bastard into Deilcladach again and again, welcomed him, were grateful at least one of our elders had survived," Diarmot finally said, then took a deep drink to ease the hoarseness of rage from his voice. "How did the earl ken it?"

"Meg and the other women told him," Connor replied. "They told the earl Meg and I were still lovers, said I got in an argument with Neil, and, as the argument raged, the drunken Neil spilled the truth he had held tight to for years. So, enraged, I butchered him. Then, I plunged my dagger into his heart and left. After enough time had passed for Meg and her cohorts to go tell this tale to the earl and for the earl to send his men to capture me, I suddenly recalled leaving my dagger behind and rushed back to retrieve it."

"So, Meg nay only tries to get ye hanged for a crime ye didnae commit, but makes ye look a complete fool as weel," Diarmot muttered. "Why should our uncle tell Meg such a dangerous secret? Our uncle didnae trust women at all."

"Nay, but he loved his drink. I think he and Meg wanted Gillyanne gone, then they wanted her dead when she showed no sign of leaving. Mayhap *they* argued when the latest attempt to be rid of Gillyanne appeared to have failed. Neil may have let some of the truth slip out and Meg had the skill to pull the rest out of him."

"Meg didnae lose anyone in the killings. Why should she care who was responsible?"

"I dinnae think she killed Neil for that crime. I would-nae be surprised if Meg thought to use that secret against the fool and to fatten her purse with it. Then Neil said or did something to stir her rage. I also wouldnae be surprised to learn Meg stole my dagger when I banished her, thinking to sell it later. She thought of blaming me after she had done the killing. Only she can tell us why she killed Neil. I am nay sure I will e'er understand why he suddenly told her so much, e'en if he was stumbling down drunk."

Diarmot stared into his wine. "Mayhap 'twas your wee wife who loosened his tongue. Uncle disliked her from the start, was a miserable bastard to her. Weel, there is the chance he kenned her skill at sensing what a mon thinks or feels. That would make him afraid and that fear kept the memories of his heinous murder at the fore of his mind, far too close to his tongue. Then it became only a matter of time before he stumbled and let it out."

"Ye think he feared Gillyanne? I did hear talk of her skill time and time again yesterday. Word of it has spread far and wide. And made to sound far greater than it is. 'Tis said she can read the secrets held deep in a mon's heart. Aye, she has a keen sense, feelings that cannae be ignored, but the rest is all lies meant to stir up fear and hatred for my wife. I now think Neil, with Meg's aid, and mayhap Jenny and Peg as weel, spread those tales hoping that others would rid them of Gilly." Connor laughed, but it was a cold, bitter sound. "Twas David who revealed the threat such talk represented, ye recall. E'en David saw more clearly than I did." He shook his head then abruptly asked, "How fares Gillyanne?"

"Weel. Still resting, which is for the best. Fiona begins to calm, nay longer fearing fever or infection, and James agrees. Soon, James plans to go to Dubhlinn to tell the tale to his family. He fears some dark rumor may wend its way to their ears and he wants to be sure they ken the truth."

"Ah, aye, the truth being that I nearly got their daughter killed."

"Ye?" Diarmot shook his head. "What foolishness is that? Ye had naught to do with all this."

"Exactly. I did naught but give succor to a murderer. I embraced our deadliest enemy, brought him close to the wife I had vowed to protect. As I have sat here thinking,"

"Brooding," Diarmot muttered, but Connor ignored him.

"I can now see so many places where doubts should have arisen, where questions should have been asked." Connor swept his fingers through his hair. "I suddenly realized Neil ne'er really helped us and he could have, many times and in many ways. I should have questioned that."

"Ye didnae because ye probably thought the mon offered no help because he had none to give. Ye also felt it your duty to lead us, to pull us all back from the brink of destruction."

"Foolish pride. Jesu, at some time I should have at least wondered why we couldnae all huddle in his stables, behind thick walls, instead of little hovels out in the open. In my blindness, I failed everyone."

"Curse it, ye havenae failed anyone! Connor, I ne'er liked our uncle. I thought him a useless mon who did nay more than come watch us struggle from time to time, eat too much and drink far more—e'en when we had so little to spare—bed our lasses, and ne'er lift a finger to do any of the work. He felt free to tell us what to do, though, didnae he? And there were times I wanted to cuff ye for listening to the pompous drunkard. The way he acted as if poor Fiona ne'er existed enraged me at times."

"Ye saw him far more clearly than I did."

"Since I wasnae the one burdened with the care of all of us, I had the time and wit left to think of other things. Yet, in all those years, e'en on the days when I near loathed the fool, ne'er did I e'er think he was the one responsible for it all. I thought him ill-humored, selfish, useless, vain, and lazy, but I am still as shocked as ye are to hear these ugly truths. God's toes, Connor, the mon was our *uncle!* Of course ye, nor any of us, would wonder if he had anything to do with the death of his own brother, of his sister by marriage, or of much of his clan."

"But I was the *laird*! *I* should have seen it. Somewhen in the twelve long years, I should have at least looked." Connor rubbed a hand over his face. "I am nay fit to be the laird. 'Tis ye who . . ." Connor's words were interrupted by the entrance of the guard.

"The earl feels ye have visited long enough," said the man.

"Aye, I have," agreed Diarmot, glaring at Connor as he stood up and started for the door.

"Diarmot," Connor began.

"Nay, I cannae tarry. Ye sit here and brood o'er your failure to have the all-seeing eye of God Himself. *I* intend to find the real murderer and get ye out of here. Just dinnae brood so deep ye fail to notice they are trying to put a noose about your neck for a murder ye didnae commit. I would like ye to still be alive when I return so ye can see what a clever wee bastard I am. Then, when ye are free again, I shall pound some sense into you. I suspect your wee wife will help me." He slammed the door shut behind him.

Chapter Eighteen

"Ye have to tell her."

Diarmot sighed and briefly ignored his sister as he tried to eat his meal. He had returned from the earl's keep, washed, eaten something, crawled into his bed, and slept until morning. He still felt tired, but he knew it was caused more by concern and a heaviness of spirit than a lack of sleep. Connor was sunk into a dangerous gloom and accused of murder. It left him with the sorts of responsibilities he really did not want.

The hardest part, he knew, was going to be telling the rest of the family the horrifying truth about their uncle. Whether they had cared for the man or not, it was going to be hard news to accept. The man had kept three clans at each other's throats, was responsible for more deaths than Diarmot cared to think about. Harder still would be understanding that this ugly truth about their uncle gave the earl a very sound reason for believing Connor guilty of killing the man. If they could not bring the earl the real killer, the best they could hope for was that their uncle's crimes were dire enough to get Connor pardoned for his death.

"She has been asking for him, has she?" Diarmot asked Fiona as she sat down next to him at the laird's table in the empty hall.

"Nay as much as I think she would like to," replied Fiona.

"How does she fare?"

"Verra weel indeed. A verra quick healer and far stronger than I e'er would have believed her to be. Just as James said she was. I caught her up on her feet this morning and, though she was pale, she was verra steady. She needs to ken what is happening with Connor. 'Twill help."

"Ye think such ill news will actually help her recover?" Diarmot asked in mild astonishment.

" 'Tis better for her to ken the truth. At least then she willnae be left thinking Connor has been hurt or killed or just doesnae care to see her."

"Ah, of course." Diarmot stood up. "Fetch the lads, Fiona, and bring them to the laird's bedchamber. Knobby, too. And, where is James?"

"He left not long after Gilly woke. James said he could see she would be weel and wanted to take the news to his kinsmen. Oh, and the news about Connor, as weel. I thought he might believe Connor killed our uncle and defended our brother to him, but James said nay, he kenned Connor had been falsely accused. It was more trouble that his family might hear whispers about, however, and he wanted them to ken the truth. He also said the Murrays had had some experience with false charges of murder and that he might gain some hint or two about how to free Connor. If he isnae free already when he returns." Fiona smiled faintly. "I shall have to remember that and press for the tale when he returns."

"Only if I am with ye when ye do, for 'tis certain

to be a good one. Go, lass, let us gather together the family.''

'' 'Tis that bad?''

"Bad enough.''

Gillyanne felt tense and almost afraid as the MacEnroy siblings and Knobby gathered in the bedchamber. She took some comfort in the fact that she felt no grief in any of them so she felt sure Connor was still alive. There was a brief moment of lightness for her when Mairi brought in a jug of wine and tankards for all of them, exchanging a shy smile and blush with Knobby. It was evident that Mairi had finally shown Knobby she was interested in him and he was responding with an equal interest. The moment Mairi slipped away, however, the tension in the room, the unease each person there felt, rushed back upon Gillyanne.

"First, I must tell ye about our uncle,'' began Diarmot.

"We ken the mon was murdered,'' Nanty said.

"Patience. What I need to tell ye is all that was discovered ere he died. Our uncle wasnae what he appeared to be. There were things about him we ne'er kenned, ne'er could have guessed.''

When Diarmot looked at her Gillyanne felt a chill. "Oh, hell's fire, all those dark secrets came out, didnae they?''

"Aye, and they were verra dark indeed.'' Taking a deep breath, Diarmot repeated all he had learned from Connor about Sir Neil. "E'en sadder is that I truly believe now that he ne'er helped us because he simply didnae care if we survived. He didnae have the courage to kill us all himself and the feud was o'er so he couldnae use that against us, but he was probably verra disappointed that we survived that final slaughter.'' When he saw how pale everyone was, he sighed. "Mayhap it wasnae right to tell you this.''

"Nay," protested Fiona, rubbing tears from her eyes. " 'Twas right." The others murmured their agreement. "Those vile truths have been hidden too long. Now that they are free, they will spread verra quickly. Better to hear it now, from ye, than whispered into our ears later by some stranger. 'Twill only grow darker as the tale passes from one ear to the next, though I cannae see how much darker it can be," she muttered as she sat down on the bed next to Gillyanne.

Gillyanne reached out to take Fiona's hand in hers, silently offering comfort. "And this is why the earl believes Connor murdered his uncle."

"Aye," replied Diarmot. "He was told the tale spilled out whilst our uncle and Connor argued and, in a rage, Connor stabbed him. 'Twas Connor's dagger in his heart."

"Meg stole it when she left."

"Most likely. Connor feels Meg and Neil were working together to be rid of you. Tales of your skill at sensing what people feel or think have been spread far and wide. And heartily exaggerated. I do wonder if Neil believed most of it, if that fear of ye seeing the truth he hid, helped loosen his tongue. Ere ye arrived, the mon probably didnae think much on what he had done. Then, suddenly, 'twas all in the fore of his mind all the time and fear of others finding out, or that ye would expose him, kept the past alive in his mind."

"They thought that they could get terrified people to get rid of me for them or cause me to run away from the dangerous whispers."

"There is no proof, no confession of this, yet few people at Deilcladach kenned about your skills. It had to have been our uncle who started the whispers."

"And was quickly aided by Meg, Jenny, and Peg. It matters not. And, once the truth is learned about the ones who started those rumors, they will lose their power. Where is Meg?" she asked abruptly.

"The earl said she and the other women were ordered to return to their cottage and stay there, but, when I stopped there as I rode back from Dinnock, I saw no sign of them," Diarmot replied.

"That is no surprise. I doubt they have gone verra far away," Gillyanne added, seeking to reassure Diarmot. "They really have no place to go, no coin, and no kin. Meg would also wish to stay close to hand so that she might see the results of her plots and crimes."

"Do ye have a plan, Gilly?" Fiona asked as she helped Gillyanne sit up straighter and gave her a tankard of wine.

"I am certain Diarmot has one or two, Fiona," Gillyanne said.

"One or two," Diarmot replied, "but I havenae had time, yet, to sort it all out. Weel, nay past the need to find the real murderer."

" 'Tis Meg, is it not?" Gillyanne felt certain it was, but feared jealousy and dislike might cloud her reasoning.

Diarmot nodded as he sat at the foot of the bed, resting his back against one of the thick, heavily carved posts. "Aye, I think so. As does Connor. Nay for the reasons we would have killed the bastard though."

Angus nodded. "Meg and the others didnae lose anyone. Ne'er seemed to care about what had happened here."

"Mayhap your uncle spit out some of his poison concerning women once too often, or enraged Meg by heaping scorn upon some idea she had." Gillyanne shook her head. "She is capable of a rage, especially if she feels insulted, and your uncle could be most insulting. Howbeit, we can find out all of that when we find Meg and the other two. That is the verra first thing we must do."

"Agreed," said Diarmot and nodded toward the other four men. "We can start the search for her today."

"How is Connor taking all of this? Is he angry?" she asked, almost hopefully.

"Ah, nay. He is brooding."

"Oh, dear. Angry would have been much better."

"Quite. Nay, he feels he has failed us all, isnae worthy to be our laird." Diarmot held up his hand to silence the vociferous protests of his family and Knobby. "I did my best to make him see that no one could have guessed what secrets our uncle hid deep in his black heart. I e'en confessed my long dislike of the mon so that I could tell Connor that, if anyone should have questioned the mere fact that the mon survived the killings, it would have been I, yet I didnae. 'Tisnae a crime one can e'en conceive of. The mon caused so many deaths, nay just those of the MacEnroys."

"But, ye didnae change his mind, did ye."

"Nay, Gilly. The betrayal cuts deep, I think, for Connor saw the mon almost as a father. The longer he thought o'er the past twelve years, the more he saw just how little the mon had done, saw where and when he should have asked a few pointed questions, and now he feels an utter fool. Connor feels he failed in not seeing that he allowed a murderer to walk amongst us, e'en when we were at our most vulnerable. 'Tis far too easy to see how often Neil could have finished the killings done that day. As I have said, I think, in a most cowardly way, Neil tried to finish his ill work by not helping us. He didnae e'en take wee Fiona in out of the cold. And, Connor thinks on how he let the mon get near ye, Gilly. How he didnae see the threat the mon was to you. Aye, and so much more. He has been secured in a windowless tower room and is provided every comfort, but he is alone in the near dark for hours."

"And so can brood and brood and brood. Weel, that settles it. I must go see him."

"Nay. 'Tis several hours ride and ye were seriously wounded but two days ago."

"Painfully, nay seriously." She held up her hand when Diarmot began to argue some more. "The arrow went through high on my shoulder, through what little fleshy area I have on this wee, too thin body. The muscle is fine, the bone fine, and I didnae bleed all that much. Aye, it hurts. Nay as much as it did when the arrow went in or came out and nay as much as it did yesterday. As long as I am careful and dinnae reopen the wound, I shall be fine. E'en then, 'twill mostly just hurt some more."

"But, the ride . . ."

"I shall go in a cart which I shall have properly prepared to soften the journey."

Diarmot frowned. "That will add time to the journey. I am nay sure ye can go and return in but a day."

"Then I shall stay at Dinnock. Diarmot, ye cannae leave the mon sitting alone in a shadowed room brooding on what he thinks is the verra worst of failures. Since the day your parents were murdered, Connor's sole purpose in life was the protection and survival of what remained of his family and clan. He cannae be allowed to convince himself that he failed in that. We all ken that he didnae, but he obviously needs someone to slap some sense into him."

"Ye are right, but, mayhap, it would be best if I did it."

Gillyanne shook her head. "Nay. He is your laird. He is the mon who raised ye, kept ye alive, and all of that. I am sure ye can speak your mind as ye will, but, at some point, ye will stop and go no further. That is, if ye last that long ere ye get angry and walk away." She exchanged a brief grin with Fiona.

"Gilly, ye are his wife," Diarmot said, amusement weighting his voice. "That makes Connor your laird, too, and much more."

"Aye, many would think that. Fortunate, isnae it, that we Murray lasses dinnae. And, consider this. As his wife,

I have a few ways of, er, improving his mood that ye cannae use." Gillyanne winked at Diarmot who grinned as the others chuckled. "He cannae just knock me down when I say something he doesnae wish to hear, either."

"Now, *that* is a telling argument," murmured Diarmot and laughed. "Ye may go. Take Fiona, Knobby, and two other men with ye. My brothers and I will hunt down Meg while ye are gone and get the truth from her."

"If ye cannae, I will do so when I return."

"I think I can be a wee bit more threatening than ye can."

"Aye—to a mon, and, mayhap, a lass who doesnae ken ye as Meg does. She kens what your weakness is."

"What weakness?" Diarmot demanded, a litle offended.

"Why, the fact that ye will quite probably falter ere ye could actually hurt a lass."

"Ah, I hadnae thought of that." He frowned. "I am nay sure she would believe ye would hurt anyone, either."

"Trust me, Diarmot, she will. Try your best, for I would as soon nay play that game, but I will if I must. A woman will believe another woman wouldnae hesitate to hurt her, especially if the one doing that threatening has reason to believe her intended victim was after her mon or had had him. To make Meg feel e'en more threatened, I will have Joan help me." She laughed when, after a brief moment of thought, each man's eyes widened with understanding. "And, one last thing— find out everything Connor did that day. Where he was, when he was there, and who saw him there."

"Why?"

"We may be able to show that he simply didnae have the time or opportunity to kill anyone."

"Lass, ye have an admirably devious mind."

"Thank ye. Now, let us prepare me and my cart so

I can turn it loose upon the earl and my brooding husband.''

Connor gaped in stunned disbelief at the person Peter let into his room. He had to be having some dream brought on by sitting alone in the near dark for too long. Gillyanne could not be standing there looking a little pale, but otherwise quite healthy. The last time he had seen her, she was unconscious, having just had an arrow yanked out of her shoulder. She should still be in their bed, resting, occasionally suffering a meal of gruel or watery broth. Although he had lost a little track of time, he was certain she had suffered that arrow wound only three days ago.

"Jesu, Connor, didnae they give ye any candles?'' Gillyanne demanded, placing her hands on her hips and narrowing her eyes in an attempt to see him more clearly in the gloom.

"Aye,'' he replied and, somewhat mindlessly, went to light the candles set on a tall, many branched stand in the corner of the room. "Once I light these, I suspect ye will disappear, as ye cannae be more than some vision brought on by too much drinking and thinking.''

"Ye mean too much brooding.''

That tart, husky voice certainly sounded like Gilly-anne, he mused as, once the candles were all lit, he turned to look at her. She did still look a little pale, but she was steady on her feet and the look of irritation on her face was untainted by the pinch of pain. It was, however, inconceivable that such a tiny woman could suffer an arrow wound three days ago at Deilcladach, yet be standing here at Dinnock now, scowling and muttering at him.

"Why are ye nay tucked up in our bed eating gruel and groaning?'' he asked.

"Because I was told ye were brooding and decided

ye needed me to talk some sense into you. Ah, wine. Good." She moved to pour herself a gobletful and took a long drink.

Since Gillyanne had seated herself on the stool, Connor returned to his chair. "Mayhap I but dreamed the attack," he muttered.

"Nay. I was wounded. It does still hurt, ye ken, but I have always been verra quick to heal. 'Tis why James felt he could leave so quickly for Dubhlinn to tell them I was weel. As I told Diarmot when he tried to stop me from coming here, the arrow just poked a hole in me. It didnae hurt muscle or bone, I didnae bleed myself weak, and I didnae take a fever. It does still pain me some, but that eases more each day and the wound already begins to close itself."

"But, 'twas barely three days ago!"

"I told ye, I heal quickly. I always have. I was rarely e'en sick as a child and I was a verra wee child. Mither believes that, because God made me such a wee lass, He decided to make me a verra robust one, too." She undid her bodice, let it fall to her waist, and, gently, lifted the clean linen bandage covering her wound. "See? 'Tis ugly, but 'tis healing."

She was right, he thought as he looked at the wound. It was healing, looked more like a wound a week old instead of mere days. On her fair, soft skin, it did indeed look ugly. Briefly, his gaze fell to her breasts and he felt his body tighten at the sight of her nipples, hard and pressing invitingly against her thin shift. He quickly turned his attention back to her wound, back to the stark reminder of how completely he had failed to protect her. Connor abruptly stood up, moved to lean against the thick oak mantel of the fireplace, and stared into the flames. He still wanted her, badly, but he no longer had any right to touch her.

Gillyanne frowned. For one brief moment, Connor had reacted as he usually did at the sight of her thinly covered breasts. She was not sure why the man found them such a delight, but he did, and she had thought to use that to her advantage. Now she was going to have to be even more aggressive. Connor needed to be talked sense to, but he was sunk too deeply in gloom. That needed to be broken through long enough to get him to heed her words. Passion, she had decided, would be the way to do that. Connor, however, was proving to have more control than he usually did. She was going to have to be ready to take swift advantage of any brief slip in that control. With that in mind, she quickly removed her braies and shoved them into a hidden pocket in her skirts. Now she was prepared to jump him at the earliest opportunity, she thought, and had to swallow the urge to giggle at the image that painted in her mind.

It would be no hardship, she mused as she looked him over. He wore only his linen breeches. That state of undress and a lingering dampness in his hair told her he had bathed shortly before she had arrived. Gillyanne hastily gave thanks that she had decided to pause just before reaching Dinnock to have a thorough wash. As she slowly looked him over, appreciating every lean, strong inch of him, her gaze briefly rested upon the hard proof that he was not as completely in control as he would have her believe. If she could get him to sit down again, she knew exactly what her plan of attack would be.

"Ye shouldnae have come here, Gillyanne," Connor said, finally looking at her and silently cursing when he found it almost impossible not to look at her breasts. He bit back the command for her to cover herself, fearing that would reveal far too much about what he was feeling.

"Nay?" She sipped her wine. "I should have ignored the fact that ye are being accused of a murder ye didnae commit and that ye are brooding yourself into making a foolish decision?''

Connor flung himself back into his chair, took a long drink, and scowled at her. "I am nay fit to be a laird. 'Tis a laird's duty to protect his kin and clan. I failed. I blindly clutched an adder to my chest, let it slither right up and strike at my own wife.''

Gillyanne moved off the stool and knelt between his long legs. "He was your uncle, Connor.'' She set her goblet aside then slowly moved her hands up and down his strong thighs. "Blood kin. Almost everyone trusts blood kin until they do something quite blatant to break that trust.''

"He survived. That should have raised a doubt or two.'' Connor was finding it difficult to ignore her caresses and her quite provocative position.

"Nay, that should have done exactly what it did— made ye grateful that yet another member of your family survived the killings.'' She inched a little closer, moving her caresses to his lean hips, and lightly kissed his taut stomach. "Ye are a fair and honorable mon, Connor MacEnroy, who has spent most of his life fighting to keep his brothers and wee sister alive. 'Tis no surprise that ye, of all people, would ne'er e'en consider the possibility that a mon would do his best to see his brother and family dead. Aye, if he had been just another mon, mayhap ye could curse yourself for nay seeing the threat, but he was your *uncle*, your father's own brother, a mon your father welcomed into your home. Ye cannae be blamed for nay seeing the evil in him. No one else did.''

"Ye did.'' He reached out to stroke her hair, beginning to care less and less about his uncle's perfidy as his body began to ache for her.

"Nay, I saw a troubled soul.'' She slowly unlaced his breeches, deciding there was no need to voice the suspicions she held now. "I saw a tormented mon.'' She curled her fingers around his erection and stroked him, savoring the tremor that went through him and the way his legs closed around her, holding her near. "I saw that he was filled with anger and dark secrets, but I ne'er would have guessed at the fullness of his crimes." Gillyanne replaced her fingers with her tongue, enjoying the deep groan of pleasure she pulled from him.

"Diarmot said much the same," he managed to spit out between gritted teeth.

"We are right and, if ye would cease sulking, ye would agree."

"Mayhap." He was beginning to believe he had let self-pity rule him, but desire was killing all urge to talk.

Connor rested his head against the high back of the chair and closed his eyes as he struggled for some control over his rising passion. He wanted the strength to sit there for a long while simply enjoying the heated stroke of her tongue, the warmth of her kisses, and the touch of her long slender fingers. She seemed to know how badly he wanted to linger in that sensual haze, easing back now and again to allow him to gain some of his lost control. Connor almost welcomed the brief loss of her touch when she paused to fully removed his breeches.

Then, she was back, slowly taking him into her mouth. Connor clutched at the arms of the chair, fighting to hold his pleasure at a level just beneath the pounding need for release. She loved him slowly, tantalizingly. Like a child trying to make a favorite sweet last as long as possible, he mused, and found that thought so flattering he knew he had to put an end to her play.

He gently pushed her away. Cautious of her wound, he tugged her up on her feet. Gillyanne looked slightly dazed. The realization that making love to him so could put her into such a state nearly robbed him of all the control he had just regained.

"Take off your gown, lass," he ordered and watched as she shed her gown, petticoats, and shoes, until she stood before him wearing only her thin shift and ribbon-gartered stockings. "Where are your braies?" he asked when he realized he could see the shadowed place between her thighs through her shift.

"I took them off whilst ye stared into the fire," she replied in a thick, husky voice. "I thought I might have to move quickly to distract you." When he lifted her leg, placing her foot upon his thigh as he started to removed her stocking, she grasped the arm of the chair with one hand and tried to hold her shift down modestly with the other.

As he tugged her hand away from her shift, Connor murmured, "Nay, lass, allow your poor mon a wee peek at what he hungers for."

Gillyanne blushed, but did not argue, even though the direction of his gaze told her he was taking more than a wee peek. Soon, the way he stroked her leg from thigh to toe as he removed her stocking, had her so heated, she did not care what he saw. By the time he had removed her other stocking, she was trembling. When he slid his hand between her legs to lightly stroke her, she almost sighed with relief.

"So beautifully hot and wet," he said and pressed a brief kiss on her linen shrouded stomach. "Straddle me, wife."

She did as he asked, but when she tried to press down against him, he clasped her by the hips to hold her away. Gillyanne blushed as he slowly removed her shift. The way he stared at her, his beautiful eyes dark with passion, his strong hands lightly touching her, quickly eased her shyness. Still holding her by the hip so that she would not rub against him, he placed his other hand at the back of her head and brought her mouth to his for a slow, hungry kiss.

When he ended the kiss, she murmured a protest only to have the sound change to one of pure pleasure as he lifted her slightly and began to feast upon her breasts. Then he urged her up a little more, kissing and licking the skin beneath her breasts, even her ribs. It was not until he was licking her belly that she realized his plans, but, by then, she was so caught up in her own passion, she did not care. She clung to the back of the chair when he tugged her up that last little bit, groaning faintly with a mixture of embarrassment and pleasure as he stroked and explored her most intimate place with his long, clever fingers. Embarrassment fled, doused by desire, when he replaced his fingers with his mouth. A small modest part of her was shocked at how she shifted her body, and allowed him to do so as well, in order to give him all the freedom to play that he desired, but her body was too greedy for the pleasure he gave her to allow modesty any rule.

He toyed with her as she had toyed with him. Connor kept her upon the knife's edge until she thought she would scream. Even though she enjoyed the game, she could finally take no more of it. She threaded her fingers through his hair as she demanded he cease his torment. Suddenly, his intimate kiss grew almost fierce, as if he, too, was now greedily demanding what he had hitherto denied her. With a loud cry, she shattered and gave it to him.

She was still shaking from the strength of her release as he slowly lowered her down his body, easing their bodies together. He still kept a grip on her, refusing to let her move, as he turned his skillful kisses to her breasts. Gillyanne felt her passion begin to soar again. She wrapped her arms around his broad shoulders and marveled at his control, wondering if she could equal it. A moment later, he slid his hand between their bodies to touch that far too sensitive place above where they were joined and Gillyanne decided control was not so very important.

Connor held Gillyanne as still as he could as he re-stirred her desire. He was teetering on the edge of release, but he wanted her with him. Even the slight squirming she did and the way her body would clench around him were almost too much. Then her release tore through her. For just a moment, he savored the feel of her convulsing around him, of her cry of delight thundering in his ears, before shouting out his own pleasure as he allowed her to carry him to the heights with her.

Gillyanne opened her eyes to find Connor peering at her wound. It ached a little but, even in the throes of passion, she had retained enough sense to favor it. She realized they were in bed and vaguely recalled Connor washing them both off before carrying her there.

"It just aches a little, but no more than it did when I arrived," she said.

Just as he was prepared to answer, a knock came at the door, and he cursed. Connor was already up and tugging on his breeches when he realized no one had knocked before. He glanced back at Gillyanne who had pulled the covers up to just below her eyes, then went to the door. It opened for him and he found Peter and Knobby in the hall.

"Ye shouldnae have let Gillyanne make the journey," he told Knobby.

"Your wife is as stubborn as ye are," replied Knobby as he tossed a small bag into the room. "I will be ready to leave at dawn."

Peter shoved a tray loaded with food and drink into Connor's hands then shut and locked the door. Connor took the tray and set it by the bed. He then glanced at the little bag before looking at Gillyanne.

"Ye came prepared to stay the night?" he asked.

"Weel, brooding can be difficult to banish." She sat up, arranged her hair to drape over her breasts, and helped herself to a thick slice of bread.

"Weel, I believe I am done brooding for now," he said as he shed his breeches and climbed back into bed. "Still, 'tis good ye will stay the night just in case I fall back into it once or twice ere the sun rises." He winked at her when she laughed, then asked, "So, ye return to Deilcladach? To do what? I dinnae think 'tis to take your rest as ye should."

"I intend to find the real murderer and get ye out of here."

He studied her for a moment, stunned by the realization that this tiny woman was going to help him, save him. It had been a long time, if ever, since anyone had done that. Then he slowly smiled.

"If anyone can do it, ye can, wife," he said. "Now, eat. Ye need your strength."

"My wound is healing nicely," she said.

"Nay for that."

"To catch the murderer?"

"Nay for that, either. For doing your duty as my wife and banishing any brooding I may feel inclined to do tonight."

"Ah, 'twill be my pleasure, husband."

"I certainly intend it to be, wife."

Chapter Nineteen

Gillyanne sat down at the head table in the great hall of Deilcladach and filled her plate with food. She had returned from the earl's keep several hours ago, but everyone had kindly allowed her to wash and rest. Fiona had probably eased their impatience by repeating everything Gillyanne had told her. Gillyanne hoped that reprieve lasted long enough for her to enjoy her meal. She was very hungry after spending a long, sensuous night with Connor, because of her continued healing, and, she suspected, due to traveling.

She suddenly recalled how she had greeted the morning, with Connor deep inside her, and shivered with remembered delight. Connor had certainly cast aside his brooding. He had begun to get irritated, however, frustrated that he had to depend upon others to get him out of trouble. Gillyanne knew it was not that Connor did not trust them or thought they were all too dimwitted to help, but he was a man used to leading, not following, and certainly not sitting around and waiting. She was glad she had made a swift departure, however, leaving before he could say something to spoil her good mood.

"They found Meg," announced Fiona as she strode into the great hall. "They captured her a wee while before we arrived."

"Please, tell me she has confessed all," Gillyanne said, pushing her empty plate aside and sipping at her goat's milk.

Fiona sat down on the bench nearest Gillyanne and helped herself to some of the goat's milk. "On her knees whilst praying for mercy?"

"That sounds good."

"Too good. According to Angus, she demanded to ken why they had sought her out in her cousin's home."

"She has kinsmen?"

"Nay. This poor fool thought God had smiled upon him by sending him three lovely, eager lasses to shelter in his wee cottage. He wasnae thinking it so glorious when all those angry and weel-armed MacEnroys came pounding upon his door. Angus said the mon nearly tossed the women out naked and barred the door after them, but Diarmot told him to allow them to collect their things. It wasnae long, Drew said, before Meg was cursing them all, e'en tried to flee. They finally bound her hands and gagged her. That made the other two lasses verra cooperative, Angus said, although they wouldnae talk. So, Meg is here awaiting your verra special touch."

"That could easily spoil what had looked to be a good day," Gillyanne muttered and smiled faintly when Fiona laughed. "Ah, and here come the rest."

"I suspect Fiona already told ye everything," said Diarmot as he, his brothers, and Knobby sat down at the table. "I tried to get Meg to talk to me, but she just became enraged. Unfortunately, she didnae reveal any secrets whilst she ranted, just repeatedly insulted and threatened us. Oh, and taunted us with the possibility that Connor will soon hang for the murder of his uncle."

"If ye *laddies* had just kept your breeches laced, we wouldnae have to deal with this bitch," grumbled Fiona.

"I dinnae believe a lady is supposed to use the word *bitch,*" Gillyanne murmured, hoping to ease the anger Fiona had stirred up in her brothers if the four identical glares the girl was getting was any indication. "And, I think I should prefer to forget which laddies were unlacing what around Meg."

"Oh, pardon. Although, when ye talk to her—"

"Exactly." Gillyanne sighed and lightly rubbed her fingers over her temples as she looked at Diarmot. "And, I have to speak to her, dinnae I."

"I fear so, Gillyanne," replied Diarmot after one last scolding glance at his sister. "Are ye sure ye can get her to talk? I, weel, if ye arenae sure, I dinnae see why ye should suffer whate'er poison she will choose to spit at you."

Gillyanne gave him a brief, half-hearted smile. "I can make her talk even when I would verra much rather she shut her mouth. And, with Joan's help, I can make her verra, verra afraid, or verra, verra angry. Now, ere I deal with that, did ye sort out all Connor did that day so that, if 'tis needed, we can show that he didnae have the time nor opportunity to kill his uncle?"

"Aye, and, mayhap, nay," replied Diarmot. "Aye, we ken what he did from the moment he rose in the morning, but all the witnesses to it are MacEnroys. Nay the best of witnesses."

"Nay. Yet, if the blood was still wet when the earl's men arrived, we may be able to argue that the killing had to have been done after the noon hour. Meg must have near killed a horse to get to the earl's and back so verra quickly."

"The blood was still wet," said Fiona and shrugged when everyone looked at her. "While Gilly was coaxing

Connor out of his brooding, I dined with the earl and his mon Peter. I told them all about the past and all Connor did, thinking it would help if we couldnae find the real murderer and they still accused Connor. Then I got them to tell me all about the murder. The earl said I was a bloodthirsty lass.''

"Ye are, but I suspect he thought it verra charming,'' said Gillyanne. "So, the blood was still wet. Odd, for, considering how long it would take Meg to get to the earl, tell her tale, then for his men to ride back here to the cottage, e'en if they all near rode their horses to death, 'twould surely have been a long enough time for the blood to dry.''

"But, Meg didnae have to ride all the eay to Dinnock. She met the earl's men in a town but half the way there. They were on an errand for the earl. Peter sent the lasses on to tell the earl their stories whilst he and his men rode to the cottage. By the time Peter returned to Dinnock with Connor, the earl had sent the lasses back to the cottage.''

Gillyanne nodded. "Which is why the blood was still wet and why Connor couldnae face his accusers. So, your uncle was murdered *after* I was attacked. It should be easy to prove Connor couldnae have done it. He was with me, then riding to Sir Robert's, then to Sir David's. I wonder if we can get them to attest to that if needed?''

"Why dinnae ye ask them yourself?'' said Diarmot.

She looked at Diarmot, but he was not looking at her. Gillyanne followed his gaze to the door of the great hall and nearly gaped. Knobby had just escorted in Sir Robert and Sir David. She decided God must be smiling on her or Connor today. For one brief moment, Gillyanne wondered if she could forgo speaking to Meg, then scolded herself for her cowardice. Meg would undoubtedly tell her more than she cared to hear about her and Connor when they were lovers, if only to try to hurt her, but Gillyanne knew she could not shy away from that when there was a chance she could pull a confession from the woman. What she now had was good enough to free Connor, but handing the earl the real killer would be far better. The more proof of Connor's innocence she had, the faster he would be freed.

"I thought ye had been wounded," said Robert as he strode toward the table, Sir David at his heels.

"I was," replied Gillyanne, inviting them to sit down with a wave of her hand. " 'Tis healing weel."

"And quickly," he said as he sat down with David. " 'Twas only a few days ago."

"Four, and 'twas nay a serious wound. Did ye come to see how I fared?"

"Weel, aye and nay. We heard what happened to Connor and thought we might be able to help. He did spend much of that day riding to speak to both of us." Robert frowned. "Dinnae ken why anyone would think Connor would kill his uncle anyway. The mon was irritating and useless, but Connor seemed quite fond of him."

Gillyanne stood up. "I shall leave the telling of that tale to Diarmot and the others. I have to go and wring a confession out of Meg."

"Ye think she killed the mon?" asked Robert.

"Oh, aye," she answered, "though I dinnae ken why." She looked at Diarmot. "Where is Meg?"

"Tied to a chair in the kitchens," Diarmot replied. "Her two friends are tied up in the stables."

"The kitchen is good. 'Tis far enough away and, with the door shut, 'twill be impossible to guess if the screaming is born of anger, fear, or pain."

"Ye intend to make her scream?" asked Robert.

Gillyanne decided to ignore the sharp look of amusement on Robert's face. "I suspect she will do a lot of it for she will be both furious and afraid of the truth coming out. Howbeit, anyone sitting here will be easily convinced that the woman is being brutally tortured.

So," she looked at Diarmot again, "bring the other two women in here. I suspect ye can think of ways to make them believe I am skinning Meg alive in there. They will quickly tell all, e'en if Meg willnae."

"Clever lass," Diarmot drawled. "Verra clever."

"When the devil drives ye and all that."

"If ye get a confession then ye willnae need us," said David while Drew and Nanty were sent off to get Meg's two friends.

"Oh, aye, I will," Gillyanne said. "I intend to present the earl with as much proof of Connor's innocence as I can get my hands on. That way, he will not only be freed, but his name will be completely cleared."

"A good plan, m'lady," Robert said, "though I am nay sure ye will be able to scare Meg into confessing to a crime that will get her hanged."

"Nay?" Gillyanne smiled faintly. "The woman is tied to a chair in the kitchen which is filled with all sorts of threatening things, including verra big knives. Meg is about to be shut up in there with one woman whose husband Meg bedded down with whilst leaving the other woman to do all the work Meg didnae do, and me, a woman she has also wronged. I do believe Meg is going to be verra, verra scared from the moment the door is shut." She could hear the men chuckling as she walked to the kitchen.

"Weel met, m'lady," said Joan as Gillyanne stepped into the kitchen and shut the door behind her.

This was going to be a sore trial, Gillyanne decided as she nodded a greeting to Joan and looked at Meg. Meg was not bruised or bleeding, but the rough state of her clothes and tangled hair told Gillyanne that the woman had indeed fought her capture and the men had not been gentle in subduing her. The woman also shook faintly from the force of the hate and fury inside her. Gillyanne caught the scent of fear. It was strong, but not yet strong enough to conquer the rage and loathing. What seemed a little odd was that those two strong emotions did not seem to be aimed just at her and Joan, but at everyone. It was a very similar mix to what had infected Sir Neil MacEnroy. Gillyanne supposed it should be no real surprise that, after putting two such tainted souls close together for a length of time, one of them ended up dead.

"It seems a verra foolish thing to do to kill your protector," Gillyanne said as she crossed her arms over her chest and faced Meg.

Meg's laugh was harsh. "Connor killed the old fool. The bastard will hang for it soon."

"So hard ye are. Connor was good to you."

"He was just another mon who rutted on me when the mood took him. Bonny, aye, and a proper stallion, but just a cursed, sweating rutter like all the rest." She tossed her head to flip her thick hair away from her face with an arrogance that made Gillyanne ache to slap her. "I was the best he ever had and the fool cast me aside. For what? An udderless runt?"

Gillyanne realized that the insult to her lack of bosom no longer stung. She might not understand why, but she had no doubt at all Connor liked her breasts, found them highly arousing. That knowledge made her immune to Meg's taunts.

"If ye were the best, he would have kept you. Many men have a leman as weel as a wife. That is of no concern, however. Lovers are often cast aside. They dinnae then stab a drunken old fool and accuse their old lover of the crime. Why did ye kill the mon?"

"I didnae kill him. How could a woman kill a mon? Nay, 'twas Connor. He went mad when he learned the truth about his uncle. Mayhap that truth will keep Connor from hanging since the mon he killed was long o'erdue for death."

"Actually, I would think that the verra last thing ye would wish for is Connor's freedom. Connor kens who killed his uncle and set the blame on him. Once free, he might come looking for you." She noticed that Meg's fear briefly grew stronger.

"He willnae trouble himself. And, I willnae be here. Me, Jenny, and Peg are going to seek out the king's court. There is money to be made there, and fine gentlemonly lovers, nay like the crude boors that live at Deilcladach."

"I dinnae think she is going to tell us what we wish to learn, Joan," Gillyanne said.

"Then we must persuade the bitch," replied Joan.

Joan certainly sounded eager, Gillyanne mused. The woman probably did want some retribution for the pain Meg had caused her by bedding down with Malcolm, but Gillyanne trusted Joan not to get too caught up in her own grievances. After the brief talk they had had earlier, she also trusted Joan to follow where she led her.

What was needed was something to either frighten Meg into confessing, or enrage the woman so much that she babbled out the truth, even spat it out whilst in a state of defiant fury. Gillyanne knew she and Joan could not actually hurt the woman, despite the somewhat violent thoughts about Meg they had both nurtured from time to time. Then Gillyanne watched Meg toss her hair back in that annoying way she had, and knew what tactic to use. Meg was vain about her face, her body, and her hair. They could not do any damage to the woman's body or face, although Gillyanne prayed Meg would not guess that, but they could certainly do considerable damage to that hair.

"I will give ye one last chance to tell us the truth, Meg," Gillyanne said.

Gillyanne's eyes widened slightly at the curse Meg snarled at her. She walked to where all the knives and other sharp kitchen instruments were on display, studying them as Joan hurried over to join her. The assault was going to have to be carefully planned. If she and Joan made a continuous attack upon Meg's pride and vanity with word and deed, Gillyanne was sure all that rage and loathing would come spewing out. With it, Gillyanne prayed, would be enough of a confession to take all the weight of suspicion off Connor.

"What do we do now?" asked Joan in a whisper as she idly tested the weight and sharpness of a large knife.

"We are going to cut her hair," Gillyanne replied in an equally soft voice.

"Cut her hair?"

"The woman fair stinks of vanity, Joan. Since neither of us could scar her face or those cursed breasts she flaunts at every mon, we shall destroy that thick mane she is so proud of."

"Ah, I see. If she doesnae confess by the time we cut it all off, mayhap we could shave off her eyebrows, and pluck off those wretched long eyelashes. Aye, that would leave her bald as an egg."

Gillyanne bit her lip to stifle the urge to giggle. "We shall butcher her hair as slowly as we can, and, as we do it, we shall pluck away at that overweening pride of hers. The woman is fair to choking on her own anger o'er real and imagined wrongs and slights. I am hoping she will tell us what happened whilst she rages at us." She looked at Joan. "Do ye think ye can butcher her hair slowly?"

"Aye, I can do it." Joan took the knife Gillyanne held out. "And ye will cut her with words."

"I thought so, though ye must feel free to fling whate'er insult comes to mind. We need to bury her neck deep in scorn and ridicule."

"That shouldnae be too difficult," Joan murmured as, knife in hand, she moved toward Meg, Gillyanne right behind her.

Meg's laugh was so scornful it made Gillyanne grit

her teeth as the woman sneered, "Ye willnae use that on me."

Joan grabbed a thick lock of Meg's hair and hacked off a piece, then scowled at it before tossing it aside. "As I thought—lice-ridden."

Gillyanne nodded. " 'Tis difficult to keep clean when ye spend most of your time on your back with your legs in the air."

"Ye bitch!"

It did not take more than a minute for Gillyanne to decide those two screamed words were the kindest things Meg would say. And the woman did scream, which would work to scare the wits out of the women sitting in the great hall, but Gillyanne suspected it would soon make her head ache. She prayed that somewhere within the screamed curses, blasphemes, and insults would come a bit of the truth before she was deaf.

"Saints and martyrs, what goes on here?"

Diarmot stared at James who stood in the doorway to the great hall looking appalled and concerned as one of Meg's screams echoed through the room. He did not think he had ever moved so fast as he leaped from his chair and raced to meet James before the man could say any more. The two women were very close to breaking. Diarmot was certain that, if they knew anything, they would soon tell all. One wrong word from James could ruin all of Gillyanne's work.

Under the guise of heartily greeting his friend, Diarmot told him everything that had happened since he had left. Later he would allow himself to laugh at the variety of expressions that crossed James' face. Now he did his best to hide them from the women in the hall.

"Jesu," James muttered as he dragged his fingers through his hair. "Go away for a few days and the world goes mad. Do ye think Gilly's plan will work?"

"Oh, aye. Those lasses are fair to shaking their teeth loose. If they ken anything about the murder, we will be hearing all about it verra soon." Diarmot draped an arm around James' shoulder and walked him to the table. "I dinnae think the game will go on much longer."

Even as James sat down with Diarmot a somewhat chilling scream came from the kitchen. James poured himself some wine as he idly wondered where Meg had learned such appallingly crude words. A quick glance at the two other women told him that they were not really hearing the words, only the screams, and Diarmot was right. Whatever loyalty they felt for Meg was rapidly disappearing.

"She is killing her, isnae she?" asked a softly weeping Jenny.

"Och, nay, lass," James replied. "Gilly kens what she is about. Why, I dinnae believe she has e'er killed anyone."

"Jesu," whispered Jenny, her terrified gaze fixed upon the doors to the kitchen. "She is just moaning now. We didnae do anything!" she suddenly burst out.

"Hush," snapped Peg. "If ye say anything, Meg will kill us."

"I dinnae think 'tis Meg we need worry about now, do ye?" Jenny looked at Diarmot. "Meg killed that old fool. They had been plotting against her ladyship from the beginning. First they tried to make her want to leave, then they tried to get Sir Robert to take her, and then they tried to kill her."

Peg nodded. "They thought telling those lies about her would make people so afraid they would kill her as a witch. That didnae seem to be working, so they decided they needed to do it themselves."

"But, why kill Gillyanne?" asked Diarmot.

"Ye must ken why Meg wanted her dead. Meg was living like a queen here ere Lady Gillyanne arrived. She blamed her ladyship when all that comfort and ease was lost. I am nay sure why your uncle wanted her dead and gone, though.''

"He once said that marrying her made ye all too strong," said Jenny. "Said he would ne'er see the end of ye now. He ne'er really explained what he meant, just babbled about how he couldnae allow that Murray wench to make ye so strong and, mayhap, e'en wealthy. So, he hung about Deilcladach waiting for some chance to be rid of her and he thought he had found it that day she and the others were dancing in the field. When the arrow didnae kill her, he just gave up."

"Aye," agreed Peg, "and that was what started the argument. Meg wanted him to keep trying. He said there was no need, that he was weary of it all, and that he was dying anyway. Meg was yelling at him until he started to go on about ghosts and sins of the past, and how he was going to die because his bowels were bleeding, and he had failed because so many of ye were still alive. Ye ken the tale." When Diarmot nodded, she continued, "Meg grew sly, tried to make him do what she wanted, e'en to giving her a lot of money, by threatening to tell everyone of his crimes."

Jenny shook her head. "He just laughed, told her to do her worst as he would ne'er live long enough to meet the hangmon. Then he got verra nasty, ridiculing Meg and insulting her. I tried to get him to hush, kenning how such things could make Meg near blind with rage, but he just kept ranting at her. Peg tried, too. Then, suddenly, Meg was stabbing him, again and again. I dinnae ken how many times she cut him ere she buried that dagger in his heart."

"And then ye went with her to the earl and supported her lies," Diarmot said, his voice cold with anger.

"We were afraid," said Peg when Jenny started to cry again. "A belted knight was dead and Meg wasnae right in the head. We didnae ken what else to do."

"What ye will do next is tell this tale to the earl," snapped Diarmot, "and clear the accusation against my brother."

"But, Meg—"

"I believe Lady Gillyanne will be taking care of that threat."

"I ne'er would have expected her to cry," murmured Joan as she leaned against the wall next to Gillyanne and frowned at Meg. "She ne'er seemed to be a woman who would, or e'en could, weep so."

"Dinnae start feeling badly," Gillyanne said as she scowled at Meg who was slumped in her chair crying and muttering. "She isnae praying or asking for forgiveness. Those are tears of rage and she is cursing all of us."

"Do ye think she is mad?"

"Aye. For a wee moment I felt guilty, as if somehow, I brought this on her, but, nay. The seed of this madness was planted long ago. Just as with Sir Neil, the rage and bitterness finally stole her wits away, made her go mad." There was a soft rap at the door and Gillyanne opened it, almost able to smile at the cautious way Diarmot peered inside. "We are done. And the others?"

"Babbled out all we wished to know and wept and claimed innocence." He stepped inside the room and gaped at Meg. "Jesu, she is nearly bald."

Turning from greeting James, Gillyanne studied Meg for a moment. Meg did look pathetic. All that was left of her glorious mane of hair were a few scattered tufts sticking up here and there on her head. Joan had, perhaps, been a little overzealous, but it was understandable, and Meg had proven to be remarkably stubborn about confessing despite the mindless rage she had fallen into.

"We left a wee bit," Gillyanne murmured. "Careful when ye get near her. She is quite mad, I think, and 'tis a raging, dangerous sort of madness. All hate and fury, and, from some of the things she said, a lot of that is directed at men. She must be weel secured, too.''

Diarmot called in his brothers Drew and Nanty to help him and James. All four young men were needed for, the moment she was released from the chair, Meg fought like a cornered wild animal. As she and Joan tried to stay as far away from the woman screaming vengeance at them as possible, Gillyanne wished one of the men would just knock Meg unconscious. She echoed Joan's deep sigh of relief when Meg was finally bound and gagged. Drew called in two very large men to take Meg away and secure her in the dungeons.

Gillyanne was near enough to the doorway to the great hall to hear the gasps and mutters as Meg was carried through the room. When Gillyanne stepped into the room, the way everyone stared at her began to make her a little uneasy. The wide-eyed stares of Peg and Jenny were the worst and Gillyanne was relieved when Diarmot had them taken away to a small, windowless tower room. She moved to the table and helped herself to a drink of wine.

"We shall leave for the earl's at first light," said Diarmot. "Do ye think ye can ride, Gilly?"

"Mayhap I could ride with someone," Gillyanne said. "I dinnae think I will add enough weight to slow anyone down."

Diarmot smiled faintly and nodded. "Now, I just have to decide who must stay behind. Drew," he began and sighed at the protest the young man made. "Ye ken Connor's rule. One of the five brothers must always stay behind. I should probably make Fiona stay, too, but, after she gained so much useful information from the earl, I feel she has a right to see the end of this. Knobby."

"Nay," James interrupted Diarmot before he could order a clearly reluctant Knobby to stay behind, "I will stay here. Let Knobby go. S'truth, after riding to and from Dubhlinn, there is a part of me which is verra reluctant to get back on a horse.''

"Since it is all settled, I believe I will seek my bed,'' Gillyanne said, curtsied a good night to the men, and smiled at James when he moved to escort her to her bedchamber. "How fares the family?''

"Verra weel. Mither sent a salve to ease the scarring,'' James told her as they climbed the narrow stairs. "She expects to see how your wound heals with her own eyes verra soon.''

Gillyanne tensed as she opened the door to her bedchamber. "How soon?''

"Two, three days.'' He put a hand on Gillyanne's shoulder, urging her to look at him. "Still uncertain?''

"Aye. There is a change, yet there is still so much distance.'' She shook her head. "I believe I am too weary to think on it now.''

"Aye. Rest. Just one last thing. Mither says ye should decide just how much ye are willing to risk ere ye give up on Connor. She says to ask yourself if your pride will really afford ye that much comfort, that mayhap t'would be better to cast it aside and let the mon ken exactly what it is he will lose if ye leave him. Sleep weel, Cousin.'' He kissed her on the cheek and walked away.

Chapter Twenty

"Payton?" Gillyanne stared in utter disbelief when her far too handsome cousin rose to greet her as she entered the great hall of Dinnock. "Payton!" she cried again and rushed forward to throw herself in his arms.

"Ye are looking hale, loving," Payton said and kissed her on the forehead.

"Aye, I am fine." She felt him tense. "What is wrong?"

"Either your fingernails have grown excessively long and sharp, or there are six swords prodding me in the back. Nay. Seven."

Gillyanne looked around him and scowled at the small crowd right behind him. Diarmot, Angus, Nanty, Knobby, Sir Robert, and Sir David all had their swords pointed at Payton's back. Fiona was right there with the others, her dagger prodding Payton in the small of his back. If her poor cousin took one step backward, he would be bleeding from seven holes.

"*What* are ye doing?" she demanded as she moved around Payton, and shoved him behind her.

"That mon was touching you," said Diarmot. "No

mon should be embracing and kissing my brother's wife."

After waiting for the grunts of agreement to pass, including, much to her surprise, those of Sir Robert and Sir David, Gillyanne said, "This is my cousin, Sir Payton Murray. He was just saying hello."

"He was being cursed affectionate for a cousin," grumbled Sir David as he sheathed his sword.

"And, he is too cursed bonny," muttered Sir Robert as he did the same.

As soon as everyone had put their weapons away, she took Payton's hand in hers and introduced him to everyone. Knobby and Fiona greeted him cheerfully, but the others remained wary. Men often had that response to Payton until they got to know him better. Gillyanne did wonder why Sirs Robert and David were acting as protective of her as Connor's brothers, however. She began to think the two men might be closer allies than Connor, or either of them, had realized. The bond had been unrecognized for it probably had not really been tested before.

"How is it ye are here, Payton?" she asked. "I didnae think we kenned this earl."

"Oh, only noddingly," Payton replied. "From court. Spend enough time trailing about after the king, and ye will meet every titled and important mon in Scotland. I am here because the earl wrote to the king about the murder of Sir Neil MacEnroy."

"He told the king he suspected Connor?" Gillyanne was appalled for she knew how court gossip could fly from one ear to another. Connor would be fighting the accusation of murder for the rest of his life. It simply would not matter if the earl declared him innocent.

"Dinnae fret. No one was actually accused. The earl merely informed the king of the murder of one of his knights and said he would soon have the guilty one. It was naught but a courtesy, asking if the king wished to judge the person or if it could be left to the earl to decide guilt and punishment."

"Thank God." Gillyanne frowned. "That still doesnae explain why ye are here at Dinnock."

"Ah, weel, the earl's mon Peter hunted me down, explained matters, and said the earl thought it might serve all well to have one of your kinsmen here." Payton shrugged. "So, I went to the king, told him I was wandering home for a wee while, and inquired if he had any errands he wished seen to, especially ones that I could carry out for him during my journey to Donncoill. Thus I was chosen to bring his reply to Dinnock, allowing Peter to return more quickly. This is to be left completely in the earl's hands."

"Oh good."

"Do ye have proof that your mon is innocent? The earl and I dined together last eve and he told me the whole sad tale. Your husband did have good reason to want to see his uncle dead."

"That he did," agreed Diarmot, "but he wouldnae have done it that way."

"Nay, he wouldnae," said Gillyanne. "Connor didnae kill the mon, Payton. He didnae discover the truth about his uncle until the earl told him about it all. I have knowledge that shows the murder was done when Connor wasnae anywhere near that wee cottage and two witnesses to his whereabouts to add weight to it all. I also have the true murderer, although I fear her madness is quite strong at the moment. But, there are two witnesses to the murder. They are the same three women who accused Connor."

"Weel done, lass."

"Do ye think the earl will accept it all?"

"Only one way to be certain. Ye must ask him. Here he comes now." He kissed her cheek, ignoring the threatening murmurs of the crowd of her self-appointed guardians. "Ye will do weel."

"Be ready to drag in those women," Gillyanne told Diarmot and then started to walk toward the earl.

Gillyanne gritted her teeth as she and the earl performed the necessary courtesies. She curtsied; he bowed. They took their seats at the head table and the earl served her some wine. Gillyanne complimented the drink and waited for him to invite her to tell him why she was there seeking an audience with him. She decided that, at times, courtesy could be pure torture.

"So, m'lady, have ye come to stop your poor husband from brooding again?" the earl asked. "I heard ye were verra successful last time."

It was hard, but Gillyanne beat down the urge to blush and to curse. She did not really need to see the amusement in the earl's eyes or hear the inflection in his voice, to know that he had heard her the night she had visited Connor. Perhaps, she mused, she should insist upon a gag each time she and Connor made love. Soon, everyone in Scotland would know that Lady Gillyanne MacEnroy bellowed when bedded. It was mortifying.

"Is he brooding again, m'laird?" she asked, knowing by the hastily suppressed twitch of his lips that her look of sweet innocence did not fool the earl for a moment.

"Nay. He is rather weary of being my prisoner, however. Who are those people with your cousin? I recognize wee Fiona and the mon named Knobby, but who are the others?"

Pointing out each one as she named them, she then said, "They have come to help me."

"Good, good. Why are they scowling at your cousin?"

Be patient, she told herself, then relieved some of her frustration with the earl by glaring at the ones who were behaving so badly toward Payton. "Payton greeted me with affection and they dinnae think he should have, cousin or nay."

"Protective of the laird's wife," murmured Lord Dunstan. " 'Tis good. And, men find it difficult to trust a mon as bonny as your cousin."

"I ken it. Poor Payton."

"That I should suffer such misfortune," the earl muttered.

"Ye are a fine, handsome mon, m'laird," she said.

The earl grinned. "Do ye mean to flatter me into freeing your husband? That is why ye are here, is it not? To free him?"

"Aye, m'laird. Connor didnae kill the mon. He certainly didnae kill him because he was sharing Meg's bed. The woman had bedded near every mon at Deilcladach. And, he didnae kill the mon because of those old crimes we now ken Neil was guilty of. Nay, poor Connor didnae e'en realize what his uncle was guilty of until ye told him."

"I had wondered about that, yet, he showed little reaction to what must have been devastating news."

Gillyanne sighed and shook her head. "I ken it. He probably just stood there like a stone and with about as much expression as one. 'Twas shock, I expect, but e'en if he felt devastated or seared with the pain of betrayal, he wouldnae let ye see it. Connor isnae a mon to show what he feels. He is verra controlled."

Lord Dunstan nodded slowly. "I have met him but a few times, yet I sensed that about him. 'Tis nay enough to free him, however."

"Of course not. I believe I can show that he couldnae have killed Neil for he was nowhere near that cottage when the murder was committed." She looked at Peter. "Ye arrived at the cottage in the afternoon?"

"Aye," replied Peter. "We were hard pressed to return here ere full darkness fell."

"And the blood was still wet?"

"It wasnae freshly spilled, but, aye, 'twas still more wet than dry."

"And since Meg told ye she had seen Connor kill his

uncle," the earl nodded in response to the hint of a question in her voice, "that means he was killed after the noon hour."

"Aye, that would be correct," replied the earl.

"Then Connor couldnae have done this murder for he truly was nowhere near that cottage, that village, or Deilcladach. At the time Sir Neil was stabbed, Connor was either at or riding hard for Sir Robert Dalglish at Dunspier to see if the mon could help him discover who had tried to kill me. From there he rode to Sir David Goudie at Aberwellen to see what that mon might ken. Then he rode back to Deilcladach, sending Diarmot and Knobby on ahead whilst he went to the cottage to speak to Meg and, mayhap, his uncle, two people he now kenned could be guilty. I have brought Sir Robert and Sir David with me for they have kindly offered to attest to all I have just said."

Gillyanne sat quietly as the earl waved the two men over to his side. Robert and David not only supported all she had said, but made it clear they did not believe Connor would have killed Sir Neil, either. They fully supported her claim that Connor had not known about his uncle, that Robert himself had only just begun to suspect that the man had something to hide about his involvement in the bloody past of all three clans. By the time the earl dismissed them, Gillyanne knew Lord Dunstan believed in Connor's innocence. She was going to have to make sure that Connor understood that his alliances were a lot stronger than he knew, even with the earl. Gillyanne could feel how relieved he was to be able to declare Connor innocent.

"Verra weel thought out, m'lady," the earl said. "I ne'er would have thought a woman would realize the importance of whether or not the blood was dry."

"Ah, weel, I come from a family blessed with many a skilled healer," she replied. " 'Tis one of the somewhat gruesome little details one picks up whilst learning such skills.''

"Dinnae be so modest, m'lady. 'Twas a weel planned defense; precise and leaving nay room for doubt in your conclusion." He smiled faintly. "I suppose ye mean to present me with the real murderer now."

"Aye, I do, but I am thinking ye already ken who it is." She looked back at her companions. "Will ye bring them in now, please?"

The earl sighed and shook his head. "The women, of course. The one named Meg?"

"Aye, m'laird," Gillyanne replied. "The other two did lie for her, but they are verra afraid of her. There was madness lurking in Meg, m'laird, and 'tis now out in full bloom. I can understand why the women feared her and did as she told them, especially when they found themselves in the midst of a murder of a knight. Yet, their lies blackened my husband's name and could have sent him to the gallows. And, they didnae offer the truth willingly or just to do what was right, but out of fear. I presented them with a greater, more immediate threat. So, I fear I cannae decide what to do with them."

"If they didnae wield the knife or plot the murder, I willnae hang them." He smiled when she sighed with relief. "Beyond that? It depends upon how much guilt I think they share with the leader. God's tears," he cried, staring wide-eyed at the door.

Gillyanne winced faintly as she watched Diarmot and Angus drag Meg over to the earl, Robert and David escorting the very subdued Peg and Jenny. Bound and gagged, struggling fiercely against her captors, and her butchered hair visible to all, Meg did look a sad figure indeed. The look in Meg's eyes, however, and the strong feelings of rage and loathing Gillyanne still sensed in the woman, told her that any sympathy Meg's appearance might stir in others would be quickly dispelled when the gag was removed.

The earl was firm yet not terribly frightening as he spoke to Jenny and Peg. It was clear that he was very angry over the lies they had told. Gillyanne did not need to reach out to test his feelings to know that. Both women told the truth now, huddling close to Robert and David when Meg fixed a malevolent gaze on them. Their very real fear of the woman softened the earl's attitude toward them ever so slightly. Gillyanne suspected they would not be punished too severely if only because the earl was a man who could accept the women being such utter cowards as a natural thing, would never hold them to blame for it.

After he had the other women taken away by his men, the earl ordered Meg's gag removed. Gillyanne was almost able to smile at the reluctance Diarmot revealed as he obeyed that command. That touch of humor vanished in a heartbeat with the first words out of Meg's mouth. Even the earl sat wide-eyed over the filthy, blasphemous, and confused litany of hate and fury that poured out of the woman. Gillyanne hoped he was not so shocked that he missed the varied bits of confession which were scattered amongst all that poison.

"Gag her," Lord Dunstan ordered in a slightly hoarse voice. "How did I fail to see such madness?" he asked as Meg was gagged and the earl's men dragged her away.

"It was weel hidden, m'laird," Gillyanne replied, pausing briefly as the earl told all of her companions and her cousin to sit down and have some wine.

"Why is it no longer hidden?" he asked when everyone was settled.

"I think the murder brought it out," she replied. "E'en the reasons why she killed Sir Neil MacEnroy might have helped to break the control she had upon it. Then her oh-so-clever plan to see Connor hang for her crime fell apart. With each little thing that went wrong, she lost more and more control over this illness writing inside her. Once her rage grew too great to keep a rein on, it all spilled out."

"What happened to her hair?"

"Ah, weel, as one does with a fever, it was cut in an attempt to release the demons she is possessed by." Gillyanne felt terrible about lying to the earl, but she did not really wish to admit to what she had done.

"Demons, eh? Why were little tufts left all over her head?"

She could see that the earl did not believe a word she had just said. It did not help that the expressions of her companions, an intriguing array of guilt, amusement, and overplayed innocence, made it all too clear that she was lying. Fortunately, she could sense that the earl neither cared about the lie nor that she had forced Meg's confession out of her.

"Weel, we didnae wish to leave her completely bald." Gillyanne waited patiently while the earl, Peter, and all her companions laughed, then sweetly asked, "Will ye free my husband now, m'laird?"

"Oh, he will be free in a moment or two." The earl paused and smiled at her. "As soon as ye sing one song for me. Your cousin told us ye have a most beautiful voice and I should very much like to hear it."

Gillyanne sent Payton a look that screamed traitor, but he just shrugged. It was obvious that none of those who had come to Dinnock with her intended to intercede. With a sigh of resignation, she stood up, clasped her hands at her waist, and began to sing.

It was a sad tale of a lordling who lived well, fought well, and married well. His lands and his people prospered. Then, one spring day, he saw a village girl singing sweetly to the lambs while watching over her sheep and he had to have her. He took her to his castle, securing her in a tower, where he could visit her as he willed. She sang for him when he commanded it and he gave her every luxury, but he refused to free her. Days passed;

then weeks, months, years. From the window of her luxurious prison she watched her betrothed marry another. She watched her parents buried. She watched life itself pass her by as she sat gazing out the tower window. Then, one day, the lordling arrived to find the room empty, the shutters opened wide. All that remained of the village girl were the flowers she liked to wear in her hair floating upon the water of the river below the window.

Glancing around as she finished the song, Gillyanne could see that Payton had actually heeded the words of the song. He gave her an amused look of gentle admonishment. She helped herself to a drink of wine and looked at the earl. He was actually dabbing tears from the corners of his eyes.

"Ah, m'lady, ne'er have I heard such a beautiful sound," the earl said, sighed, and then abruptly grinned. "I ne'er thought I would actually enjoy getting such a verbal slap, either. Or, was that just a wee scold?"

Gillyanne blushed with guilt even as she struggled to look sublimely innocent. " 'Twas but a wee song, m'laird."

"Of course. Peter," he said to his widely grinning man, "go and fetch that huge husband of hers." As soon as Peter left, the earl turned back to Gillyanne. "I will hang Meg. It may e'en be a kindness since she is so ragingly mad. 'Twill certainly make certain that others are safe from her venom. The other two women will be sent away to a remote property of mine to be servants. They willnae be allowed to leave, but they may choose how they live—either working at honest labor or on their backs. I care not."

Neither did Gillyanne so she just nodded. She had not wanted them to hang, yet, because they had helped Meg in trying to get Connor hanged, she did feel they needed punishment of some kind. They may or may not get that where they were going, but at least she would never have to see them again.

Payton came up beside her and gave her an embrace, keeping one arm wrapped around her shoulders as he said, "Ye did weel, lass. Verra weel."

"Going to pat me on the head?" she drawled and heard the earl laugh.

"Mayhap on the backside. Ah, I do believe your husband approaches," he murmured. "Swiftly. Eager to get out of that wee room, nay doubt."

Gillyanne started to step away from Payton only to have him frown at her and hold her closer. "Will ye nay introduce me?"

"Of course. I just thought, mayhap I should do it standing beside you and nay in your arms." She peered around Payton to see Connor briefly surrounded by his friends and family. He actually smiled at them all. Then Nanty pointed toward her. Connor took one look and started to stride toward her, no longer looking very cheerful. Gillyanne had the sinking feeling that Nanty had either not spoken up quickly enough, or had completely neglected to tell Connor that Payton was her cousin. Connor certainly did not look like a man thinking he was about to meet another member of her family.

"Here he comes," she said. "I really best move."

"Dinnae be so foolish. We are cousins. What can the mon object to?" Payton asked even as he started to turn to fully face Connor.

Payton's last word ended on a soft cry of surprise. Connor picked him up by the front of his doublet. To Gillyanne's surprise, Payton began to laugh. She was not quite sure what her cousin found so amusing about being dangled several inches off the floor by a big man with murder in his eye, but decided to worry about his odd sense of humor later. Gillyanne quickly grabbed hold of the fist Connor was about to smash into her cousin's pretty face.

"What are ye doing?" she demanded.

"What does it look like I am doing?" Connor said, feeling a tickle of amusement over the way she had wrapped both arms around his fist and was pressing it against her chest. "I intend to pound this pretty runt into the floor." He pulled his arm back again and nearly laughed at the way she shuffled along with it, refusing to let go. "Release me, wife."

"Ye cannae pound him into the floor. He is my cousin. *And* a guest of the earl."

Connor glanced toward the widely grinning earl who nodded. "I think ye have too many cousins," he grumbled at Gillyanne and lightly tossed Payton aside.

Gillyanne watched Fiona help a still laughing Payton to his feet. She was increasingly curious about what he thought was so funny, but a sudden strong instinct told her not to ask, that the answer he gave could prove awkward, expecially in front of so many people. That feeling was enhanced when she suddenly recalled her cousin's tales about how Payton had stuck his far too handsome nose into their business with their husbands. Even if it had not been done in a bad way, Gillyanne did not want him prying into her business, too. She released Connor's fist, a little surprised when he kept hold of one of her hands and held it close to his thigh.

"Connor, this is my cousin Sir Payton Murray of Donncoill," she said when Payton stood before them again. "Payton, this is my husband, Sir Connor MacEnroy, laird of Deilcladach." As had happened when Connor had met her father, both men bowed a little brusquely, yet not in such a way as to present any insult.

"Why are ye here?" he asked Payton, suddenly recalling some of the tales Neil had related about this far too handsome young man.

"When the earl sent word to the king about Sir Neil MacEnroy's death, asking if judgment could be left to him, he requested a Murray be the one to bring him the king's reply. After all, ye are wed to a Murray. For now."

Seeing the way Connor's eyes narrowed, Gillyanne quickly said, "Weel, now we can have a nice wee visit."

"Nay, now we can return to Deilcladach." Connor looked at the earl. "I am free?"

"Aye," replied the earl. "Your wife brought me the real murderer. Your accuser—that woman Meg. She will hang. Her two companions will be sent far away so that ye will ne'er be troubled with them again."

Gillyanne saw the earl slightly raise one brow when Connor grunted in reply and she inwardly sighed. She was going to have to do something about the MacEnroy habit of grunting, she decided. Then something the earl was saying firmly caught her wandering attention.

"And, of course, as his heir, all of Sir Neil's property comes to you," the earl told Connor. " 'Tis a small holding, but, I suspect that, with four brothers and a sister to provide for, ye will welcome it. I cannae recall the name—"

"Clachthrom," Connor and Diarmot replied at the same time.

"Clachthrom? A heavy stone?" Gillyanne rolled her eyes. "And here I thought Ald-dabhach a name which sorely needed changing."

"What is wrong with the name Ald-dabhach?" asked Connor. "It says what it is—an old piece of land."

"Dull. 'Tis painfully dull. I have been trying to think of a nicer name, something that stirs in heart and mind a more pleasant vision. Mayhap something to honor the heather or the flowers." She almost laughed at the looks of near disgust upon the faces of all the men. "Why would anyone call their keep *a heavy stone*? E'en *an old piece of land* makes more sense than that."

"That was what marked the best place to put the tower house." Connor shrugged. "If ye can think of a better name, a *monly* name, I may consider it. Or, rather, Diarmot can do so. He will have Clachthrom, be its laird. Antony can hold Ald-dabhach for us." Connor turned back to the earl. "Diarmot will send ye a full accounting of all my uncle held, m'laird. I dinnae believe Sir Neil did one for many a year."

Or an honest one, thought Gillyanne. The way the earl and Connor looked at each other told her they were thinking the same. She was not sure what Diarmot had just been given, doubted anyone there did, but she knew he would make something good of it and was pleased for him.

"So, ye will make Diarmot the laird of Clachthrom?" the earl asked and Connor nodded. "How old are the other two lads?"

"Antony is two and twenty," replied Connor. Angus is twenty. I always leave one brother at home. This time 'tis Drew, Andrew, who is eighteen."

"Weel, Diarmot, Antony, and Angus," the earl signaled the three young men to come closer, "have ye been knighted?"

"Nay, m'laird," Diarmot replied. "Connor thought 'twould be best if we gained the honors from another laird, that the title would hold more weight in other's eyes if it wasnae handed to us by our own brother. Sir Robert saw to Knobby being knighted after he helped the mon rout some thieves upon his land, but we were still a wee bit young then."

"Weel, ye are nay too young now."

"But, we havenae fought to earn it, m'laird."

"Nay? With your brother ye fought to survive, to prosper, and to keep a wide swath of land beneath my jurisdiction peaceful for twelve long years. 'Tis more than enough. In two, three years send the lad Andrew to me," he told Connor, then shrugged. "Or sooner if he is of a mind to do a wee bit of training away from Deilcladach. I will see that he gets his spurs, too."

Gillyanne moved to stand next to Fiona as the three brothers received their honors. She smiled tearfully when Payton, rolling his eyes, gently dabbed the tears from her and Fiona's faces with a fine linen cloth. He then draped an arm about her shoulder and kissed her cheek.

"I will see ye soon," Payton told Gillyanne when the ceremony was done and, after hearty congratulating his brothers, Connor looked their way and scowled.

"How soon?" she asked, watching Connor stride toward them and hoping he was not going to try to knock Payton down.

"The day after the morrow. Two nights. 'Tis up to you what ye do with them, loving."

"If we leave now, we can be home in time for ye to give me my bath," Connor said as he tugged Gillyanne away from Payton and started to lead her out of the earl's great hall.

Although still in shock over the news Payton had just given her, Gillyanne managed a hasty farewell and words of gratitude for the heartily laughing earl. Two nights, Payton had said. Two very short nights to try to gain some hint of affection from her husband before she had to make a choice. Tonight, she decided, she would simply enjoy the fact that Connor was free and safe. After all that had happened since she had been wounded, she did not have the strength or wit left to either decide or plot anything.

And, it would be especially difficult with her husband's hand sliding up under her skirts, she mused, then gasped, and grabbed at his arm in a vain attempt to stop him. Gillyanne quickly looked around and realized they were riding alone, several yards behind the others. Connor had also arranged their cloaks to shield them from view. It was obviously dangerous to be distracted around the man, she thought, and shivered as he slid his hand inside her braies to slowly stroke her.

"Connor," she protested faintly, "the others."

"Cannae see us," he said. "I missed this."

"I will make a noise."

"And I will smother it with a kiss."

"They will guess what we are doing."

"If they look our way, they will just think I am wooing my wife."

"This is wooing?"

"Aye." He nibbled on her ear. "Now, hush, wife," he slid a finger deep inside her, savoring her soft moan, "and ride."

Chapter Twenty-one

The brightness in the bedchamber puzzled Gillyanne as she stretched. Then she gasped and sat up. It was sunlight, the bright full sunlight of late morning. Connor had obviously decided she needed to rest and ordered everyone to leave her alone to sleep. It was considerate of him, kind, and might even be a sign that he felt some softness for her. It was also the very last thing she wished he had done. She had too much to plan to sleep the day away.

As she scrambled out of bed, her two cats rose up from the hollows of the rumpled bedcovers and also stretched. Since they did not sleep on the bed when Connor was in it, they had obviously taken some delight in her sleeping late. She stroked each of them and talked nonsense to them for a minute. Connor was very good to them, which had surprised her a little. He had not ordered the cats to stay off the bed, but his large size and restlessness had quickly convinced her pets that they preferred to sleep on the sheepskin bed Connor had made for them in a corner. She had also caught him patting them and slipping them little treats from time to time. Gillayanne wondered if that could be considered a sign that Connor was not as hard as he seemed to be.

Cursing softly, she moved to tend to her morning ablutions and get dressed. It was too sad for words that she was trying to find hints of Connor's emotions in the way he treated her cats. That was like trying to anchor thistledown in a high wind. Gillyanne knew the time had come to cease guessing and press for some statement or clear indication of what he felt for her.

Ask yourself if your pride will really afford ye that much comfort. Decide just how much ye are willing to risk ere ye give up on Connor.

Gillyanne cursed again as her mother's advice sounded in her head. Her mother was right and she knew it. She just wished she was not. Unfortunately, she had the examples of both Elspeth and Avery proving her mother's advice sound. Both of them had swallowed their pride to win their husbands and she doubted they regretted it for one single moment. Gillyanne suspected they had both been as torn as she felt now. In fact, she herself had witnessed much of Avery's confusion. The situations had been different, the obstacles varied, yet the choice had been the same in the end. Was the man worth subjugating her pride for, if only for one night? The answer was *aye.*

After tying back her hair, Gillyanne opened the door and followed her cats down to the great hall. It was frightening to think of opening her heart, exposing her feelings, to a man who had given her so few indications of what he might feel for her. He was very possessive, but most men were. He was possessive about his horse, too. Connor was no longer hot at night and icy cold during the day, but neither was he affectionate. He did tell her more now, but only when they were alone in the bedchamber, and very little of it was a true sharing of concerns, hurts, or joys. Their passion was hot and fierce, but she could not be sure he felt it as deeply, as completely, as she did. Her passion was all tangled up with her love. Connor's could easily be no more than simple male lusting. And that was where the gamble was, she supposed. She would hand him everything, despite not knowing the state of his heart, simply praying that he had something to give her in return for her gift. If he gave her nothing back, it would hurt her more than she cared to think about. No wonder she was frightened.

"Ah, Joan, good," Gillyanne said as that woman came out of the kitchens carrying a tray of bread, cheese, apples, and oatmeal. "I need to talk to you." Gillyanne sat down and filled a tankard with cider. "My cousin Payton told me that my family will arrive on the morrow."

Joan set the tray down a little too quickly, then sank into the seat next to Gillyanne. "Are ye leaving us?"

"Is naught secret here?"

"Verra little. We have all heard what Sir James told our laird. Ye can have this marriage ended because 'twas forced on you."

"Aye," Gillyanne replied a little reluctantly as she picked at her food. "If my fither is returning, 'tis almost certain he brings me the right to end my marriage to Connor. I would just as soon Connor didnae learn that I will face that choice on the morrow."

"I willnae tell him." Joan grimaced. "Feels a wee bit disloyal, but only a wee bit. Do ye *want* to leave him?"

"Och, nay. I do love the great brute, but—"

Joan nodded. "Aye. But."

"Is it so wrong for me to want something from him, some wee glimmer of affection? Do I truly ask for so much?"

"Nay, m'lady. If ye had no choice, I would tell ye to make the best of it, find what happiness ye can. Mayhap in the bairns ye would have, or in keeping a verra fine household, or e'en in using your healing skills. But, ye do have a choice. Ye also didnae make the choice to marry our laird, nay fairly, nay e'en by your own kinsmen's choice. Ye brought him a fine piece of land and many a new helpful ally. In truth, ye have given the mon a lot, e'en to showing him that it doesnae hurt to enjoy life a wee bit. He could give ye something more than making ye bellow with pleasure and being faithful. Though, neither of those are poor gifts.''

"Nay, and I treasure them," Gillyanne said. "But, if there is naught else, then neither of those will endure, will they?''

"True. Sadly, I think there is more. I would swear to it. Yet . . ." She shrugged.

"Aye—yet. Is it there and, if it is, will he share it or will he keep it as buried as he has so much else? There is a lot that is good about this marriage, certainly compared to many another. I need more, Joan. I need to ken that I truly matter to the mon, that I hold some piece of his heart. Honestly? I wish it all, but, for now, I would accept a piece, a solid hope.''

"I dinnae think it will work just to ask him."

"Nay. I have a plan." She laughed softly at Joan's exaggerated expression of concern. "Wretch. I plan to follow my mither's advice. She suggested that, mayhap, 'twould be best to cast pride aside and let the mon ken exactly what it is he will lose if I leave him.''

"A wise woman. Just how do ye plan to do that?" Joan suddenly grinned. "I think he has seen almost everything ye have, m'lady.''

Gillyanne giggled. "Sadly true. Nay, I mean to show that mon all that is in my heart. I have nay been as guarded as he has, but I have been cautious, protected my heart. Pride. No one wants to offer all only to have it disregarded. There lies a pain it takes courage to court. I will do it, though, on the chance that, if I bare all, mayhap he will soften a wee bit and give me something to hang my hopes on. If he doesnae, weel, the humiliation willnae last so verra long for I can walk away from it all on the morrow."

"And if he doesnae give ye e'en that hope, then he deserves to have ye leave him. What if he comes to his senses later?"

"I willnae torture myself with that hope, but I willnae turn him away. If he comes to offer me e'en a little of what I need, I will return. I love him too much not to."

"And how can I be of help?" asked Joan.

"Weel, I begin to fear all of Scotland kens there is one place Connor and I seem weel matched. Feeling— shall we say—warmly, will make it easier for me to speak freely. Mayhap, if I do it when we are both feeling warmly, he will be at ease enough to do the same. I also want everything to be a wee bit different—seductive, romantic."

Joan nodded. "Because, if it is, ye may feel the same and gain that courage ye will need."

"Exactly," Gillyanne said. "Mayhap a few herbs for the bath. Monly ones, of course. He sniffs out roses or lavender and he will probably run all the way to Edinburgh." She laughed along with Joan. "Candles."

"Good ones, mayhap a hint of scent. Aye, we have a few of those."

"All his favorite foods, especially the sweets. No strawberries. With my luck, I will accidentally eat one and they make me come out in itchy spots."

"Nay verra seductive that."

"Nay. A few soft coverings added to what is already there. My cousin Payton once told me soft things please a mon and that women enjoy the feel of them against their skin. And, if anyone should ken such things, 'tis my cousin Payton."

"And he tells ye such things?"

"Usually only after a few large tankards of good wine.

He ne'er gets too precise. Oh, and something enticing to wear. I have that.''

"Ye do?"

Gillyanne nodded. "Aye. My cousin Avery occasionally gives me enticing things to wear. She says I am to use them when I start to *foolishly think I am nay pretty.* She says such clothing makes a lass feel pretty and alluring. And, she says, sometimes it can stir a mon as much, if nay more, than if ye stand there naked. Something about teasing them with a glimpse of what they want."

"Your cousins told ye some verra odd things considering ye were just a maid." Joan blushed a little. "Mayhap, if ye stay, we could have a talk. Mayhap if I am a wee bit more, weel, clever, my Malcolm willnae seek out another lass again."

"Ah, Joan, I will gladly tell ye all ye may wish to hear. But, I truly dinnae think Malcolm really sought out Meg, and he didnae end up with her because ye lacked something or she was clever in the bedding. From what little I gathered, and some of that came from Meg herself, that woman was nay more than a kiss, a fondle, and a rut. I also think Malcolm, like Connor, believed much of what that vile fool Neil told them o'er the years— such as how having lemans and a wife is perfectly acceptable, all men do it, and the wife kens it, allows it, e'en wants it."

Joan smiled faintly. "When Malcolm was groveling with apology, he did say such things. He truly thought I wouldnae care, that I kenned it was what men did. I fear I burned his ears with a few harsh words over that idiocy."

"Good for you. I feel 'tis a woman's sacred duty to let a mon ken when he is spitting out nonsense." She breifly shared a laugh with Joan. "Now, to the plans for my night of confession."

"Ah, m'lady, I do so hope this works."

"Nay more than I, Joan. Nay more than I."

* * *

Connor stepped into his bedchamber and stopped, stilled by surprise. Slowly, he closed the door behind him. His bath was ready for him, but that was all that remained the same. There was a scent in the air, a crisp herbal scent he found very pleasing. There was no fire lit for it was a warm night, but candles were all around the room, bathing it in a soft light. He was not sure where it had all come from, but there were soft sheepskins on the floor, even draped over the chairs, and a swath of deep red velvet was thrown upon the bed. The table near the fireplace was covered with a vast array of food and drink. Gillyanne stood by the tub wearing a night shift and robe all made of the sheerest linen he had ever seen, and it seemed to be precariously held on to her lithe body by little more than thin ribbons.

"What is this all about?" he asked as he slowly walked toward her and began to unlace his doublet.

"A small celebration. Ye are free and the danger is passed," she replied as she took over the removal of his clothes.

Just watching her move, her garments and long thick hair swirling around her in an intoxicating dance was making Connor eager to toss her down onto one of the sheepskins and bury himself deep inside her. "Ye have already bathed."

"Aye." Gillyanne carefully folded his clothes and set them aside as he climbed into the bath. "Tonight is for you."

"For me?" As she began to wash him, he had to fight the urge to drag her into the water with him. "*Me* wants ye in this tub."

"Nay. Slow. Tonight we try to be patient. We have all night."

That sounded very intriguing, thought Connor. One thing he did have was patience and control, or so he used to until he had discovered what it felt like to make love to Gillyanne. He also liked the idea of celebrating his freedom, the clearing of his name. He had wanted to *celebrate* last night, but, after one very satisfying tussle, he had realized that Gillyanne was exhausted. After all the running about she had done to extract him from the trouble he had fallen into, he had almost forgotten that she had been wounded barely a week ago. It was clear that she was well rested now, he mused, as he stepped out of the bath and she began to dry him off.

His eyes widened slightly as, following the cloth she used to caressingly wipe the water from his back, came the warm touch of her lips. He closed his eyes and reached deeply within for every scrap of control he had as she both dried his back of the cooling water and heated his skin with her kisses. When she even kissed and playfully nipped his backside, he trembled.

She stepped in front of him to carefully dry then kiss each arm. "Just how slow do ye intend to be?" he asked in a thick voice as she kissed the hollow at the base of his throat.

"Verra slow," she replied as she dried then kissed the ridge of his collarbone. "Would ye deny a lass the chance to enjoy this fine strong body? Such smooth skin, such beautiful warmth for a lass to press herself against."

Connor trembled faintly when she licked his nipples. She continued down to his stomach, drying him, caressing him with her lips, and murmuring flatteries. He knew he was big and strong, that the lasses seemed to like his looks well enough, but none had ever said so in such heated tones. Gillyanne was saying aloud what he had often thought he had seen in the looks she gave him and he found it produced a very heady feeling inside him. She thought he was beautiful, all that was perfect in the form of a man, and he was deeply stirred by that. It was, of course, nonsense, and he did not believe it for a moment, but Gillyanne did and that made him feel very good indeed.

"Ye missed a place," he said when she went from his stomach to his legs, ignoring the part of him that ached for her touch.

"As if I could miss that," she murmured as she dried his long legs then kissed and gently nipped the inside of each strong thigh. "I was but saving the best for last."

She began to dry his groin with far more care and attention than was needed. "So wonderfully big here. All any lass could ask for," she said as she replaced the stroking of the drying cloth with the gentle caress of her fingers. "I think ye are beautiful here, too. All silk and steel. When I see it like this, hard and arrogant, all I can think of is how it feels deep inside me, stroking me to pleasure."

Connor groaned softly, tangling his fingers in her thick hair as she licked him. "Lass, ye have me so full and aching already, I am nay sure how much of this I can enjoy."

"Enjoy all ye wish, my love. I can wait. Enjoy it to its fullest, if ye so desire."

He wanted to ask her exactly what she meant, if she really was offering a pleasure he had only heard about and had not had the courage to ask for or try to steal, but he managed only a soft groan as she began to love him with her mouth. The heat of her mouth, the stroke of her tongue, and the caress of her clever soft hands made all his attempts at grateful flattery for her gift sound like drunken gibberish. For as long as he could, he watched her love him, even though he knew the sight made it even more difficult to grasp any control. Many would think her in a subservient position, but he was the one enslaved. Then he lost all ability for coherent thought, sinking deep into the pleasure she gave him, praying he could find the will to endure the passionate onslaught for a very long time.

It was several moments after a blinding, shuddering release, that Connor realized what he had done. Gillyanne had kept him teetering on the edge of release for so long, he was not exactly sure when he had fallen into it. Cautiously he opened his eyes, taking courage from the fact that she was softly kissing his belly and stroking the backs of his legs. When he tugged her to her feet, she simply looked a little dazed and flushed with desire. There was not the faintest glimmer of disgust. Inside, he did a little jig of delight and relief as he led her over to one of the two chairs set near the table of food. He sat down on the sheepskin-draped seat and pulled her down onto his lap.

Connor started to feed Gillyanne and let her feed him, watching as her breathing slowed and the blush of desire faded from her cheeks. He was a very lucky man. He had never had such an exciting, passionate lover and never would have expected to find one in the tiny, gently bred Gillyanne. Shyness and modesty occasionally raised their heads, trying to confine her passion, but Gillyanne did not let them win. He did, however, have her drink deeply of the wine for he wanted both of those blood-cooling emotions well drowned. Connor intended to pay her back in full for the loving she had just given him, and, considering the plans forming in his mind, a hint of wine-induced euphoria in his wife would make it easier for him.

Something was gnawing at him, however. Some faint twinge of dissatisfaction. That made no sense at all. What could he possibly be dissatisfied about? He had a wife who brought him a fine dower land, one he shared a fierce passion with, one who was restoring the rebuilt Deilcladach to a genteel glory he was not sure it had ever enjoyed, one who thought him beautiful, and one who called him her love.

He nearly choked on the wine he was drinking. *My love.* She had called him *my love.* Connor suddenly knew that he badly wished that to be true. He wanted her to be more than passionate, more than appreciative of his body, more than dutiful He wanted her to care for him, to love him. There was the root of his dissatisfaction. He did not really know how she felt about him, could only guess from the way she looked at him or touched him. In thinking of ways to keep her at his side, he had considered the passion they shared, even considered getting her with child, but now he knew what was needed to hold her at Deilcladach was love. Gillyanne had to love him or he could never be truly certain that she would stay. Connor decided that, before they left this room, he would know what was in her heart.

" 'Twas a fine meal, lass," he said, and stood her on her feet.

Gillyanne was unsteady on her feet for just a moment, but quickly steadied herself, and frowned when Connor started to clear all the things from the table. "Ye dinnae have to do that."

"Aye, I do." Once the table was cleared, Connor sat down and looked at her. " 'Tis a night for me, aye? To celebrate?"

"Aye."

"Then take that bonny thing off, lass."

"It was supposed to entice you."

"Oh, it has done that. 'Tis why I want it off."

Connor watched as she carefully unlaced the robe and night shift, letting them slide down to her feet. Her long hair, gleaming with hints of red in the candlelight, provided some covering as she folded each piece and set them on a chair before facing him. He ignored her blushes as he sat there staring at her for a few moments before leaning forward to turn her around. She was slim and small, but he found her sleek little body beautiful. A shiver went through her as he kissed his way down her elegant spine then kissed and nipped at her taut little backside before turning her around to face him.

He pushed her hair back over her shoulders and slid his hands down to her breasts. Connor watched with appreciation as her nipples hardened beneath the touch of his fingers and her breathing quickened. Slowly, he trailed his fingers down her taut belly and slid them between her legs. He watched himself stroke her until she tried to press her legs together. A quick glance at her face told him she was slightly embarrassed.

"Ah, lass, ye say ye think me beautiful. To me," he stroked her again, "this is beautiful." He stood up, took the soft sheepskin from the chair, and spread it on the table, then picked her up and set her down on it. "I mean to wallow in that beauty," he said as he pulled his chair closer to the table and sat down.

"Connor," she gasped, but his broad shoulders between her thighs prevented her from closing her legs.

"Now, lass," he removed the hand she tried to shield herself with, "I didnae deny ye your pleasure of me."

"Weel, nay, but ye are a mon. Men dinnae have any modesty."

"I am going to have to teach ye nay to have any whilst in this bedchamber."

Connor leaned closer and feasted on her taut little breasts until he felt her body soften. Stroking her legs, he draped them over his shoulders. By the time he began to kiss his way down her slender body, she was wriggling on the table and making those soft sounds of need he so enjoyed hearing. Her whole body tensed, however, when he finally reached his goal and kissed those soft reddish brown curls.

"Bonny Gilly, be true; ye like this as much as I do. I but return the gift ye gave me." He kissed her again. "Tell me, Gilly. Tell me how much ye like it."

Gillyanne cried out with a soft mixture of pleasure and reluctance as the heat of his intimate kiss spread throughout her body, stealing all resistance and leaving only the pleasure. "Aye, Connor, aye. It fair drives me mad."

She threaded her fingers through his hair, stroking his head as he loved her. A part of her was reeling in shock over her brazenness as she watched him have his way with her, but a greater part of her suddenly understood why he watched her when she pleasured him. It was intoxicating, heightening the pleasure. Soon the strength of her own desire closed her eyes. When her release tore through her, she collapsed on the table, crying out his name, but he was relentless, restoking her desire before it had completely waned. The second time she reached desire's summit, she told him she loved him.

As Gillyanne came to her senses, she felt Connor soothing the lingering heat in her nether regions with a cool cloth. When that caused a flicker of interest to stir in her sated body, she cursed herself for a wanton. Some little memory pinched at her mind and Gillyanne began to think she had done something that would cause a wrinkle or two in her grand plan. She blushed, then smiled, when Connor leaned over her and kissed her cheek. In a moment, she told herself, she would find the strength to arrange herself with some attempt at modesty.

"So, my wee wife loves me," Connor said as he nibbled on her ear.

There was that wrinkle, she thought, shivering a little with pleasure when he traced the shape of her ear with his tongue. More than a wrinkle, she decided. More like a complete rending of every little plot and scheme she had devised. It was true that she had planned to tell him how she felt. She had planned, however, to do it in a romantic way, at a time when she was holding the reins in their lovemaking. Bellowing it out while lying sprawled on a table like a filleted haddock lacked dignity. Worse, it gave Connor the upper hand and did not make him feel compelled in even the smallest sense to offer her some words of affection in return.

"Your wee wife said that, did she?" She was a little surprised there was enough strength left in her legs for them to stay in place when he wrapped them around his waist.

His palms flat on the table, Connor watched her closely as he eased into her. "Aye, she did."

"Mayhap ye imagined it." Her greedy body started to come to life and she stroked the backs of his legs with her feet.

"Since ye bellowed it out, I suspect I could go ask the people in the great hall to verify it. Possibly the stable lads as weel."

"And I am beginning to think I may have been mistaken," she drawled and gasped softly when he withdrew almost completely, then, grasping her by the hips, thrust back inside.

"And I think I will have to make ye tell me again. Just to be sure, ye ken."

Gillyanne stared up at the ceiling of the bedchamber and repeated every curse she knew. He had made her tell him again. In fact, that time he had tied her wrists to the bedposts and licked thickened cream off her, she suspected she had told him a half dozen times. Her only consolation was that she had gained some control of her voice so that she had not screamed out her capitulation to the whole of Deilcladach.

And what declarations had she gained from him? None. Not one. Thinking over all he had said to her throughout the exhaustingly sensuous night, she could find not one word that expressed any true depth of feeling. She knew his passion, knew what stirred it, even knew a few things that could swiftly fray his great control, but, of what lay in his heart, she knew absolutely nothing.

Slipping out of bed, she had a brief wash. The urge
to fall down weeping was strong, but she refused to give
in to it. She had not been able to pull any words of love
from Connor with passion. She certainly did not want
to be dragging some weak, vague declaration out of him
because he pitied her or just wanted her to stop crying.

After pouring herself a goblet of sweet cider, she
started back to the bed, pausing when she caught sight
of the two strips of soft linen hanging limply from the
bedposts. Her gaze went to them, to her sleeping husband sprawled on his back, to the pot of sweet, thick
cream set on the table by the bed, then back again.
Gillyanne had no hope that one last round of mindless
passion would wrench any words of affection from Connor. Yet, at some time during the night, she had lost
control of the game she had so carefully planned. Perhaps it was time to regain that control. At least later,
when she was tormented by the memories of this night,
she could remember that it ended with her holding the
reins.

Connor woke to the feel of a cool damp cloth moving
over his body. He opened his eyes in time to see Gillyanne toss aside the cloth she had just washed him
with. She knelt at his side, beautifully flushed, beautifully naked, sipping on a drink. When he moved to
reach for her, his eyes widened. One quick look told
him he was well secured to the bedposts. It appeared
his little wife knew how to tie a good knot. He looked
at her again. She set her goblet aside and picked up
the cream he had so enjoyed licking off her. He felt
the warmth of desire rush through his body. When he
met her gaze, he thought he saw a deep sorrow and
pain reflected there, but it was gone too quickly for him
to be sure.

"Revenge, lass?" he asked.

"Aye." The thought of the lovemaking to come was

pushing her sadness aside and Gillyanne welcomed the reprieve.

"Weel, may the poor prisoner ask for a wee boon?"

"Do ye expect mercy?"

"A wee bit. When I cannae bear the torment any more, lass, take me inside. I want to be buried deep in your tight heat when the end comes."

"I shall consider it," she said, and quickly cleared the telltale huskiness from her voice.

"And, mayhap, ye will have mercy enough to bring a sweet bit of yourself close enough for me to taste now and then."

When she found herself wondering which *sweet bit* to offer first, Gillyanne inwardly cursed. So much for regaining the reins.

Chapter Twenty-two

"Connor, I think ye have some trouble."

Yanked from a pleasant memory of his wife saying she loved him while he was buried deep inside her, it took Connor a moment to understand the importance of Diarmot's words. "Trouble?"

"Aye. The Murrays have returned."

Slowly closing the ledger he had been unable to concentrate on, Connor turned to look at his brother. "Where is Gillyanne?"

"Gone out to meet with them." Diarmot hastily got out of the way as Connor leaped from his seat and strode out of the small solar where he dealt with the business of Deilcladach. "She was out the gate ere they had reined to a full halt. She kenned they were coming."

And now Connor knew the full meaning of last night. Gillyanne had either been saying farewell or had wanted something from him, something he had failed to give her. He quickly discarded the idea that it had all been a heated farewell, even though he liked the other possibility even less. A woman did not speak to a man as she had, love him as she had, or bare her soul as she had, if all she meant to do was walk away. She had been trying to get him to give her a reason to stay, something beside the passion they had glutted themselves with, and all he had done was take.

At the gates he stopped and stared down at her things, all neatly packed. Her cats stared up at him from their basket. Connor thought they looked accusing, even disappointed, then told himself not to be a fool. That was his own guilt and fear twisting his thoughts. He looked to where Gillyanne was talking to her father, a small woman he suspected was her mother, James and the annoyingly handsome Payton. Ignoring Diarmot's soft warning to tread carefully, Connor walked toward the Murrays, vaguely aware of his brothers and Knobby falling into step behind him.

"Weel, lass, I can take ye away from here now," Eric said after Gillyanne had embraced and kissed her mother in greeting.

"Coercion was acceptable?" Gillyanne asked, trying to swallow the pain swelling up inside her.

"Aye." He smiled slightly at his wife when she slipped her arm through his. "Your wound?"

"Healed enough for riding."

"Gilly, sweet," said Bethia, "answer me three questions."

Gillyanne sighed and stared at her feet, wondering why she ever thought she could hide her feelings from her mother. "Must I?"

"Aye, ye must. Do ye love him?"

"Aye."

"Do ye want to leave?"

"Nay."

"Are ye carrying his bairn?"

It was a question Gillyanne was afraid to even consider. The moment her mother had asked it, Gillyanne had felt as if her stomach had just plummeted into her boots. She tried to think of when she had had her last woman's time and the only one she could recall had ended just before her marriage. For a moment she tried to drown her growing suspicion with excuses from the rigors of travel to her wounding, but failed miserably.

She continued to stare at the ground, envisioning herself down there, kicking and screaming like a furious child. It was not fair, she thought. Marriage to a man she adored, but who did not, or could not, love her would be a hell on earth. Her father had the means to free her from that dire fate, but, now, she was not sure she could make her escape.

"Ah, Gilly," Bethia murmured, then sighed and shook her head.

"I cannae be sure," Gillyanne protested, but knew it sounded as weak as she suddenly felt.

"Ye are sure. I can see it in your face. 'Tis nay so easy now."

"It wasnae easy before," Gillyanne muttered, crossing her arms over her chest and fighting the urge to cry.

"Ye cannae get him to say anything to make ye stay? Is there truly no hope that he might care for you, if nay now, later?"

"I certainly didnae see any and I tried verra hard to find a scrap or two."

Bethia smiled faintly. "I am quite certain ye did."

"Ye said he was a hard, tightly controlled mon," said Eric. "Mayhap ye arenae looking hard enough. Ye cannae sense what he feels and thinks. Are ye expecting him to act like the men in your own family?" He reached out to stroke her cheek. "Ye havenae had much luck with men."

"I havenae had any luck at all, Fither," Gillyanne drawled.

"Fools, the lot of them. Yet, mayhap that disappointment clouds your judgment." He grimaced and swept his hands through his hair. "Ah, Gilly love, I ken what ye fear, ken why ye should dread facing it year after year, yet, are ye absolutely certain that is what ye would face? Ye love the fool. 'Tisnae something ye can just walk away from. And, if there is a bairn . . ."

"It changes everything," she finished for him. "What do ye wish me to do, Fither? I ken it wouldnae be right to walk away if I am carrying his bairn, yet, if I stay until I am sure . . ." she shrugged. "If I stay, then, if I am nay with child now, I soon will be."

"Oh, dear," murmured Bethia. " 'Tis like that, is it?" she asked, but her gaze was not on Gillyanne. "He certainly is big."

Gillyanne sighed. "He is coming out here, isnae he?"

"Aye. Who are those people clumped behind him?"

"Knobby and Connor's brothers," Gillyanne answered after turning to watch her husband stride toward her. "Diarmot, Nanty, Angus, and Drew. I dinnae see Fiona. Wheesht, and it looks as if near every mon, woman, and bairn of Deilcladach is looking this way. I suppose it was foolish to think this business could be somewhat private. And, Connor certainly doesnae look like he intends to be pleasant."

"It can irritate a mon when his wife decides to walk away from him," murmured Eric, gaining an identical scolding look from both his wife and his daughter.

Connor stopped but feet away from Gillyanne and her family. She had that sad, hurt look in her eyes again and he knew he had put it there. What he was not sure of was how to take it away. She was asking for something he was not sure he could do. The feelings she sought were all there, he could no longer deny it, but he did not know how to let her know it without baring his soul. It was acceptable for a woman to speak of such things, but he was a man, a laird. To let the world know how badly he needed her would make him look weak, soft. She had to understand that he could not do that.

"Wife," he said, "come here." He held out his hand.

Gillyanne took a step toward him before she realized what she was doing. She stopped and glared at him. "Why?"

"Why? Ye are my wife."

"Not for verra much longer."

"Ye took vows."

"Coerced."

"Curse it, Gilly!"

His words were cut off as his brothers and Knobby encircled him and forced him back a few feet. He saw the look of irritation on all their faces. Connor knew he had started to let his temper get the best of him, but being angry was far better than revealing the fear gnawing at his innards. Yelling was certainly more manly than dropping to his knees and begging her to stay.

"Ye didnae heed a word anyone said to ye, did ye?" grumbled Diarmot.

"Since none of ye are married," Connor snapped, "forgive me for thinking that ye may not have been experts on the matter."

"Laird," Knobby said, "ye willnae stop her from leaving if all ye do is yell at her."

Connor took a deep breath to calm himself, but it only partly worked. He was filled with the urge to grab Gillyanne and lock her in their bedchamber. Then he could have time to figure out how to be the strong laird Deilcladach needed and give his wife some of the caring she needed. He did not have that time now. He felt as if he were pushed hard into a corner and he did not like it.

"Fine. Agreed. I will cease to yell at her."

"A few words about feelings wouldnae hurt," said Diarmot even as Connor moved back to face the Murrays.

"Come back to Deilcladach with me, Gillyanne," he said in what he hoped was a calm tone of voice. "We will talk. Ye dinnae want to leave."

"Nay? What have I got to stay here for?" Gillyanne was surprised to actually feel something from him. Connor was highly agitated.

"Ye are my wife. Ye love me."

"Aye, we heard ye tell him so," said Drew. "Near everyone at Deilcladach heard ye bellow it."

Gillyanne almost thanked Diarmot for knocking his brother down. She heard her father murmur the word *bellow* and forced herself not to look at him. The important thing now was Connor and whether or not he would give her some reason to stay.

"Aye, dinnae forget that," Connor said and ignored the muttered curses from behind him. "I can make ye yell."

It was almost painful to resist the urge to kick him, especially when she heard her father choke back a laugh, telling her he now understood Drew's talk of bellows. "I suspect, in time, I could find another to do the same." Despite the tension and sadness gripping her, she was almost able to smile at the looks of outrage on Connor's brothers' and Knobby's faces.

"Nay, ye will not," he said, grinding out the words from between gritted teeth. "Ye are *my* wife."

"Connor," she said quietly as she stepped closer to him, "I need a reason to continue with this. Aye, I love you. But, while that is why I ache to stay, 'tis also why I must leave."

"That makes no sense."

"It does. I cannae stay, loving ye as I do, when I get naught back from you. Nay," she said when he started to speak. "I do not speak of the passion we share. In some way, that can be gained almost anywhere. If I stay, my love for ye will soon become more curse than blessing. I see before me days of giving to ye all I have within me and slowly being starved for some return. I cannae bear the thought of it. Mayhap I am selfish, but I *need* something from you. It doesnae have to be all or nothing. I but ask for some wee piece of your heart."

He looked at everyone standing there, then at her. Connor knew what she needed, but the words would not come. Instead, he grew furious, at her for pushing him to this point, at the Murrays for trying to take her away, and even at his family for expecting so much from him. He had become what Deilcladach needed and it had saved them all, yet, now, everyone seemed dissatisfied with who he was, wanted him to change.

"Then go," he said in an icy cold voice. "Break your vows." He turned and strode back toward Deilcladach.

"He will be back," said Diarmot as he and the others trotted after Connor.

Gillyanne felt her mother put her arm around her shoulders, yet she felt no immediate need for comfort. The man she loved had just told her to go and walked away from her. She should be feeling torn apart, yet she did not. To her surprise, she actually felt hopeful. Then she realized that she had actually felt what Connor was feeling. For the first time, he had been open to her senses. The feelings were not particularly pleasant ones, for Connor was battling anger, frustration, confusion, and, to her surprise, fear, but it did not matter. She had felt him and she was certain that could only be good.

"Are ye upset, Gilly love?" asked her mother, frowning a little as she studied Gillyanne's thoughtful expression.

"Nay," she replied. "I think, mayhap, I have been a wee bit unfair, expecting Connor to toss aside twelve years of training in but two months and a little. For the very first time, I could feel what he feels, Mither," she added softly.

"Ye have set the poor lad on his ear, then," said Eric, crossing his arms over his chest and smiling faintly when

Connor was brought up short at the gates of Deilcladach by a large group of women. "Your allies, I suppose."

"Oh, dear," murmured Gillyanne, recognizing Mairi, Joan, and Fiona at the fore of what appeared to be every woman and girl at Deilcladach. "This willnae make him happy. He is the laird. 'Tis *who* he is. 'Tis *what* he is. He is verra precise about what he must do and be to fulfill his duty as their laird." She frowned slightly when she caught her father staring at her rather hard. "What is it?"

"*It* is your answer, lass. Recall the tale ye told me of his life," Eric said. "He set himself rules so that e'en as a lad, his people would follow him. Those rules kept them alive, or so he believes. In truth, loving, I was watching that lad order ye home and I saw a young mon who would probably give ye whate'er your wee heart desired, but he doesnae think he can."

"Not if he wants to remain a strong laird and keep Deilcladach safe."

"Exactly." Eric nodded toward Connor. "And, I dinnae think 'tis ye who can force a complete change. 'Tis up to his clan to make him see that he will lose no stature in their eyes if he softens to his wee wife."

"Mayhap they have to show him that he doesnae have to fight for their approval and loyalty any longer. He has it."

"Ye seem to have left your wife behind, Connor," said Fiona, scowling at her brother.

"She wants to leave," he said and his eyes widened at the vast array of scornful noises erupting from the group of women he faced.

"If she wants to leave, 'tis because ye do naught to make her want to stay. Why cannae ye just say something nice once in a wee while? Tell he she is bonny." There was a murmur of agreement from the women.

"I tell her that," he protested and decided that watching so many women roll their eyes in a gesture of feminine disgust was a little disturbing.

" 'Tis no good telling her that when ye are in a bedding mood," said Joan. "Wheesht, a mon will tell a lass with a huge, hairy wart on her chin that she is the bonniest thing he has ever seen if it will lift her skirts. Ye have to say it at other times so that she kens ye mean it."

Connor wondered when matters had gotten so out of hand that his people felt bold enough to instruct him. "I am a laird, and a mon, and a mon doesnae— Ow!" He stared at the tall thin woman who had just whacked him on the leg with a gnarled walking stick. "Mother Mary!"

Knobby tried to grab his mother's walking stick only to receive a jab in the stomach. "Mother, ye cannae hit him. He is our laird."

"I ken it. He is also young enough to be me own lad," the woman said. "I was with his mother when he was born. I was his milk mother. And, *that* is the right I claim now, the right of an old woman who changed his soiled cloths and held him to her breast." She grabbed Connor by the ear. "That woman is intending to have a wee word with ye, laddie," she said as she pulled him a few feet away from the others. "If I hear one more word about what a mon does or doesnae do, Connor MacEnroy, I will beat ye bloody. Bury that foolishness with the evil mon who told it to ye, may his poisonous soul rot in hell."

"Aye, ye are right," Connor agreed as he rubbed his abused ear. " 'Tis just hard to forget things one learned while growing."

"Some should have ne'er been taught. Och, laddie, the wee lass loves ye. Dinnae ye care?"

"Ye dinnae understand. I have to be strong for the clan. A strong mon . . ."

"Doesnae let his woman leave him."

"Mother Mary, a laird cannae have any weaknesses. A laird has to think only of his clan, of its survival."

She pressed her long bony fingers against his lips. "Ye are strong, Connor. Wheesht, I think ye are one of the strongest people I have e'er kenned. When we stepped out of hiding to see naught but death and destruction, I could almost see the steel forming in your spine. A part of me wept for the lad who was fading afore my eyes, but another part of me said, aye, 'tis the way of it, lad. Get hard, get tough. 'Tis what we need. And we did. We needed hard to survive the rough times, the hunger and cold, the grievous loss of so many. But, laddie, 'tis over. We survived. We are at peace. Ye dinnae have to be the only rock we have to cling to. The widows are strong again, the lads and lasses are men and women now, and e'en most of the wee bairns are still alive."

"But, we need to be strong to stay that way. I need to be strong."

"Did the lass's father seem like a weak mon? One ye felt you could just ignore?"

"Nay," he replied without hesitation.

"Then have a hard look at that laird. See how he strokes his lass's hair, how he holds his wife close. He smiles at them, gives them wee kisses right in front of the men, jests with them and the lads. All that softness right there to see. Yet, the lass has complete faith in the mon's ability to help her, protect her. He commands and his men obey. Those two women ken they are cared about, mayhap e'en cherished, but they still look up to the mon."

"They have to. They are shorter than he is," Connor mumbled, but he knew what Mother Mary wanted him to see, and he did see it. He could watch that man stroke his daughter's cheek, his expression soft with affection, yet know instinctively that, if he ever came to swordpoint with the man, his added height and weight would not matter, that he would be in a hard fight for his life.

Laughter briefly darkened the woman's eyes. "Wretch. That lass loves ye, foolish boy. 'Tis a fine gift she gives ye. From what I have heard ye suit each other verra weel in the bedchamber. Are ye fool enough to toss that aside, too? She rose from her sickbed to come to you when ye were so sunk in gloom o'er the truth about your uncle. Mended that, didnae she? And, she didnae rest until she had ye set free, your name and honor scrubbed clean. She looks a wee, delicate lass, but all I hear tells me she has as much steel in her spine as ye do."

"Aye, she is verra strong," he said. "Clever. Full of life."

"She is a perfect wife for a laird. And, a good laird would think hard on those fine lands she brings to the marriage and all those new allies who can only make his clan stronger."

There was a soft murmur of agreement and Connor sighed. "They have all crept nearer, havenae they."

"Aye."

"When did I lose control?"

"Ah, laird, we owe ye our lives. Mayhap we just want to be sure that ye dinnae ruin yours. Go, lad. Spit out a sweet word or two and bring your wee wife home." She patted his cheek. "Trust an old woman. It willnae hurt too badly."

The soft chuckles that comment brought stopped abruptly when Connor turned to look at everyone. "If I succeed in bringing my stubborn wife back, the Murrays will be requiring food and beds. We wouldnae want them to be disappointed in the hospitality at Deilcladach, would we?"

He felt a little better when everyone hurried away, a chuckling Mother Mary following them. Then, straightening his shoulders, he walked back toward his wife, finding some hope to cling to in the simple fact that she was still there. It was a little embarrassing that he had needed to be lectured by Mother Mary before he saw the truth. He just wished she could have given him the courage to speak freely to Gillyanne, or, even more helpful, the right words.

"Your husband is returning," said Eric. "I wonder who the woman was who dragged him off by the ear?"

"It looked like it might be Knobby's mother," replied Gillyanne, tensing in anticipation and a rising hope. Surely, he could not be striding back just to tell her that she was taking far too long to leave. "He looks rather grim, doesnae he?"

" 'Tis a serious business he is about. Lass, ye willnae press him too hard, will ye? If he doesnae say any more foolish things."

Gillyanne diverted her attention from a rapidly approaching Connor long enough to give her father a quick smile. "I have learned enough o'er these last weeks to ken that, sometimes, with Connor, a little can mean a verra great deal indeed. I just remind myself now and again that no mon could have done what Connor did for his clan if he didnae have a verra big heart indeed."

"Wise lass," Eric murmured as Connor stopped about a foot away from them.

"Have ye come to say fareweel?" Gillyanne asked him, crossing her arms over her chest and steadily meeting his gaze.

As usual there was little to read in his eyes or expression, but she did feel the turmoil inside him. Despite the discomfort such confused yet strong feelings gave her, she reveled in it all. His shell was cracking. It might be only a brief glimpse, a short-lived bonding, but it could not have happened at a better time.

"Nay, that was said because I was, weel, irritated," Connor replied, somewhat resenting her apparent calm.

"Irritated?"

He ignored the hint of sarcasm in her voice. "I dinnae want ye to leave." Connor held out his hand to her. "I dinnae want ye to leave me," he said softly.

There was a longing in his voice that moved her and she cautiously put her hand in his. "I dinnae want to, Connor."

"Because ye love me."

"Aye."

"I need you," he whispered after pulling her close.

Gillyanne was deeply affected, not only by his words, but by the emotion behind them. The odd thing was, he looked almost ill. There was the glint of sweat upon his face and he was pale. Speaking his heart was obviously proving to be an ordeal, she mused, and had to bite back a smile. Gillyanne knew he would never understand that her amusement was born of love, of joy that that love was obviously returned, and a touch of sympathy for how difficult it was for him to reveal something when he had spent nearly half his life trying to hide everything.

"Ye love me," he said.

"Aye, I believe that matter has been weel settled now."

"So this shouldnae be so cursed hard."

Sympathy won out over her other needs and Gillyanne stepped closer to wrap her arms around him in a tight embrace. " 'Tis alright, my Viking. It can wait. Ye can try again later, when we are alone."

That was a very tempting offer, but Connor resisted the urge to accept it. Gillyanne openly confessed her love for him. At least once, he could do the same for her. He also refused to let fear and confusion lead him. They were just three little words. He *would* say them.

"Nay, I *will* do this." He took a deep breath, tipped her face up to his, and said, "I love ye."

Gillyanne pulled free of his light grip and pressed her face against his broad dchest. She was not surprised to feel the sting of tears in her eyes. All her fears had been banished and all her hopes restored with those three little words. All that kept her from crying like a baby was a touch of humor. Connor had looked grey enough to swoon as he had spit out the words between gritted teeth and the sigh of relief he had given afterward was so huge she was sure he had emptied his lungs.

" 'Tis settled now?" he asked.

She looked up at him and smiled. " 'Tis settled."

A soft cry of surprise escaped her as he picked her up and started for Deilcladach, breaking into a run after only a few long strides. She caught a glimpse of Fiona skipping out to her family and knew they would be seen to. Several objections to this mad dash occurred to her, but, when she realized he was headed for their bedchamber, she decided not to make them.

"Do ye think he said it?" Bethia asked her husband as she watched her daughter being carried away.

"Aye," replied Eric. "He was looking verra sick there for a moment." He shared a laugh with Bethia before smiling a greeting at the pretty young girl who stopped in front of them. "Weel met, lass."

"Weel met, m'laird," said Fiona. "I am Lady Fiona MacEnroy, sister to the barbarian who just left. I welcome ye to Deilcladach and beg ye to come inside." She curtsied, then clasped her hands at the waist of her dark blue gown, smiling proudly at the Murrays. " 'Tis pleased I am to welcome ye to the family as weel. Gillyanne is our treasure. She is teaching me to be a lady."

Fiona blinked when the brief silence of the Murrays was ended by hearty laughter, even the men at arms joining in. Gilly had been right; her family did find the thought of her teaching anyone to be a lady absolutely hilarious. Then Fiona grinned. Connor had his Gillyanne, but there was more to be gained from this union of the Murrays and the MacEnroys than a loving wife, good lands, and strong allies. Here was joy. Here was a love of life. Soon Deilcladach would share in those gifts as well. As she linked arms with the parents of her new sister and led them to Deilcladach, she knew fortune had smiled on them all when Connor had ridden to Ald-dabhach to claim its laird. But, she suspected Connor knew that. For a brother, he could be surprisingly clever at times.

"Did I see Fiona wearing a gown?" Connor forced his sated body up on one elbow and looked at his wife.

"Aye," was all Gillyanne could manage to say, her body still weak and tingling from their lovemaking.

Connor was tempted to get dressed and go down to the great hall to have a good look at that wonder, then looked at his wife and decided she was far more tempting. "Would ye really have left me?" he suddenly asked, trailing his fingers down between her breasts to her smooth, taut stomach.

"That was my plan."

A certain tone in her voice prompted him to ask, "Ye were changing your mind?"

Gillyanne sighed as she stroked his back. "Aye. Mother asked me a few questions."

"What were they?"

"Do I love ye?"

"And ye said *aye.*"

"I did. Then, did I really wish to leave ye?"

"And ye said *nay.*"

I did, although I was still terrified of staying, of loving ye so much and not kenning how ye felt about me."

She accepted his slow kiss for the silent apology she knew he intended it to be.

"And the third question?" he asked as he kissed her neck.

"Are ye carrying his bairn?" Gillyanne was a little surprised at how utterly still Connor went.

"And?"

"That was when I began to think I might have to change my plans."

Connor straddled her, his palms flat on the bed on either side of her shoulders. "Ye would have gone, taking my bairn away?"

She stroked his chest. "Nay. That I couldnae do."

"Yet ye still pressed me."

"Wouldnae ye have done the same?"

Recalling last night, he murmured, "I did." He sat back on his haunches and placed a hand on her stomach. "Are ye certain?"

"Aye. I havenae bled since the day before we married."

He settled himself on top of her and held her face in his hands. "Ye *will* be well."

"Aye, because ye love me."

"As ye love me."

"Aye, as I love ye."

Connor grunted and kissed her. Inwardly, Gillyanne laughed with delight. Her Viking would probably never be skilled at stroking her with sweet and tender words, but she had all she needed. And, she thought as he began to make love to her in earnest, she was becoming a strong believer in the saying that actions speak louder than words. They could certainly be far more enjoyable.

Epilogue

"There is an army approaching our walls."

Connor looked up from teaching his six-week-old son Beathan how to frown with the appropriate amount of dignity and stern authority. Diarmot looked remarkably calm considering what he had just said. When Diarmot said no more, simply helped himself to a tankard of ale, Connor wished his hands were free for his brother was begging for a sound clout offside the head.

"Since no alarm has been raised, I will assume we are nay being attacked," Connor drawled.

"Depends upon how ye wish to look at it."

"If ye dinnae start giving me some answers, ye will be looking at it through two blackened eyes."

Before Diarmot could reply, Gillyanne burst into the great hall. "My family is here, Connor," she cried.

A moment later, he found himself holding his daughter, too, and watching his wife run out of the great hall. She neither looked nor acted like a woman who had birthed twins a little over a month ago. He looked at his children who stared back at him with their mother's slightly mismatched eyes. Connor doubted he would ever cease to be astonished that his tiny wife had given him healthy twins, and done so with an aplomb that many of the clan still talked about.

"I suppose I had best go and greet them," Connor said and, after Diarmot took his son, stood up.

"Ye best prepare yourself," Diarmot warned as he walked out of the great hall by Connor's side.

Connor stepped outside and nearly gaped. His bailey was crowded with people, carts, and horses. Diarmot had been right to call it an army. Deilcladach had been invaded by Murrays.

He was still in shock as Diarmot nudged him down the steps to greet three of the few people he recognized. As Gillyanne's parents and James admired the twins, Connor calmed himself and looked over the crowd. There were far too many handsome men, he decided, and began to look for his wife.

"My, he is big."

Gillyanne smiled at Elspeth and nodded. "My own verra big Viking."

Avery nodded and shifted her infant son Craig to a more comfortable place on her hip. "And ye love him."

"Oh, aye." Gillyanne joined her cousins in staring at her husband. "I am so glad ye came. I really didnae expect you."

"Weel, when we heard how few of your family could come, Elspeth and I said that wouldnae do at all. Cameron agreed and he was verra curious to see what sort of mon was wise enough and strong enough to take ye on as a wife. It rather grew from there. 'Tis a busy time of the year, but, one by one, others plotted ways to make the journey. Uncle Balfour and Aunt Maldie were going to come, but he took a mild fever and she threatened to tie him to the bed. So cousins Ewan and Liam, their wives, and older children came instead."

"I see Cameron brought Malcolm, but nay Katherine."

"Katherine is too close to her childbed. Since the land Cameron gave them is nay so far from here, he felt it important Malcolm meet with your husband." Avery shook her head. "It is astounding how much Katherine has changed."

"She grew up," said Elspeth as she picked up her three-year-old son Ewing who had been swinging on her skirts. "And, your husband has finally spotted ye in this crowd, Gilly."

Gillyanne waved at her husband then linked arms with her cousins. "Let us get everyone introduced and settled. Then we can talk, I can show off my bairns, and ye can show off yours."

"That priest doesnae seem too fond of you, Connor," Cameron murmured as he, Cormac, and Connor stood by the huge fireplace in the great hall drinking ale and waiting for the feast to begin.

"We have a difference of opinion," Connor said, wondering if Lady Bethia would be successful in soothing the priest's ire as she seemed to be trying to do. "He claims I keep abducting him and I say I am merely fetching him to come and do his priestly duty. I fetched him and held him near a sennight when I went to claim Gilly. Then I fetched and held him a few days when the twins were born so he could tend to their wee souls the moment they were born. Then I fetched him for this, what Gilly says is a proper christening. He has only been here two days. I suspicion Beathan wetting his fine robes didnae soothe his temper much, either." He smiled faintly when the other two men laughed.

"Do ye think our wives are talking about us?" asked

Cormac, nodding to where the three cousins stood together.

"Probably," said Cameron.

"Who is that lad talking to my sister?" asked Connor.

"My son Christopher," replied Cormac. "He came with me to the marriage after my mistress, his mother, was hanged."

"And the lad next to him is the son I brought to my marriage," said Cameron. "Alan's mother was once my mistress and she was hanged, too."

Connor stared at the men. "My mistress was hanged, too."

"Jesu, there is an eerie coincidence," muttered Cormac. "No bastard though."

"Nay."

"Did ye nearly lose your lass? I was fool enough to let Elspeth go."

"And I let Avery go, too," Cameron said quietly.

"I nearly let Gilly leave me," Connor confessed then smiled faintly. "All our names begin with a C and we are all tall."

"And handsome," added Cameron. "And excellent lovers."

"Aye."

"And far, far luckier than we probably deserve to be," said Cormac and hefted his tankard in a silent salute to their good fortune which Cameron and Connor quickly returned.

With the feast nearing the end, Connor swallowed nervously as the time for the celebratory toasts came. He was pleased to hear the ones offered by friends and family, gratified to know that, no matter what happened, his children would always have someone to turn to. Each toast given, however, brought him closer to the time when he would have to speak. He could feel a trickle of sweat run down his back.

"Are ye all right?" Gillyanne asked, thinking he looked a little ill.

"Fine, wife. Just preparing myself to speak."

"Ye dinnae have to, Connor."

"Aye, I do."

When his turn came, he straightened his spine and stood up. "I thank ye all for coming to help us bless our bairns. And I thank ye for all the fine gifts. Most of all, I wish to thank ye Murrays for my wife. She is my joy, my heart, and the finest gift any mon could e'er have been blessed with." He looked at Gillyanne and raised his tankard to her. "I love ye."

Gillyanne barely heard the cheers as her husband drank to her. She grabbed his hand the moment he sat back down. He was a little grey and obviously sweating, but she thought he had never looked so beautiful. He scowled at her and she kissed him.

"That wasnae supposed to make ye cry," he muttered as he wiped the tears from her cheeks with his napkin.

"Oh, Connor, that was so beautiful."

"Weel, I wanted to thank ye. I kenned everyone would be honoring the bairns and 'tis ye I honor. I love the bairns—"

She placed her fingers over his lips. "I ken it." She kissed his palm. "No one has e'er given me a finer gift."

He inwardly cursed for he could feel the heat of a blush on his cheeks. "Weel, ye deserved it."

Gillyanne smiled. He had told everyone that he loved her. She doubted he would ever know how much that meant to her. It was a gift so pure and grand, she was not sure she could ever repay him. However, she mused as she exchanged a grin with her cousins, she would certainly give it her best try later tonight.

* * *

Connor sighed with satisfaction as he entered his bed-chamber. Gillyanne's mother had calmed the priest, the feast had been sumptuous and well prepared, he had pleased his wife with his words, and all his wife's family seemed content. He did find it a little daunting to think that he had not met all of them yet. The ones he had met had accepted him, though, and he could see the promise of strong alliances.

He shut the door behind him and then frowned. There was something different. He turned to stare at the door.

"We have a new door." He glanced at the other door in the room leading to the nursery and Gilly's solar. "Two new doors." He opened the door, suddenly aware of the weight of it. "Jesu, 'tis thick." He shut it again.

Idly wondering when her husband would notice there was a bath set out and she was wearing nothing but a drying cloth wrapped loosely around her, Gillyanne replied, "It certainly is. Verra, verra thick. Ye cannae hear anything through it."

"Are ye sure?" He studied the door one more time.

"Verra sure. And, there is a fine new bell to call the lads in to dine. I willnae be the bell anymore."

Connor started to laugh. "Ah, Gilly, ye are my joy."

She ran over to be enfolded in his arms. "I love ye."

"And I love ye." He kissed her then became aware of how little she was wearing. "Gilly?"

"I thought ye might want a bath."

"The bairns are only six weeks old. Are ye sure?"

Since she was already unlacing his clothes, she thought that a foolish question. "I am nay only sure; I am desperate."

"Weel, we cannae have that," he said as he helped her finish removing his clothes and carried her to the bath. "Ah, wife, ye are my heart, my joy, and my blessing."

"As ye are mine, my Viking. Always and forever."

"That will do for a start. Now, let us give those new doors a proper testing."

Please turn the page for an
exciting sneak peek of Hannah Howell's
newest historical romance
HIGHLAND ANGEL
coming from Zebra Books in May 2003!

"Are ye Sir Payton Murray?"

The fact that the voice coming from behind him was female stilled Payton's initial fear that he had been caught by the husband he was about to cuckold. Then it occurred to him that *anyone* catching him lurking beneath Lady Fraser's bedchamber window could cause him a great deal of trouble. Well, he mused as he tamped down the desire he had begun to feel at the thought of spending a few rollicking hours in the fulsome Lady Fraser's arms, he had developed a skill for talking himself out of trouble. It was time to use it.

As he turned to face this possible nemesis, he opened his mouth to begin his explanations only to leave it open, gaping at the vision before him. The woman was very small and very wet. Her hair hung in long dripping ropes over her equally wet gown. He suspected it was not just the moonlight which made her delicate heart-shaped face look so pale. The dark gown clung to an almost too slender body, but the hint of womanly curves was there. He wondered if she knew that she had more mud than slipper on her small feet. And, if he was not mistaken, that was marsh grass sticking out of one sleeve.

"Weel? *Are* ye Sir Payton? The bonny Sir Payton?"

"Aye," he replied, then wondered if that had been wise.

"The gallant and brave Sir Payton?"

"Aye, I . . ." he began, wishing she would discard the accolades as they always made him uncomfortable.

"The bane of all husbands Sir Payton? The lightning quick and lethal with a sword Sir Payton? The Sir Payton the ladies sigh o'er and the minstrels warble about?"

There was the distinct bite of mockery behind her words. "What do ye want?"

"So, ye *are* Sir Payton?"

"Aye, the bonny Sir Payton."

"Actually, I dinnae care if ye are as ugly as a toad's arse. I want the honorable, gallant, lethal with a sword, and willing to leap to the aid of those in need Sir Payton."

"The minstrels exaggerate," he snapped, then felt guilty when he saw her slender shoulders slump a little.

"I see. Ye did notice I was a wee bit damp, didnae ye?" she asked as she wrung out a handful of her skirts.

"Aye, I did notice that." He bit back the urge to smile.

"Didnae ye wonder why? 'Tis nay raining."

"I concede that I am a wee bit curious. Why *are* ye wet?"

"My husband tried to drown me. The idiot forgot that I can swim."

Although Payton was shocked, he forced himself to be wary. He had suffered far too many women trying all sorts of tricks to get close to him, to entrap him in some situation that could force him to the altar. Payton looked her over again; no one had ever tried dipping themselves in a murky river before. Nor, he mused as he recalled her words, had such a full bucket of sarcasm ever been poured over his head before. If she was trying to lure him into some trap, she was using some very peculiar bait.

"Why did your husband try to drown you?" Payton asked.

"Payton, my sweet courtier, is that you?" called Lady Fraser softly as she peered out her window.

Inwardly cursing, Payton looked up to see Lady Fraser's sweet face looking down at him, her long fair hair spilling over the sill of the window. He glanced toward the other woman only to find her gone. She had left as quietly as she had arrived.

"Aye, 'tis I, my dove," he replied, wondering why he felt disappointed that the girl had left.

"Come to me, my bonny knight. The warmth of my chamber eagerly awaits you."

"And a sweet temptation that is, my beauty."

Even as Payton stepped toward a cleverly arranged set of kegs, he heard a soft gagging sound. He looked around, expecting to see that sadly bedraggled girl, but saw nothing at all. Uneasy, he turned back to the kegs, musing that Lady Fraser was clearly no novice to the intrigues of cuckoldry. There before him was a deviously constructed stairway consisting of the kegs and several thick boards artfully nailed to the wall of the house.

"Are ye planning to just leave me here?"

That husky whisper startled him so much he stumbled a little as he again looked around for the girl. "I have an appointment."

A heavy sigh escaped the thick ivy on the wall to his left. Looking closely, he was finally able to make out her shape tucked neatly, and very still, within the shadows and foliage by the wall of the house. It was unsettling how well she used the shadows and how quickly and silently she had done so. Payton did not really wish to contemplate the reasons a woman would learn such a trick.

"Go then," she said in that same soft whisper. "I will wait here. Enjoy your conquest. I just hope I dinnae catch the ague."

"I doubt ye will."

"Of course," she continued as if he had not spoken, "my deep, wracking coughs will nay doubt disguise your cries of illicit passion and thus keep ye safe from discovery. I am ever ready to be helpful. If her husband should return, shall I just hurl my weak, shuddering self upon him to allow ye the time to escape?"

"I am beginning to see why your husband should wish to drown you," Payton muttered.

"Och, nay. Ye could ne'er guess that."

"Payton, my *beau chevalier,* are ye coming?" called Lady Fraser.

"I worked hard for this." Payton looked up at the window and knew he would not be climbing through it tonight.

"Oh, I doubt that, although she does like to play the coy one," said the girl. "Go on. I will just huddle here in the ivy, though I doubt ye will be much help to me when ye crawl out of there. 'Tis said she is insatiable, fair wrings a mon dry."

Payton had not heard that. Although he had not thought he was the first to coax the woman into breaking her vows, he had not realized she had become so well known for doing so. Insatiable sounded intriguing, he thought, then sighed. Payton hoped Lady Fraser would not be too offended when he forced himself to leave without partaking of her favors.

"Are ye talking to someone, my braveheart?" asked Lady Fraser, leaning out of the window a little more to look around.

"Just my page, my sweet," Payton replied. "I fear I must leave you."

"Leave?" Lady Fraser's voice held a distinct shrillness. "Tell the boy to say he could nay find you."

"I fear the lad is an abysmal liar. The truth would soon be told to all and ye wouldnae wish your husband to learn where the lad found me tonight, would ye?"

"Nay. I dinnae suppose ye will return later, will ye?"

"It fair breaks my heart, my little dove, but, nay. This problem could take hours, e'en days, to solve."

"I see. Weel, mayhap I will allow ye to make amends. Mayhap. Later."

Payton winced as she slammed the shutters closed on her window then he turned to the shadowed figure near the wall. "Let us go and get ye dry and warm. 'Twould please me if ye wouldst stay to the shadows until we are weel beyond her sight."

It was not easy, but Payton fought down the unease he felt as he walked away from Lady Fraser knowing the girl was with him yet unable to see or hear her. There was a part of him that began to ponder on ghosts and other creatures that could slink unseen through the night, but he wrestled it into silence. The girl was simply very adept at hiding, he assured himself.

Once on the narrow street which led to the house his family owned, he stopped and looked for her, picking a spot where light from a house would aid him in seeing her. "Ye can come out now."

The first thing he noticed was that she was pale and shivering from the cold. Payton quickly took his cloak off and felt a twinge of relief as he wrapped it around her. She was real. He could touch her. Placing his arm around her slender shoulders, he hurried her along toward his house, deciding he would get a good look at her once he got her warm and dry. He noticed, with a twitch of amusement, that she had to hold his cloak up to keep from tripping over it for she barely reached his armpit.

Payton ignored the astonishment on the scarred face of his man Strong Iain when he entered his house. The condition of the woman he had brought home was intriguing enough, but Payton suspected the man was more startled by the fact that Payton had brought her into the house at all. None of his women were allowed across his threshold, not in any of his houses. It was an old rule, one he clung to faithfully. When asked about it by friends or family, he glibly excused it by claiming he did not wish to soil his own nest. Payton strongly suspected there was more truth to that than he cared to acknowledge.

"But, I need to talk to ye," protested the girl when Payton ordered Strong Iain and his wife Wee Alice to see to a fire, a hot bath, and dry clothes for his guest.

"When ye are clean, dry, and warm ye can meet with me in the hall," Payton assured her. "What is your name?"

"Kirstie, but my brothers call me Shadow."

Thinking of how silently she moved and how easily she hid, Payton was not surprised. He nudged her toward Wee Alice then went to find himself some ale and food. Payton felt a surge of curiosity, both about her tale and how she would look when clean and dry. He hoped it was worth what he had given up, for Lady Fraser was to have enabled him to put an end to a surprisingly lengthy bout of celibacy . . .

ABOUT THE AUTHOR

Hannah Howell is an award-winning author who lives with her family in Massachusetts. She is the author of thirteen Zebra historical romances and is currently working on HIGHLAND ANGEL, the first book in a new Highland trilogy. Look for HIGHLAND ANGEL in May 2003. Hannah loves hearing from readers and you may write to her c/o Zebra Books. Please include a self-addressed stamped envelope if you wish a response.